CORRUPTION

By the same author

ANDREW KLAVAN

CORRUPTION

WILLIAM MORROW AND COMPANY, INC. / NEW YORK

It is the policy of William Morrow and Company, Inc., and its imprints and affiliates, recognizing the importance of preserving what has been written, to print the books we publish on acid-free paper, and we exert our best efforts to that end.

Library of Congress Cataloging-in-Publication Data

Klavan, Andrew.
    Corruption / Andrew Klavan.
        p.   cm.
    ISBN 0-688-11816-X
    I. Title.
    PS3561.L334C67   1994
    813'.54—dc20   93-24128
                                                                             CIP

Printed in the United States of America

First U.S. Edition

1   2   3   4   5   6   7   8   9   10

BOOK DESIGN BY SRS DESIGNS

This book is for
George Dawes Green.

Acknowledgments

The author is grateful to Sergeant Carmine Restivo, Jr., and the Putnam County, New York, Sheriff's Department for their generosity, hospitality, and assistance.

PROLOGUE

THE HUDSON

FRIDAY, JULY 13

One summer evening, a boy went out to play. His name was Barney. He was nine years old.

It was getting late when he went out; it was almost dark, in fact. He had to tiptoe down the stairs and sneak past the living-room doorway without anyone seeing him. Mom was sure to be in the living room, doing her needlework in front of the Wheel of Fortune show. And Dad would be in there in his easy chair, the paper over his face, taking his nap before the game. Rosemarie—not that anyone cared where Rosemarie was—but Barney was almost positive she'd be in her room in the back, stomach down on her stupid pink bed, swallowing the mouthpiece of her stupid pink phone, so even though she was a definite Big Mouth, she was not going to be a problem.

He touched down at the bottom of the stairs. Scrunched up his face, his whole body—creeping, creeping past the door. As he passed, he could see the dancing TV light from the corner of his eye, the shadow of his mother, and then . . . then he'd made it. Made it to the front door.

Carefully, carefully, he pushed out the screen.

"Get back by dark," his mother murmured.

Only Barney couldn't really hear her too well because of the screen door banging shut behind him.

It was great out tonight, Barney thought: unholy. Unholy fog all over everything. He went into it, prowling. He was the Night Ranger. Down the porch steps, stalking across Adams Street, crouched. Unholy. The rows of square houses, the square porches on every house; the smokestacks from the textile mill up on the hill above the neighborhood: They were all whited out, all made weird by the mist. Strange shapes, like of some kind of creatures being born out of the ground, coming to get him. He whirled and fired. Zzzzzt. Ran across the sidewalk, leapt over the curb onto the Raffertys' lawn.

The grass was wet on his bare ankles; the wet seeped quickly into the canvas of his Keds. Ducking down, he ran past the side of the house, under the kitchen window. Jack Rafferty's mom was right there, right at the sink, wearing her red apron, washing dishes. . . . But he managed to sneak by her, into the backyard. There, the Rafferty's swing set in the mist—it was just crazy cool: like a giant space spider crawling toward him until . . . Zzzzzt! Night Ranger. Barney fired again and ran for the back fence.

He was over it with two steps. Jumping down into the Bardazzis' yard. Blasting his way past their picnic table. Nearly bunking his shin on their sandbox. He was running faster now. He wanted to get to the river before the guys went home. And anyway, some of these shapes, when he stopped to think about it, were actually kind of scary in real life. Like that one near the barbecue that was probably a tree or something but could also have been some kind of guy just standing there, staring at him through the mist. . . .

He started running faster down the slate path past the house. Out over the front lawn and right to the edge of the big state highway.

He had to stop there a second to check the traffic. He didn't want one of those giant tractor-trailers to suddenly come airhorning down on top of him. He checked left and right along the road. Then he also took a quick look over his shoulder—just in case that tree or whatever it was had sort of decided to come stealing up behind him. But it was hard to tell. The mist was so thick that even the Bardazzis' houselights seemed quiet and dim and far *away from him. He faced front again and he dashed for it, across the pavement to the railroad embankment on the other side.*

He grabbed handfuls of crumbly black dirt, sent cinders rattling under his feet as he climbed up the embankment. He crossed the tracks at the top and rattled down the cinders on the other side. Braked himself at the edge of the tall grass. He was out of breath now and sweating in the humid air. He started forward again, into the grass.

The grass reached up nearly to his crotch. Probably full of deer ticks with Lyme disease, he thought. Not to mention slavering hell demons ready to rear up right in front of him and rip his throat out. He started walking fast again. The stalks whipped at his thighs. The hoppers flung themselves out of the weeds hurrying to get away from the stomp of his gigantic Keds.

Another few steps, and he was at the brink of the short, steep scarp that led down to the river.

The mist thinned as it spread over the water. The Palisades on the far bank chested out of it, a rugged wall. Beneath them, the broad, winding Hudson still glinted silver in the last light, only slowly going dark, growing drab.

Barney stood where he was, breathing hard, squinting down the slope. He could just make them out down there: Willy Hanrahan and Mike Riley. Standing together on the riverbank, skipping stones. He could hear them talking in loud, high voices.

Barney threw his head back and let out a war whoop: "Night Raaaaanger!"

He went charging down the hill.

"Die, Rathgar!"

"Bzzzzzt!"

"Bzzzzzt!"

"Mwrawk, Mwrawk, Mwrawk!" Willy stiff-legged forward like one of Rathgar's robot henchmen.

"Bzzzzt! Bzzzzt!" Barney fired again and again.

"They keep coming!" Willy screamed. "Aaaaagh!"

Barney dashed to the riverside and plucked a fist-sized stone from the tarry mud. "Death bomb!" he shrieked—and he hurled it expertly into the water, sending a fan of spray up over Willy's head.

13

"Hey, shit, Barney!" The robot henchman waggled his hands, stumbling toward the foot of the scarp.

"Awww, he's wet," said Mike.

"What is this? How come your hair's not wet?" said Barney.

"Shit, Barney," said Willy. He kept shaking off his hands.

" 'Cause he's too chickenshit to go in, that's why." Mike ran his fingers over his own black hair to show how the water dripped from it. It dripped from his pale, pug, freckled face and ran down his white chest too.

"It's frigging cold!" Willy said. He tried to swagger as he said it. "And it's too frigging dark now anyway."

"It's cooold," said Mike. "And it's toooo dark."

"Awww," Barney said.

"Well, kids drown'd!"

"Kids drown'd."

"Aww," said Barney. "Kids drown'd. Awww."

"I don't care. Kids drown'd." And that was that: Willy squatted sulky in the gravel at the scarp bottom, snatching up a handful, shaking it, spilling it bit by bit. His square, carrot-haired, carrot-freckled face was set: He wasn't going in for anything. That was that.

"Wulp," said Barney—and he just kind of sauntered along the riverbank casual-as-you-please. "I guess I'll go in for my swim now."

Mike skimmed a stone out toward the distant palisades. "I told you you were chickenshit," he muttered at Willy.

With a snort, Barney lifted one heel then the other. Wrestled off one sneaker then the other. Peeled off his shorts and his Sea Glob T-shirt. Laid them together neatly on the ground. He stepped right up to the river. Stretched a little. Taking his time about it, his own sweet time. Not that he was scared or anything. But it was getting dark. And kids did drown. . . .

And it sure did look creepy out there, all wide and empty, the mist kind of swirling around on it and the mountains of Orange County hunkering and getting darker and darker across the way.

He looked down. There was his own reflection, dim and wavering, on the surface of an eddy. Minnows and crappies hung and poked and darted underneath it. Yeah, it really was getting to be dark, all right. It really was.

But hell, he was no chickenshit. No way. He rushed out, naked, and dove in.

*   *   *

14

Cripes, the cold! It closed over his head. He kicked, reached. Stretched up for the light. He broke into the air, screaming.

"Awwwwww, God! Oh God!"

Willy and Mike were both on the shore. They were both laughing at him.

"Cold!" *he screamed.*

"Awww," *shouted Willy,* "he's coold."

"Chickenshit!" *Barney shouted back.*

Mike laughed and slugged Willy's arm. Barney heard Willy say "Ow!" *all the way out there.*

Barney trod water for a few seconds. The current tugged him gently; downstream, away from shore. He turned himself around until he could see the Palisades. They sure were big. Big and dark and looming. And getting darker every minute too. And the way little snakes of mist sort of wriggled across the surface at him; and the way the misty sky hung over him so huge and deep; and the way the guys, when he turned around again, were way the hell away, just small dancing figures, their faint laughter drowned out by the lapping of water as he paddled and puffed; and the way the river lay quiet all around him as his feet worked in the invisible places below—well, Barney was just about ready to paddle on in; he had just about had his swim for this particular evening, thank you very much. He would just paddle on in and dry himself off . . . and then make fun of Willy some more for being such a chickenshit.

There was a hollow pop behind him, a thick splash.

"What?"

Barney whipped around. A large log, black with mud, was floating there suddenly. Not two yards from him. It rolled and bobbed on the waves.

Barney shivered. Musta fallen . . . he thought. He tread the water. Must be some tree, musta fallen . . . His teeth started chattering . . . musta gotten stuck on the bottom and then . . . Slowly, gently, the river current pulled him closer and closer to the floating log. Yeah, it musta come free when I . . .

The log shifted and rolled. River muck oozed down the sides of it. Barney noticed now how close he was to it. It was kind of disgusting. Kind of spooky too to be out there alone with it, all the quiet everywhere around, and the log oozing and turning. He could've reached out and touched it.

Jeeze, maybe I better get. . . .

The log rolled over and Barney saw its eye.

15

It was a second before he understood what it was—that small pulpy marble staring at him through the caked mud. It was a second before his mind could make sense of what he was looking at. But then he knew. And he knew that that gaping black O beneath it—that used to be the mouth . . . And now the arm too, the arm was coming away from the rest of it, floating out toward him, reaching for him, its fingers, fat as sausages, reaching out. . . .

Barney could only stare at it as he hung there treading water. As the arm floated closer to him. He could only stare at the fingers of the hand.

They touched him. The fingers. They tickled his chest.

"Oh," he said. He barely breathed it. "Oh. Oh. Oh . . ."

He opened his mouth to scream—but the water rushed in, spilled down his throat. He choked and went down, his face under the surface. Terrified, he started to fight, to thrash, to batter at the river. Down he went, deeper.

The river closed over his head. He clawed at it, trying to get out, he had to get out, he couldn't breathe, his lungs were pumping in his chest. . . . He clawed up and burst into the air, sucking the air, coughing, gagging. He looked around. Where was it, where the hell was it?

And then it was on him, on top of him, grabbing him. Barney started to scream again trying to push away from it, trying not to touch it. Again, his scream was snuffed by the water as it filled his mouth. He tried to spit it out, but he was going down again.

It's drowndin me, Jesus.

He was going down and he couldn't find the thing, that thing, where was it? He couldn't breathe. Where was it? He couldn't breathe and, Christ, he felt like his head was blowing up inside like a balloon.

Help Jesus help me.

His head was going to blow apart just like a balloon does.

I can't breathe I can't breathe Mommy help me.

He got out, out into the night, the air. The sweet air rushing and spinning around him. He wheezed in a breath but then started hacking, gasping. He couldn't stop. The water felt like it was boiling in his windpipe. He saw the sky going crazy, whirling around.

Where is it oh help help it's coming Mommy where is it? . . .

He kept his chin up. He was still coughing, but he stretched his neck, kept his chin up above the water. He could see the sky, the little lights of Gilead burning on the shore. . . .

16

And then a white arm rocketed out of the river and coiled tightly around his chest.

His hoarse, strangled wail was silenced at once as the thing dragged him under. He beat at it, clawed at it, kicking and twisting helplessly, a wild tantrum. It had him, though. He couldn't get loose. His strength began to ebb away as the arm's grip grew even tighter, as it began to tug him, carry him. . . .

Mommy . . . why couldn't his mommy just be here? . . .

Suddenly, the night came crashing down on top of him. The thing had brought him to the surface again.

"Barney! Jesus! I gotcha!"

He punched weakly at the arm, thinking, Mommy . . .

"I gotcha, Barney! Don't fight!"

Water dashed against his face, then the air again and the noise.

"Don't fight! Don't fight, Barn!"

Mike?

"I gotcha." It was Mike. Gasping. Holding him. "It's okay. I gotcha."

Barney took hold of the arm across his chest. Mike's arm, Mike's living arm. He gripped it hard, held onto it. He was on his back. He saw the faint stars far above him, the faint stars living and dying as the mist sailed over them, sailed by.

Where's the thing? Where's the thing, Mike?

Far away, Barney heard the steady rhythm of Mike's swimming, his panted whisper, "I gotcha. I gotcha."

Barney just held onto the arm around his chest. His mouth hung open and he felt muddy drool running out of it, down his chin. He felt his legs trailing limply in the water.

Mike?

"Almost. Almost, Barn. Hang on, man."

A body, Mike. A body.

"Oh Jesus," Mike gasped, kicking out, panting. "Oh Jesus. Almost. Almost there, Barn."

A body.

PART I

THE HEMLOCK CATHEDRAL

ONE

The Arrival of Merriwether

MONDAY, JULY 9

1

IT ISN'T QUIET IN the country. That's just a story they let out to fool the city folks. Realtors probably spread it to bring the fools north. Or maybe city landlords, trying to get their tenants out so they can raise the rents or go co-op. Whoever perpetrated the thing, though, it's a damnable lie. That much, thought Merriwether, is obvious.

Lying on his back on the mattress, peering up into the mysterious recesses of the cathedral ceiling, studying not the blackness itself but rather the utterness of the country dark, Merriwether believed he could make out no fewer than thirty-seven separate noises coming in through the window screens. There was the sort of blanket of whistles, of *breep-breeps,* like a distant traffic-cop convention; that was the crickets, even he knew that. Then there was a rhythmic buzzing and he was willing to surmise—it being far too early to call the forestry service and ask—he was willing to surmise that those were cicadas. There was also some sort of bird giving a low whistle now and then and a bullfrog or suchlike doing a truly remarkable impersonation of the

21

last trump. After that, when it came to the ceaseless chorus of *wonks* and *whoops* and *bzzts* and *blats* and *chiggas* that had been pouring through the screens incessantly ever since Johnny Caterpillar's Insect Bar and Grill closed down for the evening and its inhabitants staggered out into the grass. . . . Well, Merriwether would not vouchsafe any specific identity for these except to declare they were One More Reason Why This Was the Most Uncivilized Place With Which He Had Ever Been Associated.

He turned onto his side, fluffing his pillow under his head. It didn't help. He turned onto his other side and snuggled close to his wife, flinging an arm across her. The warmth of her thighs, her soft, friendly murmur, the little smile she always gave him in her sleep—not that he could see it in this incomprehensible dark—afforded him a momentary comfort.

But then, with a sigh, he was on his back again, staring up into the high ceiling, listening to the insect chorus, dreading the coming of dawn.

Oh come on, he told himself, *it won't be so bad.*

He had tried this tack around midnight to no avail, but he was hoping conditions had changed since then.

It won't be bad at all. The new job is sure to be . . . interesting, at least. And life in the country—why, it's good for you. Healthy. Natural. Fresh as a cornpone shooting a raccoon off a farmer's fence. Or something of the sort.

Really, he had to snap out of it; he was being ridiculous about the whole thing. He had grown up in the country after all. Well, some people did not consider Philadelphia the country per se, but where he had lived, Evergreen, his family estate, there had been acres and acres of lawn and garden. An entire rolling valley of greenery running between two raised roadways.

Of course, he hadn't exactly liked Evergreen either, come to think of it. With its hunkering shrubs and threatening nooks; its great white mansion lowering from a rise of ground, massive columns flanking the door, arched, soaring windows curtained at all times . . . God, it was a forbidding castle, especially when his father, the Dragon King, was fuming and snarling in the study on the third floor. . . .

Corruption

It was no better on the inside either. The proud entranceway paved with rose marble, the foyer ceiling somewhere in the ether beyond the chandelier, the mahogany banister sweeping and twisting up into the farthest reaches. Even the portrait of his mother at the top of the stairs was haughty and forbidding, a painting of a woman in a shining white dress, her blond hair piled up on her head, her bosom bedecked with jewels, her eyes pained, her smile icy. Not at all like *his* memory of her anyway, even though he only had the one memory to go by, that one moment when he was four that seemed to have stuck with him so entirely. In that portrait, that portrait that hung as it were within his own stately mansion, well, she was another woman altogether. Sitting rather quietly, rather modestly, by the window in the nursery. Watching him stack blocks on the carpet, her head tilted to one side, the sun from behind her dashing out in rays from the loose strands of her hair, her smile wistful as if she ached about something . . . his innocence . . . her loss. . . .

Ah, good, good, thought Merriwether savagely. A wonderful way to get yourself to sleep. A quick review of the Twenty-fifth Annual Parade of Anguish.

He closed his eyes desperately. *Wonk,* went something in the grass beyond the window. *Whoop, bzzt, blat, chigga,* came the myriad replies. Merriwether opened his eyes, took a deep breath. He would've killed just then for a cigarette, he would have done murder. He could almost taste the smoke, feel the comfort of it. The slow, meditative raising of the filter to his lips. The slow, luxurious draw . . .

And the image of his mother returned to him. Not a memory, but that other image he had built up over the years. The slow, luxurious draw of her cigarette. Lying on the couch in the sewing room, closing her eyes with the sybaritic thrill of that last deep, steady inhalation. Her hand falling slowly too. Slowly, slowly, lowering to her side as her thoughts drifted away behind the closed eyelids. The hand slowly dropping, the cigarette slowly dropping . . .

And then the quick flames springing up around her, surrounding her, swallowing her.

But, of course, that was just his imagination, his jolly little five-

23

in-the-morning imagination. He hadn't actually been there. He hadn't actually seen it. He had only seen his father, standing erect in the doorway when the nanny had brought him home from the park. Standing in his elegant black suit, his red tie; standing with his broad shoulders back and his head back, his great leonine head with the wavy silver hair framing it, and his square handsome chin jutting out like a dare.

Son, he had barked. *I'm afraid your mother's dead.*

Spoken curtly, in a subtle tone of reprimand, as if he had wanted to add, *And a rather good thing all in all, I think. You were far too dependent on her.*

Ah, dear old Dad, thought Merriwether. Always such a charmer. The Dragon King. Well, now the Dragon King had won the day for good and all, hadn't he? Forced his only son into this . . . this clamoring boondock. With all these drunken bugs serenading in the grass. And with tomorrow, the sickening, terrifying prospect of tomorrow already beginning to tinge the blackness with the first faint threat of gray. . . .

Merriwether ran his hand up through his long hair. He was starting to have the sneaking suspicion that he was not going to get any sleep at all tonight. Or rather, not until about fifteen minutes before the alarm clock went off. Then—and this was the way it always happened, wasn't it?—then he would slip into a doze just in time to be shocked awake by the blare of music from the radio, to realize he had seized only so small a moment of sweet peace, so tantalizing a rest before having to rise, before having to face what in this particular instance, he was certain was going to be a disaster. . . .

2

I have this problem expressing anger, thought Sally Dawes. *Otherwise, I would rip his fucking heart out.*

She brushed the second layer of eye shadow over her upper lid. There was nothing in the convex makeup mirror but that circular section of her face: one sad brown eye, one overbroad nose. She blended the color into the first layer with a finger.

He just better not try to shift the blame upstairs, that's all. He's the editor in chief. It's his responsibility.

She had the mascara brush now and was leaning into the glass making the minced strokes on her short, thin eyelashes. Not that it helped, but it was almost a superstitious ritual now: dutifully going through the routine as it had been prescribed for her last year by the Official Sprightly Shopgirl at the Macy's Cosmetics Counter.

And he better not try to bully me either, she thought. *Or get me to laugh at his jokes. I hate that.*

Stupid, sprightly little twit with her condescending, humiliating advice . . .

And if he brings up Jerry again . . . God, just don't let me blush when he does that, please.

She threw the brush down in its tray, stepped in front of the medicine chest mirror to examine her work. She tilted her head this way and that. Her pale face seemed to her pinched and grim, her cheeks scarred with wrinkles, her features soft and shapeless.

Still forty-one, she thought. Still plain as a brick wall.

And still scared shitless of Randall Shank.

She heard a floorboard creak and looked up at the ceiling. Her mother was awake. It was time to get the hell out of here.

By now, of course, the whole paper knew what Shank had done to her. How could you keep anything secret in a building full of reporters? She practically *had* to make a fuss about it, if only to save face with the staff. Just the same, the impression she wanted to make on her colleagues was one of serene indignation. As she brought her boxy little Horizon into the massive parking lot, she glanced into the rearview and tried out her serenely indignant smile.

At the center of the lot sat number one Sutcliffe Park Lane—the only address on Sutcliffe Park Lane. It was a huge, deadpan fortress of concrete striped with mirrored glass. The Plant, they called it. The headquarters of the *Daily Champion*. Unmoved, unmovable as a bureaucrat, it lorded it over this so-called park: this lot, the scraggly, new-grown ash and sumac trees all around it, and the long, flat expanses of yellow grass. It sat silent, and the steady whisk and fade of traffic washed against its walls. Cars down on the interstate at the end

25

of the drive. They rushed south to New York City, and a little ways north into the city of White Plains, and north from there into the suburbs of Westchester and then Putnam and Auburn and Dutchess counties—all in the *Champion*'s domain, Sutcliffe's domain.

Sally walked across the lot to the building, her serenely indignant smile frozen on her face.

She strolled as casually as she could past the security guard, down the hallway, to the city room. Her hands in the pocket of her skirt, she moved quickly along the wall, with the room to her right. In the flat, windowless vastness of the place, among the clusters of desks under banks and banks of fluorescents, early reporters and editors sat or gathered or milled about. Some leaned their heads together and spoke in low voices, others tapped their keyboards, peering into their monitors. Some raised their eyes to her—she nodded them a warm good morning. The rest, she felt, were watching her secretly. And all of them—she was sure of it—were waiting eagerly to see if she would beard the lion in his den.

She was approaching Randall Shank's office. There was a hallway to her left, the hallway to Sales, and the office was on the far wall just beyond it. It was a glass enclosure, but it was screened by venetian blinds: She couldn't see if he was there or not.

Sally took a deep breath as she approached. At the last minute, she felt her smile begin to falter. She braced herself. . . .

And the editor in chief stepped out of the hall, right in front of her.

"Morning, Sally," he muttered. His egg-shaped head and his egg-shaped body swiveled to her. His stumpy legs kept carrying him officeward.

"Randall? Randall? Could I please talk to you?" The sound of her own voice almost made her despair. It was so soft, so tentative; she sounded like a bashful schoolmarm. "Randall?"

Shank waddled through his door, leaving it ajar. Sally stopped outside it. She felt the eyes of every reporter in the place on her back. If she turned around now, they'd probably feed it to the wire services: *Bureau Chief Chickens Out.*

She pushed into the little cubicle.

"Sally, my ass was on the line."

He was standing behind his desk, already confronting her with the point of a rolled-up paper.

"Randall, I really don't think it was very fair." That voice—so milky and girlish and *nice.*

"His uncle is on the goddamned board of directors, Sally. Of the whole chain. My ass—Sally, they had a fire upstairs just this high, already burning, waiting to cook my ass."

"Well, I mean, you're the . . . the editor, and I just think . . ."

"Me? Me?" Shank tossed the paper down. It whapped on the wood veneer of his desk, nearly blew down his family photo: the shot of his frumpy, sneering "ball-and-chain" and their two sullen "little fuckers." He pointed his finger at her now, kept it trained on her as he moved from behind the desk, past the wall of AP plaques and Community Service awards, until he stood with his back to the big window. Framed majestically against the view of the parking lot—the only view there was from any side of the building—he kept pointing at her. "You're the Auburn bureau chief, Sally. I depend on you to run that bureau without coming down here to worry me about every little thing."

"I don't come. . . ."

"I mean, if I have to swat every bug in the backwater . . . hell, I'll never finish doing the crossword puzzle."

A laugh broke from her. *Shit,* she thought. She tried to recover, stroked a handful of hair behind her ear and—mildly, softly—said, "Well, Randall, I just think that with the election coming up and with the sheriff, you know, in the position he's in, that you, of all people, should give me some support."

"Support?" Shank started pacing back to the desk again. "Support?" His eyebrows had shot up nearly to the top of his baldish head. "Oh now, you're going to come down here and tell me I don't give you support. Who the hell made you bureau chief in the first place? Who took you back in after you ran off with that . . . that what's-his-name, that Jerry guy or whatever?"

"That's not . . ."

"And came back in here a sniveling, crawling, quivering . . . did I turn you away?"

Sally felt the hot rush of blood to her cheeks. "No, Randall, but . . ."

"Well, there you are. No support!"

She pressed on desperately: "You have ten reporters down here, Randall. And five in north county. I've had two since Liz left, and I've got the most important election in county history coming up in just five months. The county executive! The *first* county executive! And now, without even consulting me, you bring in this . . . this . . ."

"What? This what?" He leaned across the desk.

"Well, he has no experience, Randall."

"No ex— no . . ." Appalled, the little man yanked a drawer open, snatched a folder, tossed it like a gage onto the desktop, next to the paper. Sally hesitated, then reached for it, opened it. Ran her eyes over Sidney Merriwether's job application. "He ran a whole magazine for a year," said Shank.

"*Helios?*"

"What?"

"A poetry magazine. And it says here it folded."

"Well, and he . . . he speaks languages."

"Homeric Greek?"

"So he'll cover the zoning boards."

"Oh fine. If he's so great, why don't you assign him down here?"

"Are you crazy?"

"Oh, Randall." And now she sounded like a disappointed mother—worse, like her *own* disappointed mother. "How could you?" she said.

She perused the form a little more: the Harvard education, the major in classics, the failed magazine—and not one real job anywhere. Ever. Not even a paper route. Her shoulders sagged hopelessly. The sheriff was going to eat this one alive. He would eat them all alive and his man, Purdy, was going to romp into the executive's office come November.

The thought sent a little chill of panic through Sally's stomach. She looked up at Shank one more time, appealing to him silently with all her heart.

"I fought for you, Sally," Shank began. "I went in there and I said to them, I said . . . I said . . ." But he saw the look in her eyes. He stopped. He sighed. His hand ceased gesturing, fell to the desk. He sank slowly into his chair, his ovoid head lowered, his pudgy chin on his chest. He stared sorrowfully at his own feet.

"My ass was on the line, Sally," he muttered. "His uncle is on the goddamned board of directors."

My ass was on the line, Sally. She mimicked him as she drove up the interstate. *His uncle is on the board of directors, my ass was on the line, nah, nah, nah.*

The tall ash-gray buildings of White Plains were gone from the sides of the road. In their places were long lines of willows, branches sweeping back and forth above the grass; an easy green meadow rolling into easy green hills; rich clusters of trees rising up toward the soft white clouds, sloping away into the grass and rising again to the blue sky. The Hudson Valley.

Sally steered the Horizon tightly, gripping the wheel until her knuckles were white. She clung to the right lane, letting the great trucks rush by, rocking the little Horizon in its tracks.

I should've confronted him. I should've just said, It's my bureau, Randall. I can't let the sheriff just walk all over us. You dump this Merriwether character on someone else or I'm history. You management toady.

Why *couldn't* she just say that? Why was she still afraid of him after all these years?

She let the breath hiss out of her, shook her head at the sunlit windshield. She knew why. She knew, all right. Because she remembered him as he was, that's why. When he was still doing real newspaper work, before they'd promoted him into slavery, into management chains. She remembered the way he was when *he* was the Auburn County bureau chief, the first chief of a brand-new bureau. And she had just come back to town. That was seven years ago. It was just after Jerry, just after it was finally over with Jerry and she was quaking inside and had nowhere else to go and no strength to get her there. Randall had fought for her then. It was true. Management was in no big hurry to rehire someone who'd quit on them, and Randall had said: Send her up to me, she's the one I want to start the bureau with me, let me have her. And they had let her go up to Auburn County.

29

She remembered the first day she had walked into that broken-down box of an office and seen him there. He had jumped up from behind his gunmetal desk, slamming down the phone he'd been holding. He'd pointed a thick finger at her, stuck it about an inch away from her nose and shouted, "Didn't I tell you, girl? Didn't I tell you that man was garbage? Jerry! Shit! Garbage!"

She'd tried to take the joke, but her smile began to tremble, her vision blurred with tears. Shank saw it and let up on her. He slapped her gently on the shoulder.

"Well, all right then," he said. "Go grab a desk and get me some news for this thing."

Maybe it was because his ball-and-chain hadn't given birth to his little fuckers then; maybe he hadn't needed the job so much; or maybe it was just the fact that he was in the thick of the news hunt and not worrying about the management blue suits down in White Plains and how they were fixing to burn his ass—but whatever it was, Randall really had been different then. He'd been fierce then. He'd been all energy. Just the sound of his voice made her jump, and when he pointed that finger, held it an inch from her nose—she didn't dare argue with him, she didn't want to; she was so grateful.

And she was so busy too. Because Randall was hungry—hungry for news. News to make his bureau work. News to fill his paper. He wanted it desperately, needed it. The suits in White Plains were all cheerleader talk: We're a hundred percent behind you; all that crap. But they were cautious really, nervous. Auburn County wasn't White Plains, after all. It wasn't the rich suburbs of Westchester, not by a long shot. This was the exurbs, the boondocks. Miles and miles of winding roads through thick forests. Vacation spots. Retirement homes. Little towns by little lakes where the hardware store closed down on the first day of bass season. This was the kind of place where the police came to your house if you got a raccoon caught in your garbage can, for Christ's sake. The Sutcliffe Suits of White Plains were not going to put out an edition with raccoons on the front page. Not for long.

Randall was hungry, all right. And Sally could remember when he first began to suspect that the sheriff was withholding information from him. Just little things mostly. But big enough. Local pols arrested for drunk driving. A big shot's kid busted for vandalism. She could remember how Shank slowly became convinced that he had a scandal on his hands, that Dolittle was trading favors with the county elite, covering up their little indiscretions in return for political support. Oh, she could remember him stomping up and down the aisle; charging between the desks until the storefront window rattled; shaking both fists at the ceiling tiles; screaming, "That son of a bitch is trying to kill my news bureau! That son of a bitch is going to die the death! Do you hear me? Are you taking notes?"

That was why he sent her out on the rape case that night. Normally, when something like that came over the police scanner, they would wait and get the details from the Sheriff's Department press officer. But Shank was determined not to settle for that this time. He wanted the sheriff to know he meant business, and he told Sally, "Haul your heartbroken ass out to the scene."

The scene had been Bullet Hole Road, a long, snaking strip of blacktop that ran through the town of Hickory's northern forests; Sally had pushed her jalopy—an ancient, sputtering Monza—up to full speed to get there. She had come whipping past black trees blown by the raw October wind. She had wound around a corner to where the night pulsed red with cruiser beacons. She had hung back, killed her own lights and pulled to the curb. She had gotten out and crept closer on foot. And she had gotten there just in time to see the girl brought up out of the woods.

The girl was strapped to a stretcher. A blanket covered her up to the chin. Two medics and a deputy were carrying her. They had crushed a thin trail in the underbrush and they hauled her along it, up a hill, out of the trees. When they reached the street, the girl's face was lit red by the beacons. Sally could see she was a young girl, no more than twelve or thirteen. In the red light, the bruises around her eyes and mouth looked black. So did the blood that was streaming from her broken nose, that had been smeared over her cheek. Her head was thrashing back and forth. She kept grunting, "Ana, na, na." As they carried her to the back of a waiting ambulance, Sally could see that her lower jaw was dangling loose; it had been broken. She was probably trying to say, "No, no, no."

The whole weight of the past horrible year seemed to sit in Sally's stomach as she watched. Finally, she turned away, heartsick. She stayed like that until the ambulance sped off, and only looked back as the flashing lights vanished around the first curve and the siren faded slowly. Then she walked over to where the other deputies were milling by the side of the road. She approached the nearest one, a tall, husky young man in regulation khaki.

"I'm Sally Dawes of the *Daily Champion*," she said gently. "Could you tell me what happened here please?"

The young man—a boy really, his brown hair cropped close, his face still young and chubby and lightly freckled—turned to her with wide eyes. He tried to speak in that monotonous, faintly ironic mutter that cops cultivate. But instead, he said, "Well, that girl . . . well, jeeze, she was beaten something terrible. Just . . . a . . . a little girl, you see her? No older than my sister. Hell. I don't know how he could do something like that."

"You mean you know who did it?"

The young deputy opened his mouth to speak again, but he never got the chance. There was a sound from the woods, from the same path through the dark trees whence the girl had come. The deputy paused and turned to look. Sally followed his gaze.

And that was the first time she saw Sheriff Cyrus Dolittle.

The path dipped down away from the flashing lights, down the hill and into sable forest. Thin oaks and maples, the wind blowing over them, bowed and waved and rattled, sending red light and black shadow dancing along the way. As Sally watched, a form rose up out of the dark below. Just a gray outline first and then, as the red light whirled over it, the solid figure of a man. She watched him climb the hill steadily, his strides even, his arms swinging loose and easy at his sides.

He stepped out into the street. He was a tall man, she could see now. Over six feet tall and lean, with a relaxed, fluid stance. He was wearing black pants and a black vest, his white shirtsleeves rolled down and buttoned. He was also wearing a small silver badge on his chest, the old-fashioned kind, shaped like a star.

He paused as the deputies gathered around him. He spoke to them briefly and, as he did, he lifted his eyes and let them travel in a long, slow sweep over the area. They lit on her, almost immediately: on Sally. At once, he started coming toward her.

Sally felt something—fear or excitement or both—shoot up into her throat, acidic, hot. The sheriff walked through the red light until he was standing directly over her. She could see his face more clearly now, a pleasant face really. A thin, bullet-shaped head with sandy hair brushed straight back to reveal a widow's peak. His mouth seemed to curve naturally in a smile and his eyes were surrounded with upturned crow's-feet as if he were used to smiling. But he was not smiling now. His lips were set, his eyes were hard and the red light seemed to fall into the blackness of them and vanish.

"I'm going to count to five," he said. His voice was a low whisper, almost a rasp. "Then I want you out of here."

Sally looked up into those deep eyes and she could not help it: Her knees started to wobble. She pressed her notebook to her chest with both hands. "I'm a reporter," she said. "I'm with . . ."

"I know what you are," the sheriff said. "And I'm going to count to five."

She shook her head. "You can't talk to me like that."

"One," Dolittle said. The other deputies began to move in around her. Two came up behind the sheriff. One moved close to Sally's left side and another—the young man she had been speaking to just a moment before—moved up to her right.

"Two."

The deputies' faces were streaked with red. Their eyes were stony and their mouths set. The wind rattled the trees around them.

"This isn't fair," said Sally. But it was barely audible. She was about to start crying.

"Three."

She was not up to this; she knew she wasn't. She felt like someone who has been recovering from a disease and gets out of bed too soon. She was afraid her knees were going to give way.

"Four," Dolittle said.

Sally turned before he could see the tears begin. She walked to her car with her notebook clutched to her chest, her head hanging down over it. When she got behind the wheel of her Monza, when she

33

turned the engine over, she heard the deputies laughing. She did not look at them again. She drove away.

Now, Sally had crossed over into Auburn County. She guided the Horizon off the interstate and turned onto Route 6, a desolate corridor of gas stations, car dealerships, shopping malls, and fast-food restaurants. She drove past them all, up the hill to the traffic light, and there turned right onto Main Street.

In those days, she thought—and it was only seven years ago—but in those days, Shank knew how to act in a crisis. When he found her out in the parking lot that night, when he saw her sitting behind the Monza's wheel and sobbing into her hands, when he had listened to her confess the entire humiliating episode, he had simply nodded, scraping his chin thoughtfully with his knuckles.

"All right, Sally," he'd said to her finally. "Pull yourself together, kid. We're gonna sharpen our fucking pencils on that bastard's heart."

She was in the center of the town of Tyler now, the county seat. To her left, up ahead, was the spreading water of Lake Tyler. To her right was the County Courthouse, a crumbling Greek Revival shack more than a century and a half old, its dusty white stairs struggling up to the chubby Doric columns that barely held up the slumping portico. She glanced at the building only briefly as she drove past. The Sheriff's Department was housed in there.

That's right, she thought. Back then, it was "Sharpen your pencil on his heart, kid." And now—now when Sheriff Dolittle was about to take over the whole county, now when his puppet, Purdy, was going to become Auburn's first county executive, and the new county charter was about to become just a weapon for the sheriff's personal coup d'état—now all of a sudden it was "My ass was on the line, Sally. His uncle, Sally. Management demands it, Sally." And because Sally didn't have the guts to stand up to him, she was stuck with a novice reporter as the days before the election ticked away one by one.

She turned the corner onto Stillwater Lane and there, near the corner, was the *Champion*. The same crummy cube of a place, the same storefront window, the same flat tar roof. She turned down the alley beside it and into the parking lot. Stopped the car near the rear door.

Paused a moment to gather up her purse, her briefcase, her accordion files full of notes and clips . . .

Well, she thought, as she kicked her way out through the door, her arms full; *well, I've got enough guts for this Merriwether character anyway, board of directors or no board of directors.*

Somehow, she promised herself, she was going to whip him into shape before the conventions in August, before the campaigns got up to full steam.

She kicked the car door shut, weaving a little under the pile of papers and cases in her arms. She made her way slowly to the rear door of the office and snuck a hand out from under her briefcase to pull it open.

That boy is going to read every goddamned story ever written in this newspaper. Before I'm through, he's going to know so much about Auburn County he'll think he was born in the . . .

She slipped into the office then—and she saw him. He was standing right there, in the aisle between the desks.

Sally stopped dead in her tracks.

Jesus, she thought, *he looks like . . . He looks exactly like . . .*

She felt the color rise in her cheeks, she felt as if the wind had been knocked out of her. Quickly, she started moving again, moving toward her desk.

She thought: *Uh-oh.*

3

He was beautiful, Merriwether was. Even Emily could see it and she'd been married to him for two whole years.

Just standing at the window, as he was this morning, his hands jammed in his trouser pockets, his expression morose—just like that, he got her going. She was all the way in the kitchen. She had the coffeepot in her hand; she was ready to pour from it, was holding it in a hover above their two mugs—and the sight of him, that profile, the powerful brilliance of the brow, the cool blue of the eye, the strong, the regal, nose, those rich, those sensuous, lips . . .

That human face dee-vine, she thought. *Woof. Gimme shelter.*

The sunlight fanned in over him. The skin of his cheeks gleamed like marble. His hair, spilling to his shoulders nearly, shone like gold. In his dark pants and white shirt, his slender body slouched gracefully; it flowed like a passage of music.

Emily raised her shoulders and shivered. Turned away to fill the mugs. Thought of how they would make love tonight, of his breath on her neck, of the rise and falling of his ivory hip under her hand. She licked her lips.

Woof.

Then she put on a sympathetic frown and carried the coffee out to him.

"So, would 'dying inside' be a fair description of your emotional state?" she asked him. She was standing beside him at the living-room window now.

"It does have a ring to it," Merriwether said. He took the mug from her. "But I prefer to think of myself as grimly determined."

"Stalwart. Off to work with the other fellows."

"That's it. With Gimpy and Sloop-eye and Red."

"At one with the Common Man," said Emily.

"Right." He sipped the steam off the coffee's surface. "Naturally, I detest the Common Man, but think what a dinner story it'll make when I finally shake the little bastard."

"That's the spirit."

"Unless of course I die a wizened failure out here among the savages."

"That's not the spirit, Sidney."

"Sorry." He faced the window again.

"Come on, it's exciting," she told him. "I'll be here, waiting for you by the hearth. Fighting the good fight. Writing the good dissertation." She gestured around the little living room. Crates from the Somerville Shop N Save were piled high in every corner, almost covering the cottage's white floorboards. "Unpacking the good box," she said. "It's going to be an adventure."

"For you, perhaps: a blithe spirit, running so wild and free you don't care whose life lies shattered in your wake. But for me, a poor peasant lad from the wilds of western Albania . . ."

She laughed. "Think of the new grant money I'll get. And think of your first-ever actual paycheck, Sidney."

"Yes, but that won't be for two weeks yet. Two weeks, mind you, without cigarettes."

"Well, then it's a good time to give them up."

"Yes." Merriwether sighed. "It's also a wonderful time to smoke them incessantly."

It *was* kind of sad to say good-bye to him actually. When they were standing out on the front path together, she remembered him as he was, back at the Wine Cellar, their basement café off Harvard Square. He was at home there, surrounded by the dank and deep-stained walls, by the yellow lantern-glow, and by the ardent young faces everywhere. She remembered how his clear voice would rise above the general murmur as he proclaimed, *"Scenery is fine but human nature is finer."* Keats, that was. The letters of John Keats. She remembered how he rattled on about that so intensely. *It's in the letter to Bailey,* he declared. *1818, March, I think.* The candlelight trapped in the red wineglasses, the wineglasses rimming the great round table: Emily could almost see it. *But then, scarcely a year later, he goes and writes "Ode to Autumn," which is pure scenery and just . . . genius.* And everyone— not just her but everyone—the Harvard Jews themselves, bearded like young sages, their eyes like wells of brown fire—had been riveted on this Merriwether with his "golden tresses famed," with his shirt open gallantly and his cigarette spiraling smoke in the dim air. *You see? You see?* he'd said. *That's my point. Where beauty is truth and truth beauty, there is no scenery, only human nature perceived at a distance.*

Emily smiled to herself, rather sadly. She remembered that too now. "Human nature perceived at a distance." No doubt he would have preferred, she thought, a somewhat greater distance than this.

Because there he was, cast out into the cool July, with scenery, nothing but scenery, everywhere—and he looked so alien, so forlorn. To his left was their cottage, no more than a shabby three-room trailer, sided with white aluminum, roofed with red tar paper. Behind him in the dirt drive was their miserable Volkswagen Rabbit, a wreck with the gay old irony of its Harvard days long gone. And then, to his right, all around him, was the hilltop. A huge oval of lawn, half ringed by a stand of hickories. A field out beyond, its grass grown high and wild. And wildflowers—Emily remembered them from the fields behind her father's church: yellow daisies, golden St. John's wort, shaggy purple clover and orange daylilies—all set against the low, rolling mountains in the distance, their summer beryl and the misty blue of the sky.

It was not so bad for her, a poor minister's daughter from the wilds of western Massachusetts. To her, it was a jolly enough setting for a brief exile. A quiet place to work on her dissertation, a stopover on their way back to Cambridge or on to New York. But for Merriwether . . .

He was a heavy presence amidst it, slumped in his dark, sleek-lapeled Louis suit as in the ruins of his own urbanity, lifting a game salute to her as if he thought he would never return. . . .

"Well . . . Tallyho," he said.

She didn't know what to answer. He turned away from her and plodded toward the car.

Emily was almost relieved to see him go.

4

To Merriwether, of course, it was the merest chaos: all this field-and-flower nonsense. He drove his rickety Rabbit along a pitted snake of a road and there was nothing else on either side of him. Hills of trees. Seas of weed. Disheveled barns sinking into the overgrowth. Houses, grandiose Victorian-style houses, decaying at the edges of the pavement. And a huge sky, swept with clouds, fringed with green mountains, in which some enormous bird was circling like a vulture—probably even *was* a bloody vulture, for all he knew, waiting for his car to fail and for him to perish in the wilderness.

Tallyho! he thought. Was that really what he'd said to poor Emily? Tallyho? *My God, but I'm an asshole.*

Still, he did have to make some kind of show of it. He didn't want her to think he had lost all heart, that he was an utter failure. Which he was, of course, but he didn't want her to think it. Didn't want her to feel it was all over for him.

But now—now when he looked out through the windshield on this . . . this . . . "living hell" seemed to express it rather neatly . . . well, he could hardly believe it was only two days since he'd been in the house on Massachusetts Avenue. Sitting on the parlor floor, slowly laying the books into the open crates from the Shop N Save. Nestling his Blake beside his Bloom, his Bible by his Frye, his Plato by his Derrida, his Poe beside his Lacan. Casting his eyes over what had been the front office of his magazine, over the dismantled computer, the printer with the electric cord wrapped around it, the dusty piles of manuscripts tied together with old cords, boxes filled with the unsold copies of *Helios*. Sighing like a girl in a gothic, and feeling his soul turn to lead. And hearing his father's voice echoing thunderous all around him: *No son of mine . . . No son of mine . . . No son of mine . . .* The Dragon King Triumphant.

The road—County Highway 17 (Hickory Kingdom Road, it was named)—coiled and snapped beneath his tires. Vast, undulating, interminable fields rolled and rose around him into vast, undulating, interminable hills.

Welcome to the town of Hickory, thought Sidney Merriwether. *Where we count no man happy until he is dead.*

Then, just as he figured the landscape could get no bleaker, he turned the Volks left onto Stillwater Lane and saw a sign in the high weeds to the right: ENTERING THE TOWN OF TYLER. POP. 19,000. He crossed the line from one town into the other and, almost at once, the wilds of Hickory vanished. Instead, there were suddenly small parcels of mown grass chiseled out of the hillside with houses at the center of them. Unbearable houses. One after another of them, on lawn after lawn: spunky, simpering rectangles of empty-hearted aluminum or self-satisfied shingles. And, as if they weren't bad enough by themselves: accessories. Accessories on the lawns. A plaster gnome, grinning under its peaked red cap. A plastic deer listening by a scum-laced birdbath. Wooden geese in a row; plastic flowers in a pot; a satellite dish snatching God-knew-what inanity from the inanity-riddled air

. . . This was Tyler. And even as Merriwether battled his way past its horrifying display of human degradation, he came around a bend in the road and, Good Christ, there it was, right there. Just before the intersection with Main Street; just beyond a glass-and-metal barracks of a post office to the right and a brick bunker of a high school to the left; just through the gateway formed by their two towering flagpoles; just before the pool of Chevys and Buicks collecting under the corner stoplight: a tar-topped cube of steel with a dingy storefront window. The Auburn bureau. His new place of employment.

It was set on a plot of litter-riddled gravel, squatting behind a sidewalk shot through with grass. There was a board wired up above its glass door, handpainted like a sign on a boy's backyard clubhouse: THE DAILY CHAMPION.

Merriwether, gaping, slowed the Rabbit as he approached.

"I can't do better until your father calms down a bit, Sidney." That's what his uncle Oliver had said to him. *"It'll be a good place to ride the storm out anyway. It's a good little paper. Really."*

Merriwether forced his mouth closed, licked his lips. *Maybe there'll be a nuclear war before I find a place to park,* he thought.

The noise. That's what struck him first as he came through the door. The phones jangling. A radio hissing and snapping like a downed wire. Typewriters clattering—actual IBM Selectrics, the kind Cro-Magnon Man used. Mr. Coffee gurgling in the back somewhere. And some woman with an accent that was pure Long Island squawking at intervals like a seagull. "Awn wun, Chris! Rumple awn two!"

The inside of the place was even more repulsive than the outside. Two rows of four gunmetal desks apiece squatted against either wall. An aisle no more than three feet wide ran between them. Papers were stacked and crumpled on the desktops. More papers were tacked and dangling on the wall. Ribbed fluorescents fluttered purple in the white-tiled ceiling. A tannish carpet lay pocked with stains and burns upon the floor.

And then . . . then there were these people.

O! that the Everlasting had not fix'd his canon 'gainst self-slaughter! thought Merriwether.

They didn't even greet him when he came in. They didn't even pause. The young red-haired hulk, second desk left row, went right on battering at his typewriter, squinting through the smoke of the cigarette clenched in his teeth.

O! That the Everlasting would give me a cigarette! thought Merriwether.

At the desk behind him, some wild-eyed troll, all beard and hair, went right on rocking madly in his squeaking chair, a phone pressed to his head. Aisle right, the seagull, a pair of scarlet lips underneath an enormous hairdo, kept squawking. "Awn wun. Loin tu. Awn tree." The aging housewife behind her typed and talked gently into the phone wedged between chin and shoulder. And the silver-haired old gentleman at the very rear went on smoking his pipe and reading the paper, his feet up on his desk.

"Excuse me?" said Merriwether loudly—to the red-haired hulk as much as anyone. "I'm here to see Sally Dawes."

"On her way," the hulk shouted back. He didn't look up. He went on typing. Then he stopped typing. Then he looked up. "Hey. You're the new guy."

On the instant, the tumult ceased. The troll stopped rocking, the seagull stopped squawking, the housewife stopped typing, the silver-haired gentleman set his paper down. Everyone but Mr. Coffee fell silent and turned Merriwether's way. Merriwether shifted under their stares.

"Gawsh," the seagull murmured dreamily, "yu rilly aw hentsum."

Merriwether smiled painfully, praying for death.

"That's Doreen." The red-haired man whiplashed a thick finger at her. She smiled and batted her lashes. Then he pointed to the rest of them. "Alice, our feature department. Les, the Silver Fox, our man on county sports. Mr. Coffee on the table in back. Ernie Rumplemeyer behind me and I'm Chris Shea: We're newsside. You smoke?"

Shea snatched an open pack from the litter on his desk, held it up. Merriwether tapped at his shirt pocket. "Yes, I . . . I do seem to be out." He forced his hand to stay steady as he reached for one. Leaned down almost casually into the small domed flame of Shea's plastic lighter.

But that first inhalation—it made him drunk. He tilted back, closing his eyes a moment, tumbling down inside himself. . . .

41

"Can I just ask you one question?"

It was a high, reedy whine. Merriwether pried his soul from the nicotine's spell and opened his eyes to see the troll, Rumplemeyer, grinning at him. The little man had hung up his phone, but he was rocking back and forth again, his chair sending out a noise that sounded like a chimpanzee having a coronary. His corduroy coat, enormous and deplorable, billowed around him. His eyes seethed in the tangle and frizz of hair and beard.

Before Merriwether could reply, the troll went on. "Just one question. I just wanna ask . . . I mean: If your father is so rich, how come your magazine folded?"

Merriwether took another swig of smoke, blasted it from his nostrils. *And off to a lovely start.* "I'm sorry," he said, "I must have missed something: How is that your business?"

To Merriwether's surprise, the others in the room chuckled their approval. The seagull laughed outright. "Thet's tellin im," she said.

But this Rumplemeyer person just lifted his shoulders and grinned some more into his beard, rocking and squeaking. "No, no, no, no, I just meant: Your father is that big, that magazine guy from Philadelphia. Sidney Merriwether, right?"

"Yes, he is."

"So, like, you're Sid Junior."

Merriwether suppressed an interior cringe. "Not exactly," he said.

"Oh. You mean, like, Sid the Third?"

Who *was* this gremlin? "No."

"Jesus," said Shea. The sportswriter chuckled again. The housewife seemed to be bracing for it.

Rumple grinned and rocked, nodding now too, a bouncing furball. "Fourth? The Fourth?"

"Yes. The Fourth," sighed Sidney Merriwether. Damn it, now everyone would know he was their better and dislike him for it. That was always so tiresome.

"So, I mean, I just wanna, like, ask you," said Rumplemeyer, grinning, "like, with all that old money, you know, like, how come you have to work here? I mean, like, how come you can't afford a pack of cigarettes even?"

42

"Listen to me, you toad . . ." Merriwether was about to say. But before he had a chance, a thick metal door in the back of the room cracked open. A woman came through it, and the others in the room spun about. Almost in unison, they called out, "Morning, Sally."

She was a homely little creature, this new boss of his. Limp brown hair framing a round, pudding face. Brown eyes nested in crow's-feet. Lips thin and pale. A small, slender figure, nearly frail in a white blouse and a peach jersey dress—a scoop-necked dress down to her ankles, about two years out of style. She staggered, huffing, through the rear door under an enormous weight of purse, briefcase, and loose accordion files. The door banged shut behind her as she hauled these to the rear desk, the one behind Rumplemeyer's.

Rumplemeyer kept rocking, grinning, waiting for an answer. But Merriwether plugged in his cigarette and kept silent. Unless he was very much mistaken, he'd been saved.

Rumplemeyer whined: "So Fourth—I just mean, I just wanna know: how come? Why won't you answer that one simple . . . Ow!"

Merriwether nearly laughed aloud. The woman—Sally Dawes— had leaned over her desk and given the troll a sound rap on top of his hairy head with the back of her hand. Rumplemeyer's chair shrieked as he spun to her.

Good Lord, what a smile she has, thought Merriwether. It really was a sweet one. It transformed her whole face; made her look like the mother on a box of oatmeal.

"Call off your dogs, darling," she told Rumplemeyer gently.

And, lo and behold, Darling obeyed her on the instant and swiveled around to swipe his phone from its cradle. As he began punching the numbers, he grinned wickedly at Merriwether. The grin said, *Wait till next time.* Merriwether pursed his lips in return.

Shea, the big red-haired one, had meanwhile started typing again. Doreen and Alice were on their phones and the sports man was reading the paper. Sally, Merriwether saw, was bending into one of her desk drawers. Merriwether drew the last wisp of smoke through the filter of his cigarette and watched her. He shifted his weight from foot to foot.

Then Sally straightened. Merriwether had to fight to keep from

43

staring. Suddenly, this woman was tottering down the aisle toward him under a stack of manila folders that towered above her head. She leaned out from behind them. She was not smiling anymore and her face had become homely again.

"Hello, Sidney. I'm Sally Dawes."

She had a girlish whisper, thick as cream. It was even sweeter than the smile.

She went past him, dumped the folders on the desk behind him. They landed with a loud slap and spilled across the surface. Sally Dawes turned around and faced him.

"You can begin with those, okay?" she said softly.

"Begin . . ."

"I mean read them."

"What, all of them?"

"Yes."

"Aha," said Merriwether after a moment.

She came a step closer to him. He looked into the dull brown of her eyes. They were not as pleasant as her smile had been or her whisper. Not just at that moment anyway. Just at that moment, in fact, her eyes were not very pleasant at all. They were not looking at him the way women's eyes usually looked at him—with the fanning lashes and the wide pupils, the steady, receptive gaze. They were narrowed and flat—daring him, it looked like, to say the wrong thing.

And yet when she went on, it was in that same gentle whisper.

"Listen to me, okay?" Merriwether didn't answer. He looked in her eyes. "Okay?" she whispered again.

He blinked. "Uh . . . yes. Of course."

"There's going to be an election in November. That's five months from now, okay? It's a very important election, Sidney. Up until this year, the county has always been governed by a board of supervisors: the supervisors of each town—do you know what a supervisor is?"

"Uhp . . . aaahh . . ." Merriwether said.

"It's like a mayor."

"Yes, of course," Merriwether said.

"The supervisors would meet together every month as a board to govern the county."

"I see, yes, of course," said Merriwether.

Corruption

"Now," Sally continued, "we have a new charter, okay? For the first time, instead of the board of supervisors, there's going to be a county executive and a legislature, the same way that there's a president and a congress governing the country."

"Ah. Uh-huh," said Merriwether.

"There's also going to be new zoning, countywide, and that will create a commercial corridor that will cut through all five towns in the county. Okay?"

"Right. Right, right, right," said Merriwether.

"So whoever wins the county executive's office is going to have a major impact on the way the county is developed over the next few years. And naturally he'll also be able to put a political machine in place that could become a dynasty."

"Naturally, naturally," said Merriwether.

Sally's expression became even grimmer, her voice more earnest, and her face more plain. Her thumb and index finger formed a circle and she was punctuating her words with little motions of the circle in the air. Merriwether thought she looked for all the world like a spinster schoolmarm. And the only thing he wanted just then was to get away from her before she discovered that he didn't know what the fuck she was talking about.

"Now the sheriff of this county is a man named Cyrus Dolittle," she went on. "And he's . . . well, I can't describe it, but he's been very powerful around here for a very long time, okay? And he's backing a candidate named T. Whitman Purdy, who is the supervisor of the town of Tyler. The other candidate is probably going to be Ralph Jones, who is the supervisor of Hickory."

"Hickory. Right," said Merriwether. *Is she insane? Is she babbling?* he thought. *Supervisors? County executives? What are these things? What is she saying? Why am I standing here with this ugly little woman?*

"And the thing is," said Sally, "I don't want you to walk into this situation without understanding who the players are, because it's very important to the whole county. A lot is riding on this election. Okay?"

I'd like to tender my resignation now, Merriwether thought. He smiled at her. "Fine. I'll get right to work," he said.

At that, finally, she smiled again. And what a relief it was, what a transformation. The sun shone, birds sang in the trees, spring came,

45

and calm smoothed the surface of the tumultuous deep. Even her eyes seemed to soften a little. "Good," she said.

"Tally . . . uh . . . right," said Merriwether.

But she was already hurrying away from him, up the aisle to her desk. And Merriwether was left standing there alone—alone with the huge stack of folders.

"Jesus Christ," muttered Christopher Shea. He hunched his heavy shoulders, shook his head. "Good luck, pal."

Merriwether sighed and nodded. He walked sadly over to the desk with the folders on it—his desk, his new desk. He tentatively lifted the cover of the first folder and nearly groaned aloud. Inside was a stack of newspaper clippings approximately the height of the Prudential tower. He closed his eyes, rubbed his forehead. Opened his eyes . . . and noticed that there, right there on the top clipping, was a photograph of this sheriff fellow, this County Sheriff Cyrus Dolittle, as the caption said.

Merriwether studied the face in the photo, lowering himself into the desk chair as he did. Well, the man looked pleasant enough, he thought. Just a lean, craggy-faced farmhand with a receding hairline and a lopsided smile crinkling the corners of his eyes. Sort of bloke who says, "Yes, ma'am," and makes clicking noises with his teeth a lot.

Still, as Merriwether looked at him, as he recalled to himself what Sally had said, the image came into his mind of an enormous, a veritably titanic, figure. A Zeus of a sheriff, enthroned in a marble chair. Up in the clouds perhaps. Overlooking the insectile minions below. His brow thunderous, his mouth in an iron frown. Ready to hurl lightning, ready to unleash the plague, ready even to back Purdy, whoever he was, for county executive, whatever that was, in revenge for the Promethean sins of merely mortal man.

Merriwether smiled and chuckled softly to himself. He began to read the paper.

TWO

In the Hemlock Cathedral

MONDAY, JULY 9–FRIDAY, JULY 13

SHERIFF CYRUS DOLITTLE stood that morning in his home on Wapa-taugh Mountain. He stood before the picture window, looking out, his left hand in his pants pocket, his right by his side. He was already dressed, wearing his usual dark vest and pants over a white shirt. His thinning sandy hair was combed straight back. His crags and crow's-feet were cut deep in his face as his eyes narrowed at the view before him.

His wife, Liz, and his daughter, Cindy, were in the kitchen behind him. Liz—Dolittle figured—was probably sitting at the table. Head propped on her hand, elbow propped on the table's edge. She'd be staring into her coffee with that slack, stupid look she had in the morning: before the bennies and caffeine kicked in and cut into the effect of last night's tranquilizers. As for Cindy—well, Dolittle could picture her too. Banging around between cupboard and refrigerator, cursing under her breath, frowning as deeply as a large-mouth bass, and stomping back and forth to let the whole world know how pissed off she was about her big fight with Mean Mr. Daddy last night.

Dolittle sure as hell didn't want to go in there and face the two of them. One corner of his mouth lifted in a wry smile at the thought of it. No, sir, that was not his idea of a breakfast of champions. He figured he would just stay put awhile, at least until Liz was ambulatory and Cindy was on her way. He'd just stay right here at this window and look out over his county.

He could see a broad section of Auburn from here. The trees on the mountainside were in the full foliage of summer and the big maple on his sloping front lawn flared out so far that some of its branches scratched the pane. But he could peer between one starry leaf and another, and over the tops of the oaks on the ridge below, and he could make out a wide, peaceful vista of countryside that seemed to reach halfway to Gilead. There was the Hickory Pine Forest to his right, a green-blue swath, almost as dense again now as when the Indians hunted deer in it. North of that, farther to his right, there was the range of hills that marked the northern border of the Dutchman's original patent. At the forest's southern end, train tracks were visible for a bit, weaving down toward the town of Lincoln along the same old path as the nineteenth-century milk trains. And he could see where the milk farms used to be too: the overgrown fields in Hickory to the west, lining Hickory Kingdom Road.

Further south—the left border of the big window—there was Meadowbrook Reservoir. In the southwest, there was Lake Wannawan. And way off in the misty blue on the southwestern horizon, he could catch the silver flash of the early sun on Lake Tyler as well. Peaceful pools, sparkling in the morning light. They were part of New York City's watershed: whole farms, whole towns, flooded in the 1870s for the convenience of Tammany Hall. The crooked little sachems in their brown derbies—the machine pols from New York City chomping their cigars—had been caught short of water and had induced their cronies up in Albany to steal the earth right out from under Auburn in order to fill the city's need. Then, after they'd flooded perfectly good farmland—and after they'd ruined what agriculture there was and chased the big dairies away—then they had the gall to try to pay lower taxes on the reservoirs because the value of the land had dropped. Once, Dolittle remembered, about six years ago, the Army Corps of Engineers had had to drain the Cow Corners Reservoir in Auburn Hills in order to repair the dam there, and as the water neared bottom, Dolittle could see the fieldstone walls of the old farms rise up out of it, a crisscrossing network still standing in the cracked, the almost lunar, mud: like a ruined city from the county's Golden Age.

It wasn't until after the war, with the building of the interstate and other new roads, that the county had started to come back. Now, especially, in these boom times, the eighties, there was development everywhere. Just to the right of Lake Tyler, neatly nested in the maples of Tyler's flatlands, Dolittle could see the steely glint of National Paper's Corporate Park, its mirrored windows in the rising sun. It was just one of three corporations that had moved their headquarters here in the last five years. He could make out the three-year-old neighborhood planted just to the east of it—the edge of its lawns, a few rooftops: nice houses, good solid homes for workers and their families . . .

There was a metallic bang. A screen door had slammed. Dolittle blinked and glanced back over his shoulder. Through the window across the room, he caught a glimpse of Cindy storming off across the front lawn. He saw the chopped back of her dirty-blond hair bouncing.

Well, that was one down, he thought. And he could probably handle Liz by herself. Anyway, he was hungry.

He turned from the window and headed into the kitchen.

After breakfast, he drove to the Elks' hall in Tyler. An old green colonial house at the end of a dirt cul-de-sac. In the first deep heat of the day, the cul-de-sac had turned dusty. Dolittle's black Caddy kicked up a cloud as he pulled up to the hall.

Dolittle parked at the end of a row of Caddies and Town Cars. He walked through the settling dust cloud to the hall, up the front stairs, through the front door.

The gang was all there. They were gathered in the meeting room just off the foyer. It was a broad, bare auditorium with wood planks on the walls and floor. On one wall, there was a small painting of the Founding Fathers signing the Constitution. On another, there was a photograph of some of the Elks at the convention in Kansas City five years ago. An American flag hung from a pole in the wall up front.

The whole room, everything in the room, wavered and faded behind a thick greenish-gray haze of cigar smoke. Dolittle coughed into his hand, taking a place at the back, just inside the door.

The long folding table had been set up for a dais up there under the flag. There was a podium at the center of it. T. Whitman Purdy stood at the podium, begging for campaign funds and convention support.

He was a good-looking candidate, Purdy was, you had to give him that. He had a great shock of red, almost orange, hair falling over his forehead. A distant twinkle in his bright blue eyes. A wry half-smile on his lips with bright flashes of white teeth when it was called for. And he was trim and muscular too, his biceps bulging from his blue short-sleeve shirt.

"Some people in this county," he said, shaking his finger in the air. "Not to mention Ralph Jones by name, you understand—but some people will tell you that new development in Auburn means trouble. They'll tell you that growth is not the way to go. It doesn't matter how many new jobs we plan to bring in, how many homes we plan to build. These Jonesians just pull a long face and say, 'What about crime? What about our rural heritage? What about the environment?' "

Purdy leveled his upraised finger, poked it at the audience. "Well, I say these *aren't* problems. I say these are *challenges*. And they are challenges that I can meet."

The rest of the boys sat in their metal folding chairs and listened impassively. Rows of men with cigars rolling damply in the corners of their mouths. Rows of fat men mostly, thigh next to thigh, wheeze next to groan. Men so obese, some of them, that their white shirts all in a row made Dolittle think of a line of medicine balls.

He absently patted the tidy middle of his vest, running an eye over the pols.

There was Marcus Borden up front, the county party chairman (who was netted twice in the last five years during raids on a Manhattan whorehouse; three times for Driving While Intoxicated since a year ago May). There was Lincoln supervisor Albert Schneider (exposed himself to a boy in a moviehouse men's room seven years back; DWI'd two summers ago). And Greg McManus, a realty lawyer (big campaign contributor in return for zoning tips; blacked his wife's eye last year in a dispute) . . .

Lord, the lot of them, Dolittle thought: The combined tonnage of the county's politicians could sink the whole state into the Atlantic. And Christ, those cigars.

He took a breath, as best he could. Even without the smoke, it would have been stuffy in there. The summer sun beat at the window. The air conditioner snored fitfully, dripping water on the wooden planks of the floor. And Dolittle's lungs, anyway, hadn't been feeling right lately. As if there were a cloud floating at the bottom of them, a sore point that his breath couldn't quite get to. The shortness of breath was making him irritable, angry. Probably why he got so mad at his daughter last night. That and the fact that his wife was so drugged up that she hadn't had sex with him in six weeks . . .

Purdy finished his speech and the gang applauded heavily. A couple of them shouted. Borden had the good sense to let fly with a whistle. They rose to their feet with a sound like thunder.

Dolittle watched as they gathered around Purdy. Purdy's smile flashed white through the greenish-gray smoke.

When it was all over, Purdy and Dolittle stood together outside, leaning their backs against the sheriff's Cadillac.

"We have a problem with Sally Dawes, that's all I'm saying," Purdy said. He ran his hand up through his shock of red hair. "I mean, lookit, these guys here: no problem. Most of these guys—they'd nominate their aunt Sadie's shorthairs if you endorsed them. I mean, if you didn't intimidate them, their lives would lose their meaning. You know?"

Dolittle snorted softly, shaking his head at the dusty ground.

"So, all right, fine," said Purdy. "So the convention's in the bag. But after that . . ." Dolittle started to speak but Purdy held up his hands. "After that comes the election, Cy. And no matter what you think, Ralph Jones is an attractive candidate. With all that country-bumpkin bullshit of his. And you can just bet that Saint Sally of the Frostbitten Inner Thighs is gonna be backing him. And gunning for us. She's already started with that series she's doing on drug dealing in the county. You know? I mean, what's that do? It makes us look bad and Jones look good. That's all. That's all it's for." He let out a breath, sagged against the car, as if he were giving up the argument. "All I'm

51

saying, Cy, is: If we got something on the opposition, on Ralph Jones, let's use it. All right? Before Sally lets fly with whatever she's got on us. That's all I'm saying."

When Purdy stopped talking, Dolittle studied the dust a little longer. Then he raised his eyes and looked into the distance. Maple and oak trees lined the dirt road that led to the hall. The trees were heavy with leaves. Dolittle could hear the birds singing in them. Chicadees and titmice burred and twittered. A mourning dove on a nearby phone wire sent three sad notes into the pauses.

"We don't need anything on Jones, Whit," Dolittle said in his soft, rasping voice. "I've told you that. You're gonna be elected county executive in November. Just relax and we'll get there."

"Okay," said Purdy. "Okay." He threw up a hand and scratched his forehead with it. "You're calling the shots here, Cy. Really. But, I mean, if this is some kind of friendship thing for Ralphie Jones, some kind of auld lang syne thing, well, I wish you'd forget about it. That's all I got to say. I mean, Jones didn't hew too close to the friendship line when he gave Sally that story about the Hemlock Cathedral. Okay? That's all I got to say here."

"It's not friendship, Whit. It's just the best way to run the campaign. A scandal now won't help anyone." Dolittle smiled and slapped Purdy on the shoulder. "Would you relax? I'm telling you. It's guaranteed."

Purdy looked like he might start in again, but he thought better of it. He pushed off the car, shaking his head. Dolittle chuckled and patted him on the back. Purdy walked off across the dusty road.

Poor asshole, Dolittle thought as he drove back toward the Sheriff's Department. It was small wonder he was worried about Sally. If she only knew it, she could get Purdy solid any day. Influence peddling; unauthorized use of town funds; unauthorized use of the town car; seven DWIs in two years; two statutory-rape complaints in six years; one hushed-up paternity suit . . . Jesus. The poor rancid little son of a bitch was a walking blotter.

Still, Sally didn't know any of that. Purdy figured to survive the campaign well enough. He was attractive, eloquent; he followed instructions well. The only real problem with him was the one that was dangling between his legs—when it wasn't standing up around his navel, which was most of the time.

Dolittle could remember one night before the campaign began. He'd been having a beer with Purdy in Seymour's Bar and Grill in Lincoln, feeling him out about being willing to run and all. After a while, Greg McManus's secretary came in. Purdy and she exchanged one glance with each other. Then Purdy excused himself to go make a phone call. After sitting alone at the table for about ten minutes, Dolittle finally got up and strolled over to the phone booth. It was in a dark corner, a little hallway near the bathrooms. Dolittle looked through the booth's glass door and there, sure enough, was T. Whitman Purdy, his zipper undone, and the secretary, skirt up, panties down, planted on top of him. The two of them were stacked up in there one on the other like some kind of totem pole.

Dolittle laughed to himself as he drove, shook his head at the windshield. If Purdy could just keep that zipper of his closed until November—that zipper of his and that mouth—and if he could just keep from panicking and blowing the whole deal with his blackmail schemes—well, then even Sally, with the worst will in the world, would have a hard time getting at him.

The big car wound around Church Road smoothly and quickly. A canopy of maple trees threw dappled shadows on the stretch of pavement ahead. Warm air blew in through the open window. Dolittle drew in a breath as deeply as he could. He coughed a little. He thought about Sally Dawes.

Purdy did have a point about her, no question. She *would* be gunning for him. She always was. She had never liked Dolittle, never. And the feeling had been mutual. Right from the start.

That time, that very first time he'd met her, she'd been trying to sneak a story about Fred Denkinger's daughter. Not even five minutes after Dolittle and his boys had pulled the little girl's battered body out of the woods. Betrayed, raped, crying out, poor thing. And there was Sally Dawes, just trying to get the story in the newspaper, just trying to write it up for everyone to see.

Dolittle hated that shit, he hated it. Big-city shit, smearing a family's misfortunes over the front page. Sally had probably been trying to get good clips so she could get a job in New York or down in

White Plains or something. She didn't understand that the Den-kingers had neighbors here who cared about them, friends. Even if you don't name the girl in the paper, everyone who matters is going to know who it was.

Dolittle had been mightily pissed to see that woman standing there. And maybe he'd been a little rough on her, scaring her off. But damn, ever since then she'd just been obsessed with him, obsessed with getting him. That story Purdy mentioned, the one she did about the Hemlock Cathedral . . . Dolittle's lips twisted as he drove.

He had turned onto Route 6 now. He was heading for Main Street. He stopped at a light beside the Tyler Corners mall. He let his eyes travel over its long line of stores. Cars cruised back and forth across its huge parking lot. Women pushed strollers on the sidewalk from the Ben Franklin five-and-dime to the Duane Reade drugstore to the Bookworm to the Stitch in Time and so on, store to store. Ralph Jones, Sally Dawes, and all the rich folks who had apartments in the city, and all the summer people who only spent a few months up here—they hated this mall, they hated all the places like this. Dawes had even written an editorial about it, calling Tyler Corners an eye-sore.

But the thing was, the mall wasn't meant to be beautiful. The mall wasn't meant to serve rich people and summer people and news-paper people and pols. It was meant to provide convenient shopping for the young families who'd been transferred up here to work at the paper company and the computer company. It was meant to provide movies their kids could go to so they didn't hang out at the train tracks and get in trouble like the kids did in Hickory. Dolittle had had to pull a lot of strings to get Commercial Corridor zoning for Route 6. And Sally and Jones and all of them could get ready, because there were going to be a lot more Route 6's too in this county, after the election was over and the rezoning plan went into effect.

The light changed. The Cadillac cruised forward, up the hill toward the corner of Main.

It must be driving Dawes crazy, he thought with some satisfac-tion. To see him moving in on the executive's office like this. It must've driven her crazy these last seven years, watching him consol-idate his power, guide the charter, work out the rezoning—and now to see him make his move. She probably thought she had finished him off right at the start with that piece on the Hemlock Cathedral. Homely, lonely little spinster, taking out her frustrations on him . . .

Maybe that was the solution right there: Maybe he ought to give her some satisfaction. Maybe they ought to have a fling, he and Sally. God knew, they could both use a little of it. . . .

Dolittle tried to draw a deep breath again and coughed into his hand. This thing, this breathing thing, it really was making him irritable. And Sally Dawes too—he was getting tired of thinking about her all these years, tired of worrying about her, worrying she might come up with something, worrying he'd finally make a fatal mistake and she'd nail him.

Suddenly, he thought of his daughter again. He really had lost his head with her last night; he really had lost his temper.

He turned onto Main and cruised toward the Sheriff's Department. He cursed quietly.

He thought of the Hemlock Cathedral.

2

Cindy was there today. Cindy Dolittle. She was in the Hemlock Cathedral. It was a huge circle of suddenly open ground in the Hickory Pine Forest, and in Cindy's opinion it was the fucking greatest.

Most of the kids who hung out at the Hickory train station came here sometimes—the leaves around the fringes were littered with their beer cans and roaches, their condoms and cigarette butts. But Cindy liked to be here alone like she was now: just sitting at the center of the ring of hemlocks and pines, her knees drawn up, her arms wrapped around them. She liked to sit and gaze at the tree trunks shooting up like rockets through the light and shadow, their ragged branches black up there against the high sky, swaying, the sun angling down through them in misty pillars of light, and the big white boulders sitting here and there on the brown needles, frowning at her like old men.

She liked to come here and sit like this when she was depressed. Depressed like she was now. About Daddy, about everything.

He wasn't even supposed to have been home last night. Mr.

Tough Guy Sheriff. Mr. John Wayne Walking Tall Shithead. He was supposed to be out sucking off one of his fat political friends so they'd bow down to him and nominate that asshole Purdy to be his puppet government. Purdy, who once drove Candy Nolan home and fingered her when she was only thirteen, and everybody knew about it, too. Although Candy had already been doing it by then.

Anyway, Sheriff Duke Daddy was supposed to be out till eleven, and Mother, aka the Walking Drugstore, was supposed to be so tranked up as per usual that you could trust her to be found sprawled out across the double bed upstairs, one hand flung over the side, and a snore coming out of her wide-open mouth that sounded like a logger's saw.

So Cindy had had Teddy over. And they hadn't even been doing anything. What did he think, that they'd never fucked before? She was practically fifteen, for Christ's sake, and Teddy wasn't some old fart politician trying to get his finger wet. But they hadn't even *been* fucking, that was the thing that had Cindy so pissed off. They'd had all their clothes on. And they'd just been lying on the bed together and Teddy had just been kissing her neck and, okay, maybe giving her a little knee action between her legs. They hadn't even heard him come in.

The next thing anybody knows, Sheriff Dad has dragged Teddy off her. And he's got him by the front of his shirt, holding him up against the wall, banging him against the wall. Big tough guy. Cindy had cried and screamed, pounding at Daddy's arms with her small fists. But Daddy was crazy; he just kept slamming Teddy against the wall, his eyes all nuts and on fire.

And he kept saying, "I know you, you polack piece of shit. I know. You're one of Scotti's gang. Drug-dealing piece of garbage. Garbage! If I ever see you around my daughter again, so help me God, I'll ram my fist so far down your throat you'll shit my knuckles."

Big tough guy, big cock. As if Teddy couldn't have killed Daddy if Daddy weren't a cop.

And then, when Daddy had dragged Teddy to the door and thrown him out, he had turned on her. Cindy had been practically hysterical by then, screaming in his face, feeling her own face turn scarlet, her tears flying. She spun and ran away from him. Ran into her room, slamming the door behind her. But that didn't stop Buford

Tough Guy Daddy, no sir. He just shoved the door in after her, almost hurting her too. And when Cindy had flung herself face down on the bed, he had stood over her, hissing at her like some kind of snake or something in that snaky, raspy voice of his.

"Let me tell you something, little girl. That boy and his boss Scotti, and all their drug-deal friends, your goddamned . . . train-station pals . . . they are all about to take one big fall, do you hear me? A little weasel named Billy Thimble has just turned over on them, you hear? And your lover boy and all his buddies are going to be spending the school year in Sing Sing, and if you're not goddamned careful, you're going with them too. You hear? You hear?"

Cindy hated him. She hated him. She hoped he lost his goddamned election. She hoped they came to him and said, "Not only don't we want Purdy to be county executive, but we don't want you to be sheriff anymore. You're fired. And you're a shitty father too."

She smiled grimly at the thought, hugging her knees tighter. Gazed up at the treetops as they bowed and rattled in the slow summer breeze. She breathed the breeze. Oh, she did love it here. It was the only place where they all left her alone, where everything was just far away and left her alone.

Sometimes—sometimes she even had a dream about the place—or not a dream, a daydream, or a fantasy. She'd be in danger. She'd be running through the fog. And there would be this . . . *thing* after her. This bear or this killer or a rapist or something. Just this shadowy shape behind her in the forest and the forest all covered with mist and the mist all moonlit. And the mist would sort of thread its way eerily between the trees or just lie draped over the branches like in a wolfman movie. And the bear-thing would come through it, come after her. The shape of it getting larger and larger and larger until she could hear its slavering breath, its disgusting snorts and noises. And then she would come into the clearing, into the Hemlock Cathedral, and she would stumble . . . (When she was alone and she got to this part of the fantasy, she would begin to touch herself, she would touch her cunt, play her finger over the fleshy nub. She would think about how she'd stumble) . . . and just lie there, panting, helpless, while this thing, this maniac shape, got larger and larger in the mist and then suddenly . . .

Suddenly, a branch snapped. She spun toward the sound.

There he was, coming along the path, ducking under a branch now to step into the cathedral.

She jumped to her feet to greet him.

"Teddy."

Teddy Wocek: She thought the guy was unholy. The way he hunched his shoulders and hung his head when he walked into the clearing, his long hair swinging. The way he looked from under his hair in that sort of shy, sort of hunted way. He was short but he was very broad and muscular. She had seen him do twenty-six pull-ups once. And he lifted weights too. His rocky shoulders bulged from his cutoff T-shirt; his tight hips bunched and rippled in his tight jeans. Even the grime on his clothes—because he'd just come from the gas station—and the smudge of grease on his cheek looked good. He was three years older than she was—he was seventeen. And since Cindy hated the way she looked, with her square, chunky face and her small, scrawny body and her chopped-off dirty-blond hair that just *hung* there, for shit's sake, whatever she did . . . Well, she thought it was pretty amazing that Teddy wanted to be with her at all.

He stomped up to her. She couldn't help smiling. He smiled back down at her and took her by the shoulders and kissed her, kissed her for a long time, sliding his hand down to her ass, pressing her hips up against his. It was kind of gross when he put his tongue so far into her mouth, but aside from that it was just like a movie. To have him doing it to her in the woods like that, in the Cathedral, with the columns of sun coming in and the birds singing and the steady burr of crickets and peepers. All they needed was actual music.

Teddy broke away, pulled back. Gazed deeply into her eyes. "Ey," he said.

"Ey."

"Are you, like, fucked up?"

She shrugged in his grip. "Fucking parents. You know."

"Ey, tell me about it."

"Fuck them. I mean, you know?"

"Forget it. Fuck em, Cinj. We're okay. You know? Fuck em."

He moved in again, burrowing into her neck. Working his

hand—his rough hand, dirty hand, cold hand—up under her T-shirt now. Cupping it over her breasts—which was just *so* embarrassing; they were just *so* small. Making her cunt start to run a little.

"Ey, Teddy, wait."

"I don't wanna wait," he whispered.

"I gotta tell you something."

"So tell me. I can listen."

"Ted-dee!" She laughed and pushed against him. It was like pushing against a house or something.

He pulled back again. "Ey. What's so important? I'm a fucking adolescent here, I got animal urges."

She tried not to laugh this time, but she did anyway. "Really, Teddy. I'm fucking serious." She pushed against him some more. "Really. Okay? Really."

He gave up with a sigh. Letting go, leaning back on his hip, crossing his arms on his chest. "All right. What's so fucking important?"

"Well I mean Jesus, Teddy, it's about fucking Vince Scotti."

"Oh great!" He stalked away from her, threw up his hands, dropped them with a slap against his jeans. "I thought we weren't gonna fucking talk about this anymore."

"Well, you wanna hear? About that he's gonna get arrested? You wanna hear or not?"

Arms crossed again. He eyed her. "You know that?"

"It's around."

Teddy tried to shrug it off. "Ey. Vince is a fucking drug dealer. You know? That's what that's like."

"Yeah." Cindy ran her hand up through her hair. She frowned—to keep from smiling at that intense look of his. "Only I don't think he's gonna be so happy about this. I think this time Billy Thimble is gonna go to the cops about him."

That surprised even Teddy, as Cindy was glad to see. He jutted his face out at her, his mouth open suspiciously, his eyes narrow. Yeah, she thought back at him, that's right, Billy Thimble. Everybody thought Billy Thimble was so fucking great. Because he wasn't like the rest of them. He was a big lawyer, and he wore suits and ties and was educated. And he always looked clean and had a fancy haircut and his eyes sparkled when he smiled. Even Vince was proud of having Billy Thimble around. Even Teddy was always telling her about some joke Billy Thimble made, and how much Billy Thimble liked Vince and did what Vince said, even though he was a lawyer and everything.

Teddy gave her the squint-eye another second. Then he pulled back. "Are you shitting me?"

"No, Teddy."

"Are you shitting me? You heard that?"

"Yeah. I swear."

"Ey . . ." He shrugged again, but Cindy could see it really bothered him.

Shoving her hands in the back pockets of her jeans, she bit her lip. She tried to look very serious. "I mean, I'm, like, scared, Teddy."

"What." He lifted his chin at her. "What."

"Well . . . I mean, fucking Vince Scotti, you know? He gets in trouble or something? He could tell about you."

"Ey." Teddy leaned forward. He counted the fingers of one hand with the other. "First of all, Billy Thimble doesn't know shit, okay? No way they're gonna arrest Vince Scotti because fucking Billy Thimble is saying something, no way. That's one. Number two: The New York cops couldn't outsmart Vince when he operated down there, right? So—what? He's gonna get nailed by these fucking woodchuck cops up here? Forget about it. Okay? Next: There's no fucking way Vince Scotti rolls over on me because I'm his friend. There's no fucking way Vince Scotti turns in any of his friends. Everybody knows that. That's world famous. All right?"

Cindy rolled her eyes. Vince Scotti was a gangster piece of shit who would roll over on anybody—that's what she wanted to say.

"And third—or fourth or whatever," Teddy said, "what the fuck would he tell the cops? Vince. What the fuck is he gonna say? I didn't do nothing. What did I do?"

She put her hands on her hips and gave him a Real Look now.

"What," he said again.

"Well, I mean: you know, Teddy."

"What? What?"

"Ted-deee."

"Ey. Look. Vince is a close personal friend. I did him a couple of favors a couple of times. And I mean, it was, like, marijuana, not a big deal."

"Well, I don't know if the cops are gonna see it like that, Teddy."

"Ey." He started counting his fingers again. "First of all . . ."

"All right, all right. Forget it. Forget it."

"No, wait. No, wait. I'll prove to you what I'm saying."

"I said forget it, Teddy. It's okay."

"I'll prove it."

"It's okay, really."

They stood apart for a few more moments. Then Cindy went closer to him.

"Okay?" she said.

He wagged his head back and forth.

"Come on," she said. She hated for him to be mad at her. "Come on. Forget it. Let's do something. Okay? Before somebody comes by. Let's do something."

He sighed at her, but he nodded. He pulled his T-shirt up over his head, baring his rippling stomach, his flat, stony chest. She pulled off her T-shirt too, embarrassed again by how small her breasts were. She turned away from him when she stripped off her jeans.

Naked, then, they lay together on the conifer needles. It was kind of uncomfortable: The needles prickled her ass. Teddy worked his finger around in her pussy until she got wet and then he climbed on top of her and guided his cock into her. He laid his head on her shoulder and pumped in and out. It scraped at first until she got wetter. Then he pumped a little faster and slumped on top of her.

They should use rubbers more, she thought, holding him. But it was too romantic in the Cathedral. Lying here, looking up at the high trees with the sun falling in over them. It was like a movie or something. You didn't want to ruin it.

After a minute or two, they got up and brushed the pine needles off each other and put their jeans back on in case anyone came. Then she lay bare-chested with her head on his bare chest. It really was romantic.

Out at the edge of the forest, out on Hickory Kingdom Road, a truck went by, a big one by the sound of it. Clutching with a stuttered roar, it drowned out the birdsong and the cicadas for a second and drove away the little sound of the breeze in the branches. When it was gone, the quiet wafted down over them like a sheet. The quiet went on, it seemed to her, a long time.

"So you gonna tell him?" she asked. "You gonna tell Vince, I mean, about Billy Thimble being a rat and everything?"

He didn't answer right away. He stroked the back of her head. "I gotta tell him. I mean, Vince is a man who has taught me a lot of things, Cindy. I mean it. He knows a fucking lot about life, okay? What else am I gonna do?"

"Not tell him?" She watched him gazing up at the treetops. "Like, you know? Just not tell him."

He sighed, shook his head. "I gotta tell him, Cinj. He's, like, my friend."

"Vince Scotti is not your friend, Teddy. He's not anybody's fucking friend."

That, anyway, was what she wanted to say. But she didn't. She just lay there with her head on his chest, hearing his heartbeat. Feeling their good nakedness together.

3

The Hemlock Cathedral, Sally thought. *Oh damn.*

At first, when she saw Merriwether take the *Hemlock Cathedral* folder from the pile on his desk, she tried to ignore it. She trained her attention on the copy before her: the second piece in Rumplemeyer's series, "The Rise in Drug Use Among the County's Teens." Very important stuff. Crucial stuff. Let people see what the sheriff's greedy development policies were turning the county into. . . .

She skimmed her red pencil over the typed words:

Though the Sheriff's Department says (make that "claims") *it has not yet compiled figures on drug arrests* (which is a definite lie), *Hickory supervisor Ralph Jones says these arrests have risen* ("soared") *nearly 25 percent in a single year. Jones, who is favored to win his party's nomination for county executive, has seized on the increase as a political issue* (Why did I leave the Hemlock Cathedral piece in there? Damn it. Damn it.) *in expectation of a campaign against Tyler supervisor T. Whitman Purdy, who has the backing of Sheriff Cyrus Dolittle.* (That sentence is two days long, Rumple, stop reading the goddamned *Times.*) *Purdy has responded by charging* (And anyway what do I care what this Merriwether guy thinks, he's not even a real reporter, he doesn't even know . . .) *that the problem is centered in the towns of Hickory and Gilead because* (. . . he looks like that, that's why, I mean, Jesus, he looks exactly like . . .) *they have not "responded to the need for development and opportunity."* (I'm turning into a walking Tennessee Williams play. . . .)

"Oh hell," she whispered. She had lost track of the paragraph. She raised her eyes again in time to see Merriwether open the folder on the desktop.

The Hemlock Cathedral, she thought again. *Damn.*

They were alone together in the little bureau, Merriwether at his front desk, Sally in the rear. Christopher Shea was off having his Friday fish dinner with the in-laws. Rumplemeyer, who lived in White Plains as she did, was down at the Plant, writing his connector road story directly into the computers. She had stayed up here because— well, because it was quiet, for one thing. The phones weren't ringing. The smell of Shea's cigarettes was fading away. The long last light was folding to peaceful purple at the storefront window. The traffic passing to and from Main was growing sparse, a car going past now and then, a whisper. No noise but the police scanner hissing on the file cabinet behind her. A good place to get some work done.

And it just so happened that Merriwether was also here, also working late. It was very diligent of him really. With his wife at home waiting and all. Waiting patiently, faithfully. Here he was, going through the million folders of old news stories she had dumped on his desk. Down to the last few folders and going through them just as intensely and thoroughly as he had all week. She couldn't fault him on that at all.

And now he had opened this one, this one godforsaken folder with the frayed gray edges . . . Sally had recognized it from clear across the room.

Why didn't I hide it, why didn't I leave it in the drawer? . . .

She lowered her face again quickly. Blushing. She was blushing, for Christ's sake.

After all this time, after seven years, she could still remember—she could still feel—what it was like to go after that story. Those stretches of wooded county road, far from service stations and phones. The feel of the steering wheel clutched in her hand, her knuckles bugging out like eyes. The cool necklace of sweat beneath her Peter Pan collar as she willed that jalopy—that decrepit, practically antebellum Monza— willed it to serve her another hour, another day.

"This is your big chance, Sally," Randall Shank had told her. "I told you we'd sharpen our pencils on that bastard's heart, didn't I? I told you. Now go out there and get me the story on the Hemlock Cathedral."

She could remember the faces—she could still see the faces, hear the voices of the people she had interviewed. Ralph Jones, the fat old country-boy Hickory Town supervisor. He was chief among her sources, her main source, his square, fat, jowly face blinking at her from behind his desk in the Hickory Town Hall. Then there had been Maria MacMillan, a creaking, raisin-faced neighbor of the sheriff's family, serving tea in her musty parlor. And the victim's brother, Bert Marsh, dour and ashen outside his struggling seed business. And there were others. Sally could see them all, could hear them talking even now. And she could see herself scribbling diligently in her notebook. She could feel them, her sources and herself both, subjects and re- porter together, building, word by word, the core of the story: an idea; no, an image—that image that had seemed to her then, that seemed to her to this very day, the crux of the Matter of Auburn County. That image—the image of Cyrus Dolittle.

Back then, seven years ago, in that miserable time of hers, in all her panic to beat the deadline and give Shank the news he wanted so feverishly, in all her desperation to succeed at what she knew was her last chance with the Sutcliffe Suits in White Plains, in all her efforts to bury herself in her work again and forget Jerry and the way she had been with Jerry, and even in her efforts to fall back to sleep at night when she lay in her bed with her fist screwed into her mouth for fear her sobs would wake her mother—in all the concentrated insanity of her thirties, that image of Dolittle had become her focal point. She would think of it constantly to take her mind off her personal pain.

She would conjure it to dissipate the ceaseless slide show of her stupid mistakes. Slowly, as the days went on, as the story of the Hemlock Cathedral grew clearer, she would use the image to bring together the seemingly meaningless scraps and fragments gleaned from her sources, to arrange them like jigsaw-puzzle pieces in the frame of the story, to *make* them into a story when a story was what Shank—and her own mind—demanded of her.

And so that image—that image of Dolittle—it came to seem to her not only the origin point of the county's recent events but the symbol, in some indescribable way, for her own life up to that time, her own pitiful life.

And yet it was not an image of Dolittle as he was then, seven years ago. It was a far older image. A primordial image (or so she put it to herself). It was an image of Dolittle as he had been a great thirty-six years in the past. Back in the Auburn County of the 1950s. The Auburn County of history. It was an image of Dolittle when he was strong and youthful and lean and loose. Or that's how she pictured him anyway: rising from the snowy ground of the Hemlock Cathedral like a wisp of woodsmoke. Alone at the center of the circle of great trees, his deer rifle slung over his arm. The body of the little girl he and Jones had discovered lying pathetic and broken at his feet.

That was the image she had constructed as she tracked down the old story:

Dolittle, alone, inexorable. Coming to his conclusions.

Thirty-six years ago. Back, back in time. That was the year after the feds finally got around to approving funds for the new interstate. It was a big event for Auburn. The county had responded with a four-year, $1 million plan to overhaul its own roads, all seventy miles of them. And both Cyrus Dolittle and Ralph Jones, both around twenty then, had quit their jobs with the Hickory Highway Department and answered the county's call for new road workers.

In this they followed, as they always followed, the lead of their best friend, Hank McGee.

McGee was twenty-eight, and the two younger men idolized him. When Sally interviewed Ralph Jones thirty years later, Jones frankly admitted that McGee was a kind of father figure to him. His own father, a dairy farmer, was a "real good fellow," Jones said, but irritable and worn out from a lifetime of kicking and cursing the rickety milker that barely squeezed a profit out of his dozen or so recalcitrant udders. Young Ralphie needed someone like McGee, he told her, "to sorta, sorta, whatcha might call, see me through, if ya understand me."

And as for Dolittle—what must McGee have meant to him? Maybe Sally just got a sort of voyeuristic kick out of the rites and rituals of male bonding, but this question fascinated her all those years later as she interviewed Jones and the others. What must McGee have meant to young Cyrus Dolittle?

Dolittle's father was Hickory's town drunk, a onetime dairy man who barely survived by raising chickens and peddling scrap. The rot-eaten clapboards of his old house were visible to the world at the edge of Hickory Kingdom Road. The windows of it, covered with plastic in the winter, stared out on a lawn cluttered with empty car bodies and rusted lampstands and dented filing cabinets—and sometimes the old man himself, lying facedown in the crabgrass, his blue work clothes grimed black and his flesh reeking. Dolittle's mother had died of emphysema, and for many years while her son was growing up, she'd been forced to stay in bed, staring at the ceiling through the dark of a curtained room, wheezing softly, drowning in her own lungs. The boy, Cyrus (this was according to Mrs. MacMillan, Sally's neighbor-source), had grown up to be a wary-eyed, taciturn slat of a young man "with a real chip on his shoulder."

What—Sally asked herself over and over—what must McGee have meant to him?

McGee, in Sally's opinion at least, was everything a young man could ask for in a hero. Rugged, handsome. A hunter, an athlete. He had grown up in the South somewhere—no one ever did know where exactly. He had wandered around the country as a boy and had been in the war also, before settling in Auburn where, he said, he liked the rolling hills and the weather. He told great stories about hopping freight trains, about hammering across Sicily with General Bradley, about traveling the south and making it with girls named Mary Lou and Lucy May in towns named Gurley and Hoxie and Zebulon. McGee taught his two protégés how to drink and how to hunt, and he taught them about women—the women at the roadhouse on the county line, Jones said (but that was as much as he *would* say, the fat old blushing bumpkin, no matter how Sally pressed him).

And, McGee talked. A great talker, full of stuff. Told them the county, this Auburn of the fifties, was on the rise. Yessir. And these new roads they were building were just the beginning of it. For fifty years, ever since Tammany Hall came up and legislated the county's ground away, ever since they condemned the farms and flooded them to make the city's reservoirs, the county had been depressed. The farmers had been only too happy to take the city money and move west in search of less stony ground. The big dairies had gone north and, with the war over and the need for wool slacking off, the sheep farms and most of the mills on the river had started closing down as well. By the 1950s, there was nothing left in Auburn but the stately mansions of the rich and a lot of city-owned lakes for the Irish and Italian workers to build their summer cottages around.

But all that was gonna change now, said McGee, and he said it (according to Ralph Jones) with such verve and conviction that you almost had to believe him. The new roads would put Auburn within striking distance of New York and White Plains, he said. And with the automobile taking over the way it was, and the suburbs taking over the way they were, Auburn wasn't going to need farms and industries and all that wash—no, sir. All it was going to need was land—land with roads on it. That's right, McGee said. Land with roads on it. Why, they were building the county's future with their very own hands!

Dolittle and Jones were convinced anyway. They adopted McGee's tartan lumberman jackets, his stiff-legged way of walking, his way of squinting off into the distance as he talked. They hunted with his kind of rifle—a Winchester bolt action 30–06—and they called it "the Ought-six," the same as he did. McGee told them he was going to be sheriff one day, when Bart Thompson finally retired. And that the county was going to grow too big for a two-man force. The state police wouldn't be able to cover the place alone, and the new sheriff was going to need a whole lot more than one deputy, and what did they think of that?

Jones was kind of happy where he was, in the Highway Department. But Dolittle said, Sure. Sure, yeah. He would be pleased and proud to be deputy to a Sheriff Hank McGee, if that should come to pass and. . . .

Well, Sally, all those years later, she just had to wonder: What must Dolittle have really thought, really dreamed?

What must McGee have meant to him?

Now, pretending to edit Rumple's piece, she snuck a peek at Merriwether from under the fall of her hair. He was laying the front page clip aside (*The Hemlock Cathedral: The Murder That Made a Sheriff. First of two articles*) and had begun poring over the clip from the jump page (*Sheriff, cont. from pg. 1*). She could not see his expression. It was possible he was finding this part of it grotesque. A brilliant young man like him, after all, would enjoy the first part, the character study, more than the mere sensationalistic details . . . or maybe he would think the first part was shallow and overwritten . . . or maybe he would be disgusted by the whole thing and simply jump to his feet and stride up the aisle to her, his bronze brows lowering over his piercing blue eyes, and hurl the folder in her face and cry, "How could you, Sally? How *could* you?"

Sally lowered her head again quickly as Merriwether shifted in his chair. He was right, she thought. It was overwritten. Shallow. Unfair. Why had she let Shank force her into it? It was the biggest mistake of her life. . . .

Oh, Sally, she thought, *how could you?*

She had been trying to convey her sense of genesis, her feeling that all things in modern Auburn had begun somehow with this. A Saturday in early December, thirty-six years ago. The Hickory Pine Forest, silent and white with an early snow. First light, just dawn.

Dolittle and Jones had been hunting for over an hour. They'd already changed their spot twice but had not even sighted a doe. Following the cloven hoof prints and spoor, they made their way to the Hemlock Cathedral. The boulders made good blinds and gave them a wide range of vision.

They came into the clearing and stood still together, one slim, one pudgy, both turning their heads slowly, surveying the area for a place to settle. It was Jones who first spotted the mound of leaves and dirty snow at the rim of the open circle.

"Cy," he hissed.

Dolittle followed his friend's pointed finger and saw a shiny red shoe protruding from the top of the mound.

Quickly, each man leaned his rifle against a rock. They went to the snowpile, dropped to their knees. Clawing like dogs, they began to scrape the frozen humus away from around the shoe. First, they uncovered her ankle, clothed in a pale blue sock. Then her bare leg, the skin chilled to the color of quartz. Then her naked torso—the clothes had been torn off her. They kept digging, their fingertips stinging and numb.

Her vagina, they saw, was lacerated and brown with dried blood. Her chest was blown open by a rifle shell: There was a slanting black cavity into the darkness beneath her flesh. Finally, they settled back on their haunches and looked at her. Her face, Jones said, was just the face of a child asleep.

Her name was Carol Marsh. She was seven years old. She'd been sent to spend the night with her grandmother and, because of crossed signals, had not yet been reported missing.

Both men picked up their rifles and stood together, watching the snowy woods. Finally, after a few minutes, Jones ran off to call the police, leaving Dolittle alone.

The sun was visible through the trees now. The snow sparkled with it; the snow-covered conifers sparkled and shone. Water dripped from branches and glittered. Icicles flashed on them. (Sally could always picture this; it sent chills through her.) Dolittle stood alone, his ought-six hung in the crook of his right elbow, his head bowed a little, his narrow brown eyes steady on the child's form. His right hand was clenched, pressed to his left breast. In it he held the brass shell casing of a 30–06 Springfield bullet.

He was coming to his conclusions.

Merriwether, reading, sighed. Sally heard him. She was sure of it. Maybe, she thought, the child's death had moved him. Maybe he had been touched by her fine, her impassioned, prose. She peeked up to

69

see him lift his head—yes, he was touched, he was taking a moment for solemn consideration. It had grown dark enough outside so she could see his face reflected in the storefront window, could study the noble sadness of his frown, the intelligence of his bearing, and that gorgeous mouth . . . Jesus. He looked just like . . .

She lowered her eyes. She'd been staring at him. He had probably seen her, seen her reflection in the window, staring. They might even have been staring *at* one another. She had to stop acting like this. She had to get back to work, back to Rumplemeyer's fascinating and urgent analysis of how cocaine traffic could become a major campaign issue. . . .

She raised her eyes to look at Merriwether again. If only there were not that incredible resemblance, she thought. If only he did not look just like . . . just like . . .

Yes. By God, yes: He looked just like *The Man of Her Dreams!*

It was true; it was uncanny: Every feature was the same. Whenever she lay in her bed at night, or touched herself in the shower, or drove to work, or walked in the park and fantasized about the man she wanted—he was it, he was the guy. Whether it was the Sinister Fellow Watching Her Through Her Bedroom Window or the Drifter Coming to Town on a Hot Summer Day or the Dashing Scientist She Had to Interview in a Deserted Lab or (one of her favorites) The Mysterious Stranger Who Followed Her Home from Work—they all had his smooth, impossible beauty, his easy elegance, his musical grace.

Christ, she thought, how could he show up now? The exact right man. How *dare* he show up now? So many times in the past she had actually *believed* he had come to her. She had overlooked so many flaws, made so many allowances for one son of a bitch or another on the off-chance it might be he. And now here he was? In the flesh? When she was too tired? When she was too old? It must've been some sort of punishment for her sins. She wanted to march to the front of the room and tell him, To hell with you, buster. Go back whence-ever it was you came. And take your goddamned wife with you.

Maybe a stake through the heart would kill him, she thought.

She let out her breath as he lowered his eyes to the clip again. He must be reading the end of it, the end of Part One. Oh, God, and now he was going to see Part Two, the notorious, the terrible Part Two? He was going to see it and recoil from her in disgust. That was it. That was the sin she was being punished for. . . .

She looked on in agony as Merriwether kept reading.

The article—Part One—ended like this.

Hank McGee lived in the Sunshine Trailer Park in the northeast corner of Hickory, in the shadow of Wapataugh (or Injun) Mountain. Around noon on the day Dolittle and Jones discovered the body of Carol Marsh, McGee had come home to his trailer there, carrying a grocery bag full of beer. (This Sally got from Dolittle's testimony at the inquest, the only official version of the story there was.) McGee set the bag on the fold-down kitchen table. Then he turned around and saw Dolittle.

The young man was sitting in the trailer's only comfortable chair, a shapeless orange easy chair McGee had salvaged from the side of a road. He had one foot up on the long coffee table in front of him, and his ought-six was lying across his lap. Beside him, on the lamp table, was one of McGee's own pistols. His favorite, in fact: a replica of the old 1875 Remington Outlaw. Long-barreled, nickel-plated. And loaded with .45 caliber bullets.

McGee's face went gray. He spoke his friend's name once: "Cy?" Dolittle tossed the ought-six shell casing across the room. McGee, taken by surprise, clapped at it and caught it between his two palms.

Outside, just then, the state police were fanning out through the Hickory woods, flagging down motorists on the icy roads, canvassing neighborhoods with photos of seven-year-old Carol Marsh, broadcasting calls for help over the local radio.

Inside, McGee looked down at the casing in his hand.

It was a common gauge, the ought-six. The Winchester Model 70 was considered one of the best mid-priced hunting rifles there was. But later ballistics tests matched the slug that had killed the girl to McGee's rifle. And McGee, according to Dolittle, wasn't prepared to argue the point anyway.

According to Dolittle, the man just tossed the casing down on the tattered sofa against the trailer wall. His chin sank to his chest; he shook his head, his lips trembling, his eyes filling with tears.

Dolittle picked up the Remington Outlaw, dropped his raised

foot, and laid the revolver on the coffee table in its place. He slid it down toward McGee.

"You're a friend, Hank," he said. "I thought you might want to handle this yourself."

McGee nodded. "Thank you, Cy," he said.

He reached down and slipped his hand around the walnut stock, his finger through the shining trigger guard. He raised the pistol . . . and then, suddenly, pointed it at Dolittle. He pulled the trigger.

Dolittle fired the Winchester. McGee was slapped back against the kitchen table, his arms pinwheeling. A window pane blew apart as the Outlaw's .45 slug crashed through it. McGee stood upright for another second, wavering like a tree about to fall. Then he tumbled to the floor, his eyes open, his shirt spattered with blood, his chest ripped wide by the impact of the ought-six.

THREE

The Floater

FRIDAY, JULY 13

GOOD LORD, THOUGHT Merriwether, *how long do I have to pretend to read this stuff?*

Folder after folder of yellowed newspaper clippings lay scattered over the surface of his desk. Faded photographs of dewlapped bumpkins and their astringent wives. Columns of prose which, if read, could drive a man blind with boredom. Thank God he was only staring at it.

The last time he had actually happened to read part of one of these so-called *news stories*—oh, it had been a living nightmare of intolerable dullness. That was about two putrid days ago. He had been sitting here pretending to study the clip in front of him, his mind in transition from a daydream about love-raping the actress Molly Ringwald to wondering whether the poststructuralists had not somehow lost their grounding in the physical particularity of Freudian thought, when suddenly his unsuspecting eye happened to fall on this masterpiece of a sentence penned by that perfidious gnome Rumplemeyer: "The 1965 decision by the Court of Appeals, the state's highest court, which deemed the Supreme Court's one man, one vote rule applied to local governments and so set Auburn on the long road to a legislature

73

and a charter, has also been held responsible for the board of supervisors' current predicament." Fascinating, no?

Merriwether was convinced he was in the sixth circle of hell: *Unmanly Failures Who Defied Their Fathers, step this way.*

There had been five solid days of this—and now it was Friday evening and he couldn't even get home for the weekend. The Dawes woman was positively standing guard over him as if he were some sort of mischievous boy held late at school. She hadn't yet asked him to *do* anything, thank heavens. In fact, since that first day, she'd hardly said a word to him at all. But she kept *hovering* there behind him—he could see her reflected in the storefront windows—sneaking peeks at him, making sure he was still hard at work, still putting in a full eight hours. . . .

Had he looked at this clip long enough to be convincing? he wondered. *The Hemlock Cathedral,* it was called. *The Murder That Made a Sheriff.* Clearly, he was dealing with cheap melodrama at its cheap melodramiest. He glanced over a paragraph toward the bottom:

"Dolittle's courageous and tragic confrontation with his best friend caught the public's imagination."

It certainly has engaged mine, Merriwether thought.

"Ironically . . ."

Ironically? My, my, my.

"Ironically, by killing Hank McGee, he had made himself a natural candidate for the post McGee had coveted: county sheriff."

So that's how it's done here. Dear God, these people are savages.

"After Bart Thompson's retirement, Dolittle served as deputy for nine years before his election to the sheriff's post."

Then, underneath the last sentence, were the almost incredible words: "Next Week: The Second of This Two-Part Series."

Merriwether lifted the clip and, by golly, there it was *The Hemlock Cathedral.* Part Two: *It Snowed the Night of the Murder.*

It snowed? he thought. *What in heaven's name . . . ?*

"You don't have to read that one."

Startled, he looked up to see Sally Dawes standing right beside him. Before he could react, she reached out and took the folder away from him, tucked it under her arm. She turned her eyes down; her cheeks were mottled with red—was she blushing?—her voice was even sweeter, shyer, more whispery than usual.

"I don't know how that one got in there. I did it . . ." She made a gesture with her hands to indicate the distant past. ". . . long ago."

Merriwether didn't know what to say. Was she *justifying* herself? To *him?* Who didn't even know what the hell she was talking about? "Well, it's . . . a very interesting story."

She nodded. "The sheriff is a, uh . . . an interesting man."

"Yes," he said carefully. "I see that." He didn't want to get into a discussion of too much detail, after all.

There was a pause.

"Well," Sally said then. "Anyway. I hope I didn't . . . overwhelm you with reading."

"Not at all. I've truly enjoyed it."

That smile, that kindly smile of hers, it really did transform her face. Sent a little punch of warmth up him, in fact: She was not, it turned out, as hideous as she'd first appeared.

"Well," she said. "I didn't want to just send you out with no understanding of how things . . . came about here. You know? I mean, did you get any sense of that?"

"Yes, you mean, the sort of . . . flow of events from the one man, one rule decision to today, to the charter?"

"That's it."

"I think I'm beginning to get a picture of it."

"Because some of the people you'll cover, they really try to keep you from . . . knowing anything. I mean, the sheriff is just . . . I mean, he won't even let us see his blotter, okay?"

"Oh Christ, you're joking." *His what?*

"He could just, you know, arrest some pol for drunk driving and let him go, and we'd never know it. Then he's got someone in his debt, you see?"

Well, Merriwether didn't, but she looked pretty worked up about it so he lowered his brows and nodded.

"It's against the law . . ." she was about to say—but then she stopped.

*   *   *

75

She stopped and turned to the rear of the room, taut, attentive.

"What's that?" she said.

He followed her gaze. She was looking at that thing, that box that was sitting atop the file cabinet in back. A black doohickey with all sorts of blinking red lights on it.

"Oh that," he said. "It's some sort of radio, I think, but it doesn't seem to get very good . . ."

"Ssh."

She walked quickly up the aisle—and Merriwether took the opportunity to observe the switch of her skirt. (Nice switch. Cheap skirt. Peach linen. Looked as if she'd sewn the thing herself years ago.)

She put her ear close to the radio. Merriwether listened too. There was a quick flare of static—*sssssst*—then a male monotone: "All cars in Harry sector . . ." More static: *brrrack!* "This is Central . . ." *Brrack.* "Repeat, we have report of a floater at the . . ." *brrack-ssst!* ". . . end of Route Thirty-two, approximately one half mile north of the Gilead train station . . ." Ssssst. "All cars responding acknowledge, over."

Whatever it was all about, Sally reacted with reassuring calm. Gazed into the middle distance, tapped her chin with a thin finger. Brushed a strand of hair from her forehead. Tilted her head this way and that as if to say, *Ah well.*

Then she went to her desk and opened the drawer. Lifted a camera out of it. Brought it down the aisle to Merriwether's desk.

"I need you to cover this for me, okay? I don't have anyone else. It's a floater in the Hudson." She spoke in sweet, slow, soft sisterly tones. They did nothing to still the sudden hammering of his heart. "Route Thirty-two is that road by the lake. All you have to do is take it straight across the county to the river. Just find out what you can, take some pictures if you can, and call in. Okay?"

Okay? thought Merriwether. *Good Christ!*

He found himself standing, his legs unsteady. She was putting the camera in his hand. Smiling that warm, delicious smile at him: the oatmeal mother sending her child off to play. He muttered something—"Well, I'll do my best"—and swallowed. She patted him on the shoulder gently.

With a quick nod—it was all he could manage—he started up the aisle, the camera in his hand. He was at the back door. The cold metal of the push bar was against his palm.

"Sally!" He spun around, his voice cracking.

And there was that same sweet smile. "Yes, Sidney?" That same sweet smile—and that soft voice speaking his name. . . .

More calmly, Merriwether said, "I don't know what it is. A floater. I don't know what a floater is."

"Oh, that's all right." She laughed gently. "It's a body."

"Ah," said Merriwether. "Of course."

And he turned and pushed out the door, his eyes like saucers.

Maybe I can just keep driving and never be seen again, he thought.

He rolled the Rabbit to the corner, to the stoplight. There was Main Street. Desolate. Darkened stores to his right, their quaint white-brick faces; the purple neon glow from the Italian restaurant; the street lamps haloed in the warm, hazy evening.

Get me out of here.

The stoplight turned green. Merriwether turned left. Ahead of him now, a paltry Greek-style courthouse. And opposite, on his right, the big black body of the lake; houselights sparkling on it; the sky above moonless; faint stars.

I need you to cover this for me, okay?

Her calm, unworried voice. Even the thought of it soothed him.

Okay, he thought. *Okay. But pardon me a moment, would you, while I snivel in terror of failure and humiliation?*

Now Route 32 was up ahead: Lakeshore Road.

The Rabbit putted around the corner onto the narrow two lane, curled slowly along the shore. Merriwether saw some sort of low boathouse squatting under tree branches. Then a large white manse, empty it looked like, its porch overlooking the water.

Just find out what you can. Okay?

Okay. That's what he would do. He would find out what he could. He would ask questions. That was simple enough. That's what a reporter was supposed to do, right? Okay. Okay. It was going to be fine. He read the newspaper, after all. He'd even watched TV now and then. He knew the sort of thing to look for. There would be "Witnesses at the Scene" and "Officers in Charge of the Case." There would be "Attempts to Recover the Body" and "Speculation as to the Cause of Death." He could do this. He could handle it. It would be okay.

His eyes darted nervously as he drove. He took in the passing scene. The willows by the waterside. The houses on the wooded hills across the street. Door lanterns gleaming yellow through the branches. Window lights gleaming warmly through the curtains. Suppertime in Auburn County. Ma and Pa probably settin round the table, chucklin at the kids, those rascally varmints . . .

Get me OUT OF HERE!

Just take some pictures if you can and call in. Okay?

Okay. Okay.

He glanced down at the camera on the seat beside him. A 35mm Pentax. He knew how to use it at least. He'd been quite proud, in fact, of his photo-art for Bertram Metzenbaum's "Mode as Catharsis, Catharsis as Mode" (*Helios* Vol. I, No. 2): a whorl of rose petals superimposed on a woman's unsmiling face. He took a deep, shuddering breath, watched the white lines on the pavement zip beneath him. He could do this. Ask questions, take pictures. It would be okay.

Okay?

Okay.

The road veered off from the lake and plunged him into a black savage forest emptiness from which, he was certain, he would never emerge again.

Straight across Route 32, she'd said. Christ! That serene, milky voice of hers! And now look at this. There was nothing but night here, night and the hills of trees, the shadows of hills, the shadows of trees, pressing in on him, blocking out even the hope of light, leaving only his car beams to pick out each sudden whiplash of the crazed pavement and then suddenly . . . a truck.

Jesus Christ!

A truck the size of a mountain came tearing around a blind curve, straddling the midline, bearing down on him. Merriwether, hands on the wheel, heaved his car to the side of the road with a muscular motion of his whole upper body. His tires jarred on the gravelly shoulder teetered on the edge of a muddy ditch. And then the truck was past and the Rabbit righted itself and Merriwether chugged breathlessly on through the night.

Okay?

I'll kill her. I swear it to God.

He really was nervous now, no doubt about it. Sweat in his sideburns. His teeth gritted. His body rigid behind the wheel. It was worse with every mile. The road corkscrewed deeper and deeper into the oppressive emptiness. Trees, the hills of trees, rolled dimly by the window. Spectral shapes flashed past him: cabins on the hills; a junk pile just within the woods; the shell of an abandoned pickup by the side of the road; the ghostly stillness of a deserted gas station; a graveyard in the night mist.

And always, waiting for him at the road's unavoidable end, the phantom of Mean Mr. Failure and his faithful sidekick, Disgrace.

And then—out of nowhere—came the fog.

"Damn it!"

The fog washed over him, over the Rabbit. The windshield went soupy, white. The forests vanished. Merriwether had to bring his foot down fast on the brake as the beams of his headlamps were forced back on themselves. The needle of the speedometer wobbled down from 45 to 35 to 20. All but a yard of the road ahead disappeared from sight.

He was lost for certain, for good and all.

There was this fog, Sally. By the time I got there, the body was buried, and everyone had gone home and really I couldn't . . .

He could imagine how she'd nod, with her lips thinning. He could hear her tell him softly that it was "okay." The sweat poured out of his sideburns, down his jaw. . . . He could almost hear his father laughing at him from within the mist.

But wait. Wait. Wait ho, fellow news lovers. There was something—a light—up ahead to the right. The Rabbit took an easy curve, and for a moment the fog was glowing, lit from within by the bright windows of a two story clapboard house at the roadside. Even as Merriwether passed it, he spotted another house just beyond . . . and another—or at least the dim radiance of another in the fog—just beyond that.

Gilead! It was the town of Gilead. Oh. Oh, balm in Gilead! He'd made it.

He went round the next curve and the fog turned blood red.
"Shit!"

He hit the brakes hard. The red went out, flashed on, went out
again. The Rabbit's tires screeched and Merriwether was thrown forward against the wheel.

What . . . what the hell . . .

The thick mist dimmed, went scarlet, dimmed. The Rabbit
stopped. Merriwether squinted through the windshield. His stomach
took a clammy plunge as he saw . . .

Our old friend Mr. F.

Not three feet away from his front fender was a red-and-white
Sheriff's Department cruiser. It was parked lengthwise across the road,
blocking his way. Its dual beacons whirled, flashing red and white over
the shroud of mist. Merriwether sat with his mind racing, searching for
a way through, trying to comprehend the suddenness and complete-
ness of his own impotence when . . .

Out of the mist like a reproach stepped the most rugged icon of
male effectiveness he had ever seen: a tall, hard figure in khaki,
swaggering; a deputy, whose cowboy hat shaded a face as featureless as
stone.

The man—that is, the *man*—leaned down at the open window.
"I'm sorry, sir. This road is closed. You can't go through here."

*I'm a journalist protected by the First Amendment, and the public has
a right to know,* Merriwether thought. "But I live here," he said.

"No." The deputy shook his head slowly. "No, sir, you don't."

"Oh. Well, I'm a journalist. I'm here to cover the floater."

"Yessir." The deputy straightened, stepped back from the car,
pointed back whence Merriwether had come. "All press information
will be handed out by the Sheriff's Office. Now, if you'll just turn
around and clear the way please. We have other vehicles coming
through on *official* business."

The Rabbit retreated forlornly through the fog. The speedometer read
barely over 15. Merriwether's forehead nearly touched the wheel as he
peered, morose, out the windshield. There would be no way off this
route for miles. Even if there were, he would not have been able to
find an alternate path to the river; not in this dark, not in this mist.

The best idea he could come up with was to ditch the car and wander up into the forest to become a mysterious local character dressed in rude jerkins and living off edible plants. It was a bit extreme, but it would be better, anyway, than watching Sally hide her annoyance at him. Better than having to resign into penury as a point of honor. Or hearing Emily offer her sympathy—*I can put my dissertation aside for a while, get a job myself;* anything was better than that. And anything was better than touching his father's money too, even the trust fund in his own name. And having to come up with more wry remarks about how badly he had handled everything, blithe comments about how unsuccessful it had all been, fa-la . . .

Merriwether pulled the Rabbit over to the side of the road. He put his hand over his lips as they trembled. He squeezed his eyes shut, fighting back the tears.

"Ah God," he said softly.

Then he heard a sound.

It was a sound like music, first. A single note, sustained, unwavering. Then . . .

What is that?

. . . a dip, a slow fall almost to silence before the note rose up again full bodied and

A siren

started growing louder in the mist.

A siren. He raised his head to listen. Yes, it was. A siren. Another cop car must be approaching the barricade. A "vehicle." On "official business," no doubt.

Merriwether ran his hand once over his eyes, took hold of the wheel. Sat paralyzed with excitement, barely able to swallow, barely able to breathe. He had had an idea.

You won't do it, he thought. *You can't. It's madness.*

Fuck you, he thought back. *Just watch me, you old son of a bitch.*

He nudged the car forward, onto the road again. He killed the headlights. He rolled along the road in the fog, in the dark.

The siren was louder now. There was a first faint tinge of pink before him—the oncoming cruiser's beacon through the wall of fog. He didn't have much time. But that house. That first house he had seen, it was just up ahead somewhere. At least he thought it was. He clutched the wheel hard, stared into the morass until his eyes ached and . . . There. That glowing spot: the house. He pushed the Rabbit nearer to it.

The siren grew louder. The red of the beacons flashed in patches, vanished, flashed in other patches, vanished again as the cop car neared. Merriwether reached the house and turned his car into the driveway. Loose gravel crunched under the tires as he started to come around in a three-point turn. The white beam of the porch lantern glared at him through an iridescent halo. The lion knocker on the front door made a gravid shadow; he sensed its blank eyes. . . . He backed up. There was no time, no time. The siren was deafening. Its pulsing red light was on the fog all around him; his heart pounded and the very air throbbed red right back at him. Merriwether swung the car forward, turning, turning, his beams off, only the light from the house to guide him, and the feel of the gravel, then grass under his tires. . . .

And the beacon broke through. Merriwether spun the Rabbit around just in time to see the Sheriff's Department cruiser burst from the mist—a smear of red and metal—and shoot into the mist again, its wail doused by the doppler shift to a lower moan.

Merriwether hit the gas and shot after it.

It was caught—all of it—that one careening instant—frozen in Merriwether's mind by the strobic flash of the scarlet beacon. There was the cruiser, the red glow from the cruiser, speeding away from him, round the bend; the Rabbit, beams dark, screaming after as fast as it could; himself at the wheel, his face twisted and taut; the road-block, the red glow of the roadblock, that first police car flung across the road, the second police car rocketing toward it, Merriwether rock-eting right behind; the screech of brakes, the jarring crash, the shat-tering of glass, the wrenching of metal, the final paroxysm of white pain—that did not come because the roadblock, the first cruiser, had been pulled aside, pulled aside just as Merriwether had calculated, had prayed it would be so that the oncoming cruiser could pass on through. . . .

And in that same, single instant that it did pass, that instant captured for Merriwether in the light, Merriwether himself, Merri-wether and his Rabbit, were sailing right after it, flying past the obstruction too, past the roadblock on the tail of the cruiser, past the roadblock and on into Gilead, heading toward the river, unchallenged, unstoppable, his fist pumping the air, his eyes jacked wide.

"Ha ha ha ha ha!" remarked Sidney Merriwether the Fourth. "Ha ha ha ha ha ha ha!"

2

"The recurrent mythic structure thus signifies Structure itself. It is at once Structure and thus the deconstruction of the outer limits of narrative—in effect, of our perception in time. This accounts for its supersession, its ordering, its reconstruction, as it were, of the attempts to deconstruct it. While the concept Truth repeatedly collapses under the identification of the self-referential signifier, the experientiality of Vision depends, in fact, on the affect of the signified called forth. Paradoxically, then, we find that only Story transcends Narrativity; to see, *sans* the concept Truth, we must, in Milton's phrase, 'be lowlie wise'; we must, that is to say, tell the story."

Wo! thought Emily. She leaned back from her computer. *Wo! Get down!* She pushed her glasses to the end of her nose, looked over their rims. Her eyes ran across the amber characters on the monitor yet again. *The structure and the deconstruction of the outer limits of narrative—I say, Wo! Baby! I wrote that!* It had taken her three hours, that paragraph. She'd been at it ever since she'd gotten Sidney off to work at ten.

She glanced up, through the cottage window. *Identification of the self-referential signifier.* The misty green hills. The hazy blue skies. A hawk making ominous circles beneath the clouds.

Emily, limp in her chair, took a deep breath, sighed.

I wonder if it's too late to plant a garden, she thought.

Someone—some previous tenant of the cottage probably—had had one, a garden, out beyond the drive. There was still a rectangle of tilled earth just at the edge of the lawn near the stand of hickories; a patch of about four yards by two, overgrown now with weeds. Emily wandered over to it after lunch. Stood by it for a while, contemplating the chaotic tangle of green stalks and leaves, the laboring creep of a brown caterpillar.

She had had a garden herself once, the years she was twelve and thirteen. Tomato poles, low domes of lettuce, sprigged carrot tops. She'd planted them by the stone wall, just on the other side from the churchyard. At that age, the other girls were going to the McDonald's together; sitting at a table together on half-swiveling chairs, sipping their Cokes together; bending their heads together, giggling, when the boys came in; waggling their backsides at the boys when they walked out together. They were poor girls, most of them, the daughters of gas jockeys and restaurant workers and house servants. Emily knew they didn't feel comfortable around the PK—the Preacher's Kid—not when she talked the way she talked and wrote the kinds of essays she wrote in school.

So just about every day after school, the PK had been alone in her garden out behind the parsonage. A solemn little woman tending her vegetables, kneeling by the low wall with the gray monuments visible over it in the neatly mown field beyond. Those monuments, the faded escutcheons, the carved steles inlaid with grime, the one angel mourning on a cenotaph she could see in the far corner when she raised her head: They were somber watchmen over her solitude. She liked their company. And she liked the pleasant breezes in the strands of her hair and the damp earth on the tips of her fingers and the mint and marigolds mixing their scents together in her nose—the details that had time to become important to her when she was alone. With these to occupy her, she could work her way into the ground for hours on end—sometimes right up until her mother called her in to practice the piano before suppertime. . . .

Standing above the remnants of the cottage garden, she touched the silky leaves of the nearest weed. It was only July. Too late for seeds maybe. But she could get some plants . . . A shovel, a trowel, a rake. Tear up some garbage bags for the mulching. It wouldn't cost too much. She'd enjoy the feel of her hands working in the earth again. She could use the chance to make plans for the future, recharge her brain. . . .

And one more week of this dissertation bullshit and she'd go plumb crazy anyway.

A breeze rattled the hickory leaves. She raised her face to it and felt it fresh on her cheeks. The air was warm and faintly damp. The trees and grass were loud with birdsong, cricket burr, the crackle of cicada. The idea of going back inside the cottage, back to her desk . . . She'd forgotten how lonely it always was in the country. She lowered her eyes to the old garden, toyed with the viny weed, tugged at it, gauged its resistance.

Slowly, she lowered herself to her knees and began to dig at the roots with her fingers. She worked the weed out, tossed it aside to where it lay limp on the lawn. Tomatoes; lettuce, she thought. Green peppers. Onions, maybe. Maybe some marigolds to keep the aphids away. And she could grow impatiens in the shade over by the house . . .

She began clawing at the ground again, uprooted another weed, dropped it on the lawn beside the first. Gloves—she needed gloves; maybe her dishwashing gloves would do it. And an older pair of jeans. And maybe she could find a trowel in the cellar. . . .

Sidney phoned around six-thirty.

"It's going to be another hour, at least," he said.

She tried to keep the disappointment out of her voice. "Okay. Whenever you can."

"Well, I didn't get here till ten-thirty, you know."

She didn't say anything. She nodded with the phone to her ear.

He went on in an undertone: "She keeps watching me, Em. This Sally character. She watches me all day long. I have to look at least a little diligent."

"Okay, okay." With as much cheer as she could muster, she added, "I'll see you later."

She replaced the phone. Wandered out of the kitchen into the living room. Looked around it, a little desperately. Not much left to do in here, she thought. She'd done the best she could with the place, given what she had to work with. The shag rug (which needed cleaning) was centered on the floor, the leather sofa (worn) was against the back wall; her three chairs (old canvas chairs) were strewn casually about, and the board and cinder-block bookshelves were all filled practically to overflowing.

Her shoulders sagged as she completed her study of the room.

Between the cheap paneling on the walls and the white paint on the wooden floors and her own ratty furniture—well, it looked about as good as it was going to look for now.

Not that that was an excuse for idle hands, of course. There were still three boxes of books to unpack; and she did want to make some curtains for the windows. And there was always the computer, still moaning, somewhat plaintively, on the desk by the window. . . .

But after all that weeding she'd done, and then the bath she'd taken. . . . Her body felt so tired and warm. And it was so quiet here. . . .

She got the little Sony out from the bedroom closet, set it up on a chair by the sofa. Turned it on and watched the image flash out over the eight-inch screen. She was grateful for the sound of voices, even the sound of canned laughter. She lay down on her side and—not that there was anyone to look in besides that old walking stick climbing up the pane—smoothed her bathrobe down over her legs, adjusted the towel turbaned around her hair.

She settled in, head on the bolster, trying to focus on the tiny picture, the comical faces gawping at each other as the canned laughter was touched off again. Poor Sidney, she thought. Stuck in what he called "the hellhole." With "Shea of the Common People." And "Rumplemeyer, the Profligate Jew." And "that mousy slavedriver," Sally Dawes.

Emily smiled a little and closed her eyes.

There was a burst of laughter from the television set. She propped herself up on the sofa, her towel falling to the floor, her hair spilling down around her cheeks.

"It's all right," he said. "I'm all right."

"What? . . ." *The Late Night Show?* . . . "What time is it?"

"Almost one. Don't worry. Just go back to . . ."

"Sidney?" She sat bolt upright. Dazed—she was dazed—and he—Oh God, he'd been beaten up. "What happened? What happened to you?" She twisted the heels of her palms in her eyes. Peered and blinked at him.

There was a smudge on his cheek, a light scrape on his forehead that his hair drooped over. His jacket—the tan one from Louis she liked so much—one shoulder of it was brown with mud, one lapel was grass-stained. His pants were torn and soiled at the knee. His loafers were caked with mud.

"It's all right. It's the clothes mostly." He limped to one of the canvas chairs, and sat down gingerly. Fingered one of the jagged tears in the pants. "I don't suppose they can be dry-cleaned though." He started to peel off the loafers. . . .

He was so casual about it. She could only stare at him, her lips moving. "Where *were* you, Sidney?"

"Oh, I had to cover a story. You know. A floater."

"A body?"

He paused in stripping off his socks, frowned at her, annoyed. "Well, yes, as a matter of fact." He dropped the socks on top of his loafers. Started to work off his jacket. "Didn't get back to the bureau till an hour ago. I would've called, but I was afraid I'd wake you."

The bureau? What had happened to the Hellhole? Emily kept moving her lips silently.

"Sally is certainly right about the sheriff in this county," he muttered. "He definitely does *not* like us. The press, I mean."

Us? The Press? Us? "Uh . . . really?" she said.

"I actually had to run a damned roadblock to get to the river." He added the jacket to the pile, began to unbutton his shirt. "Then I had literally to crawl under the police lines to take my pictures."

"Of the body?" she said.

"Yes." He could barely restrain a proud smirk. "Unpleasant-looking thing it was, too. Bloated beyond recognition. The police kept trying to bring it in with grappling hooks but the flesh just broke open like . . . rotten fruit."

"Oh, yuck, Sidney, don't tell me that! Why are you telling me that!"

He worked his shirt off, baring his chest. Oh, he was just *so* pleased with himself. Him and his bodies and his roadblocks . . .

"There were these deputies," he went on more quickly. "They were watching from the train embankment like me, only down a ways. And I had to casually stroll over to them, you see—because they wouldn't talk to me otherwise—I had to hide my camera and just sort of—make conversation with them. Using small words, of course. That's how I got the information out of them. And then, just as I was doing that, up drives the deputy from the roadblock."

Emily crossed her arms, tightened her lips. He just *sat* there, wearing nothing but the pants now, all eager and dashing—as he probably damn well knew—with his hair tangled on his bruised brow and the streak of dirt on his cheek and his blue eyes bright. And all this had happened while she was pulling weeds.

"So," he said, "out he jumps, this deputy, crying, That thar's one of them dadblamed journalist fellahs. Or words to that effect. You see? Well, Brer Merriwether—he made tracks, I don't mind telling you."

While she was arranging furniture. While she was deconstructing *Milton*, for Christ's sake. Had he *any* idea how dull that was?

"And you'll never guess what happened then?"

He smiled a white, a gleaming smile. Gave a laugh so boyish, so genuinely delighted with himself that a small laugh nearly riffled out between her own clamped lips, and she said, after a moment, "All right, what?"

"Well, you know, there I am, running for my life, terrified of having my pictures confiscated, dodging hither and yon through people's backyards with all these men in cowboy hats shouting 'Hey!' in back of me . . ."

"You were chased by the police?"

"Oh, they were after me in force, I'm telling you. And I was scrambling over fences and slogging through mud and barking my shins on . . . sandboxes and—plaster elves and God knows what else. . . ."

She really did laugh now—once—shaking her head at the idiot.

"Finally, I stumbled out into some street or other—and what to my wondering eyes should appear but another deputy's car—parked right at the curb across from me."

She pinched her eyes shut, shook her head again, trying not to smile.

"Well, I thought I was done for," Merriwether said. "But then—as I stood quivering, the car simply drove away. And I saw, standing on the front walk of this little aluminum box of a house, a man and a woman and a boy, waving farewell."

She opened her eyes and he was standing. Standing and unfastening his belt buckle.

"And I noticed that the boy seemed to have been swimming, you see. His hair was tangled as if it had been wet, and he was hugging a towel around his shoulders. And I thought to myself maybe . . ."

It was the boy who found the body, she thought.

". . . maybe it's the boy who found the body. So I . . ."

"You didn't interview him," she said sternly. "He must've been so upset."

"But the police wouldn't tell me *anything,* Emily." He was tugging the torn pants off now, bending first one leg up then the other to work them over his feet. When he was done, he swaggered toward her, marble-skinned in his Jockey shorts—already, she noticed, getting an erection as he sat down on the sofa beside her—playing the big macho man with his police chasing him and his roadblocks and interviewing poor little boys. . . .

Well, deconstructing Milton is a dirty business too, ya know.

But she smiled again with a corner of her mouth because it was sort of funny of him to be so proud of it like a boy—and to be so hard so fast, pressing against her, wanting her, conquering-hero-style.

"You shouldn't have bothered him," she managed to say. "The boy. The poor thing. You should've left him alone."

He leaned toward her, lips on hers, tongue warm in her mouth suddenly. Her hand rose to the side of his face, and it felt good: his breath in her mouth, his eagerness, the soft terry cloth under her, not to be alone. His hand was parting her robe and his cock was pressing against her thigh.

She gave in, stretched and murmured as he withdrew his tongue, as he kissed her lips gently.

"Oh," she heard him whisper, "but what a story he had to tell, Emily."

Her eyes were closed but she felt him gazing down at her. She was breathless, ready.

"Good God," he murmured. "Good God, what a story."

PART II

THE HOUSE
ON SHEEP PASTURE
ROAD

FOUR

The Body of Billy Thimble

MONDAY, JULY 16–TUESDAY, JULY 17

DOLITTLE FELT LOUSY. His stomach hurt. So did his chest. It was an effort to look relaxed as he sat there at the end of the long table. He sat tilting back in his chair slightly, his thumbs hooked in his belt. He fixed a small, wry smile on his lips and made the corner of his eyes crinkle. One way or another, he thought sourly, he was just going to have to deal with this.

He was in the Sheriff's Department conference room. His eight investigators—the Bureau of Criminal Investigation, to be fancy about it—were ranged up the table's sides. Curtis, Rozek, Wayward, Conti, O'Hara, Flanagan, Dean, DiMola. BCI. Eight hard-faced men in their thirties and forties. Wrinkled linen jackets in navy or green or loud plaid. Wrinkled white shirts, loosened ties. And cigarettes, every goddamned one of them. The conference room—a big rectangle of a room—was thick with their smoke, the bright blue walls dimmed practically to gray. Dolittle felt like he was strangling on the stuff. Goddamn cloud in his lungs; it just kept sitting there. . . .

Still, he sat tilting back in his chair and smiling. Watching Benoit, listening to Benoit.

Benoit sat at the opposite end of the table. Undersheriff Henry Benoit, who ran the department's investigations. He was reviewing the information on the body they'd pulled out of the Hudson last week, the one the boy had found.

"Okay," he said. He spoke out of the side of his mouth. "The guy'd been down there since Wednesday sometime, the M.E. says. So, you know, the water's, like, warm, the guy's really decomposing, bloating up, lot of the evidence got washed away. And there were a lot of, a lot of fuckups at the scene too. I mean, like: a lot."

Dolittle watched him, his stomach churning.

"The fucking Gilead town cops got there before us," Benoit went on. "Then you got half an hour practically from the time the first deputy got there till an investigator shows up. Which is just a lot of time for fuckups. A lot of, lot of time. They're using fucking grappling hooks to bring the body in. I mean, fucking grappling hooks! They're punching *holes* in the guy. I mean, wait'll the D.A. gets to court with that and the defense starts in: Is that a bullet hole, or did you idiots make it with a grappling hook?" He shook a weary head, smiled a hard-boiled half-smile.

"Assholes," muttered Curtis, shaking his weary head, smiling his hard-boiled half-smile, too.

"They said they were afraid he'd float away before we got there," Benoit told him.

"Bunch of assholes, the lot of them."

And the other investigators shook *their* weary heads and smiled *their* hard-boiled half-smiles. And smoked their cigarettes. Dolittle coughed softly.

"Okay," said Benoit. "So the M.E. says he's not sure about the blow to the head at this point. But there was a definite shotgun wound to the chest with recovered pellets. And a .38 wound to the head with recovered slug."

"So he was shotgunned in the chest and then pistoled in the head," said Flanagan.

"And then they drowned the poor bastard." O'Hara laughed.

Benoit snorted back at them. "Hey, don't laugh. There was water in his lungs too, I'm telling you."

"You're shitting me."

"I'm telling you. Only the M.E. says it may not mean much at this point. He can't say, only he can't say no either."

"Jesus."

Benoit took a drag of his cigarette, narrowing those sharp eyes. "What else have we got here? The divers recovered the cinder block they used to sink him with. And they got the rest of the rope too."

The investigators around the table nodded. Narrowed their eyes as they dragged at their cigarettes. Or exhaled through their mouths and noses. Or held their cigarettes between rough fingers sending zigzags of smoke up to the white-tiled ceiling.

Dolittle took one hand from his belt, covering his mouth this time as he coughed into his palm.

"Oh, also, the M.E. hadda peel off his fingers, you hear about that?" Benoit smiled with one side of his mouth. "Guy's fingerprints are so fucked up, he's gotta peel the skin off the guy's fingers, like, whole. Puts the skin over his own fingers, see? Like little gloves. Then he prints himself—to get the guy's prints."

"So, what you're saying, it shouldn't be long before *we* finger the bad guy too." This was Rozek, with his donkey laugh.

"Oh yeah. We'll nail him," added DiMola. "He's under our thumb."

"We'll put him in the joint," said Curtis. He sucked on his cigarette sharply.

The others chuckled. Dolittle, his thumbs hooked in his belt again, tilted back farther in his chair. Smiled a hard-boiled half-smile of his own. The others kept muttering, laughing, joking around.

Dolittle just kept thinking, This could really be trouble. They were almost sure to have the body identified as Billy Thimble by tonight, tops. And if Sally Dawes got hold of it . . .

I'm gonna have to deal with this. I'm gonna have to deal with this real fast.

Like it or not, he thought, he was going to need Benoit to help him.

Henry Benoit was forty-two years old. A big fellow, husky; big heavy arms. A round face sculpted in sandstone, pug and pebbly. A snide smile and sharp, careful, beady black eyes. He had been Dolittle's undersheriff for the last four years. Second in command, the head of BCI. Ever since he left the NYPD.

Benoit had been a sergeant, the whip, in his old Bronx precinct. He'd retired from the force in a real hurry, without full benefits, in fact. Just six months after his retirement, the papers down there broke a hellacious scandal in, coincidentally enough, Benoit's old precinct.

It was quite a story, Dolittle remembered. Cops were confiscating drugs and then franchising crack dealers to sell them on the streets of other precincts. They were hiring themselves out as strong-arm men and bodyguards to high-stepping black dudes with gold chains and gold teeth. After a while, these officers of the law were even packaging and selling confiscated drugs on their own, in vials with a brand name on the label: Midnight Blue.

Well, that was bad stuff. But it wasn't quite as bad as the story about the Brave Bodega Owner.

The Brave Bodega Owner had been scheduled to meet with investigators from Internal Affairs. He had information about the police carryings-on in the area; he wanted to discuss it with them. All of a sudden, though, the Brave Bodega Owner had changed his mind. Instead of coming to the meeting with Internal Affairs, he apparently decided to distribute his body parts among several different garbage bags and hide them in a garbage dump out in Queens. It was too bad. No one was ever indicted for killing the Brave Bodega Owner. The Brooklyn D.A. said he hadn't enough evidence to indict.

Dolittle had read all about these scandals when he came across Benoit's résumé in his files. He made some phone calls to his contacts in the city. Then he called Benoit in to interview him for the undersheriff's job.

When Benoit came into the sheriff's office, he was wearing a tan leisure suit. He looked confident and relaxed. He had shot his cuffs with real style before sitting down in front of Dolittle's desk.

The sheriff of Auburn County had sat across the desk from Benoit and smiled into those black marbly eyes of his. Benoit had smiled back, even chuckled. Dolittle had nodded and chuckled too.

"Henry," Dolittle had said, "no one has ever taken a bribe in my department. No one ever will. No one has ever sold drugs in my department. And if anyone ever does, I'll use his testicles for a paperweight."

Benoit had chuckled again, replacing his friendly smile with a smile of understanding and agreement.

Dolittle had continued. "Now you may be thinking that I am a hick upstate sheriff, Henry. And, Henry, you may be right. You may be thinking that I don't know the way things work. And maybe you're right about that too."

Benoit had smiled a new smile then, a disclaimer smile to show that he'd never thought such a thing in his life and never would.

"But Henry," Dolittle had said, "if I even sniff you taking money —or selling drugs—or doing anything contrary to the rules of this department, then I will not only have you indicted for the murder of that bodega owner, but also for bribing the District Attorney's Office to cover up the case against you."

Benoit had stopped smiling.

Dolittle had leaned forward, his hands clasped on the desk before him.

"What you are going to do as the undersheriff of Auburn County," Dolittle had said, "is just exactly what I tell you to do. And not one damned other thing."

Sure enough, the I.D. on the body came in around five o'clock that afternoon. Dolittle was sitting in his office, gazing out the window at the time. His chest felt a little better but his stomach was still at it. He was just going to have to deal with this, he kept thinking. He was just going to have to deal with this step by step.

He was sitting in the highbacked leather swivel chair. The state flag stood to one side of him, the county flag stood to the other. He was swiveling gently back and forth, his fingers bridged under his chin. His desk, a massive mahogany desk, stood all but empty in front of him. Nothing on it but a phone and a blotter, a calendar, and a pen set from the State Sheriffs' Association.

The rest of the office was sparsely covered too. There were a couple of wooden armchairs facing his desk. A filing cabinet. An ancient coatstand hidden behind the open door. One wall, the wall across from him, held a cluster of framed certificates and awards. There was also a photo of his wife, Liz, with her arms around Cindy. Cindy was giggling with her hand raised to hide her braces. That had been taken when she was only nine years old.

Dolittle looked out the single window on the wall to his left. Through it, he could see Main Street and, across Main Street, Lake Tyler, its sloping banks of grass, its rippling water murky under the gray sky. Someone was out there in a rowboat. Fred Denkinger, it looked like, on a day off from the Auburn First National. His fishing pole was over the side, his hands were cranking away at the reel; he was working a spoon through the bottom weeds, trying for bass.

Dolittle gazed at Denkinger and his thoughts drifted to that night years ago when they had dragged his raped and beaten daughter out of the Hickory woods. He thought about Sally Dawes coming to the scene trying to get the story. He thought about what she would do when she found out about Billy Thimble.

It was no good. It was just no good. He couldn't let it happen. The convention was just a month away and there were still people, plenty of people, who didn't want Purdy to get the nod for county exec. Dolittle had to be in control; he knew he had to be in complete control, had to show that the party was completely behind him. He couldn't be sick. He couldn't be weak. And he couldn't be under attack from Sally Dawes.

God, he thought, *God damn. It's been a long time since I've been fishing.*

Benoit rapped loudly on the wooden jamb. Dolittle blinked and looked up at the big man standing in the doorway.

"Sheriff?" Benoit's voice was quieter than it had been in the conference room. More respectful. "We got an I.D."

"Come on in, Henry," Dolittle said.

Benoit strolled across the threshold, but he didn't go for one of the chairs. He walked over to the window and perched his anvil-heavy ass on the sill. Blotted out all but a sliver of Dolittle's lake view. He had a cigarette in his hand. He held it at the middle of his wrinkled navy-blue suit. He watched the sheriff carefully, warily, as if he thought Dolittle might suddenly fly across the room at him. "It's a guy by the name of Billy Thimble," he said. "Ever hear of him?"

"Only vaguely," Dolittle lied.

"O'Hara says he pulled him in a while back on cocaine possession."

"That's right. Yeah, I remember."

"We don't have a record of it, so we must've let him go?" It was a tactful way to put it: Benoit knew better than to ask too much about the record keeping around here. There were some things only the sheriff knew.

But Dolittle said simply, "Yeah, that's right. I told O'Hara to drop it. Thimble was a family man. Wife and kid. Good job."

"A real estate lawyer," said Benoit.

"That's it. Young guy. Kind of sharp, slick. I gave him a break. Told him to get off the shit or we'd bust his ass for keeps."

"Well . . ." Benoit cocked his head. "He's off the shit, anyway."

Dolittle laughed. "Whatever works, I guess."

Benoit laughed too, relaxing. "So, anyway, it isn't exactly a case for Sherlock Holmes or anything. Like we used to say back in the Bronx: You get strangled for hate, you get stabbed for sex—but if you're shot, it's strictly business."

"You were a witty bunch of guys back in the Bronx, Henry."

"We were, it's a fact."

"So that means: what? You think Vincent Scotti killed him."

"Hell yeah. Who else?" Benoit shrugged, raised his cigarette to his lips and sucked on it deeply. "If it's business, like I said, then it's probably drugs, right? And up here in Sticksville, Vincent Scotti *is* the drug business. Maybe Thimble couldn't pay him for his supply, maybe he tried to rip him off, I don't know. Maybe Scotti wanted to borrow his tie and Thimble wouldn't give it to him. But it was Scotti all right, that's almost for sure." He cocked a jaded eye out the window at the lake. Fred Denkinger's rowboat drifted out from behind him and into view. Dolittle saw the banker lift his fishing rod above his head, whip it forward. The yellow line looped out against the dark sky.

Benoit kept talking. "I had a couple of guys—on a hunch, I had em go down to the Hickory train tracks this afternoon, ask some questions. We got some good informants now down there with the kids."

"Uh-huh." Dolittle was only half listening. He was watching Denkinger.

"The word is that our man Scotti has taken himself a little vacation, right?" He snorted. "Gone to get himself a little sun, I guess."

Benoit paused. The sheriff glanced at him, trying to remember what he'd just said. "You want a bulletin on him?" he asked finally.

"Nah. The word is he'll be back. The word is he's just waiting to see how the land lies. I think we ought to lay low a couple of days. Ask our questions but keep the heat down. Play possum."

"Okay," said Dolittle. "Sounds right."

"Few days. Scotti feels secure. Comes back. And, by golly, Sheriff, America's finest will be on the scene."

The undersheriff grinned his snide, sandstone grin and laughed again, roughly, down in his throat. His black eyes flashed with the laughter.

Dolittle leaned forward in his chair, his hands clasped on the desk before him. He nailed Benoit with a stare. He coughed sharply.

"Here's what you're going to do, Henry," he said.

Benoit stopped laughing at once. "Uh . . . yeah . . . what, what do you need, Cy?" he said. His eyes stopped flashing too. They were wary again.

"Listen to me," Dolittle said. "There's a boy by the name of Teddy Wocek."

Benoit's eyes shifted as he thought about it. "Yeah. Yeah. He's one of Scotti's guys, deals stuff for Scotti. We talked to him."

"Okay. Now don't talk to him."

"Uh . . . what?" said Benoit.

"Don't talk to him, Henry. Wocek has been hanging around my daughter—Cindy. Understand? I don't want his testimony in this case at any time. I don't want to hear what he knows, I don't want to know what he says. You got that?"

Benoit waited, but Dolittle just sat there, staring at him, his hands clasped on the table.

"You want him protected," Benoit said finally.

"No," said Dolittle carefully. "No, not exactly. It would be more accurate to say I don't give a fuck what happens to him. As long as he's kept out of it. However it happens. He is not part of this investigation. At any time. Do you understand now?"

A long moment passed. Then, the undersheriff inclined his rubbly chin. "Whatever it takes, you're telling me. Just . . . that's it. That's what you're telling me."

Dolittle nodded. "That's what I'm telling you, Henry."

Benoit suddenly threw his cigarette hand wide. "Hey." The round rock of his face broke into a jagged grin. "You know me, Sheriff. Whatever you say, right?"

"Right," said Dolittle. "That's right." He broke into an easy smile. His eyes crinkled. His stomach turned over. "I know you, Henry."

2

Down at the old Hickory railroad station the next day, Cindy Dolittle was hanging out with her friend Bobbi Scorsese. They were in the parking lot next to the train tracks, leaning against Bobbi's old boat of a Pontiac. Actually, the car belonged to Bobbi's big brother Herman, but he wasn't allowed to drive it because he'd been in jail and was on probation now. He let Bobbi use the old car instead.

So it was a warm summer's day, the sky hazy, and Bobbi and Cindy were leaning there, smoking cigarettes. Bobbi had just come from the Burger King on Route 6 where she worked and she was still wearing her red-and-brown uniform. She liked to wear it, Cindy thought, because it showed off her legs, still chubby with baby flesh but shapely for all that. The cap set off her cute pug nose and her short, curling raven-black hair too.

She was telling Cindy about her latest adventures with her creepy boss. Bobbi said he was making her do all the scut work—cleaning the grill, mopping the bathrooms—just because Bobbi had cursed at him when he "accidentally" brushed his hand over her ass.

Bobbi went on and on about it, but Cindy wasn't listening. She was thinking about Teddy. About Teddy—and about the body in the river. That was all she *could* think about, ever since Friday when the body was found. She had known right off whose body it was. It wasn't exactly hard to figure out. First she tells Teddy that Billy Thimble is going to testify against Vince Scotti; then, the next thing anyone knows, a body turns up in the Hudson weighted down with a cinder block. It wasn't exactly a brain-twister. Billy Thimble was now deader than shit, that's all. And Teddy—her own Teddy—had disappeared.

It was making her feel almost sick inside, sick and leaden. He just *vanished*—Teddy—the day the body was found. He didn't call her, he didn't answer her calls. What was she supposed to think? That he was running from the cops or something? Or from Vince? Or what? It was making her sick practically.

"Ey! Ey, Cinj? Ey, Bobbi? Did you hear this?"

Cindy looked up and saw Al Delgado coming out of the variety store across the street.

"Did you hear this? Ey! Listen."

He was shouting, walking toward them with his imitation black dude strut. Cowboy boots kicking up stones in the dirt lot. Denim jacket patched with skulls and Death Angels. He was waving his fresh pack of cigarettes in one hand.

Cindy's heart just turned to ashes the minute she saw him. Behind him, the Main Street of Hickory, the sagging row of storefronts—the diner, the barber shop, the grocery, the variety store—stood shit-depressing under the cloudy sky.

Oh fuck, Cindy thought. She already knew what Al was going to say. She bit her lip hard. She could practically throw up about something like this. Where the fuck was Teddy? Where the fuck was he?

"Did you hear this? Did you hear this?" Al kept shouting.

Bobbi flicked her cigarette onto the train tracks. It sent a line of smoke drifting up from the cinders.

"No, Al," she said. "We just stand out here waiting for you to tell us things, okay?"

Al—pimply Al—he didn't give a shit what Bobbi said. He just went on. "You know that dead guy? That guy they found in the river?"

"Yeah," Bobbi said, "like, everybody knows about the guy in the river, Al."

"Yeah, but you know who he is? You know who they say he is now?"

Oh please, Cindy thought. *Please, please, please, please, please don't let it be Billy Thimble. Please. Let it be a stranger. Let it be someone we don't know.* She waited on tenterhooks.

"I just heard it on the radio," Al said. "They're saying it's Billy Thimble."

Oh, God, thought Cindy. She winced and held her stomach. She really was going to be sick.

Bobbi shrugged. "So what? Who's Billy Thimble?"

"Don't you remember him? Remember? That was that guy. That was that guy Teddy brought around that time. The slick lawyer dude."

"Oh yeah. With the briefcase."

"Yeah, snapping open his briefcase full of dope. Mr. Suit and Smile and that shiny briefcase and it was all full of shit, remember? Wasn't that the guy, Cindy? Teddy brought him around here that time with the dope, didn't he?"

Cindy shrugged. "I don't remember," she said softly. But Bobbi was looking at her too, looking at her hard with her big brown eyes. Bobbi did remember. Cindy could tell.

Al let out a high-pitched giggle. "Boy, I'll bet Teddy's nervous today," he said. "Fucking cops are gonna be asking some pretty heavy-duty questions, man. And Teddy's fucking old man, shit, he's gonna rip his heart out if he finds out Teddy was selling stuff." Al laughed again, sucking it in with a short, hoarse sound.

"Have you seen him?" Cindy blurted out. "Do you know where Teddy is?"

"What, you don't know where he is?"

Bobbi glanced at him. "No, she knows, Al. This is a contest."

"Ey, I'm just saying. I mean, Teddy knew the guy, right? He brought him around that time."

Cindy gave him a dull glare. Him and his pimply face, his long, filthy hair. He was jealous of Teddy because everyone admired him, that's what she thought. That's why he was saying all this shit. Fucking Al. She couldn't believe she had let him feel her up at Bobbi's party last year.

"So maybe he doesn't want the cops to ask him questions," Al went on with another stupid laugh. "Like maybe he's hiding out—like in a hideout somewhere."

And Bobbi said, "Good thinking, Al. If you were a TV show, you'd be canceled."

Cindy smirked. Bobbi was really good at saying things like that. And the way she looked at him too: like she couldn't care less. Leaning back in her Burger King uniform, showing him her legs, sneering at him with her glossed lips. And Al had actually *fucked* her: Just before school ended, he got her so drunk she could hardly walk. That was the kind of thing Al was always doing.

He gave her a shit-eating grin and was about to say something . . . and then he stopped. And the grin melted away.

First Cindy, then Bobbi, turned around to follow Al's gaze.

"All right!" said Cindy under her breath. "Finally."

Out of the shadow of Mount Wapataugh, down the long stretch of Hickory Kingdom Road, racing under the wide white sky came Teddy Wocek's Trans Am.

Cindy straightened—with a proud toss of her chopped blond hair at Al.

"He was up in the mountain," she said. "He musta been looking for me."

There wasn't anything Al could say to that.

Cindy stood and waited, feeling her heart beat. The green sports car, the throaty hum of it, rose out of the distance, came on faster and louder toward the intersection with Main . . . then the car was thudding over the train tracks. Squealing as its big rear wheels grabbed the road. It spun, leaving a track; spun halfway round until the driver's door faced the three teens where they stood.

The door cracked open. Teddy leaned out at her across the gear stick, his hair spilling into his eyes.

"Ey. Cinj," he said.

"I'll call you," Cindy told Bobbi. She didn't even bother to look back at Al.

Teddy wheeled the car around, lead-footed the gas. She heard the tires spit gravel—heard the patter of it under her—as the Trans Am shot off down the road.

Hickory Kingdom pitched and curled. Dove under the old freight trestle. Out past the big old houses at the edge of town, out toward the fields. Clotheslines, tricycles, lawns, garages—they all blurred and the wind rushed in through the open windows and Cindy thought she would strangle on her own heartbeat they were going so fast, racing around the curves like in some kind of chase scene in the movies or something. She had to shout over the air and the pounding engine.

"Whyn't you fucking call me, Teddy? Whyn't you call me? I was, like, 'Christ, where is he?' All weekend."

With his hair blowing back from his face, she could see his expression: He looked so *dramatic*, so much pain in his eyes, his lips practically trembling.

"I don't know," he said. "I had to think."

"You could fucking call me at least."

"I had to think, okay? Jesus, I'm telling you. I couldn't . . . I couldn't think."

"Well, what happened?" she said, her hands moving up and down. "I mean, what the fuck happened, Teddy?"

"I don't . . . Oh man. Oh, Jesus."

"I mean, I tell you Billy Thimble is gonna turn around on Vince Scotti, and now Billy Thimble is fucking dead?"

Suddenly, Teddy pounded the dashboard with his fist. He cried out, "Fucking Vince!" They climbed up past the old graveyard, the bleached stones slanting behind the iron gate. The Trans Am strained at the grade. "Fucking, fucking Vince!"

"Did you tell him, Teddy? Did you really go ahead and tell him what I said? About Billy Thimble? Did you?"

"Fucking . . . Vince, he's got no . . ." Now Teddy hit his chest with his fist. "He's got no . . . *things*, you know. He's got no . . . *things*, like . . . *things* . . ." He hit his chest again to show what *things* Vince was missing.

"Oh shit," Cindy said. "Oh shit. Did he really kill him? Oh shit, Teddy."

Teddy hit his chest again. "Ya know? Ya know what I'm saying?"

"What happened, Teddy? Are the cops gonna question you? Don't tell em anything. Jesus. Don't get Vince mad. Oh Jesus. What're we gonna do?"

"I dunno. I dunno . . ." he said.

They screamed round a curve; out of it; past a field of high grass and purple wildflowers. Sick, she was practically sick about this really. . . .

Teddy said something too low for her to hear.

"What?"

"I gotta go to a meeting first. . . ."

"Whataya mean? What kind of meeting?"

Overhanging trees. Rushing shade. The wind, the engine. Her own breathing.

"Tomorrow night," he shouted to her. "Eight o'clock. Vince wants us to get together."

"Jesus, Teddy, don't . . ."

"Vince called a fucking meeting at the house over on Sheep Pasture Road. What'm I gonna do? I gotta go."

"No. No. Don't go to no fucking meeting with him, Teddy. Jesus. The guy's a fucking murderer. He's fucking crazy, man. Don't go to no fucking meeting."

"I gotta."

"You gotta stay out of this, Teddy. You didn't do nothing. You just told him. You gotta just keep out of this. You gotta keep away from everybody."

"I gotta go, Cinj. It's Vince."

"Oh, Jesus, Teddy." She started to cry. The tears really welled up in her eyes and, when she squeezed her eyes shut a little, one or two of them actually spilled out. "Oh Jesus, Teddy. Don't go."

They were out of the trees—and the wild purple fields whipped by on every side and all at once . . .

He came off the gas. The guttural thunder of the engine dropped to a deep murmur. The Trans Am slowed, pulling to the side, jouncing, in another moment, along the road's shoulder.

And then it was quiet: It was weird the way it got to be so quiet all at once. The car stopped. At the window, there was high grass waving in a gentle breeze. Cindy could hear the hum and chatter of insects. She was breathing hard.

"Don't go," she said again, softly.

Teddy leaned his forehead against the steering wheel. "I gotta."

*　　*　　*

Later, that evening, the air was cool and damp and still. The Hemlock Cathedral smelled of leaves and pine. Cindy perched on the edge of a white boulder. She sucked a joint.

"Now he's gonna go to a fucking meeting with him," she said. "Tomorrow night at that house on Sheep Pasture Road. I told him. I said, keep away from that guy, man. That guy is so fucking bad."

"He's going to a meeting?"

"Yeah. I told him. He's gotta just stay out of it. He's gotta keep his mouth fucking shut. Scotti's a fucking *murderer*, man. Teddy could be some kind of accessory or something."

Bobbi Scorsese was in her jeans again now. She was sitting cross-legged on the ground in the center of the clearing and she looked serious, impressed.

"Jesus, Cinj," she said after a while.

A chickadee sang a three-note song in the high shade of the trees. Another one answered.

"Don't tell nobody about this," Cindy said. "All right, Bobbi? Just don't tell fucking nobody. Understand?"

FIVE

Rumplemeyer and the Widow

TUESDAY, JULY 17

WHAT, RUMPLEMEYER WONDERED, would it be like to be whipped by the widow?

Pushing his Volkswagen through the moonless dark, the bearded little reporter could just imagine it. He could see her—she was, ooh, so fine—her white skin contrasting with her black leather bikini, her silky voice cooing, "Naughty, Ernie, bad, bad, bad." She flicked the birch across his bare ass as he twisted in his shackles, begging for mercy. . . .

Hee, yeah . . . Rumplemeyer thought.

He had to shift in the cramped seat behind the Beetle's wheel: One of the problems with these cars was that they didn't have room for erections. Built by the Germans, he thought, that's why.

The Volks wound into the night, over Bullet Hole Road, through the savage wilds of northern Hickory. Hulking forests crept up on the edge of the pavement like goblin armies. Canopies of black leaves blocked out the starless sky. Only Springsteen—*Born in the USA. I was . . . Born in the USA.*—screaming hoarsely on the little AM car radio was there to remind him that civilization was still nearby.

108

Corruption

He plucked at his pants to free his stiffening cock from his underwear. He tried to imagine the widow's face. It would've made it sexier if he'd known what she looked like, but he hadn't met her yet so he had to invent something. Maybe he'd give her Sally's face, with her sweet smile, her tender eyes. . . . But he was tired of her. He'd been using her for his fantasies ever since he came to the paper a year ago and her whip arm was probably getting tired by now. And anyway, Sally was too busy mooning over this new Sidney the Fourth character to take time out to flagellate him even in his dreams.

And also anyway, here came the turnoff to the Orchard Hills Development.

Born. In the USA. I was. Born in the USA . . .

He slowed the Volks. Reached down to adjust his pants again. It was time to put Mr. Penis to sleep for now.

He banished the image of the Whipping Widow from his mind. Tried to will his erection to soften. When that didn't work, he conjured up something unpleasant. His psychiatrist, for instance. That was perfect: the distasteful Dr. Schuster; leaning back in his easy chair, stroking his mustache, gazing at the ceiling, uttering utter bullshit into the air: "And so you see you have these masochistic fantasies because you feel guilty about your sexual attraction toward your mother, which you felt *caused* your father to desert the family when you were only five."

Yeah, Rumplemeyer thought, or maybe he had these masochistic fantasies because he felt guilty about trying to interview this poor widow woman just four days after her husband's body bobbed up in the Hudson tied to concrete and filled with lead. . . .

The Volkswagen chugged around the corner into the development.

Or maybe. Rumplemeyer thought, *I just have these masochistic fantasies because—lash!—they feel so fine.*

The fact was, though, he did feel guilty about badgering the widow. He never would even have thought of doing it, he told himself, if the great and powerful Sheriff Siren Donothing hadn't been such a prick about the whole story. It was just that, after the press conference this evening, he really felt he had no choice. It was a question of self-respect. That's all. A question of self-respect.

This evening, just as evening came, Rumplemeyer got a call from the Sheriff's Department receptionist: Press conference in ten minutes, she said, come on over. Naturally, the little reporter rushed from the *Champion* office and headed around the corner to Main Street. Bowlegged, humpbacked, his wild hair and beard blowing in the twilight wind, his enormous corduroy coat fluttering out behind him, he hustled past the darkening shadow of Lake Tyler to the old courthouse that faced it from across the street. He skipped and grunted up the stairs, under the colonnade. Pushed breathlessly through the front doors and tumbled into the Sheriff's Department anteroom.

The anteroom wasn't much more than a collection of dead cigarette butts on an ancient linoleum floor, a dispatcher's booth encased in glass along one wall, and the receptionist encased in glass along another. But the county's assembled press corps had gathered there— Dog Saunders of WAUB Radio, Buzzy Farquharson of the *Weekly Trader*, Debbie Pullman of the *Hartford Examiner* from across the state line, and now the intrepid representative of the Sutcliffe Journalistic Empire, Rumplemeyer himself. They were all accounted for. The press conference was supposed to start in seven minutes. Rumplemeyer stood bouncing on his toes.

Forty minutes went by. Forty-five. Rumplemeyer grinned at the receptionist. The receptionist looked bored.

Then a buzzer sounded. The gate to the back rooms swung out, and out past the receptionist stomped Undersheriff Henry Benoit. In Rumplemeyer's opinion, an unmitigated asshole.

Without a word, the lumbering thug in navy-blue polyester thunked around the anteroom from reporter to reporter. He handed each of them a single sheet of paper. When he handed one to Rumplemeyer, he looked the smaller man in the eye and snorted. Rumplemeyer grinned. He bounced on his toes. He looked down at the paper.

On it were written thirty-one words: "Sheriff Cyrus Dolittle announces that the Sheriff's Department, in conjunction with the Westchester County Medical Examiner's Office, has now identified the body discovered in the River Friday as one William Thimble."

"That's the news, don't wear it out," Benoit said. He started walking back toward the gate.

"Can you give us his age?" Debbie Pullman called after him.

Benoit paused at the gate and looked back at them, sleepy-eyed. "Nothing else can be released at this time due to the ongoing nature of the investigation. Have a nice day."

"Wait a second." This was Dog Saunders. He was holding up the microphone to his cassette recorder. "Could you say something I can put on the radio here, Undersherrif? I'd appreciate it."

The undersherrif sighed. He waited, eyes heavenward, while Doggie approached with the mike. Then he said: "Ya ready?"

"Yeah," said Dog.

"Working with the Montclair County Medical Examiner, the Sheriff's Department has now established that the victim's name is William Thimble. No other information can be released at this time due to the ongoing nature of the investigation. Okay?"

"Thanks," Dog said. He tucked the mike back under his arm.

Benoit pulled the gate open.

"Well, thank you so much for keeping us up-to-date," said Buzzy Farquharson. Sad-eyed little Buzzy. He loved the sheriff to death. A doormat, thought Rumplemeyer. A doormat who dreamed of being a boot.

Benoit deigned to wave at him. He was about to go through the gate again when his eyes passed over Rumplemeyer. He hesitated. "What's the matter, Ernie? Haven't you got any questions for the six or seven readers of the *Chumpion?*"

Rumplemeyer, still bouncing on his toes, let fly a grin that hoisted the top of his shaggy beard right up into the bottom of his shaggy hair. "Yeah," he said. "How you feeling this evening, Undersheriff?"

Benoit snorted. "Seeya, Ernie." And went through the gate.

After the press conference, Rumplemeyer stormed over to the Courthouse Restaurant next door. Sally was in there, sitting at the end of the long counter, sipping coffee. Shea was standing next to her at the very back of the room. He was playing Jungle Man, an old-fashioned pinball machine: five balls for a quarter, a field of chutes and dropcards decorated with tigers and palm trees and gorillas; a backdrop with Jungle Man swinging on a vine with a scantily clad Jane under one arm.

Fred, the owner of the place, was standing by the cash register reading the paper. He glanced up and smiled as Rumplemeyer went by. The rest of the place—the counter and the tables—was empty.

Rumplemeyer humped toward the back of the room. "Can you believe that bastard Dolittle? Listen to this."

"God damn it!" said Shea. The big man slapped the side of the pinball machine. "Why does Jungle Man hate me? Why? What have I done? Just tell me."

"He gives us this bullshit press release and then he won't answer any questions." Rumplemeyer flung the paper down in front of Sally.

She picked it up and read it, sipping her coffee, shaking her head.

"That fuckhead," said Rumplemeyer. He slid in between Shea and the machine and took the controls away from him. Shot a ball up onto the field. "He's a Nazi, Chris. I don't care what you say. The Sheriff and Hitler are the same fucking person. Why do you think you never see them together?"

The ball ricocheted off the top bumpers. Shea read the press release over Sally's shoulder.

"That son of a bitch," Sally said.

"He's Hitler," said Rumplemeyer.

"Come on, you guys," Shea said. "Who gave you the release?"

"Benoit. He's Goebbels. This is where they all went after the war." The ball dropped to Rumplemeyer's flippers. He shot it back up at the dropcards. It ricocheted down and he shot it back again, downing the cards one after the other.

"Well, you can't blame Dolittle for what Benoit does," said Shea. "Benoit's a jackass. The sheriff doesn't know half the shit Benoit pulls."

"Oh right. And Purdy is acting totally on his own too."

"You can't blame Dolittle for Purdy all the time either," said Shea.

The red light on the extra ball hole went on. Rumplemeyer slapped the ball right into it. The machine gave a loud pop and racked up an extra ball.

"Yeah, sure, Chris," Rumplemeyer muttered. "And I can't blame Reagan for Iran-Contra."

"That's not the same thing. Reagan was trying to implement a perfectly legal . . ."

"Boys!" Sally whispered. She held up her hand. "Don't do Iran-Contra, okay? Don't do Watergate and don't do Iran-Contra. Okay? Please?"

Shea sighed. Rumplemeyer muttered some more. The pinball dropped down a side chute and Jungle Man began to ring up thousands of bonus points.

"Goddamn it, Ernie," Shea said. He slapped the counter. "How do you do that? Just tell me. How do you *do* that?"

Rumplemeyer spun around and grabbed the press release out from under Sally's nose.

"I don't do it, man," he said, heading for the door. "I just, like, acquiesce."

He humped back to the office through the night. The problem with Shea, he thought, is that he's Irish Catholic. That's it. Those people think anyone in authority is second to God. Well, Rumple would be damned if he'd file this press release as a story. Christ, even Pretty Boy Merriwether the Fourth did better than that with the body story on Friday night. He could still remember Sally beaming at him. Oh, tee-hee-hee, I'm so proud of you, flutter flutter flutter. Shit.

Deadline wasn't till twelve. He had hours to work. He was going to nail this story to the sheriff's ass.

He flew in through the front door, hitting the light switch as he came. Even as the fluorescents flickered on overhead, he was at his desk. He shoved piles of paper and folders to the side until he uncovered his Rolodex. Spun it around till he found the number he wanted. After he'd punched it in, he planted himself in his chair and started rocking, tugging at his tie. The phone began to ring. It rang five times. Then, finally:

"Hello?"

"Dr. Schneiderman!" cried Rumplemeyer.

"Rumpelstiltskin is your name!" cried Schneiderman. "Now will you go away? I'm having dinner."

"Can you tell me just one thing?"

"I thought if I guessed your name you'd fall through the floor."

"Can you give me the cause of death on Billy Thimble?"

"Oh. Hell. I'm not supposed to talk about that. All information on that comes through the Auburn County sheriff."

"Please," said Rumplemeyer. "I'll be your best friend."

"God, what a prospect. All right, it's public information anyway. Can you leave my name off it?"

"I'll just say an extraordinarily youthful and brilliant source in the Westchester County Coroner's Office."

"No, then everyone'll guess it's me. Anyway, I don't know all that much. The guy was all fucked up by the water. What was there? You had a head injury with him . . . forty–forty shotgun wounds to the chest. A .38 wound to the head. What else? Oh yeah, there was also some water in his lungs."

Rumplemeyer, scribbling furiously on his notepad, stopped short and looked up at the plate-glass window. The street outside was dark; the pane reflected an image of the messy little office back at him.

"You mean, like, he was still alive when they threw him in?"

"Possibly. Or the water could have just seeped in there over time. Could just be an anomaly. You got me."

"When did he die?"

"When did they find him, Friday? He was dead around two days. Make it last Wednesday."

"Anything else?"

"Uh, Yeah. Cocaine. Lots of cocaine. He was a cokehead."

"Like a user?"

"Definitely. I mean, there wasn't much left of him, but what was left of him definitely looked like a user. Anything else?"

"What are you having for dinner?"

"Calf's liver."

"You're a disgusting individual."

"Talk to you later, Rumple."

"Thanks, Doc."

Rumplemeyer hung up. He was rocking faster now, practically vibrating in his chair. He reached out on the downswing and spun the

Rolodex again. State Trooper Margaret Hartigan's number came up this time. She picked up on the first ring. Rumplemeyer began singing.

"I'll be calling yoooooooo-ooooooooo-oooo."

"I'm not charmed, Rumplemeyer."

"What do you mean? Why not?"

"Because you're short, bowlegged, humpbacked, and ugly."

"It's 'cause I'm Jewish, isn't it?"

Hartigan laughed. "You asshole."

"Can you just tell me one thing? One thing."

"What is it? You wanna know what we got on Billy Thimble."

"Dolittle's not giving us anything."

"Yeah, I know. We were strictly prohibited from giving out any information."

"I won't use your name. I'll just say: the best-darn-lookin trooper in the state whispered it in my ear."

"Hold on, guttersnipe. Let me get my notebook."

"Mwah." Rumplemeyer waited, rocking back and forth. "Born in the USA," he sang under his breath. "Born. In the USA."

"Okay." Trooper Meg was back. "There's not much yet. He was I.D.'d as a twenty-seven-year-old lawyer with Rainbow Realty in Hickory. You got the cause of death and the cocaine and everything."

"Yeah."

"Then you got everything that's on the wire."

"I have dreams about your holster," Rumplemeyer said. "Hello? Hello?"

He giggled, rocked forward and pressed down the phone plunger. He got Rainbow Realty's number from information, but it was after eight by now and when he called there, no one answered. As he was hanging up, Sally came walking in.

"Sally! Where's Chris?"

"He had to go home to have dinner with his wife and baby, or he'd rot in hell for all eternity. Then he's got the Tyler zoning board at nine."

"What's the difference?" said Rumplemeyer. "Could you, like, look in his Rolodex and just sort of steal the number of the Hickory planning commissioner?"

She leaned over to the Rolodex. Rumplemeyer studied the curve of her rump and sighed.

"Harold Haskins," she said. She read him the number. He started punching the buttons.

"So, like Sally," he said as he listened to the phone ring. "Are you, like, in love with the Fourth?"

"What?" She waved a hand at him as she walked past him to her desk.

He swiveled around, following her. "Well, I mean, you stare at him all the time. Ooooooh, you're blushing!"

"Shut up, Rumple, that's not . . ."

"Hello?"

"Harry!" Rumplemeyer cried into the phone. He swiveled back to his desk as Sally sat down at the desk behind him. "This is Ernie Rumplemeyer at the *Champion?*"

"Oh no."

"Listen, could you just tell me one thing?"

"I don't know anything about this, Rumple."

Rumplemeyer plucked a blank sheet of paper off his desk and studied it. "Well, it's just, I'm looking at this photograph we took at the Rotary picnic last year? And you've got your arm around Billy Thimble's shoulders."

"What? I don't remember that."

"Well, like, they're gonna run this picture and I said . . ."

"What?"

"I told them, you know, the guy was a cokehead, it really makes Harry look bad."

"Ernie. Really. I didn't even know the guy."

"That's what I said. So I was just, like, wondering, you know, could you maybe put me on to someone who did know him, like someone else at Rainbow Realty. . . ."

Harry gave him the home number of Sandy Ferguson, a secretary at Rainbow Realty. Rumplemeyer called her.

"The Rotary picnic?" said Sally behind him.

"Isn't there a Rotary picnic?"

"Hello? . . ."

"Sandy? Hi. This is Ernie Rumplemeyer over at the *Champion.*

Harry Haskins gave me your name. I'm trying to find out something about Billy Thimble."

"Oh, gee, I'm sorry," said Sandy Ferguson—she sounded as if her tongue was in her nose, "the people from the Sheriff's Department said we're not supposed to talk to you. They were very strict about that."

Rumplemeyer dropped his voice to a confidential whisper. "Listen. Could you just tell me one thing. I mean, my boss here says I have to find out if Thimble was married and if he had a family or anything? So he, like, wants me to call, like, his wife, you know?"

"Oh God," said Sandy Ferguson. "That's terrible."

"And I don't want to disturb her in her time of grief," Rumplemeyer said. "So if you could just tell me, like, if he was married or anything, then I wouldn't have to do that, see?"

"Oh," said the woman after a moment. "Oh. Well, I guess that's all right. Yes, he was married and they had a little boy. Will, Jr. He's only three. Such a precious boy. Nancy . . . his wife? She would bring him in to work sometimes. He used to play around on the floor."

"What a terrible tragedy," said Rumplemeyer, sounding stunned, dismayed, surprised, and/or bereaved.

"Yes," hummed Sandy Ferguson through her nostrils. "We were all very, very shocked."

"Oh, I'll bet. Had he been working there long?"

"Three years. Ever since he moved here from California. He was a very hard worker."

"Really?"

"Oh my yes." Now the woman's voice became confidential. "If you ask me, I think he was worried about money."

"Really? Nervous?"

"I shouldn't be telling you this. You won't put this in the paper, will you?"

"You mean, like, he owed people money?"

"Well, he was always working. Harder and harder, longer and longer hours. Always making jokes about making his mortgage payments and men breaking his legs about it and like that. I mean, if you ask me, there was something to it." She clucked with her tongue. "Oh, now I hope I haven't told you anything. I'm really not supposed to tell you anything. I really have to get off the phone."

"Can you just tell me one more thing?" said Rumplemeyer. "Can you just: did he have any friends, people I could talk to?"

"No. No. I don't know anyone. Anyway, no one's supposed to say anything except the Sheriff's Office. I really have to get off."

She meant it this time. He let her go.

That was when he decided to try the widow. A drug killing in Auburn County was big news, after all. Especially with Purdy going around telling everyone that development wasn't going to bring in big-city problems like drugs. Especially when Rumplemeyer himself was countering with a series on how kids were using drugs more and more these days. No wonder the sheriff wanted to hush this up.

He found Thimble's address in the phone book. Jumped to his feet and started stuffing notebooks into his huge coat's huge pockets.

"What now?" said Sally softly.

"Uh," said Rumplemeyer. "I've gotta go."

"Rumplemeyer," said Sally.

Rumplemeyer waddled away from her toward the back door, the door to the parking lot.

"Rumplemeyer," said Sally, her milky voice rising.

Rumplemeyer knew that tone. He stopped. He turned. He grinned. "Uh, like, Sally?"

She cocked her head, her plain face sweetened by that smile of hers. "Uh, like, Rumplemeyer?" she said.

"Uh, well, you know how sometimes there are things, like, a reporter has to sort of do and, like, if his editor asks him what they are he has to tell her and she might say no and then he won't get a really, really, really great story so she shouldn't ask?" said Rumplemeyer.

Sally sighed. Rumplemeyer rushed out the back.

Born. In the USA—hey. Born. In the . . .

Now, Rumplemeyer and his Beetle were cruising slowly along the newly minted lanes of Orchard Hills, looking for Nancy Thimble's house. His stomach had started gurgling at the thought that he was actually going to go through with this thing. Still, he scanned the rural mailboxes for their numbers, slowed to read the names on street signs, peered at the houses that he passed even though each of them looked pretty much the same.

The whole development seemed to have been slapped up about ten minutes ago. The "gently sloping hills"—sure to feature in the brochures—looked scarred and naked, their spindly trees stuck in grassless dust that still bore the track of the bulldozers. The ten or twelve "graceful homes in Early American style" plunked down in the hills here and there were all more or less identical: two stories of reddish wood, the second floor overhanging "garrison-style"; some with hex sign reliefs above the door, others with flanking carriage lanterns.

Rumple drove past them slowly, thinking, *Maybe I won't be able to find it. Maybe she won't be home.*

But then, there it was: 33 Appletree Lane. Another house like all the others. The name THIMBLE was on the mailbox out front.

A spunky little red Tracer was parked in the driveway, leaving plenty of room for Rumplemeyer's Beetle. But he parked on the street all the same, in case he had to run for his life. Twisting in his seat, he reached into the back; rooted around in the humous of old newspapers, McDonald's cartons, unreturned morgue files, and yellowing notebooks, until he found one notebook that had a few blank pages in it. Then he sat still for a while, cowering.

I hate this, he thought. *I hate this.*

Then he stepped outside.

The night was warm and humid. A sheet of haze had covered the sky. Rumplemeyer plodded slowly up the slate front path. With each step, the image of Nancy Thimble became clearer in his mind. He tried to imagine what she would do when she saw him. She could have a stroke or a heart attack. She could kill him or call his mother. She could tear at her own flesh with her fingernails. . . .

The possibility that she would actually shackle him naked to the wall and flog him was probably just the cockeyed daydream of a born optimist.

He reached her doorstep. He bounced nervously on his toes. He rang the bell. Waited in the yellow light from the carriage lanterns. The air was thick and damp around him. His stomach was twisted in him now like a wrung rag. He worked a belch out of it. The door opened.

"Yes?" she didn't even have a chain lock on. She just stood in the opening. A pretty brown-haired woman, maybe twenty-five. Pale lips, soft eyes—already developing the kind of maternal character lines that could fuel Rumple's masturbatory fantasies for weeks.

She gazed at him directly, but wearily, he thought. And he thought he could feel the oppressive loneliness of the house behind her. Where were her relatives? Why had they left her alone in her time of grief? Christ, and now *he* was here too. He felt so bad for her.

But he braced himself and spat it out through his best shit-eating grin. "I'm really, really sorry to bother you, Mrs. Thimble, I really am, really, but I just came to ask you, like, just one or two questions, okay? My name is Ernie Rumplemeyer and I'm with the *Daily Champion*, okay?"

"Oh!" A whispered syllable. She put her hand to her mouth and shook her head. Stared at him with large, damp blue eyes.

Oh no, thought Rumplemeyer.

"I'm sorry," she said. Her tears rose up almost instantly, as if she had barely stopped crying a moment before. "It's just, I realize . . . This must be so hard for you."

Ooooh noooooo! thought Rumplemeyer.

"I don't know what I can tell you, I . . ." She had to stop, covering her mouth again as the tears fell. "I'm sorry." And now she was reaching into the pocket of this incredibly sweet blue housedress and taking out . . .

OOOOOOH NOOOOOOO!

. . . an already sopping Kleenex. She wiped her eyes with it. "He was such a nice man. We have a little boy. He's only three. I don't think he understands really. Billy was so nice to him." She squeaked—she couldn't finish.

Rumplemeyer grinned till the sides of his mouth ached. "Do you, like, uh, have any, you know, I mean, idea why anyone would . . . ?"

"Oh, that." And for a second, just in the gesture of her hand, just in her wry laugh, he thought he could see the way she was, the way she usually was. A great Mom type, he thought, domestic and insecure and funny: the heartbeat of the house. He wished he were dead. "That was the drugs," she said.

"Really?"

"Once he was—addicted . . . Once he owed them so much money . . . He had to start selling it for them, and it was . . . it was killing him. He just hated . . . for Will Jr.'s sake, especially, but he couldn't . . ."

"Do you know who, who he sold for . . . ?"

"I can't talk to you about that. I just can't . . ."

"Okay, okay. Uh . . . Do you know, like, why . . . why they would want to . . . ?"

"No. But it had to be about that somehow. That was the only thing. Everybody's been asking me all these questions, I can't really . . . Oh . . ." She was completely overcome; leaned her head against the doorpost, sobbing with abandon, holding the Kleenex to her lips.

"Mommy?" A little voice trailed out of the interior of the dark house.

Aaaaaaaaaaaaaaaagh! thought Rumplemeyer.

"I have to go," she whispered. "He's only three. I don't think he really understands. Excuse me. I'm sorry."

The little voice came again. "Ma-ma? Is Daddy home yet?"

"Really. I have to go. I'm sorry."

She slipped behind the door and shut it softly. Rumplemeyer stared at it.

She's sorry? he thought.

He turned away.

He limped rapidly up the path to his car.

He thought; *Okay, okay, okay. This was good, this was a good thing. The guy got involved with drug dealers, and they killed him. It shows that Auburn is not immune to big-city crime, it's important information, the public should know, so it's good, it's good. Good job. Good.*

He reached the Volks, yanked the door open. Dropped into the seat. Dragged his legs in after him. He sat then with the key in the ignition, his hands resting on the wheel, shivering.

Okay, and tomorrow. Go to the Hickory train tracks, ask the kids if they had any dealings with this guy, just, just, I mean, if it only shows the sheriff he can't, like, do whatever, whatever he wants all the time. . . .

He took hold of the key, turned the engine over.

Okay, okay. It's good. Good.

He let the key go. He made a fist. He punched himself in the forehead as hard as he could. The blow made him grunt. He fell back hard against the seat. He sat for a second, his head throbbing.

Then he straightened.

Okay.

He put the car in gear and drove off.

SIX

"Here I Am."

THURSDAY, JULY 19

IT WAS THURSDAY evening. Seven twenty-five. A day, thought Sidney Merriwether, like any other day.

The rays of the late afternoon sun were slanting through the storefront window of the newspaper office like a premonition of danger. The beams were falling on the gunmetal gray of a desk. A desk, thought Sidney Merriwether, like any other desk. Except that here, at this desk, sat Sid "Get the Story" Merriwether, ace reporter for the *Daily Champion*. His battered snap-brim was pulled low over his brow—actually, he didn't have a battered snap-brim, but if he had, it would have been pulled low over his brow—his gnarled fingers pounded at the keys of his typewriter. He squinted through the smoke of the coffin nail plastered in his kisser as another hot story rolled out of the machine in front of him.

Suddenly, the Ameche rang. He reached out and snagged the receiver.

"*Champion.*"

"Sidney?"

"Oh—uh—hi." It was his wife. *Damme*, he thought.

"Well, I'm sorry to bother you." She paused, no doubt waiting for him to say, "You're not bothering me."

"Oh, you're not bothering me," he said. "It's always a delight to hear from you."

"I was just sitting around counting the little dots in the TV picture and I sort of got to wondering if you were ever going to come home again."

Merriwether cleared his throat. "Um . . . sorry, darling," he said with a laugh. "Just trying to finish up this story. Shouldn't take long."

There was another pause. A rather cold pause, he thought. Then Emily said, "All right." And he could just imagine her eyes—he knew how they got—those melting brown fawn's eyes she had—how they got all loyal and bravely smiling and hurt . . . "I'll see you whenever you get in then."

He hung up. Leaned back in his chair with a sigh. Smoked and looked through the smoke at the page sticking up from his Selectric:

Hickory supervisor Ralph Jones pledged today to fight to maintain the "rural traditions" of the town of Hickory. A likely candidate for county executive, Jones spoke at a gathering of the town's Shamrock Society. . . .

Merriwether raised his eyes to the ceiling.

What was Emily's problem anyway? he thought. Good Lord, did she think this was fun? Hour after hour of sweaty fat men discussing landfill sites. Arguing over zoning maps. The Shamrock Society, for Christ's sake. Did she think he was having a good time here?

He stole a glance around the office. Chris Shea was still manning *his* post, after all. He hadn't gone home yet, and he was supposed to be Mr. Family Man Extraordinaire. He wasn't even working, just sitting tilted back in his chair, his feet up on Rumplemeyer's desk, his cigarette bit in his teeth. Just chatting away with the profligate Rumplemeyer. Who was also at his station, by the by, vibrating back and forth in his chair. That horrible hairy head bobbing, those grisly teeth showing in that scraggly beard. And that corduroy coat . . . really, what could one say? But the point was, he was there, not rushing home to sup with the wife, if one could imagine him having a wife, which one couldn't but still . . .

124

And Sally too. She was here, or at any rate, over at the CR (the Courthouse Restaurant, to the uninitiated), where she had gone to pick up a sandwich—which she would eat, it should be mentioned, at her desk while editing the day's copy.

He looked out the storefront window, watching for her. He could see the bright green of the small elms lining Stillwater Lane, the redbrick backdrop of the professional building across the street; he could see their colors slowly, slowly starting to dim and blend with the oncoming dusk. . . . Well, it was getting late, it was true, but the mill of journalism couldn't just grind to a halt. The Public had a right to know . . . things.

He came forward and laid his hands on the typewriter keys. But he didn't begin typing again. He turned to watch Shea and Rumplemeyer as they talked. He even smiled stupidly, in the hope of being included in the conversation.

". . . So I go over to the train station to interview the kids," Rumplemeyer was saying. "And I'm, like, getting out of the car, right? And who should come up to me but your good old buddy Henry Benoit, okay? Comes right up to me, the shithead, and he points at this gum wrapper that's lying in the gutter? And he says to me, he says, 'You know, son, that's littering. I could run you in for that.' "

Shea waved him off. "Ah, so what, Ernie? He's an asshole. He's just giving you a hard time."

"So, you know, I'm scared shitless because, like, I don't want to die, so I said, 'Well, sorry, Undersheriff, I didn't realize.' And this asshole—he says to me, 'Ignorance of the law is no excuse, Rumplemeyer.' So I said, 'Spell ignorance, Henry.' He just looked at me." Rumplemeyer grinned.

"All right, so Benoit's Benoit, that's what he's like. I don't know why Dolittle even hired that guy."

"Because if you advertise for a stormtrooper, that's who shows up."

"Well, Dolittle's just pissed at you, Ernie," Shea said. "I'd feel the same way if I were him. I mean, one day you write this big series about how drugs are getting out of hand in Auburn, and we make it sound like it's all Dolittle's fault. Then the next day, there's a murder, and Benoit hands out this stupid press release—so you go out and dig up this drug shit on Billy Thimble and then write . . . I mean, you made it sound like Dolittle was trying to cover that part up or something."

"He *was* trying to cover it up."

Shea glanced over one of his huge shoulders and took notice of Merriwether. "Don't listen to this guy, Sid. Ernie's father abandoned him when he was young. I diagnose a deep-seated hostility against authority figures."

"The worst people to follow are leaders," Rumplemeyer said.

"Well, I am sorry your father abandoned you," said Merriwether. "But there's no need to extrapolate. I'm sure, in your case, it was purely personal."

"Thanks, Fourth." The vibrating troll grinned even wider. "So, like, how come Third wouldn't give you, like, a zillion dollars for your magazine, huh?"

"It's just such bullshit, Ernie," Shea went on. "It's all Sally, it's all Sally and Dolittle, that's what it's all about. It's like the whole paper has to go haywire whenever she wants to get at him. Which is all the time."

"Sally didn't even know I was writing the story," Rumplemeyer cried.

"It's her *attitude*. It's a fucking virus around here. I mean, Purdy's campaigning around saying, 'We can develop the county without having big-city problems because Sheriff Dolittle, who supports me, is on the ball.' Okay, that's his campaign. So all of a sudden, Sally's gotta make a big deal out of any little drug story that comes down the pike. She even has me doing it sometimes. It just gets into your blood. I mean, if Dolittle said the sky was blue, she'd front-page a cloudy day."

"You know, I must admit," Merriwether chimed in—and glanced quickly out the front window to make sure she wasn't coming back, "I have noticed that Sally shows some symptoms of this deep-seated hostility business. She really doesn't like him. The sheriff, I mean."

"It's a neurosis," said Shea.

"Yeah," said Rumplemeyer. "It's called Democracy."

"Ah, Jesus!" Shea swiveled away from Merriwether. "She's obsessed, Ernie. She's one of these . . . these women . . ."

"What women?"

"These frustrated women. I know: We're not supposed to say it—but that's what she is. Oh hey," he said, his tone changing suddenly. "That reminds me . . ." He dropped his feet, leaned forward in his chair, toward Rumplemeyer. "Have you heard about Purdy and Susie Wyman? Oh, you'll like this. . . ."

The two reporters put their heads together, and Shea murmured low. Which left Merriwether out of it again. He was alone again with Ralph Jones and the Shamrock Society. He went back to reading the page in his typewriter.

Jones said he refused to let "greedy developers destroy the traditions of our past and the environment of our future. . . ."

He planted his coffin nail in his kisser again . . . but whenever he tried Shea's trick of smoking and typing at the same time, he nearly asphyxiated. So he swiveled around to look for an ashtray in the fastidious mess of papers on his desk . . . and that's how he spotted Sally.

He saw her through the storefront window. She was trotting toward him, toward the office, along the opposite sidewalk. Slowing a second as the headlights of a pickup rushed past on the way to Main. Hurrying across the street then. Coming close enough for him to see her clearly in the twilight, for him to notice that—well, first of all, to notice that she made a rather appealing figure out there, slender and grim and full of news, running in that cute way women have with their arms half out. . . .

And to notice that her hands were empty: She hadn't gotten her sandwich.

"Hm," said Merriwether, hoping one of the others would pay attention.

". . . and right while our ever-grim councilwoman Wyman is sitting there," Shea was saying, "going through this big, big lecture about the evils of deficit spending—the girl from the clerk's office is on her hands and knees under Purdy's desk . . ."

"Uh, gentlemen?" Merriwether said.

"You're kidding," said Rumplemeyer.

"She's blowing the good supervisor off," said Shea. "It's true."

"Gentlemen." Merriwether rose from his chair. "I do believe something is up."

"I just saw Curtis, Wayward, Flanagan, and Dean . . ." Sally was moving up the aisle before the door closed behind her.

Shea was on his feet. "Christ. That's half of BCI."

"Must be the Thimble killer." Rumplemeyer catapulted out of his chair.

". . . they were walking, two by two," said Sally. "They turned onto Sheep Pasture Road."

"There's just that ghost house there." Shea was heading for the door. Rumplemeyer stepped to Sally's desk.

Merriwether stood in his place, shifting his weight from one foot to the other.

And still Sally's voice stayed even and creamy; her smile remained serene. She handed Rumple the camera. "You and Chris run over there. One of you find a phone and call me as soon as you know what it is." Shea was already gone; the door was swinging shut behind him. Rumple was rumpling up the aisle after him. "I'll call down to the plant and reschedule," Sally said. She picked up the phone as the door swung shut again. Now Rumplemeyer too was gone.

Merriwether still stood there. He ran his hand up through his hair. He looked at Sally with frantic eyes.

She was speaking into the phone in the slow, friendly drawl of a gossiping housewife: "Ha-aye," drawing out the syllable, singsong. "We've got something going on up here, and I think we may need the page-one lead for it. Yes." Almost delicate—almost fragile, she seemed to him—in her puff-sleeve shirt, peach lace at the collar. Her thin arms bare and downy. The makeup so careful on her poor plain face—he could imagine her putting it on so carefully. . . .

She's one of these women. . . .

". . . I guess we'll know for sure in half an hour," she said pleasantly. "Okay?" She set the phone down.

"I want to go too," Merriwether blurted out.

"What?"

"You have to let me, Sally. I have to see . . . I want to see."

For a moment, she eyed him curiously, her head tilted to one side. Then she shook her head: no. "I don't need more than two people on this and if something happens while they're out . . ."

"Please, Sally."

She began to shake her head again, looking at him, gauging him. . . .

And then, all at once, there was that smile, the unexpected sweetness of it. She was going to say yes. Merriwether was taken off guard by a surge of warm affection for her.

"Okay," Sally said. "Go ahead then."

And he just stood there, looking at that smile.

Pardon me a moment, would you, while my loins burst into flames.

"Go ahead, I said."

But it was another moment before he could tear his eyes away from her. When he did, when he headed for the door, she called after him:

"Sidney."

He stopped, looked back, terrified that she would stop him.

"Bureau of Criminal Investigation," she whispered.

"What?"

"BCI. That's what it means."

Merriwether laughed.

In Cambridge, at Harvard, and later when he was running *Helios* too, he hadn't really had much of a chance to do this sort of thing. This running to crime scenes through the night with a grim look on his face. It just didn't come up all that often. Turned out it was sort of exhilarating once you got the hang of it. Dashing along the lakeside. Fireflies dancing over the grassy shore. That tawdry old Greek Revival courthouse across the way, the first stars above it in the violet sky . . . The chirp of crickets, the lap of water. The deceptively quiet facade of a small town about to explode in passion and violence—the whole *Bad Day at Black Rock* experience. It had a certain undefinable charm.

He was out of breath, and his tie was rather gallantly blown back over his shoulder, when he got past the lake and reached the corner of Sheep Pasture Road. A forbidding little lane it was. Quite dark—much darker than Main Street—all overhung with the twisted limbs of maple trees, and not a street lamp anywhere. It was a dead end too.

He moved off the sidewalk to avoid the deepest shadows. Proceeded more slowly down the middle of the street. Nothing was moving. No birds were singing. Even the occasional frog or whatever let out only a dispirited blip from the grass. They sounded as if they'd rather be somewhere else entirely.

Smart frogs, Merriwether thought.

He walked with his body tense, his hands raised from his side at the ready.

There seemed to be more light up ahead. Softer shadows at least. A break in the trees, and then beyond it . . .

Beyond it was a dismal vision. Shea had called it a ghost house, and that's what it was, all right. Merriwether stopped cold at the sight.

He found himself aware suddenly that Shea and Rumplemeyer, not to mention these stalwart well-armed BCI people he'd heard so much about, were nowhere to be seen. He was alone with this house, this Gothic shambles of a place. A three-story monstrosity sitting in a barren field at the end of the lane. It stared at him through black windows—a dozen windows—dormer windows, gable windows; windows lost and reappearing in the hips and valleys of the tortuous roofs. Each one of them seemed to him like a skewed and shattered eye, and there was no way to tell what lurked behind any of them.

Down below, on the front porch, obscure beneath its roof, strange shapes hulked between the supporting columns or leaned beside the door. They also seemed to pin him with their stares while an impenetrable silence dropped down over him—*like a shroud* was the image that came to mind.

An arm snaked from nowhere. A hand wrapped around his elbow.

"Ya!" screamed Merriwether.

"Shut up," said Shea.

The husky Irishman yanked Merriwether under a maple tree.

Merriwether was rigid, his mouth open, his breath quick. The boughs hung down around him, enclosed him in their deep shade. Slowly, only slowly, did he begin to see again: the gray shape of Shea's head above him to his left; to his right, the white glow of Rumplemeyer's eyes, bobbing up and down.

"Nice going, Fourth."

"Oh, be quiet, Rumplemeyer."

"Shut up," said Shea. "They're going in."

"Who's going in? There's no one . . ."

"Shut up."

"Nice going, Fourth."

Merriwether turned to peer out from beneath the leaves. There indeed, across the street, were three men—the featureless figures of three men—striding out of nowhere. They marched past the wild growth of hedges, up the weed-entangled front path to the porch steps. They went up all abreast and disappeared under the porch roof. Another second and Merriwether saw the white rectangle of the door swing inward. He saw a motion in the dark: the men were slipping inside.

Somewhere a whippoorwill had the temerity to sigh. The house— the soulless windows of the house, falling from sight among the roofs, suddenly reappearing—glared out at them. As if hypnotized by that lowering gaze, Merriwether stood staring back, feeling his heart beat. In his mind, he was composing the story he would tell his wife:

. . . and then, for the first time, I noticed the faint wavering glow of candlelight in one of the dormer windows and . . .

His thoughts droned on senselessly. Cricket song, hushed and tentative, rose from the grass and died.

And yet nothing happened. Second after second, there was nothing but that shroud of silence, that faint, wavering glow of candlelight at one of the upstairs windows.

Merriwether's pulse began to slow. He began to shift uncomfortably. He wanted to look away—at something other than those staring windows, that rambling, tortured shell; that house—but he was afraid he would miss the thing, the main event, whatever it turned out to be. He was afraid he would not be watching at the crucial instant, would not, in the end, be able to describe to Emily the thrilling incident that would make her look on him with envy, admiration, and, finally, forgiveness.

But still, nothing happened. His body relaxed. He sighed, shrugged, and shook his head.

And then the house erupted in gunfire.

First, there was a shout. A single wordless shout: Ha! Then— *crack!* A gunshot—and red lightning in the dormer window. Suddenly, they were everywhere on the street: men, running. They came

131

from behind bushes and trees, vaulted out of parked cars. They wove across the unmown lawn, crouched down, arms out, pistols in their fists. The white beam of a spotlight shot up from the curb, slapped against the house wall. Now Merriwether could see more men, racing from under the maples, dodging behind the hedges, pressing close to the wall of the house . . .

At the same time, from within, there came a rending crash. Wood splintered, and there were more shouts—Ha! Ya!—the words unintelligible. Gunfire, a steady crackle of it now, etched the jagged glass in the window's frame as staggered red flashes burst within balls of smoke.

"Oh man," said Rumple.

"Holy shit," said Shea.

"Good Lord," said Merriwether.

Whereupon, the dormer window exploded.

There was a soft, almost musical, crash, and the glass gushed from the house's dark body. The shards sprayed out into the spotlight's beam, seemed to tumble—glittering, colorful—down and down through the harsh, unswerving light.

The men converging on the house, the crouched and running cops, stopped, stood in the grass. They looked up, their arms across their brows, their guns waving at their sides uncertainly. They looked up as the window shattered and the glass flew. . . .

And they saw, above their heads, a terrible figure.

He had flung himself out among the spray of shards, falling and tumbling as the shards tumbled and fell, caught, like them, in the light that pierced the blackness as if the blackness, the night, had been torn in half to set him free. He fell, curled in a ball, his arms crossed at his face.

Like a bat, thought Merriwether. *He looks like a bat.*

Falling and falling, unfurling as he fell. Spreading his arms as he plummeted toward the porch roof, stretching his legs . . .

Or a gargoyle or . . .

Until he landed on the roof with the sound of a mallet blow.

At once, the spotlight slashed down to pin him. Pinned him, hunched and pivoting, his eyes wild, his fingers curled like claws.

or possibly the living incarnation of universal evil, thought Merriwether.

The man bared his teeth, snarling down at the cops below him.
"Freeze!" someone shouted.

"Hold it!"

"Freeze!"

The cops were closing in across the grass again. Their guns were clutched in both hands now. Their arms were raised as if to make salaams.

"Freeze!" they shouted.

"Hold it!"

"Freeze!"

The man on the roof twisted to one side. He looked to the left for a way out.

"Freeze."

He looked to the right, his hands before him.

"Hold it!"

"Freeze!"

"Freeze, motherfucker!"

Now, in the shattered dormer above, a heavyset detective leaned out carefully through the last jags of glass. He pointed a pistol down at the man.

"Hold it, Vince," he said. "You're nailed."

But the creature swung around yet again. Squinted past the blinding beam. Scanned the distance, as if for some source of help, some final avenue of escape.

Merriwether, watching him, shook his head: It was over. There was no way out. The thing was at bay.

And in fact, the man began to straighten out of his crouch. He lowered his hands. The cops moved closer, cautiously. They kept their pistols trained on him, a half-circle of gun barrels, tightening around the house. The man on the porch roof watched them. His hands were at his sides now. The snarling grimace on his lips was easing away. He watched the men steadily. Slowly, he sneered.

Look at him, Merriwether thought. *Just look at him!*

The policemen swarmed around the base of the old Gothic. The dark man shook his head at them as if in disgust. He raised his hands again, held them out from his sides.

"All right, you bastards," he said quietly. "Here I am."

133

Part III

THE WOCEK PIECE

SEVEN

Getting the Piece

SATURDAY, JULY 21–
MONDAY, JULY 23

1

Shit, thought Rumplemeyer.

He couldn't *believe* the deputy was going to check on the house again. He just *did* that, fifteen minutes ago. At 12:30 A fucking M. And here was Rumplemeyer lying belly-down behind the hedges all this time in tall, wet grass that probably had deer ticks in it, and it was dark and a hydrangea branch kept poking into his nostril and something like gelatin with legs had just crawled across his hands, and if he moved, this idiot minion of Adolf Dolittle was going to wheel around and empty his revolver into the bush and then shout, "Halt, who goes there," and then they'd take his bullet-riddled body to his mother and say, "Sorry, Mrs. Rumplemeyer, but we asked him who he was and he wouldn't answer," and she'd say, "Oh yes, he was always like that, never came when you called, I could tell you stories. Believe me, I thought of shooting him once or twice myself." Christ, he hoped his underwear was clean.

But now, finally, Deputy Vigilant had done his duty. He'd walked around the Terrifying Haunted Mansion of Death yet again. Danced his flashlight beam over the busted windows and the junk piled on the porch and the yellow police tape wrapped round the whole place like a ribbon. Jutted his Dick Tracy chin at a few suspicious whistles of the wind and was returning to the cruiser parked at the curb.

He slid into the cop car and the door clunked shut. But he kept his dome light on, and Rumple could still see him in there from where he lay getting Lyme disease. He continued to watch as the deputy opened a lunch bag and pulled out a sandwich and a pink note from his wife reading, "Have a nice day, dear. Kill a Jew for me." Or words to that effect.

This seemed like as good a time as any.

Rumple pushed to his feet and started creeping through the high grass toward the house. Faster and faster he went, his heart beating hard, the ramshackle beast of a place looming nearer, the sky broad and clear and full of stars, the maple trees everywhere around him at the edges of the night.

Ah cha cha cha, I move like the wind, he thought.

And, like the wind, he went swirling up into the air: He had slipped on the grass. He came down hard, his arms wheeling. *Whump*—the air went out of him (also like the wind). He lay on his back, gasping through a slack mouth, staring at the stars.

He heard the cruiser's door snap open.

Oh, I am in trouble. I can't believe how much trouble I am in.

"Someone out there?" the deputy called.

Yes. It's me, asshole. Someone out there?

The flashlight beam shot out over his head. He lay still, on his back, looking up at it as it passed over him to the left. Passed back toward him. Over him to the right. Then it went out.

Good, good, good. It must've been a squirrel.

"Musta been a raccoon," the deputy muttered.

Squirrel, raccoon, I'm having a heart attack, he's dickering.

The minute he heard the cruiser door shut again, he rolled over, pushed to his feet, and hobbled on those goddamned, mutant, clumsy bowed legs toward the side of the house. Just a few feet to go. Closer and closer. *Then a cry behind him: "Hold it." Blam! An arrow of pain in his spine. A whoop of triumph:* "A Jew, a Jew, Ah done killed myself a Jew. . . ."

And then he was safe, pressed against the house's rot-pocked clapboards, out of the deputy's line of vision, panting, panting. . . . Safe.

He paused only a second there. Turned. Lifted his eyes to the window above him. The yellow police tape cut it in half. But he grabbed hold of the splintery wood, dragged himself up, ducked under the tape, and bellied over the sill. Dropped inside into—

darkness like a madman's worst nightmare of hell

—the house.

Blinking, trying to see through the gloom, he shuffled into a maze of odd jags and sudden obstacles. Garbage, it looked like; junk lying around everywhere. The tingle of dust in his nose. The smell of—

moldering flesh trying to claw free of its cerements

—decay. The banister cracked as if it would fall. Kind of like the scene in the horror movie where the audience says, "Don't go up there, don't go up there," and then they do and a guy with a big butcher knife pops up at the top of the stairs and cuts their faces off. *Aaaagh!*

He reached the first landing. Started up the next flight and . . . Outside, faintly, there was the *thunk* of that damn cruiser door again. The guy couldn't sit still for two minutes! Rumplemeyer climbed faster, the stairs setting up a steady moan beneath him.

He stepped onto the third floor and saw it. Right there, to his right. The Shattered Door. It hung aslant, fastened to the frame by the bottom hinges only. A ragged hole had been blasted through the bottom panel. A bullet hole—it was a bullet hole for sure.

Rumple approached the door slowly, almost with awe. Touched it, pushed it. Pushed it harder so that it moved in, scraping loudly against the floor. He stepped through the opening gingerly. And now, he was in the room. The actual room where it had happened. A long, low space with the eaves of the roof pressing into it. A table with a broken leg, tilted onto its side. Wooden chairs, two on their backs, two standing. And the windows, the wedges of glass jutting up in the frames, the faint starlight playing on them, passing through them, falling over the gray and splintery boards of the floor.

The way the police told it, the three men had come to this room in the dead of night, or around the dead of night anyway. Vincent Scotti, the ringleader, and his two accomplices John Barnes and Teddy Wocek. They had come together to discuss the murder of Billy Thimble. What they would say to the police if the cops arrested them. Where they would go if they had to go into hiding. How they would get in touch if they had to. And, most important, how they would divide the late Billy Thimble's drug business among themselves now that he was gone.

That table, that broken table, thought Rumplemeyer, practically shivering with excitement, that's where they'd been sitting. A single candle had stood between them. Their three heads had been bent together, their faces half in shadow, half illumined by the wavering flame. Scotti, the cops said, had brought some cocaine and some money with which to buy the silence of the two younger men. No one knew exactly who had brought the gun.

All of a sudden. . . .

His eyes wide, Rumplemeyer glanced back at the shattered door.

All of a sudden, there had come a heavy pound at that door, he thought.

"Open up. Police!"

Chairs scraped. The table pitched. The candle yawed, its flame-light careening over the open mouths, the frenzied stares of the three conspirators.

The police said one of them grabbed a gun. *Blam!* Rumplemeyer could almost hear it. *Blam!* He had fired right through the door at the cops.

Bang. Bang. Bang.

The cops fired back through the door. Kicked the door in and charged into a hail of bullets, firing back steadily as they came. . . .

Rumplemeyer turned from place to place, awestruck to be right here, right here where it had all happened. There was the window through which Scotti had crashed out into the night. There was the chair which John Barnes had turned over in his hurry to surrender.

And there, right there in that dusty spot on the floorboards . . .

Right there, two days ago, was where Teddy Wocek had died.

2

Now he was in that box, Cindy thought. Inside that box with the white sheet over it, the red cross stitched on top. Closed up in there. Her Teddy. His same face, that she knew, with its long hair and the shy twist of his lips, and the lowered eyebrows—and the eyes, staring up at the coffin lid that was tight on top of him . . .

Cindy sat in the back row of the church and cried until she thought it would shiver her to pieces. Her mascara pooled under her eyes, ran down her cheeks in lines. She had to hold a handkerchief to her mouth to keep from sobbing too loudly.

Bobbi Scorsese sat beside her. She was crying too, but Cindy thought she was making too big a show of it. Rocking back and forth with her hands to her face. She hadn't even known Teddy that well, Cindy thought. All the kids were doing a big crying number, as far as Cindy was concerned. All the girls were anyway. And the guys were being sure to look all serious and solemn with their ties and jackets and washed hair. The whole last three pews were filled with kids from the Hickory High School and half of them hadn't known Teddy at all, Cindy thought. They probably just wanted to be in on something exciting.

Most of them, since they were kids, didn't have real funeral clothes. The rear pews were a strange array of colored jackets and dresses: navy, dark green, brown corduroy, tan, and so on. About halfway up to the altar, that's when the pews turned pure black with the suits and dresses of the adults. Cindy recognized most of them. Bobbi's parents; the Pulaskis; the MacDonalds . . . And right up in front, Teddy's mom and dad. Cindy had never met Mrs. Wocek, but she'd seen her at school and at the mall. She wasn't forty yet, Teddy had said, but her face was all round and saggy with wrinkles. There was a lot of gray in her short reddish-brown hair, too. She sat there—with the box right next to her, right at the head of the center aisle, and her son right there inside it—she sat there and she bent over and sniffled into her handkerchief. Cindy wished she could go to her, sit down next to her and put her arm around her shoulders so they could cry together. But Mrs. Wocek never knew about her and Teddy;

Teddy didn't want to tell. So Cindy could only watch Mr. Wocek—his big slumped back, his crew-cut white hair—as he put his hand on her arm and patted her a couple of times. He was probably sorry now he was always such a drunken shithead who used to knock Teddy down all the time, Cindy thought. Teddy would have been glad, at least, to see that he was crying.

The last note of a single singer—Esther Morrison, the widow—rose from the oaken chancel into the high shadowy rafters. Father Flynn, a white-haired old fart with a thin smile as if he knew more than you did, slowly climbed the winding stairs to the pulpit. He smiled down at them over the top of it, the carved wooden eagle hovering just below. Cindy cried louder.

"I see that some of you are weeping," the old priest said.

No, thought Cindy, *we're dancing in the fucking street.*

"Why do you weep?" His voice was thin too, like he was talking through his nose. He even sounded as if he thought he was smarter than everyone else. "Why do we weep when we only are saying good-bye to the body of our beloved Theodore? When his soul is now free to mingle with ours without the impediment of flesh? . . ."

Cindy looked over her handkerchief, through the blur of tears, at the box with Teddy in it. His face in it, his body. His hands, which she could still feel holding her arms or rubbing her nipples. His arms—so hard with muscle—that she could still feel in her hands. Even his prick, which had been right up inside her, was inside the box now, the lid closed over it . . .

"The body is just a worn-out vehicle the soul has cast aside," said Father Flynn.

Cindy narrowed her eyes, squeezing out a few more tears.

Oh Jesus, Teddy, she thought. *First they say all this horseshit, man. And then they're gonna fucking bury you!*

Her father had brought her the news. That night, that Thursday night that Teddy had gone to meet with Scotti. For a long time before he came home, she had stayed in her bedroom, listening to the radio. Lying on her bed with the earphones on. Looking out her window into the dusk. Tracing the dark branchwork of the cherry tree on that side of the house. The same cherry tree that had been there ever since she was a little girl, its stark, witchy fingers in the winter, its pale green leaves and white blossoms in the spring, the green cherries of summer and the red cherries of fall. She stared at them all without seeing them most of the time, she was so used to them, the tree had stood there so long. She stared at them now in the twilight and they were just part of the pattern of the oncoming dark.

And she listened to the radio, looking out the window, thinking that if anything happened, anything bad, it would be on the news. But WAUB went off the air at sunset, and no one else said anything about it. After a while, she fell asleep, listening to Madonna sing about Romeo and Juliet.

The next thing she knew, he was there, her father. The shadow of her father in the doorway.

"Cindy."

"Wha—"

She was still half-asleep and she couldn't see him well. She sat up on the bed. The earphones had fallen off and she could still hear the tinny sound of the music coming from them, dim music from far away.

Her father turned on the light and she squinted, holding her hand up in front of her.

"Cindy, I have something to tell you."

It was another moment before she could see him. His long, craggy face seemed to be sagging with its own weight. She had never seen his eyes looking so dark, so tired. Behind him, she saw her mother. Her mother was wearing a pink flannel nightgown. Her dyed blond hair was falling onto her forehead. She was wringing her hands and biting her lips.

"Cindy, that boy, that Teddy Wocek . . ." she said.

"What," she said. She slid to the edge of the bed, her feet on the floor. She felt as if her blood had turned to fire. "Oh my God," she remembered saying. "Oh my God." Her voice sounded funny to her, high and squeaky.

"He fired on one of my men," Dolittle said. "They . . ."

"Teddy? Is he all right?"

Slowly, the sheriff of Auburn County shook his head, looked down at the floor. "I'm sorry, Cindy."

The next thing she knew she was standing in front of him, trying to hit him with her fists, screaming, "Teddy? Teddy?"

Her father captured her wrists in his hands. "Stop it, Cindy! Stop it!" Her mother was beside her too. Trying to pull her away, trying to put her arms around her.

"It's all right," her mother kept saying.

But it was not all right. Why was she saying that?

"It's not true," she screamed. "You liar. Fucking liar. Where's Teddy? What did you do to Teddy?"

Her mother pulled her free and Cindy fell backward onto the bed. Her mother sat over her.

"It's all right," she said.

"Cindy," said her father. "He tried to kill one of my men."

She looked from one of their faces to the other. Their faces were so haggard and serious. They were not going to stop saying it was true. They wouldn't stop saying it.

"Oh God. Oh fucking God," she cried.

She threw herself face first into the coverlet, crying and crying.

"It's all right," her mother said, stroking her hair.

"Cindy . . ." said her father softly.

"Get out, get out, get out," she cried.

She had refused to look up again until both of them were gone.

After the ceremony, they had to take Teddy out to Greenlawn. St. Elizabeth's Church had only been built ten years ago, but its church-yard was a landmark more than two hundred years old and they couldn't bury new people in it. So they carried Teddy's box out into the hearse and shut him in there, and then everyone got in their cars and drove out to the newer, bigger field.

First the family went in a long procession of black limousines, headlights on, dim in the bright of noon. Then came the big brown Buicks and the blue Chevrolets as the other adults followed after. Then, finally, the kids, their low-slung Trans Ams and rumbling rebuilt Volkswagens, and the vans with death's-heads painted on their doors, and the bright yellow Mustangs with green fire stripes along the side.

Corruption

The long line of cars wound away up Hickory Kingdom Road. The white steeple of St. Elizabeth's sank out of sight behind the hills.

Cindy rode with Bobbi in her brother's Pontiac. She wasn't crying anymore. Just leaning her head against the window, watching the onrush of the fields. The same fields she had driven past with Teddy. Where she'd pleaded with him.

Don't go, Teddy.

The same fucking fields.

As for Bobbi, Cindy was glad to see that she was finding it hard to do her sniffling routine and handle the five-speed stick at the same time. It was tough for her to keep the pumped-up crate from lurching through the Purple Rage band logo on the back of the van ahead of them.

They had to turn off at the town hall onto Milltown Road and travel along the narrow blacktop practically to the state line. When they reached the place, they pulled to the side of the road behind all the other cars. The minute Bobbi had the stick in Park, she really let it go: She went crazy with tears, boo-hoo-hoo. Burying her face in her handkerchief, the whole thing. Cindy was annoyed at her. She patted Bobbi on the arm a couple of times but after all, she thought, Teddy had been *her* boyfriend, not Bobbi's. After a while, Cindy just opened the door and stepped out into the street and left Bobbi where she was, crying.

It was warm today. Warm and dry and clear. The summer sunshine was coming down through the towering tulip trees, and the way it streaked the pavement kind of reminded Cindy of the Cathedral, the sweet Hemlock Cathedral in the woods. The graveyard was about ten cars down the road, a green field in a valley—square plots of gray stones, white crypts, sand-colored paths—basking in the full sun. From where she was, Cindy could look down the slope over the car roofs and see the hearse being unloaded, the box with Teddy in it being carried out to the new hole they'd dug for it about fifty yards in from the front gate. Mr. and Mrs. Wocek were following after the coffin. And Teddy's brother and two sisters, all clinging together. And the relatives Cindy had noticed in church, in their dark suits, all walking with hunched shoulders. And that little guy . . . who was that little guy?

Cindy squinted. Who the hell was that little bowlegged guy in that huge corduroy jacket, humping along after them? Seemed to be writing something in a notebook or . . .

"Cinj."

It was Bobbi, out of the car now, looking across the roof at her. She was smudged with mascara too now, stained with tears.

"Cinj," she said again. "I think my brother may have . . ." She couldn't finish. She choked on a sob. "I think he may have fucking said something, okay?"

For a long moment, Cindy just kept standing there, looking at her. What was she talking about? Her brother? Herman? The one who was on probation? What did she mean he had said something? Said something about what? For shit's sake, she thought, Teddy was dead, *her* Teddy. Why did everything always have to be about Miss Burger King of Nineteen Eighty whatever.

"I think he may have said something about the meeting," Bobbi said. "He may have told his probation officer, okay? That Scotti and . . . and everybody were gonna be at the ghost house that night. You understand what I'm saying?"

Cindy felt her mouth fall open. "What?"

"I'm so sorry, Cinj." Bobbi burst into fresh sobs. "I didn't know he was gonna tell, I never would have fucking told him in the first place except . . ."

She went on talking, but it was strange: Cindy could hardly hear her anymore. Bobbi was still there, she could still see her, crying and talking, trying to talk, and everything was just the same as before except the words, the sound of the words, had gotten very dim. And the dappled lane and the sounds of the dappled lane and the bright valley of gray stones below and the brown coffin with Teddy in it—it was all suddenly far, far away. Everything was far away, except this thought in her head, this thought that just kept running through her over and over:

The cops knew he was there.

That was all she could think about, over and over:

They knew. They knew. Daddy knew.

146

3

Monday, the Monday after the funeral, Sally stood in the office staring at the bathroom door. Behind her, Shea was at his desk, leaning back in his chair, his hands behind his head. A cigarette bobbed in the side of his mouth. He was staring at the bathroom door too.

Suddenly, the bathroom door flew out. Out with it flew Rumplemeyer, his finger pointed like a gun.

"*Bang,*" he shouted. "*Bang-bang-bang-bang-bang-bang.*"

Shea groaned. "There were only five shots, Rumple."

Rumplemeyer stopped. He stared down at his hand. "How many was that?"

"Like, forty-seven."

"All right," Sally said with a laugh. "Try it again."

"I can't believe this," said Shea. "This is ridiculous."

Off trundled Rumple, back into the bathroom. He shut the door.

"Ah!" Shea waved his hand, made as if to swivel back to his typewriter. That was his answer to every argument, Sally thought; look away. Just because he agrees with the sheriff's politics, he won't see what the man really *is*.

But Shea did not look away. He kept watching her. Leaning back in his chair again, chomping his cigarette. Glowering. All that Catholic morality, she thought, aimed right at her. Trying to eat into her like some sort of . . . Guilt Termite. It really was a double standard. The way he glared at her sometimes. The way he glanced away, judging her. She could just be standing around with someone or talking with someone . . . All right, say she was standing around or talking with Merriwether, but still . . . She was just talking to him, just chatting with one of her reporters, for God's sake. Just because Merriwether was married, that was no reason for Shea to give her that Look of his, that patented Shea Guilt Look. He unloaded all of his cramped, repressed sexual morality on her, and then—then, when it came to the sheriff, to judging the sheriff—well, no matter what *he* did, oh, that was fine, that was A-OK with Pope Christopher. Sell off the county to developers? Fine. Cover up for public officials and then blackmail them? Great. Make a laughingstock of the newspaper? Wonderful. You didn't hear a word, not a peep from Chris last Friday, the morning after the raid on the Sheep Pasture Road house. When they sent out the Auburn edition with that incredible headline:

SHERIFF'S MEN OUTGUN MURDER SUSPECTS.

Now, there was an actual sin for you. That head. Dolittle could hang that head on his wall, like a stag's head. She could just see him, sitting back in his office with his heels on his desk, with that newspaper, *her* newspaper, hung triumphantly on the wall behind him.

SHERIFF'S MEN OUTGUN MURDER SUSPECTS.

Oh, it made Sally furious. She had been on the phone the minute she came to work that day. Calling down to the plant, down to the city desk. Even with her soft voice, even with her gentle phrases, the desk editors had known they were getting a real scolding. What on earth did they think they were doing? she had said. They were practically writing Dolittle's campaign slogans. Smearing them all over her front page. Purdy would be able to hold that edition of the paper up over his head at campaign stops, like Truman with the paper mistakenly announcing his defeat. The county big shots would scramble like mice to get in line behind him, the candidate handpicked by the hero of Sheep Pasture Road. SHERIFF'S MEN OUTGUN MURDER SUSPECTS. It made Dolittle sound like a cowboy hero, like John Wayne. And just in time for the August convention too. Oh, but Chris—Chris had just shrugged when he'd seen it. It had been just fine with Chris, it hadn't bothered him one little . . .

"Ready?" Rumplemeyer's voice was small behind the bathroom door.

Sally glanced up at the clock. And where *was* Merriwether anyway? It was 10:35 in the morning already. Everyone else was here. Doreen was at her telephone; Alice was at her typewriter. Shea was at his desk, Rumplemeyer in his bathroom. Everyone was here but Sidney.

"Ready?" Rumplemeyer cried again.

She looked at the front door, through the glass at the street. Cars whipped by through bright sunshine, under fringes of shade. He was probably still at home, she thought. Lingering a little with his wife after the long, slow Sunday together. They were probably . . .

"Bang-bang-bang-bang."

His great big drug bust, she thought. His great big macho display. Oh, he thinks he's going to walk all over that convention, he thinks he's got Purdy nominated already. Wait'll we give the big shots a dose of this. Let Purdy hold this over his goddamned head at campaign stops. . . .

"Bang," Rumplemeyer shrieked.

"Oh, this looks jolly—can I play too?"

There he was—Merriwether—all of a sudden. Just strolling in. His jacket slung over his shoulder. His golden hair tousled by the breeze. Probably coming from breakfast with her, with Emily, his wife. He'd probably gazed across the breakfast table at her, murmuring witty, affectionate remarks. Jokes about the people he had to work with. That poor plain old Sally, he probably said. . . .

She turned and gave him her prettiest smile.

"Can you believe this?" Shea called out to him. "Rumplemeyer went to Wocek's funeral and waylaid his mother for an interview. At the funeral!"

Rumple bounced on his toes, pretending to feel sheepish. "I couldn't find her address. I figured she'd be there."

"Shrewd guess, Rumplemeyer." Merriwether gracefully swung the jacket off his shoulder, draped it over his chair with a flourish. "Well, what did she say?"

"What's she gonna say?" said Shea. "Tell me if I'm wrong, Rumple." He began to blubber in a high-pitched voice. 'He was a goooood booooy. He never did no harm to nobodeeeee. The police shot him like a dog in the streeeeeet. They don't care how much I loooooooved hiiiiiiim.' Great story: *My Son Good, Mom Says.* How close am I?"

"Well, we printed the police side of it," Rumple told Sidney.

"The police were fucking there," Shea told him.

"So was I. . . ."

"Right." Shea addressed Merriwether again. "Rumple sneaks into the Sheep Pasture house in the dead of the night without even a flashlight. . . ."

"I had a penlight."

149

"And now his expert forensic opinion is that Wocek couldn't have fired on the cops."

"Not after they came in. There were no bullet holes on that side of the room."

"For Christ's sake, he doesn't know that, Sid. They could've been anywhere. Ah!" He waved them all off again, and this time he did spin around to his typewriter. Even managed to type a few words. Rumplemeyer stalked back into the bathroom and stood there running his hand up and down the door as if examining it for damage.

Merriwether meanwhile ambled up the aisle to where Sally was standing in the back before the bathroom. He propped himself against her desk, lit a cigarette. Smiled at her, his blue eyes merry.

She sighed. *Oh boy oh boy oh boy.*

" 'Everything comes about by way of strife,' " he told her.

"Who . . ." She had to clear her throat. "Who said that?"

"Heraclitus."

"With the *Tribune?*"

"No, that was Sam Heraclitus. Are you going to print it?"

"Heraclitus?"

"This piece about Mrs. Wocek."

"I don't know." And then to her surprise, she heard herself, in that breathy schoolgirl whisper, say; "What do you think?"

Merriwether tilted his head, considered it, and Sally thought, *What does he think? Who cares what he thinks? What am I asking him for? He isn't even a reporter. He quotes Heraclitus. What does he know about news?*

And yet, and yet, on the other hand, what if he said no? What if he said, This is the same as accusing the sheriff of murder, Sally. It's like saying his men shot Teddy Wocek down through negligence—or even in cold blood. You can't do that. You have no proof. Or what if he said, I'm sorry, but I don't want to be associated with an operation that uses its journalistic powers to advance the personal and political goals of its angry, obsessive bureau chief. Or worse, what if he merely looked at her, merely narrowed his eyes or pursed his lips as much as to say, Oh, but Sally, you wouldn't. Or what if he . . . ?

"Oh well . . ." he began to say.

"You know what it is, Sid." Shea spun to him, pointing his

finger. "It's accusing him of murder. That's all it's doing. And with no proof."

Sally felt the heat rise to her face. She stole a look at Sidney, but he only had time to murmur again, "Oh well . . ." when out bounced Rumple, whining, "It's not, like, a question of us accusing him, Fourth. It's the opinion of like, an involved party."

"It's Wocek's *mother*, for Christ's sake, what's she supposed to say?"

"The evidence in the house backs her up and the sheriff isn't giving . . ."

"What evidence in the house? There is no evidence in the house."

Sally kept watching Sidney as the two reporters went at him. The heat in her cheeks grew more intense and she prayed she wasn't blushing, though she figured she probably was.

Accusing the sheriff of murder. With no proof.

She waited. What was he going to say? What did he think of her? What did he think she was? . . .

Just then, Shea's voice broke into her thoughts. "Come on, Sid," he almost shouted, "wouldja tell her?"

And Sally felt a sourness in her stomach bordering on nausea. They were arguing with Sidney, she realized—Rumplemeyer and Shea—they were trying to convince *him* . . . Because they thought she would do whatever he said.

Quickly, she raised her hands. She let out a perfect, tinkling laugh.

"Okay, boys, okay," she said gently. "I've made up my mind."

EIGHT

Reading the Piece

TUESDAY, JULY 24

Slain Suspect's Mom:
"My Son Was Innocent"
by Ernest J. Rumplemeyer
STAFF WRITER

The mother of murder suspect Theodore Wocek says her son was not a murderer and was wrongfully shot dead by police during a July 19 raid in the town of Tyler.

Margaret Wocek, 38, of Iron Mine Road in Hickory, says investigators of the Auburn County Sheriff's Department "committed murder" themselves when they opened fire on her son during the raid, which took place in an upstairs room in an abandoned house on Sheep Pasture Road. The 17-year-old Wocek was hit five times in the chest and torso and died at the scene. The S.D. says Wocek fired a .38 caliber pistol once through the door of the room, then twice more at the investigators when they attempted to enter and arrest him and two other men for the recent murder of real estate lawyer William Thimble.

"My son didn't commit murder. The police committed murder," said Mrs. Wocek, during a tearful interview. "My son was a good boy. He didn't kill anyone. They shot him down like he was some kind of an animal. I loved him. I loved him so much. They didn't even care."

In a printed statement, Sheriff Cyrus Dolittle refused further comment on the incident, saying, "A departmental investigation is still under way." The Department has also refused to reveal which of the three arresting officers—Undersheriff Henry Benoit or investigators Frank Curtis and Harry Wayward—fired the fatal shots. A reporter's examination of the house where the raid took place found no stray bullet holes or other signs to corroborate (see *Wocek* back page)

Dolittle did not "see *Wocek*, back page." Instead, he slapped the paper down on the kitchen table.

"Damn it, damn her," he said aloud.

He pushed away from the table, his chair scraping against the linoleum tiles. He went to the door, the back door, which opened up into the driveway. He yanked it open and was about to step out when he saw Cindy. She had just come into the kitchen and was moving to the table.

For a moment, he thought it was her mother, his wife. She looked like Liz with her bathrobe loosely belted and her mouth slack and her hair uncombed, falling down around her face. As she moved toward the table, toward the paper lying there, he could hear her feet shuffling along the floor.

She saw him. She looked up and saw him standing with his hand on the back door. She kept walking, kept moving toward the kitchen table, but she stared at him too, her mouth twisted in a little grimace of disgust.

Dolittle glanced down at the newspaper and started to speak. But he didn't. He couldn't think of anything to say. He couldn't think of anything.

His daughter's hand lifted, reaching for the newspaper. Dolittle left the house.

•   •   •

Behind the wheel of the Cadillac, racing down the mountain road, he felt as if he were choking, as if his own body were closing in on him. He took a deep breath—or tried to anyway. There was still that spot, that cloud at the base of his lungs that the air couldn't get to. It was an awful feeling, a feeling of panic almost. He pushed down on the gas a little harder. At the window, the evergreens of Wapataugh whipped by. He caught glimpses of the large white houses hidden in the slopes of high pines.

He thought of Sally Dawes. He thought of her almost sorrowfully. If he had had her there, he would have liked to grab her by the front of her blouse and shake her and shout into her face, Why do you do this? Why do you keep doing this? What do I have to do to make you understand?

The smooth pavement rushed beneath his tires, tar-black and rich. He wanted to say to her, I built this road. I held the gravel in my hand. I can still feel the gravel in my hand. Where the hell were you when I did that, Sally? What gives you the right? What gives you the right?

He had not only built this road, he wanted to tell her, but a dozen others. And widened and repaved the old paths under a dozen more besides. She wasn't there, she didn't know. He and his buddies, Ralph Jones, Hank McGee: They'd been there, they'd done it, with a Cat bulldozer and some buzz saws and a big old backhoe they'd nicknamed Millie. They had beat their way through the pine and oakwood, cursing and whooping . . . He could almost smell the autumn air of those days, the bulldozer exhaust; could almost hear the cracking of the trunks giving way and see the treetops sweeping down across the sky, that dizzying fall . . .

The car is king, man. They're letting the railroads die. The car is king. That's what Hank McGee used to tell them. *Four years from now, I tell you, there'll be two miles of sure-enough paved road for every square mile in this county. Wait and see, it'll change everything. Make this area young again, I'm telling you.*

But that was the thing, right there. That was exactly the thing. Hank was right, but only as far as he went. The roads did come, and they did change everything. They put Auburn within commuting distance of White Plains and even New York, linked it to trucking routes, opened it for development. But Hank didn't understand, none of them understood, what that meant, what it was going to mean for the county.

And she wasn't there, Dolittle thought. Miss Sally Dawes. She wasn't there, she didn't know. Dolittle could remember, just after he'd first been elected sheriff back in the early sixties, he could remember standing before the old Board of Supervisors . . . the old gang of five fat men in their white shirtsleeves, their armpits dark with sweat . . . he could remember standing there in front of them with the people, twenty, thirty people sitting in the pews behind him. And the people applauded him when he stood up to speak. They reached over the railing to pat his shoulder, shake his hand. The people thought he was a hero because he had solved the murder of the little Marsh girl. More than that, because he had faced down the girl's killer himself. He had asked for no sympathy and offered no explanation but the facts, and he had faced down the girl's killer and shot him dead—even though the killer had turned out to be Hank McGee, his own best friend.

And so he had stood before the five fat men, Dolittle remembered, he had stood before the board of supervisors and he had told them, There's trouble coming to Auburn, gentlemen. Trouble from your young people. The farms up here are dying, and the old communities are dying with them. There's no place for the kids to go. No recreational facilities. No way for them even to get around unless they can drive a car. That means the young girls are dating older guys who can drive—older guys who smoke cigarettes and drink liquor and get the girls into trouble. And that means the young boys are hanging out around the railroad tracks with nothing to do. And they're drinking too and getting themselves into trouble. This county needs to think about its future, he told them. We can't just be a summer hideaway for New Yorkers. We can't just be a place for the rich to build their second homes. Not if we want to raise families here and keep our kids straight. We've gotta bring in some businesses, some development. We've got to build new communities, with places for kids to play, with stores and summer jobs and corporations that offer opportunities. . . .

He had spoken for nearly fifteen minutes in his slow, cool drawl. He had spoken as well as he knew how, and even showed them statistics: the recent rise in juvenile arrests, in delinquency and drinking—and a frightening new interest in the sort of drugs that used to be reserved only for Negroes. He spoke, and when he was done, he stood before them silently and waited. And those men, the town supervisors, those five fat men—they sat there at their big table, and they smiled politely at him and nodded and clucked. And the people behind him who thought he was a hero, who'd shaken his hand and slapped him on the back—they applauded politely and then shuffled their feet and cleared their throats and looked away.

Because they all knew that the farms were in trouble—but they weren't dying exactly, not yet, not *their* farms. And the rich city folks buying houses, why, nothing wrong with that, they thought. You could make good money selling out to the city folks, if that's what you had a mind to do. And the summer people too, they had money. There was a lot of good money to be made off the summer people what with one kind of business and another.

And so they had not listened to him. None of them had listened to him. Not then. Not yet.

And Sally was not there. She was not there, and now, more than fifteen years later, she came toddling up here from White Plains, commuting up here every day from White Plains to run her paper, and she was saying, Oh, my goodness, the young people are dealing drugs! The young people are juvenile delinquents! They're carrying guns, they're getting shot! Oh my stars, it's all the sheriff's fault! The evil sheriff and his bad men with their big guns!

He coughed. He felt it deep in his chest. It's the stress most likely, he thought. Some kind of nervous thing, some kind of nervous asthma. Christ, that woman, she's killing me here.

The road leveled out in front of him, the slopes of pines and houses fell away from the window. He was crossing the highway now, moving onto Hickory Kingdom Road. Driving toward Hickory's Main Street, toward the train tracks. To his right were the first dense clusters of scraggly conifers that led into the Hickory Pine Forest.

He tried to drag in a breath, wheezing. He glanced at the forest. He thought of the Hemlock Cathedral. He thought of Sally Dawes. Coming up here with her hothouse-flower version of the way things ought to be. Writing her stories: *The Hemlock Cathedral: The Murder That Made a Sheriff.* He could still see that headline in his mind.

Corruption

Part Two. It Snowed the Night of the Murder.

He pressed his lips together, forcing down a cough. He drove on, staring at the road, at the white line slipping under the Cadillac's fender. His eyes were dark and furious.

He thought, *It snowed.*

The jail cells were in the basement of the courthouse. There were not many of them. There were not enough. One of the first things Purdy was going to have to do if he got into office was find the funds for a whole new Sheriff's Department with full jail facilities. Right now, they only had six cell blocks with four cells each. The place was so crowded they had to farm some of their prisoners out to Dutchess and Putnam, and then pay the cost of bringing them to and from court.

Still, though, Barnes was here. Johnny Barnes. The boy they'd busted with Vince Scotti in the shoot-out on Sheep Pasture Road. The boy who'd survived the gunfire. Scotti himself had made his bond—it was 250 grand, but somehow he'd come up with it—but not Barnes. Barnes was down here in the jail.

He was a miserable eighteen-year-old punk, this Johnny. Black hair flopping on his forehead, thick lips sullen, eyes like a hamster's, black and blank and buggy. When Dolittle came downstairs to his cell that morning, the kid was just sitting there, slumped on his cot in his jailhouse grays—button-down workshirt, loose-hanging slacks—working his hands together, staring at the cinder-block walls. There wasn't much else for him to do, of course. The cell was about four paces end to end and, besides the cot, there was nothing in it but a metal toilet bowl, set back in a nook. So he could sit or he could pace or he could shit, those were the choices. He was sitting when the sheriff unlocked the center panel of the heavy bars, slid it open, and stepped inside.

The punk looked up, his sullen mouth working nervously, his hamster eyes bugging. Dolittle slid the bars shut again. He leaned back against them. Crossed his arms. He kept his face rigidly under control, his lips thin and grim, his eyes expressionless. He didn't give the kid anything to hope for.

The kid kept looking at him. Dolittle didn't say anything. The kid rubbed his hands together. Snapped his head back to clear his hair

157

off his forehead. Dolittle leaned against the bars, arms crossed on his chest. Studied him, keeping that dead expression on.

Finally, the punk couldn't stand it anymore. "Yeah?" he said. "Yeah, what?"

The sheriff bowed his head a moment, then eyed the kid again. "Son," he said—and he kept his voice even, cold, and slow. He enjoyed watching the punk squirm. "Son, there comes a time when every young man has to look into his future. You understand me?"

The kid's mouth hung open. He managed to nod.

"Now when I look into your future," Dolittle went on, "I see a young man lying facedown over a prison toilet bowl with a large black hard-on being rammed repeatedly up his ass." The kid stared. Dolittle raised a finger. "Now, you may not be aware of this, but scientific tests have shown that one drop of a nigger's jism has more AIDS virus in it than the entire city of San Francisco. So when I picture you in future years, my friend, all I see is an empty space where John Barnes *used* to be. You understand me?"

The hamster-eyed punk opened his mouth a little wider—even managed to say something. "I want, like . . . uh, my lawyer, okay? You know?"

"Yes, I do know," said Dolittle. And now, finally, he favored the poor creep with one of his friendly country smiles, his crow's-feet crinkling, his eyes dewy and bright. "You can have your lawyer," he told Barnes. The rodent never blinked; his mouth never shut. "You can have your lawyer," the sheriff told him. "Or you can have half a chance at redemption."

Fifteen minutes later, when he got back to his office, he started to cough. He felt something stick in his throat, so he coughed once to try to clear it out and then he couldn't stop. He just kept coughing hoarsely, the phlegm seething in his chest. He shut the door, closed the venetian blinds. The last thing he needed was for someone to see this, for word to get out that he was sick, weak . . . Christ, what would Sally Dawes make of that if she had it?

"Uh-huh!" A loud, guttural old man's noise came up out of him. He leaned against the desk, bent over, his fist in front of his mouth. He was going to bring up blood, he was sure of it, he had lung cancer, he was sure. He fought to keep the noise down, wheezing and gasping into his fist until the air was emptied from him, until his head felt light and the big mahogany desk and the state flag and the county flag and the plaques on the wall all started to tilt and shift and he thought he was going to pass out.

He sat down hard on the desk, pulled in a breath. Coughed. Pulled in a breath again. No blood. There was no blood; maybe it wasn't cancer. Emphysema, maybe, like his mother had. Now, he took two breaths in a row, both of them stopping at that strange, frustrating, scary clog at the bottom of his lungs. But still, it was breath; still, he was breathing. Maybe it was just some kind of asthma or something. Or an allergy maybe.

He moved around the desk to his chair. Dropped down into it, his hand covering his eyes, massaging his forehead. He was breathing again. Steady, shallow breaths. It was stress. That's what it was. That's what it was, all right. He dropped his hand to his chest and moved in slow circles. All this political bullshit; his wife all tranked up; his daughter angry at him all the time; no sex . . .

He smiled with one side of his mouth. It was true: He and Sally ought to just get together and fuck each other instead of just . . . fucking each other all the time.

He snorted—and coughed a little more.

Then he looked up and saw Undersheriff Henry Benoit standing in the doorway.

Benoit walked in—he sauntered in, the heavy pillars of his legs dragging, the cigarette held casually at his waist. The round, rough face was screwed up in an insinuating smile. A new smile, a smile he hadn't worn before. He wandered easily over to the window. Propped his butt on the sill.

Dolittle felt his gut go sour at the sight of the man. He steadied himself with a few more breaths, fought down the whistling sound as the air came out of him. He watched Benoit carefully, as the undersheriff glanced out at the lake, glanced back.

"I knocked," Benoit said, "but there was no answer."

Dolittle forced himself to smile. "Well, then just come on in and sit down," he said. *You crazy motherfucker,* he thought.

159

The son of a bitch laughed. Met his eyes easily. Arrogantly. Oh yes. This was a new Henry Benoit altogether. A changed man. A man who felt powerful and dangerous. This was the man who had gunned down Teddy Wocek in the house on Sheep Pasture Road. The sheriff managed to keep his smile in place. He waited.

"I just thought you'd wanna know," Benoit said after a second. "We found the slug that Wocek fired. Pesky little bugger. DiMola had to move this big old dresser sitting there. The slug was wedged . . . there was this kind of mirror on it, turns on a pivot? . . . Bullet kind of got wedged in there. Well, anyway, it's all taken care of now. We just tell the press about it; it ought to take care of all their questions, nice and neat."

His sharp dark eyes held Dolittle's for a long time. Dolittle met him stare for stare; he'd rather have died than look away.

Finally, Benoit turned back to the window, shaking his head. "Only thing at this point is: Will they play fair and print it? You know? This Rumplemeyer. Shit," he said. "Fucking press, they are just a fucking problem, man. Not just here. Down in the Bronx, they couldn't tell the good guys from the bad guys half the time. They didn't know. The kind of fucking animals we were dealing with. They didn't have a clue. I hate that. Guys like that. This Rumplemeyer. I hate that shit. What do they think these assholes are we're dealing with, the Little Rascals?" Now when Benoit faced him, his mouth was twisted into a knowing grin. "I'll tell you one thing: I wouldn't want them hearing some of our conversations around here. Huh? What would they think of that, right, buddy?"

Dolittle glanced at the garbage can by his feet. He made a soft spitting sound between his lips.

"Yeah, that's the problem with these press guys," Benoit went on. "They just won't let you alone. Like this Rumplemeyer. I'm telling you. You know where he was the other day? He was down by the train tracks in Hickory. Yeah."

Oh shit, Dolittle thought. But he didn't let his expression change.

"I mean, who do you think he's looking for? You gonna tell me he's not looking for your daughter, for Cindy? You gonna tell me he's not looking for her to ask her some questions about Teddy Wocek? It's a good thing I was there. I'm telling you."

Benoit paused. Finally, Dolittle had to ask: "What did you do?"

"Oh hell, I rousted him," Benoit said. "What was I gonna do? I told him, I said, I'll haul your ass in for littering. How'd he like that?" He chuckled. "You shoulda seen him. He jumped back in that Volkswagen of his and went farting right back to Mama. You shoulda seen him." He scratched the back of his neck. "Still, I don't know. I don't know. You might want to keep an eye on the girl herself, Sheriff. I mean, I don't want to tell you your business or anything, but I know it would make me feel a lot better if we had someone watching her. Just for a while, you know. Until everything calmed down."

Outside, through the window, across the street, a line of white fire, the reflection of the noonday sun, cut the lakewater in two. Benoit glanced at it, humming under his breath.

Dolittle watched him. He could almost feel Benoit's throat in his hand, he could almost imagine what it would be like to squeeze it, to have the crazy fuckhead's eyes bug out first in surprise, then in terror. . . .

But he remembered Cindy too, the way she had looked this morning. That drugged, ravaged sleepwalking figure, shuffling into the kitchen, reaching for the newspaper . . .

The mother of murder suspect Theodore Wocek says her son was wrongfully shot dead by police. . . .

"All right," he said softly. "Watch her. From a distance, Henry."

Benoit shrugged. Hoisted himself off the sill. He came—strolled—across the room, the ashes dribbling from his cigarette onto the sheriff's floor. He stood over Dolittle's chair.

Then he reached down and patted Dolittle on the shoulder. Dolittle stared up at him.

"Sure, Cy," Benoit said. He winked. "Whatever you say."

NINE

The Huntley Hearing

SUNDAY, AUGUST 19–
MONDAY, AUGUST 20

1

"I DON'T WANT to choose between phallocentrism and deconstructionism. One's too positive and the other too negative: They both miss the point."

He wasn't even listening, Emily could tell. Sitting on the sofa in the cottage living room, elbow on its arm, cigarette held to his brow as if he were considering it all, Jove-like; working his lips at her thoughtfully, nodding every now and then at the correct intervals—while all the time he was thinking about . . . the Paper.

Still, Emily pressed on, pacing up and down across the rug in front of him, working the words out with her hands in the air.

"If there's a pattern, see, a universal Knower, than the phallus is just another signifier in that pattern, sure—but to deconstruct every signifier because it's not the unknowable pattern in itself is just an act of peevishness—it's like they're in a snit because they're not the gods. Do you see what I mean?"

He blinked. "Uh-oh. Uh . . . I suppose. I'm . . . I'm sorry, Emily."

That knocked the juice out of her. She sagged down into the canvas chair by the picture window. Under her glare, Sidney spread his hands unhappily.

"I am sorry," he said again.

"Well, they're *your* stupid ideas, Sidney."

"Are they?"

"You could at least pretend they matter to you."

"They do matter to me, Emily. I said I'm sorry."

She turned her face away from him—not that she was going to cry, she was *not* going to cry—but just to look out the picture window.

It was a hot summer Sunday, the air heavy and wet. The hickories at the edges of the lawn looked weary under the weight of their leaves. No clouds above them, the sky scorched to the palest shade of blue. But the heat was not stagnant, not suffocating, not the way it was in the city, back in Cambridge. Here, with the front door open, the air moved pleasantly through the screens, door to window, across the cottage. The smoke from her husband's cigarette drifted to her, pleasantly sharp; and the rough coughing of crows chasing a hawk from their territory—that drifted to her too. . . .

In Cambridge, she remembered, back in Cambridge, they had walked together on paths beneath the winter trees. Harvard Yard was covered with snow, and there were lights on in the big windows of the redbrick dormitories and she could see students sitting on the window seats in there, books on their upraised knees. And he *did* say these things to her. She remembered it clearly. He gazed into the empty air and quoted her own beloved Augustine to her, his face uplifted with visionary fervor: *The two times, past and future, how can they be, since the past is no more and the future is not yet?* He was just twenty and he was One of Them, One of Them with a vengeance, One of the Elect. He'd descended like Apollo to her, who was not One of Them, who was an Outcast even among her own kind. He'd descended from those redbrick halls to stroll her back to the subsidized houses. Walking, unselfconscious, shoulder to her shoulder down Cambridge Street through the snow. *Maybe it's just . . . slavery to illusion,* he'd said. *Memories and dreams; this insistence that they . . . refer to something*

163

outside themselves: the past and the future. A slavery to illusion; that's what he had said, he had said that. And there was all this urgency to it. And she, trying to catch his tone, had answered, *Without your memories, though, you'd just be . . . anyone, you'd be everyone. And without your dreams, you'd be . . . alone. You wouldn't be one of your kind.*

Well, it didn't sound like such airy nonsense back then. In fact, it seemed to have more weight than anything else, more weight than the everyday things anyway. It seemed, in fact, to have so much weight that when later, snowblown on the steps of her ramshackle Victorian house, he mentioned his childhood depression after his mother's death as an illustration of Man's Alienation from True Time—mentioned her death when he was four as an illustration of a philosophical *point,* for God's sake—she, idiot that she was, *accepted* it as an example, responded to the *point,* arguing that Illusory Time was an Indispensable Constituent of Humanity. That's exactly what she said: Illusory Time . . . Indispensable Constituent . . . She didn't even begin to realize that he was *telling* her. About his mother. That she had died when he was four lousy years old, and he wanted her to know and he was never going to discuss it with her again, never ever, and that it would squat between them sometimes like an unmentionable goblin, with all the weight, the truth and substance, of a toothache or lunch or the need to go to the bathroom . . . And that meanwhile—meanwhile these fine, these urgent ideas of theirs—they would seem to be burned to nothing, utterly dissipated by the mere presence of this summer heat. By the caw of crows, and the fields out past the lawn, and how the fields had changed over the slow July, growing all gold and white and purple now—with goldenrod and loosestrife and Queen Anne's lace; and the way the hills had become a rich and misty green behind them . . .

Maybe later, she would go out to her garden, Emily thought. Water it at least. Pick some of the lettuce, cheer on the reddening tomatoes . . .

"Well, what *are* you thinking about then?" she asked suddenly, coming around to face him where he sat on the sofa.

Merriwether smiled, embarrassed. Because it was something

about the Paper, of course. She just knew it was something about the Paper.

"Nothing," he said.

"No. Go ahead. What?"

He tapped his cigarette out in an ashtray he'd balanced on the sofa arm. He sighed out his last lungful of smoke.

"All right then. A hearing. I'm thinking about a court hearing. I have to cover it tomorrow. It's part of the Scotti case." He shrugged. "And I was thinking about it."

Emily nodded once and looked out the window again, up at the cloudless sky. The crows had retreated. The hawk was a brown speck, wheeling away on the high thermals.

The Scotti case. Part of the Scotti case.

Already she dreaded Monday, being alone here.

2

It poured on Monday—it was teeming. A black sky, hurling rain. The parking lot in back of the newspaper office was practically submerged.

Laughing, Merriwether stepped gingerly from his Rabbit and was immediately soaked to his ankles. The cuffs of his wool plaid suit were positively glued to his skin as he hopped and splashed along the archipelagoes of asphalt to reach the rear of the bureau. Then, sweeping off his snap-brim, he shoved his way in—"Ta-daaa!"—and saw the disaster.

The roof had given way. Good God, he had overheard Sally on the phone half a dozen times at least, telling that journalistic genius Randall Shank that the thing was starting to leak. It was a flat tar roof and the water just collected on it and now . . . ten, twelve, fifteen silver cascades were pattering down upon the office interior in various places. Alice was scurrying up and down the aisle on her baluster-shaped legs, carrying a wastebasket to the latest outbreak. Shea—his cigarette extinguished, sopping, crumbling in his mouth—was trying to move his Selectric to high ground. Rumplemeyer, in his chair, all that hair plastered to his head, kept rocking in and out of a drizzle as he cleared a space on his desk for the rain to fall on. And Sally, the phone to one ear and her finger in the other, was trying to hear above the rattle of water hitting the wastebaskets.

"I know, Randall," she was saying sweetly. "I know you have more important things . . . You're a very important man, Randall. Yes, I really do think so. But I have the conventions to cover in exactly one week and I . . ."

Merriwether started laughing again. "Is this why reporters always wear their hats?"

Shea spit strands of tobacco. "Go get em, Sid. Good luck."

"Hey, Fourth," said Rumplemeyer. "Don't blow it, okay?"

Merriwether squished along the aisle carpet to his desk. Snatched up a pad, a pen; snagged a copy of the paper. "Go down with your bureau, lads. I can't tell you how I envy you this opportunity for heroism. I love you all." He blew them kisses, backing toward the door.

"Good luck," Sally called. He had a second to savor that smile of hers and the look in her eyes: bit of affection for him, what? Bit of an attraction to him, ey, what-what-what? Then she plugged her ear and spoke into the phone again. "No, not you, Randall."

And Merriwether backed out the door.

He splashed swiftly along the Main Street sidewalk, using the *Champion* for an umbrella. It really was rather jolly seeing that smile of a morning, he thought. Especially after the gloom around the old homestead. Not that he was opposed to a weekend of unspoken recriminations per se, but he just . . . Well, he hadn't formed the thought before, but he *missed* her, Sally, when they were apart. He missed being around her. She made him feel good, better than he'd felt in a long time. She was good for him, she and this newspaper work. Whether Emily liked it or not.

And, of course, she didn't like it. He knew she didn't. He could see it in her eyes whenever he started talking about it. But what did she want him to do? Sit in the house all day and . . . ponder? Mull over arcane ideas he didn't even *understand* anymore let alone subscribe to? Start the magazine again, lose the magazine again? Maybe she was one of these women who secretly want their men to fail all the time, who try to make them feel guilty the minute they . . .

But he didn't think that, he didn't feel that. The point was . . . The point was: Sally believed in him. He needed that. She didn't even care that he had no experience. She never even mentioned it to him, not once. She gave him his marching orders and just had faith that he could do whatever had to be done. Like this assignment, for instance. Here was a perfect example.

He climbed the rickety steps to the courthouse and made his way under its crumbling portico.

Here he was—only six weeks on the job, mind you—and she had sent him (Sid Merriwether, ace reporter for the *Daily Champion*) sent him off to cover the Scotti case. The Scotti case! The county's most important murder in years. Decades. Centuries . . .

Well, anyway, it was very gratifying.

He entered the courthouse, the dingy vestibule of the Sheriff's Department. There he saw a hand-lettered sign—TO THE COURT-ROOM—pointing to the left, to a stairwell. Humming the tune to "An Actor's Life for Me," he stepped lively up the stairs.

One had to understand, he thought as he climbed, one had to fully comprehend the assignment's implications in order to see how supportive of him Sally had been. The reporter whom he had originally replaced had covered the court beat, the trials and so on. And while, up to now, the Scotti story had belonged to Rumplemeyer (aka the Gargoyle), Rumplemeyer was currently busy tracking down more information on this Wocek character the police had apparently gunned to pieces in cold blood. So it was not stretching things too far to say that this assignment could well be a tryout for the actual . . .

MURDER TRIAL OF VINCENT SCOTTI. The county's most important murder trial in . . .

He stopped cold at the top of the stairs. His lips parted, and a long breath eased out between them.

There before him was a short, thin hall: the court anteroom. Courtroom doors to his left. Dingy double-hung windows overlooking the street to his right. Two bathroom doors at the far end.

And Vincent Scotti. Right there. In the center of the room. Alone.

Merriwether stared at him. The man—the actual man accused of murdering Billy Thimble. The drug dealer accused of clubbing and shooting the young lawyer to death and then tying his body to a cinder block and hurling it into the Hudson River. The very same man who had crashed through the window of the ghost house on Sheep Pasture Road—who had flown out into a veritable hail of gunfire and sneered down the guns and glares of the encircling police. There he was, just standing there, a very tall, broad-shouldered man in his thirties, slightly stooped, leaning on a cane, turned half away so that Merriwether might just have a chance to sneak down the stairs, run home, pack up his wife and belongings and move to another state before . . .

Scotti turned around and saw him. Saw him through heavy, half-lidded eyes. His thick lips curled slowly.

"Well, well, well," he said. "Who the fuck are you?"

"Uh, Sid . . ." *Damn it.* He had to swallow. "Sidney Merriwether. *Daily Champion.*"

"Oh. Sidney Merriwether. *Daily Champion.*" Scotti snorted. His cane thumped on the tile floor, his left leg dragged and whispered as he approached. "And what's that?" he said. "Is that your face?"

"What, this old thing? I only throw this on when I have nothing to wear." Merriwether smiled thinly, his throat tight. Scotti was standing over him, towering over him. "Heh heh," Merriwether added.

Scotti's face pressed down—a long face, olive-skinned, black hair curling low on the brow. "Whatta they do, Face? They hire you for your face? Your editor a man who likes a pretty face?"

"Actually, she doesn't . . ."

"Ooh, a pussy editor. I'll bet she knows where to put that pretty face."

Well, Merriwether managed to frown quite sternly at that, in spite of the fact that he couldn't swim with a cinder block tied around his neck. He even took out his cigarettes and angrily shot one between his teeth for good measure. "If you were thinking of trying to win this case on charm, Mr. Scotti," he said, "I strongly suggest you make a contingency plan."

"Oooh, Face." Scotti reached out—and Merriwether jerked back. But the man only snatched the cigarette pack away from him.

"Whatsamatter, Face? You nervous?" He put a cigarette between his own lips and slipped the pack into his own jacket pocket. "You know the thing is," he said, "if you're not nice to me, I'll just have to talk to another newspaper. 'A Killer's Story.' Exclusive. And then, Face . . . you'll have to do some heavy licking to keep your pussy editor happy then."

While Merriwether stood speechless, Scotti brought out a slim silver lighter. Lit his cigarette and—how was he supposed to avoid it?—Merriwether's as well. "But that's not gonna be a problem." He blew his first breath of smoke into Merriwether's eyes. " 'Cause I know you wanna hear all about it yourself. Don't you, Face? Don't you? How he was squirming on the ground. Billy Thimble. How he was begging me not to shoot him? That kind of shit? That's good, right? That's good shit. He squirmed on the ground and he was crying and begging me, 'Please don't shoot me,' and I was standing over him with the gun pointed at his head and it was like I could already feel his blood pumping out of him and into me because I knew I was gonna pull the trigger. I was just listening to him cry for the kick of it." He tapped Merriwether's chest with his forefinger. "You shoulda heard him, Face. Just like a woman. Like the way a woman squeals when she's really getting it good. Shit, it felt like soft, warm pussy creaming all over me to be standing there. And then . . . Bang. It was just like coming." He winked. "That's good shit, isn't it, Face?"

Merriwether had pulled himself erect, his lip twisted with disdain, one eyebrow raised imperiously. *Oh, please get me out of here,* he was thinking. He smiled an insouciant smile. "Is it your statement for the record," he said, "that you are guilty as charged, Mr. Scotti?"

Scotti laughed: "Heh." A sound like a body dropping. "It ain't my statement, Face. It's Johnny Barnes's."

Merriwether blinked. "What?"

"That's right, Face. Don't you even know what you're here for?"

"Well, actually . . . no. We were just told there was going to be . . . some kind of hearing."

"A Huntley hearing," Scotti said. He smiled—or sneered—it was hard to tell. "Johnny went and sang a little song, did Johnny." Slowly, he turned. Began to limp away across the anteroom; thump of the cane, whisper of the lame foot behind. "Johnny Barnes," he muttered as he went. "Johnny went and sang a little song."

169

By noon, the rain had stopped completely. The ping and patter of water hitting wastebaskets began to slow. Sally looked up from typing the day's preliminary schedule. She surveyed her empire.

The office was empty except for her and Shea. Doreen and Alice had gone to lunch. Les had a night game and wasn't coming in. Rumplemeyer was supposed to be covering Purdy's appearance at the mall groundbreaking on Route 4, but it had been postponed due to rain so he'd seized the time to run out to the Hickory train tracks instead—he was trying to get some of the kids to talk about Teddy Wocek, who his friends were, who his girlfriend was, but so far, they were too hostile to talk, or too scared maybe or too intimidated.

Anyway, only Shea was at his desk, on the phone—with Ralph Jones, it sounded like. He'd gotten a cigarette lit finally and was tapping the ashes off into the water-filled wastebasket on his typing table.

Sally stood up, stretched. Walked gingerly down the aisle, feeling the rain ooze up from the rug, under her T-straps, onto her stockings. She grit her teeth and laughed for Shea's benefit as she passed by him to the glass front. There, she looked out on Stillwater Lane: the hangdog elms, dripping; the cars hissing past to Main. The clouds breaking up overhead; swatches of blue; rays of the sun.

"Calm descends," she whispered at the window.

She shouldn't even have thought it.

The next moment, Merriwether came running, hell-bent around the corner. Trench coat flapping out about him, hat flapping in his hand.

Damn, thought Sally. *Damn, damn, damn.*

The look on his face told her it was something big. The grim lips, the wide, panicky eyes. She cursed herself for an idiot. She never should have sent him to that hearing. She had thought it would turn out to be nothing, the usual pretrial static. . . .

Damn.

She should've sent Shea instead. What had she been thinking of? Merriwether always messed these things up, forgot the details, left out the key question. She had just wanted to make him feel good about himself. That is, she had wanted him to sigh at her with gratitude, gaze at her with those blue eyes. . . . And now, it looked like she had dropped the ball in a big way.

"Damn," she whispered aloud.

Dodging cars, Merriwether made it across the street. Sally pushed the door out to receive him. He didn't even slow down, just rocketed in. He was all over her, like a puppy, even panting, out of breath.

"Sally! Sally! He confessed."

"What? Scotti? Oh my God."

"No, no, the other one, Barnes. The accomplice. O'Day, Scotti's lawyer, is trying to get the judge to suppress it, and no one else was there—Buzzy or Dog—none of the other reporters. It's an exclusive. And the prosecutor told me . . ."

"Okay, okay. Calm down, sweetheart. It's a good story. Have you got it? Did you get everything?"

"Yes. Yes. I think so. Yes."

Merriwether sagged, propping himself against the edge of his desk. His face was red, his long hair tousled . . . it was everything Sally could do not to reach out and brush the blond tangle of forelock off his brow.

Editor Corrupts Youth, she thought. *Acts Stupid, see page 3.*

She reached out and brushed the blond forelock off his brow. He lifted his eyes, his blue eyes—and the way he looked at her—well, she let her fingers stay in his hair another moment. And he kept looking at her, breathing hard, his lips parted. . . .

Be my loooooooove, for no one else can eeeeend this yearning. . . .

Shea dropped his phone into the cradle, and Sally dropped her hand quickly. And Shea (the High Priest) barked at them.

"So what happened there, Scoop?"

"Barnes copped a plea and spilled his guts," Merriwether said.

Shea laughed. "Dat doity rat."

Sally managed to pull her eyes away from Merriwether. "It turned out to be a Huntley hearing," she told Shea. "They're trying to get the confession suppressed."

"Wo. Good story."

"There's more, Sally," Merriwether said.

His tone was solemn, almost apologetic—as if he was sorry for her. It didn't take much to guess what he was going to say next. She smiled warmly into that earnest, cerulean gaze of his. She licked her lips, her dry lips. "What?"

"The judge hasn't decided yet whether to make the confession public," Merriwether told her. "But according to the prosecutor, anyway, the senior assistant D.A., this fellow named . . ." He reached into his jacket for his notebook.

"Stern," Sally said.

"Stern?" said Shea. "Stern talked to you?"

"Right. Stern. According to him, Barnes's confession not only implicates Teddy Wocek in the murder of Billy Thimble, it also includes a description of the police raid on Sheep Pasture Road that corroborates the investigators' version of events. Barnes apparently says that Wocek *did* fire on the police when they came in to arrest him and that they then shot him in self-defense. In other words, the Mrs. Wocek story—Rumplemeyer's story—was just wrong."

Shea stood up, his cigarette bobbing between his teeth. "Stern told you that? Off the record?"

"On the record, but not for attribution."

Sally turned away from them, to the window, to the drooping trees and the sunlight falling brightly now from an almost cloudless sky. *Shit, shit, shit,* she thought.

"Oh Christ!" said Shea.

Sally faced him in time to see him dash his cigarette down into the wastebasket. It went out with a hiss as it hit the surface of the water.

"Well, it's not all that bad," said Merriwether. He offered her a small smile. "It's Mrs. Wocek who was wrong, not us. I don't think it was all that big a mistake to print what she said, even if she is Teddy's mother." He turned from one to the other of them. "Was it?"

"Well . . ." said Sally.

But Shea, of course, wouldn't leave it at that. "What did Barnes get in return for his confession? What's he bargained down to?"

"Uh . . . Manslaughter One, I think."

"Uh-huh. Great. Did he use a weapon?"

Now Merriwether did draw his notebook out. He flipped it open. "Well, according to the confession, it was Scotti and Wocek who did the actual shooting. . . ."

"Yeah, I'll bet."

"Barnes apparently does admit to a youthful indiscretion involving a tire iron and the back of Billy Thimble's head. But then, it was summer and his heart was gay."

"And all that's from the A.D.A., from Stern? On the record?"

"Not for attribution, yes."

Shea let out a rude snort. Swung away from them with a snarl and stomped up the aisle, the water spitting out from under his shoes. When he reached the back door, he cast a dramatic look back over his shoulder at them—at her—and said: "You explain this one to him, Sally." And he banged out.

"Explain what?" he asked her, almost immediately.

"Oh . . . Chris is just . . . being Chris." She waved him away, gave a soft laugh. "He thinks I'm out to get the sheriff. He thinks that I'll do anything . . ."

She bowed her head—avoided his eyes—as she walked to the back—as his eyes followed her.

"Yes. I've noticed that," he said. "That he thinks that, I mean." He waited until she reached the table against the back wall. Until she was standing in front of Mr. Coffee. The great and good Mr. Coffee, she thought. Thank God he had been spared in the flood.

"Are you?" Merriwether asked her then. "Are you out to get him?"

"No. I mean . . . No. Do you want a cup of coffee?" She held the tower of paper cups up to him, and he regarded them with such a frown, such a *serious* look, that she added, "Look, nobody's objective, Sidney. I do think the sheriff has a stranglehold on the politics in this county, but it's not like I'd . . . Look, whenever a pol gets caught out at something, it's the easiest thing to say, 'Oh, you know, the press is after them.' But *they* do these things. They're the ones who actually do them."

He paused, considered it. Brushed his own hair away.

"I would like some coffee, yes," he said.

She set two paper cups side by side on the table and poured, thinking, *Chris, God damn it! Goddammned Chris.*

"So what are you going to explain to me?" Merriwether asked. "What did Chris want you to explain to me?"

"Milk and sugar?"

"Sugar just. One."

Sally took a deep breath, let it out in a long sigh. "He wanted me to explain the Huntley hearing," she said. "Barnes's confession." She took her time spooning the sugar from the waterlogged box. "See, the D.A.'s Office is basically in the sheriff's pocket. Muncie, the D.A., was handpicked. So usually, we can't get anything out of them besides press-release garbage and some off-the-record stuff from Stern now and then. That's what Shea was upset about." She let him think it over while she stirred the coffees, while she brought them down the aisle to him. She handed him one, and he looked at her steadily. Not accusingly, just . . . steadily.

"You mean it's rather odd that Stern, that the assistant district attorney, gave me details on Barnes's confession," he said.

"Right. On the record like that. Not for attribution, but still—quotable."

"Chummy of him, in other words."

"Yes. It was."

She watched him sipping his coffee, working it out. She sipped her own, her stomach sour.

"So—in other words—this is something the sheriff *wants* us to know." He looked up at her. "He wants this in the paper."

"That's right."

"Because he wants . . . he wants us to know . . . and to print . . . that the Wocek piece was wrong."

"That's right. It's a perfect setup for him. Barnes not only confesses to helping kill Billy Thimble, he also clears the sheriff's men for shooting Wocek dead during the arrest. So he helps Dolittle get a conviction in the Thimble case, and he discredits us on the Wocek piece all in one fell swoop."

"And he'll get a lighter sentence for it," Merriwether said.

"Right. And Shea thinks the sheriff wouldn't have let Barnes roll over like that in the first place except *for* the Wocek piece. He thinks that because we ran the piece, the sheriff felt obliged to get Barnes to talk about the raid."

"Good heavens. Do you think that's true?"

Sally set her cup down with a very harsh click indeed. Enough was enough, after all. "Look," she said . . . and it was that same sweet, stupid whisper—and his hair had fallen rakishly into his eyes again . . . and why did they have to be talking about this anyway? she thought. "The sheriff has to do what he does, and I have to do what I do, Sidney. A big murder conviction now is a virtual advertisement for him and for Purdy's county-executive campaign and all their . . . bullshit about cleaning up the Hickory train tracks and blaming Ralph Jones for everything and . . . And if you think Dolittle doesn't get off on the idea that we're practically running his ad campaign for him on our front page . . . well, believe me . . ." But the way he was looking at her—as if it were all her fault—as if it were all her fault only he didn't want to be the one to say it . . . She heard her voice trail off lamely: "Well . . ."

"He certainly does seem to annoy you, doesn't he?"

She nearly rolled her eyes. Why had Shank done this to her? Forced her to nurse a beginner now, when everything was so complicated? . . . "I just don't think his version is the only version, that's all. Even this confession . . . it may just be one more cover-up."

"You mean, you think the sheriff may have induced Barnes to lie?"

"Well, it's possible, isn't it?"

"I suppose, but why? Why would he?"

"Why would he? Sidney. His men shot a seventeen-year-old boy to death. They killed Teddy Wocek in that raid—they killed him. And there's just no evidence to confirm that it was an act of self-defense. We don't know. It could have been negligence. It could have been brutality. And now, Barnes's confession just clears all that up nice and neat, and we're just supposed to accept it?"

Merriwether drank deeply of his coffee now. He smiled when he looked up again. A wintry smile . . . it didn't make her feel much better. "Of course, it's all tied together: Barnes's confession about the Billy Thimble murder, and his statements about the death of Teddy Wocek in the raid. If you prove that our Wocek story is correct, then you'll prove that the confession is false."

"Well, that may be, but . . ."

175

"Which would seriously compromise the prosecution's case when they go to prove that Vince Scotti tossed young Billy Thimble into the Hudson river *avec* cinder block."

"Well, I'm not the one who made Barnes lie, Sidney."

"Yes, but Scotti would go free then. Wouldn't he? I don't think that's such a spiffy idea."

She insisted, "I didn't make Barnes lie."

Merriwether was still smiling, but he shook his head. "But you don't know he did lie, Sally. You have no reason to believe he lied except your own personal . . ." His eyes came to rest on her, rested on her a long time.

She met that gaze as firmly as she could.

If I don't have him, I'm going to die, she thought.

"Well," she said softly. "Welcome to the newspaper business."

TEN

Cindy

SATURDAY, AUGUST 25– MONDAY, AUGUST 27

1

THIS HOUSE, EVEN the shape of this old house, oppressed her. A little saltbox on a suburban lane. Sometimes she felt it stood on the highest hilltop of her interior kingdom, that its corridors, its corners, it rooms in shadow, had impressed their blueprint on the very chambers of her self. This house, this old house. She felt sometimes that it was sapping her slowly of her life force.

Tonight was a night like that. A Saturday night. Sally sat slumped in the old armchair before the television set. Fred Astaire was dancing on the screen; the blue light of the set was dancing over the darkened living room. She was slumped there wearily.

It was almost 1:00 A.M. Finally, finally, her mother had gone upstairs to bed. After "snoozing" in the other chair with her mouth hanging open. After snoring loud enough to ruin the music from the show. After blinking awake only at intervals, only half-aware of where she was. . . .

What . . . What . . . Is everything all right?

It's fine, Mother. Why don't you go on up to bed?

No, no. I'm watching the show. I was just snoozing. I'm watching the show.

Finally, finally, she had risen with a groan. Shuffled slowly to the stairs. And started climbing. Sally had sat with her eyes half-closed in suspense, listening to the footsteps rise, wondering if they would go all the way to the top or stop or even return. . . .

I forgot something. . . .

But no. Thank God. It really did seem that she was gone. And Sally was blessedly alone. With the television. With the house.

She slumped in the chair, and the house oppressed her. She had been here too long, that's all, she thought. Her family had first moved here when her father had gotten the city-editor post with the *Tribune*. She was only nine years old at the time, and she had lived here until she went to college, until she was eighteen. After that, she had been gone for quite a while, but she had returned again in her thirties, at the same time she returned to the *Champion*, after she had finally left Jerry for good.

Her father was dead by then; the cigarettes had killed him during those years she was away. But she could still feel him here, in the house, whenever she returned to it. It was part of what held her here, his presence in the rooms. It was part of what oppressed her. She would walk into the kitchen, for instance, and suddenly remember: She had seen him there once, dancing with her mother. She had crept downstairs from her bedroom and peeked in. Her father, Terry, was a tall, slender southern gentleman with an angular and elegant face, and he had been whirling his weary beauty of a wife between the stove and the refrigerator. They were holding a carnation between their two clasped hands.

Or in the dining room. She remembered how he had sat at the head of the long oak table. How he had sipped white wine with his dinner and told them stories. Like the one about how he had proposed to her mother. It was a summer night like this, he said, a summer Saturday night. A U.S. Army bomber had crashed into the Empire State Building, and he'd been the first at the scene to cover it for the *Trib*. He had sent her a telegram later that day: "The *Tribune*'s on top everywhere. Will you marry me?" Mother pretended to blush every time he told it.

And Sally remembered how she had heard him crying in the bedroom once. She had heard him through the walls. She never found out why. And once she had walked in on him in the bathroom and seen him naked. She had never seen an adult's penis before, and the size of it astonished her; she thought it was huge. Her father had not spoken to her for the rest of the day.

In the living room, right here, they had argued at least a thousand times. When she would come home from college especially. She liked to flaunt her radical views at him and make him mad—although they were her friends' radical views really. It made him furious, and it seemed they were always fighting over her politics during those years, or over her "lifestyle." It was actually pretty ridiculous when you considered the truth of the matter. If only he could have seen her, if only he could have seen her as she really was in those days: the way she slipped meekly across the campus during the antiwar protests and the sit-ins, with the quad packed tight with students, the students shouting, bearded faces, screaming faces all around her, women in torn jeans, breasts loose in their T-shirts, fists punching the air while Sally struggled past them to her class on "Aspects of Congressional Government" or something, her books clutched to her padded bra, her eyes turned down to the redbrick pavement, her virginity still intact. Her so-called "lifestyle" never amounted to more than daydreams. All she had ever done, in fact, was dream, as far as she was concerned. That was why she had to taunt and tease her father when she came home: because she had never really *done* anything and it was driving her crazy, she was so *frustrated* about it. Every night, behind all the dormitory walls, the other girls were crying out with their brave new orgasms, and all she ever did was fantasize and dream, dream about men, dream about Merriwether, about someone like Merriwether, Merriwether exactly, inventing and reinventing his beauty, his elegance, his manners, his learning, his suddenly polite hello out of the melee. . . .

Sally leaned her head back on the chair and sighed. Imagining Merriwether. That look he had given her. The disapproval in that look.

Yes, but Scotti would go free then, wouldn't he? For no reason except your personal . . .

She could see everything in that mild blue gaze of his: the still-pristine morality, the lofty notions of the written truth, the academic idealism—she could see them all girding his mind against her, and she wanted to tell him, It isn't that simple. It isn't that simple at all. The sheriff's convention Monday night. Just a day away, for God's sake. And Purdy was a shoo-in for the county-executive nomination—especially now, especially since the *Champion*'s coverage of the Scotti arrest. And there would be the elections in November. Why couldn't he see . . . ?

"Oh, stop this," she whispered. She put the heel of her hand against her forehead.

A moment later, she stood up. She listened. There was no movement upstairs anymore. The old house was very quiet, very still. She might even be able to sneak into the kitchen and make herself a scotch without bringing out the Mother Patrol. It was a hazardous mission. One sharp clatter of ice cubes and the thin, gravely voice would float down to her from above:

Everything all right down there, Sally?

Still, she had to chance it. She moved slowly from the living room, hunching at the creak of every floorboard. She tiptoed down the short dark hall, leaving the television glow dancing over the furniture behind her. She slipped into the kitchen. Softly closed the kitchen door. Flicked on the lights.

And screamed.

"Oh! Oh, Jesus!" She leaned against the cupboards, hand to her fluttering heart. "Oh, Rumplemeyer, Jesus, you scared the life right out of me! Oh!"

He was sitting at the kitchen table, a short table topped with blue-and-white ceramic tiles. He was seated at the head of it, huddled under his huge corduroy jacket. There was an aluminum pie plate set in front of him. A single slice of apple pie was all that remained in it—the slice and a lot of crumbs.

She fought to catch her breath while he gave her that sheepish grin of his.

"Sor-ree, Sally. But I know your mom hates me."

"Really, Ernie. Oh!" She kept her hand to her chest, felt her heartbeat growing slower under the palm. God, she hoped she hadn't awakened her mother . . . but she didn't really think a scream would do the trick. Not like ice in a glass.

"She just wouldn't go to bed," said Rumplemeyer. "I was waiting and waiting."

Shaking her head, Sally moved to the cabinet beside the refrigerator. Opened it to reveal a small bar. Unsteadily, she collected a glass and a bottle. Splashed some J & B in the glass and knocked back a mouthful of it.

"I just finally got so hungry," Rumplemeyer was saying.

"You were standing outside? Looking at us through the window?"

"Well, I mean, she wouldn't go to *bed.*"

"You climbed in through the *window?*"

"I mean, the thing is: It was just open, Sally."

"There are screens on our windows, Rumplemeyer." She drank again, another large shot.

"Oh yeah," Rumplemeyer said. "It was kind of hard to open. It's kind of hard to get the screen back on. It's kind of still out there in the pachysandra." He tried another sheepish grin. "I was really hungry, Sally. Really."

She leaned against the counter. Sipping the scotch more slowly now, breathing more slowly. Eyeing him.

"You want me to make you some eggs?" she finally asked.

"No. I'm kinda full now. I mean, I had a lotta time to, like, eat, you know? She wouldn't go to bed."

"Why didn't you turn the lights on, you fuzzball?"

"I didn't want to scare anyone. I didn't think it would take this long."

She laughed. "All right." Drank again, the sweet sting of the scotch in her nostrils. Set the empty glass on the counter. "So this is how I spend Saturday night. Now you know, okay? Another scoop for the grapevine."

"Gee. Sorry, Sally." Rumplemeyer's shaggy head bounced up and down. "But it's like: Everybody wonders. The people have a right to know."

181

"No comment."

"I mean, didn't you have a boyfriend for a couple of months this year?"

"Oh come on, sweetie. That disaster was on the grapevine back in June. Don't you have any sources among the girls?"

"Yeah. I was just being polite."

She laughed. "Thanks."

"I mean, don't get me wrong, I thought you made the right decision. The guy was kind of pompous, you know? Really insecure."

"Well jeepers, Ernie. I'm glad you never actually had to meet him."

Rumplemeyer's grin got wider; his head went up and down faster. The shadow of his hunched back made a strange little blot on the flowery wallpaper and the wooden cupboards behind him. "He wasn't good enough for you," he said through his grin. "You know? He wasn't, like, classy enough. Or handsome enough." His eyes pinned her. "Or, like, educated enough. Or young enough. Or WASPy enough. Or . . ."

"Shut up, Ernie, will you?" She collared the scotch bottle, hooked the glass. Dragged both to the kitchen table and thumped them down. Sat in the chair across from him. "I've had a long week, okay?" She poured herself another shot. "And anyway, he's married." She drank. "And anyway, he hates me."

"Fourth?" said Rumplemeyer. "Yeah, right. He hates you. Right."

"He does."

"He's fawning all over you."

"He thinks I'm violating the Code of Journalistic Chivalry or something. Not playing cricket. I don't know. Whatever it is, I can see it, the way he looks at me: He disapproves." She rubbed her eyes. "Oh God, and he hasn't even read Part Two of the Hemlock Cathedral piece yet. Wait till he gets a load of that."

"Well, if he thinks that way about you, Sally, then he's, like, an asshole."

"He is not, Ernie. Stop . . . picking on him all the time. That's all you ever do."

Rumplemeyer grinned. Rumplemeyer bobbed.

"He's just . . . not a reporter, that's all," she told him. "He has no experience. He doesn't understand what's . . . what's happening up there."

"I know. I know. 'Cause, I mean, if he were a reporter? I mean, if instead of just being, like, this rich piece of deadwood we have to support during the most important election in the county's history because his uncle is on the board of directors and he can't get money from his rich father for some mysterious reason which he won't tell anybody?"

Sally dipped into her drink again, away from that laughing glare.

"If he were, like, a reporter instead, you know?" Rumplemeyer went on. "Then, instead of, like, thinking you were hounding poor harmless Sheriff Fuckhead with the unscrupulous power of the press, he would be spending every second of his spare time at the Hickory train tracks, you know? He would be risking getting beaten up by fascist undersheriffs who are intimidating all his sources? He would be courageously tracking down Teddy Wocek's girlfriend, who could be the one person who knows the truth about what happened on Sheep Pasture Road who's not, like, a major felon, you know, and could be the key to, like, a major, major story on the eve of the fucking convention when Dolittle's iron grip on his party is going to be prac-tically unbreakable? You know?"

There was a pause after that. Sally noticed that Rumplemeyer had crumbs in his beard. She reached across the table and picked them out for him. "That reminds me of something I've been meaning to ask you," she whispered gently. "What the fuck are you doing in my kitchen at one o'clock in the morning?"

Rumplemeyer reddened somewhere under all that hair. Combed his beard down with his hands. Grinned even wider.

"I just thought you might want to know, you know, that this kid, this punk, down at the train tracks, this guy named Al Delgado? He told me off the record—and it's not solid or anything; I mean, we can't print it in time for the convention Monday but I'm sure it's, like, true?"

"Yeah?"

"Well, he told me that Teddy Wocek had a steady girlfriend named Cindy?"

Sally waited. Finally repeated, "Yeah?"

"Like in, Cindy Dolittle?"

"What?"

"Yeah. Like in, the sheriff's, like, daughter. You know?"

2

Cindy was going to make him cry tonight. His big night. Convention night.

Fucking asshole. Fucking Daddy.

She hurried through the forest. It was Monday. His big night.

He fucking killed you, Teddy. He knew you were there.

She was going to make him cry, and then he'd see what it was like. On his big fucking convention night that was all he cared about.

The forest was dark, too dark. It was spooky. It was almost like her dream. That dream she had where she ran through the fog with something chasing her. It was just like that tonight. There were tendrils of mist creeping low on the ground, gray in the light from the crescent moon, twining between the trunks of trees, making weird shapes of their vines and branches. It was spooky all right, and Cindy kept looking back over her shoulder, feeling that something actually *was* moving behind her—*hearing* something, actually hearing the leaves, the duff, crunching back there. But when she looked back quickly to catch it, whatever it was was gone. There were only the motionless trees like cowled men, staring at her through the drifting mist and the fading moonlight.

She hurried on, pushing the branches away from her face. She kept thinking, Well, something *could* be back there, it *could* be like her dream, it could even be a rapist or something. Or she might step on a copperhead or something like that. They did have them out here; it was possible. But what did she care? She didn't care. She didn't give a shit anymore. She was going to do this thing. She was going to do it, and his big important night that he cared about so much, that he'd been waiting for and bragging about to everyone. Tonight it would really hurt him. It would really make him cry.

Because he knew you were there. Teddy. And he sent his men to kill you.

The Hemlock Cathedral. Suddenly, it was before her, rising around her. The straight-spined conifers looked like a circle of demons shooting up out of the dim earth. And the white boulders, they were like ghosts, the way they shimmered in the silver beams, then slowly went sinister as the fog drifted across the moon and . . .

What the fuck was that? . . .

Stumbling into the Cathedral's clearing, Cindy turned. She took a few steps backward as her wide eyes scanned the hulking cluster of trees behind her, peered into its rhythmic motion, listened past the rustling of its leaves in the warm breeze. Something—she would swear it to God—was fucking out there, coming after her. She held her arms and shivered. It was *just* like her fucking dream, only she couldn't . . . quite . . . see it . . . Not yet.

She backed farther into the clearing . . . Then she spun around quickly . . . because she'd seen those movies where that happens, where the thing creeps up on you while you think you're backing away from it. . . . But the demony trees and ghosty rocks just watched her, that was all.

Okay, she thought. *Okay.*

She got back to what she was doing. She reached into the back pocket of her jeans. Took out the paring knife. She had snuck it right from the drainer, not that that was so hard, of course, her mother would never notice, she was so fucking drugged out of her fucking mind half the time. . . .

She laid the cold point against her wrist. She held it there. Held it there. She told herself: *He fucking just killed him.* And she knew why too.

It was because he found them, that's why, together in her room. Because he found them on the bed—big fucking deal. He was such a fucking pervert. Big Mr. Sheriff Shithead. Sneaking up on them like that, like they were doing something when they were just making out a little on the bed. As if they couldn't do it in the woods any time they wanted, or even at Teddy's house when his mother was at work . . .

And I liked it, Daddy, I liked his big fucking cock fucking me, bigger

185

than yours ever was, you faggot piece of shit. You knew he was gonna be there, Daddy. Bobbi told you, she told her brother and he told you and you sent your shithead killers in there to shoot Teddy and now you're going to be fucking sorry. . . .

She held the cold blade to her warm wrist and . . .

There. She saw something. She raised her eyes quickly to catch the shadow in the woods. She had seen it. A shadow flitting across the surface of the mist. And now a sound. Getting closer. A different sound from the shifting leaves . . . twigs crackling. A squirrel or a skunk or even a deer maybe. Some kid maybe coming out to the Cathedral for a smoke. She had to hurry. She looked down again . . . But still the blade just lay there, cold against her warm wrist.

Cindy sat down, cross-legged, on the needly floor. She took deep breaths to steady herself. She tried to close her eyes in order to get her concentration going, but she kept peeking through the lids in case the creature that was following her sprang out suddenly and it turned out to be a bear or something terrible like . . .

She laid the blade against her wrist again. She had to do it. She wanted them to find her here. Where she and Teddy had been lovers. She wanted them to find her lying right here where they'd made love. Now she would be sprawled out alone on the pine needles. The morning after his big convention, and they would find her here alone. And they would put her in a box like they did Teddy, and everyone would come and look at her there and shake their heads and cry. And *he* would have to look at her. And she'd be lying there in the box with her arms crossed on her chest and her face looking so heavenly and serene. He'd cry then all right. She bet he would cry just like Teddy's father had, even though he'd been such a mean bastard before. They would all be crying. She would love that. She would love to see that.

She dug the blade down, down, down . . . until it punctured the flesh. And it hurt, it hurt, but then she jabbed herself—jabbed herself and dragged it, tugged on it more and more and it ached like anything and then finally she plucked it out and there was a second where nothing happened and then . . .

The blood. It spurted out of her really, really high. It surprised her. This big wet arc. It pattered loudly on the ground when it fell.

Corruption

Oh shit.

It had stopped. There was no more blood. Maybe it's stopped, she thought. There was roaring in her ears.

Jesus, look at it.

The blood shot up again. Then again. She could *feel* it coming out of her heart. She could feel her heart beating, and then the blood would spurt again and patter on the ground. She grabbed hold of her wrist.

Oh shit . . .

But her heart just kept pumping it out. She could feel it spring hot and wet between her fingers. She watched it, stared at it, dazed. So much blood.

She looked up at the forest around her.

Help me . . .

She looked around at the bolders, at the circle of high trees.

Mommy?

But no one came. No one answered. Quietly, steadily, her blood pumped out, spilled between her fingers. Her arm, her hands, were dark and sticky. So much blood.

What, she thought woozily. *What's that?*

She looked up through heavy lids. Oh. Yes, she thought. There it was. She could see it now. The Thing. The Thing from her dream. It was out there in the tangle of woods. A shadow. It was coming for her. A shadow growing bigger, getting closer through the mist. Crunching, tumbling, thundering through the leaves, louder and louder. A shape . . . like a man-thing. She wanted to run, to get up, to get away. But it was like her dream, it was just like her dream, she kept waiting there, she couldn't move. Her head was getting all thick and stuffy, and the blood was draining out of her, she could feel it draining through her fingers. She felt weak. She felt lazy and tired. She did not want to move. She just wanted to sit there. But that Thing, that Thing was coming. The mist was closing all around it like a curtain and the shape of it was getting darker behind the mist. A shape like a man, like a cowboy in a cowboy hat, the man who would come to find her . . .

And then he broke through. He broke out of the mist.

"Cindy!"

"Oh God!" she screamed. She held out her wrist to him. "Oh look! Oh God!"

"Cindy!"

He was over her. The bad Thing. She waved the knife at him crazily.

"Drop it, Cindy! Put it down!"

His strong hand grabbed her arm, shook it. The knife fell from her grasp. His other hand wrapped around her wrist, slipping and sliding at first in all the blood, then grabbing hold, holding tight. It hurt, it ached. He was lifting the arm up into the air . . .

"All right. All right. You're going to be all right," he said.

Her head sank forward. She couldn't . . . She couldn't think . . . She was being lifted. Lifted into the air. He had her, the cowboy. He had her in his strong arms. He was holding her to his chest, and her head was sinking against him.

"I knew you'd come," she whispered.

And then everything was gone.

3

The Lincoln Grange Hall was thick with smoke that night, but Dolittle swore he would choke to death before anyone would see him coughing. He stood in the doorway to a side room, his arms crossed on his chest, his long frame looking lean and easy in his black vest, black slacks. His lips were parted slightly, but the whistle of his breath was lost in the general noise of the room. No one could hear it but him. There was a gently wry smile playing on his mouth.

Before him, the convention was in full swing. Folding chairs packed the hall from the podium to the back door, from the cattle-show ribbons tacked on one wall to the hunting trophies in the case just at Dolittle's shoulder. Over a hundred men and women packed those chairs—men mostly, mostly fat men, those same obese men who had always run the county, their thighs the size of tree stumps, their bloated white shirts doming out in endless rows, one after the other, side by side. It really was a wonder the floor didn't just sink down into the earth.

Most of the men clamped cigars in their mouths. Some of them gripped bundles of papers in their sweaty hands. Some had very large bundles of papers. Their proxy slips, the votes of absentee members. All of the fat men had sweat their shirts limp and gray in the close, hot hall.

Their voices were ceaseless, ceaseless and loud. Deep and guttural, the sound of them rose to the ceiling, swirled in the swirling smoke. County party chairman Marcus Borden was at the podium, tapping his gavel on the podium top. You could hardly hear it. His whale of a belly was jiggling, his thin mouth opening and closing. You could hardly hear his voice.

". . . and therefore it gives me great pleasure . . ." It was a thin, distant sound. ". . . to nominate our first-ever legislator to District Four: Nick Twomey!"

There was an eruption of applause and cheering.

"Yeah," someone shouted.

"All right. Yeah," shouted someone else.

Lincoln party committee chairman Bob Hotchkiss stood from his metal chair. Hotchkiss had an excellent steak house in Hudson Corners. It violated something like thirty-six provisions of the health code the last time a deputy checked on it. That was about six years ago.

"I second the nomination," Hotchkiss called out.

"Second the nomination," several voices answered.

There was more applause, more shouting.

"All in favor of Nick Twomey," Hotchkiss screamed into the chaos.

"Aye!" The room boomed back at him with a single voice.

And they erupted in applause again. The smoke roiled and rose above their moving hands. Their voices rose to the lights hanging from the high ceiling.

Sheriff Dolittle, meanwhile, nodded to himself. He uncrossed his arms and applauded with the others. At this rate, he thought, it would only be an hour or so before they got to Purdy.

Dolittle allowed himself a small cough into his fist. Then he came off the doorframe and stepped into the little room behind him.

* * *

189

Purdy was there. Sitting at the small table, drumming his fingers on the top of it. He was wearing blue short sleeves; his striped tie hung down undone. Dolittle could see the muscles in his arms rippling as his fingers played against the wood.

"That was the fourth district," Dolittle told him.

The candidate nodded. His dark red forelock bobbed on his brow. The hair, Dolittle noticed, was a little damp.

"It's going well, Cy," Purdy said. "No bout adoubt it. No, sir. It's a lock tonight. They're falling in line every which way. Every nominee so far is on our team."

Dolittle couldn't help it: He let loose with a full-fledged grin. It made his face look younger, almost young. "They are, at that," he said. "Four districts in a row."

"And the D.A., as always. And the county clerk too." Purdy kept nodding his head as if to the rhythm of his fingers. His fingers kept drumming on the wood of the table.

Dolittle snorted, walked over to him, slapped him on the shoulder. He could feel the sweat right through his shirt. "And the county executive too, Whit. They'll fall in line on that too."

"If you say so."

"Jesus, you are one nervous son of a bitch. Hell and damnation, Whit. I got Fred Denkinger out there holding enough proxies to nominate Sally Dawes herself if that's what I tell him to do. Do you know how many bond underwrites I've thrown his way? Do you know what that man owes me? I mean . . ."

But he stopped. He'd said enough, almost too much. Dolittle was feeling good—no bout adoubt it, as Purdy would say—but he had to rein it in a little, keep his tongue in his head. It was the first rule of the game.

"It's gonna be fine, Whit, really," he said.

He slapped Purdy's shoulder again and moved back to the door. He looked out through the clouds and tendrils of smoke. Nick Twomey was at the podium now, making his acceptance speech. A squat, florid Irishman. He ran Evergood Insurance out of Tyler, and they held all the Sheriff Department's insurance and some for the town Fire Department besides. He was pounding the wood with his fist, his mouth working, the veins on his forehead standing out. Couldn't hear a word he was saying above the steady clamor of guttural voices.

Dolittle smiled and watched him and shook his head. Purdy spoke from behind him.

"Why can't we use the stuff on Jones? That's all I want to know."

Dolittle's lips tightened. He didn't turn around. "Because we don't need it, Whit. Come election time we're gonna beat him flat-out easy. It's stupid to use the stuff if we don't need it."

Purdy drummed the table with his fingers. "There's two months of campaigning still to go, Cy. And Ralph, old fat Ralph, I mean, you can't underestimate him. All that country-bumpkin bullshit he pulls. You can't underestimate him for a minute."

"I think I know that, Whit," the sheriff said.

"I know, I know. You go way back you two, back to the old Highway Department, back for a million years, I know. I'm just saying . . ."

He let the words trail off in a sigh. The sheriff turned and faced him. Slowly, Purdy lifted his eyes to peep at him from under the fallen shock of red hair.

"What?" the sheriff said.

"I'm just saying I didn't like that Wocek thing in the paper," said Purdy. "Okay? That thing about Wocek's mother and you being a murderer and all. It looked bad. That's all I want to say here. I mean, I know, I know, it all got cleared up. Barnes's confession cleared it up great, but . . ."

"But what?" said Dolittle.

"Well, darn it, Cy. You can't believe that Dawes harpie is gonna stop there. And I mean, with what we got on Jones, that stuff you showed me, those papers you showed me, well, Ralph Jones and his Save-the-County-from-the-Evil-Developers campaign, we could blow him sky high on that, you know we could. You know it. And it pains me. That's all. It pains me, Cy, not to go to the limit on this with so much at stake. Not just the county-executive office. The whole legislature, the new zoning codes. It pains me not to go all the way on this. That's all I'm saying here."

Dolittle just stood there looking at him. He forced his anger

191

down. He forced himself to smile again. He didn't know what to tell the man anymore, he didn't know how to explain. If Purdy had just been a little bit more intelligent than, say, a fart, Dolittle might have tried to put the idea across: Sometimes, most times, when you know something, when you really know it, silence is power. It's when you start talking that you get yourself into trouble.

"Whit . . ." he began.

But just then, a young man—Marty Lewis from the Seed Barn in Wannawan—stuck his head in the door.

" 'Scuse me, Sheriff," he said. "But you got a phone call. It's Undersheriff Benoit. He's says it's urgent."

He was surprised at how calm he was. Sitting behind the wheel of his Cadillac now, feeling his Cadillac race through the dark. The mist twined across the pavement. The headlights blasted it aside. It curled at the windows, laced the pane, and vanished. Dolittle steered the big car over the sharp curves. The forest leaned out of the night on either side of him. He really was surprised to feel so calm.

He had been afraid at first, just at first, when Benoit told him what had happened. Then Benoit said that it was going to be all right, and his fear went away. After that, if he felt anything, it was irritation. He was annoyed at being dragged away from the convention just as his chosen candidates were being nominated one by one. He would miss Purdy's nomination now as the candidate for county executive. He did not need this tonight, this adolescent melodrama, not tonight of all nights. But the irritation too had passed very quickly.

Maybe he should have felt sorry for Cindy then. Maybe he should have felt concerned for her, or even angry at her. But he felt nothing like that. He felt perfectly calm. He kept thinking about her as he drove, about Cindy. He kept thinking about the way she was as a little girl. He could see her, when she was just two, maybe not even two. He could see her toddling down a grassy slope at Roosevelt Park. Liz was there, Liz was on her knees, holding her arms out to her. Cindy was rumbling unsteadily down the hill, wobbling like a string toy toward Liz, toward Mommy. Cindy would go faster and faster as she came down the slope, and then she would fall down. She would look at Liz, trying to gauge her reaction. "Oopsie!" Liz would say and laugh, and then Cindy would laugh too.

Dolittle had the snapshots of it somewhere. In a closet somewhere, in a shoebox. He wished he had those old snapshots with him tonight. He would have liked to show them to her, to hold them up in front of her face. Maybe she would not understand, maybe she would not even understand what he was trying to tell her. But he would have liked her to have a chance, anyway, to see the way she had been back then, to compare it with the way she was now, with this juvenile she had turned into. He let the car's speed slacken as it approached the final hairpin turn.

No, he thought, no, he did not feel sorry for her. He did not feel sorry for her at all.

The doctor's driveway appeared up ahead. He eased his foot onto the brake. He did not feel anything. He was very calm.

Benoit was waiting for him in the dirt parking lot outside the doctor's house. He was standing in the mist, a trench coat wrapped around his large frame. He was smoking a cigarette, holding it at his waist. Behind him, the house stood brightly lit against the night.

What a house it was too. As Dolittle stepped out of his Cadillac, he let his eye run over it. It was a goddamned mansion, that's what it was. A three-story colonial mansion. White shingles painted till they gleamed. Newly planted dogwoods lining the sides. An attached office—a nice, convenient one-story wing right there, jutting off from the main body.

Dolittle strode across the lot toward where Benoit stood. His eyes stayed on the house. His mouth was a thin line, turned down. This whole damn place, he thought: It had probably been bought and paid for with the money his wife forked over for tranks and uppers. Doc Steinbach probably got coupons from the drug companies like kids who sold greeting cards: Hey, Doc, send away for your free mansion today!

Dolittle stood before Benoit. He stood only a few inches away. "What happened?" he said. His voice was flat and even. There was no emotion in it.

Benoit let out a long breath of smoke. He shrugged as if he didn't give a damn. He had the good sense not to smile anyway. "I had someone watching her like we agreed. A good thing, it turned out, huh? Deputy Modzelewski. He got there just in time. The doc says she's gonna be fine."

Dolittle nodded. He glanced up at the house. Deputy Modzelewski, he thought. A deputy of mine, he finds Cindy in the woods with her wrists slashed open, and he calls Undersheriff Benoit to report it. Not the sheriff, his own boss, the girl's father. No. He calls Benoit, as if *he* were the boss. As if they were running a little department within the department.

I'll remember that, Dolittle thought. Deputy Modzelewski.

"Okay," he said.

He moved away from Benoit. He walked slowly to the house.

Just within the office door, there was a waiting room. It was dark and close. Dolittle coughed as he moved through it. He was finding it hard to breathe.

He went past the empty receptionist's cubicle, into a hall. The lights were on in here. They shone on bright walls painted half-orange, half-yellow. There were various doors along the hall. As Dolittle walked past them, he saw darkened rooms. He saw the silhouettes of examination tables, shadowy canisters, steel instruments flashing with the hall light.

I hate this. Fucking places like this, he thought.

He walked by quickly, but he still felt calm. He was really surprised that he wasn't more agitated than this.

He reached the end of the hall. The door there, the last door, was closed. There was light coming out from underneath it.

Dolittle paused. Looked at the closed door, listening. He could hear his daughter's voice coming from behind it:

"Get away from me, damn it," she said.

He heard Steinbach's low murmur in reply. He couldn't make out the words.

Quickly, Dolittle seized the knob and yanked the door open.

The light in there was stark, bright. He narrowed his eyes against it. He saw Cindy. She was sitting on the examination table, huddled close to the wall. She was shrinking away from the doctor. She had one shoulder pressed against the wall. Her left arm was bandaged almost to the elbow. Dolittle saw a bloodstain on the thigh of her faded jeans. Another stain blotted out part of the white skeleton on her black T-shirt.

The wallpaper had a pattern of yellow giraffes, and Dolittle thought, *Giraffes. Jesus. Where does he get this shit?*

"Daddy!" Cindy cried out. Tears started to stream down her cheeks at once. "Daddy . . ." She hung her head.

Steinbach hovered over her with his stethoscope. He looked for all the world like a mad scientist in a movie. With his white smock, his limp, dark black hair falling into his glasses. His glasses had thick black frames, and the lenses were thick as goggles. His eyes looked huge and skewed.

Dolittle glanced at him. "Wait outside," he said.

The doctor blinked from behind his lenses. "Sheriff, I think it's very important that I . . ."

"If I say it twice, you'll spend the next twenty years in a federal penitentiary. You quack piece of shit. Get the fuck out."

Dolittle said this very quietly. He did not raise his voice at all. Just the same, Steinbach scuttled off like a crab. He closed the door gently as he left.

Dolittle took a deep breath. He looked at his daughter. The sight of her brought the irritation back. The way she kept cringing away from him, sniveling in the corner, it annoyed him. Her heavy square face mottled, her chopped-up hair all mussed and shaggy. Her lips quivering, her nose running. When he thought of what she had been when she was little and saw what she had become . . . He did not feel sorry for her one bit. He hardly even *liked* her when he saw her like this.

"You know what this is going to do to your mother, don't you?" he said.

She kept quivering, cringing, snuffling. It really did get on his nerves.

"A lot she cares," she said. "She's so stoned half the time."

"Hey. I don't want to hear you talk that way about her."

"You know she is, Daddy."

195

"You heard what I said."

"Daddy . . ."

"That's enough."

"Oh!" she cried out suddenly. She held her bandaged hand up to him, her fingers splayed. She cried: "Oh! Listen to you! Listen to you! Look at me! Look at me, Daddy!"

He gazed at her, stony-eyed. He did not feel sorry. He was damned if he did. "I see you," he said.

"Oh!" she wailed. "I wish I'd *done* it. I wish I'd done it, I swear to God! I wish I died and was with Teddy!" She bowed her head and began to sob loudly.

Dolittle snorted. Teddy. That's what all this melodrama was about in the end. Teddy Wocek. That lovely gentleman friend of hers. He shook his head at the floor, smiling coldly. "Cindy," he said, "let me tell you something. Teddy Wocek was a drug-dealing piece of garbage. He was a piece of trash. That's all he was. A piece of trash."

"Stop it."

"He helped Vince Scotti and John Barnes kill Billy Thimble."

"Stop."

"And then he fired on my men. . . ."

"Shut up, shut up," she sobbed.

Dolittle felt the blood rush to his face. "Don't talk that way to me. Don't you say that to me."

"You killed him." Cindy wept fiercely. "You fucking *killed* him, Daddy. Jesus!"

He waited a moment before he spoke. She really was getting him angry now, she really was. Teddy Wocek. He remembered how he had found them on her bed together, clawing at each other. He pointed a finger at her. He had to fight to keep his voice steady. "Look," he said, "I've had just about enough of you tonight. Do you understand me, young lady? If you can't behave yourself, I'm going to have to teach you to behave. Do you understand?"

"God," she said. She cried and shook. "God. Listen to you. You're a murderer, Daddy. You murdered him. You just stand there and talk like I'm supposed to listen to you, and you murdered him. And I'm going to tell." Her lips were twisted and ugly.

"All right, that's enough," he said. "That's just enough. Do you hear me?"

"I'm going to tell everyone," she sobbed. "I'm going to tell them, and they'll never vote for you again. I'm going to tell the newspapers and everybody what you did, Daddy. You killed him. You killed Teddy, and I hate you."

"I said that's enough."

"You're a murderer, and you killed the boy I loved—you killed him because I loved him!"

He stepped toward her. Before he could think, his hand flew up in the air.

She threw her arms in front of her face. "Don't touch me!" She cringed against the yellow giraffes. "Don't you touch me!"

His hand hovered. He clenched it into a fist. The fist lowered slowly to his side. "I *never* touched you." The words barely rasped out of him. He felt as if he were choking on them. "I never touched you, never. My father touched *me*. You don't know. You don't know."

He backed away from her as she sniveled and whined and cringed. He couldn't stand the sight of her.

"All right," he said thickly, slowly, trying to keep his voice under control. "All right. You're going to be sorry for this, young lady. I'm going to teach you a lesson you'll never forget."

Cindy leaned against the wall and sobbed, her shoulders shaking. "Daddy," she said.

Dolittle cursed softly. He pushed the door open and stepped out into the hall. He was fighting for breath.

"Daddy, please!" Cindy cried. "Daddy?"

He shut the door.

Steinbach scuttled up to him at once, wringing his hands, his sweating hands. The sheriff looked down at his bent back. His mouth was tight. He felt faintly nauseous.

"I'm going to get a cruiser to take her to Green Hills," he said quietly. "I want her hospitalized."

"I . . . Well, I . . . I mean . . ." The doctor's mouth hung open a moment. "I mean, I don't think she's in any real danger of . . ."

"Yes. Yes, you do. I want her hospitalized at Green Hills. The director there is a man named Dr. Jeffrey Bloom. Tell him I want her put under observation for seventy-two hours for likelihood of serious self-injury. I'll be there in the morning to sign full committal papers."

"Committal?" said Steinbach. He waved his damp hands back and forth in the air, "Oh no, no, no, Sheriff, she doesn't . . ."

"If she demands a judicial hearing, call me, and I'll arrange for the judge. Otherwise, she's not sixteen yet—I don't think there'll be any problem."

The doctor just stood there with his mouth hanging open.

"I have the files on you, Doctor," said the sheriff then.

"Of course, she *is* still looking rather shaky. . . ." Steinbach said.

"When you're done at Green Hills, I'll need you to come to my house. My wife is going to be very upset about this. She'll need something to calm her down."

ELEVEN

It Snowed

TUESDAY, AUGUST 28

1

By 10:00 P.M., it was all over but the interviews. Christopher Shea, leaning with Merriwether against the wall at the back of the Grange Hall, shook his head in wonder. In front of him, throughout the hall, the fat old men of the party were wandering around under a heavy blanket of green cigar smoke. Bumping bellies. Shaking hands. Bobbing cigars at one another's faces. Their proxy slips lay torn, stepped on, forgotten on the floor between the folding chairs. It was all over.

Every district, Shea thought. All six of them. The county executive, the D.A., the county clerk: Every single candidate who had been nominated here tonight had been handpicked by Sheriff Cyrus Dolittle. The party had not veered from his wishes on a single line.

Shea jabbed his cigarette into the corner of his mouth. His square, pasty face was screwed up with a wry expression. His pale eyes were narrowed against the smoke. Cripes, he thought. He had never seen anything like it. Not here, anyway, not in Auburn. He had grown up in this county. He had lived here his whole life with the exception of his four years at Fordham. He could not remember—he could not remember ever hearing about—so powerful a bid for control. If the party swept the election, Dolittle would be running the shop virtually single-handed from the top down. Guiding development, planning, zoning. The patronage power alone would be incredible.

The hulking redhead shifted his big shoulders under his dark sports jacket. He could feel the sweat sopping through the armpits of his white shirt. He could feel his thin tie tight around his throat. "Long night," he said out of the corner of his mouth.

He turned to look at Merriwether beside him. The smaller man only nodded and said nothing. He was slumped against the wall with his hands in his pockets. He looked drained and weary, his chin lowered. Up past his bedtime.

"Have we got everybody?" Shea asked him. "You interview Twomey and Williams?"

Merriwether put his fist to his mouth, stifling a yawn. "Interviewed and accounted for. We're only missing the big ones now, Purdy and the sheriff."

"Yeah, well, Purdy's still around here somewhere. But Dolittle. Where the hell did he go?"

"Don't know. Haven't seen him for over an hour."

"Shit. You'd think he'd hang around awhile after taking over an entire political party." Shea plucked the cigarette from his lips. Scanned the faces milling and converging under the shifting cigar smoke. "All right," he said. "I'll go upstairs and scout for him. You look around here. If you see either one of them, nail em, get some quotes." He glanced at his watch. "We gotta get back in time to write this up."

"Right-ho," said Merriwether.

"Yeah," said Shea. "Right-ho."

He began walking across the room to the stairs, his red hair rising above everyone around him. He had to turn his big shoulders this way and that to push his way through the clusters of politicoes. Marcus Borden, the county chairman, saw him, slapped him on the back.

"Write it up good for us, Chris," he said.

A burst of cigar breath hit Shea in the face. Shea smiled painfully, sidling by.

He reached the stairs and climbed up to the second floor. It was quiet up there. No one in the hall. There were doors along the walls: two or three private offices and the bathrooms. Shea went past the first two offices and peeked in. They were empty and dark. He paused at the men's room door. He actually wouldn't mind taking a whiz while he was up here, he thought.

He was about to go inside when he heard something. A gasp. It came from the last office, the one at the end of the hall.

Shea stopped. Jutted his head, listening. He dropped the butt of his cigarette to the floor, ground it out silently under his loafer.

There it was again. A gasp, a little cry. Sounded like a woman. What the hell? Shea thought. The office door was nearly closed, but ajar. He moved to it carefully. He peeked in.

There was a light on in there, just a small desk lamp. The top light was off. In the glare from the lamp, Shea could see her, a shapeless older woman with hair dyed a deep black. She was wearing a purple dress with grape clusters on it. It took him a moment to recognize Jackie Schneider, wife to Al Schneider, the Lincoln town supervisor. She was the head of the party's entertainment committee this year, Shea remembered, and clearly she took her position very seriously because she was bending forward over a straight-back chair with the skirt of her dress hiked up to her waist and her panty hose pulled down around her ankles. She had an ass like an aging tomato, Shea thought. But that didn't stop Purdy. What did? The party's newly nominated candidate for county executive—who had a prick the size of a baseball bat, it looked like—was standing behind Mrs. Schneider, and sliding said prick in and out of her with great rhythmic, slapping strokes.

Shea glanced at his watch. Shit, he thought. If he didn't get an interview with Purdy before he left, he might be screwed himself. Especially if Sid couldn't find the sheriff downstairs.

Stealthily, he returned to the men's room. When he went inside, he closed the door as loudly as he could. He took his piss, then opened the door again so that the noise from the flushing toilet would carry.

Finally, he stood in the hall, coughing and clearing his throat a few times.

"Well," he said loudly. "I guess I'll take a look around for Purdy."

"Hey, Chris!"

Purdy came out of the far office, striding down the hall with his hand extended. He still had his tie on—you had to love that. It was loosened a little at the top, but it was still tied. His white teeth gleamed as Shea shook his hand.

"I thought I heard someone up here," Purdy said.

"I was just looking for you," said Shea. "It must be fate."

Purdy laughed. The two tall red-haired men stood close together. Shea took out his notebook and pen.

"I just need some quotes about tonight. Like: How do you feel about the slate?"

"Oh, hey, how should I feel?" said Purdy. He spread his powerful arms. "It's a dream slate as far as I'm concerned. I feel very good about the future of this party tonight, and about the future of the county."

"These are all people who've been endorsed . . . Are you okay? You wanna catch your breath?"

"No, I'm fine, fine."

"Well, these guys are all backed by Sheriff Dolittle," Shea went on. "Some people would say he handpicked them. Would it be fair to call this the Dolittle slate?"

"Oh, heck, I don't think so, Chris. I don't think so. Every single one of us has a record of service and standing on our own two feet. I know I'm my own man, and I think that's true of everyone else who was nominated here today. That said, I want to add for myself that I'm in no way ashamed to be associated with the sheriff. As he's proved repeatedly, uh, most recently in his arrest of Mr. Vincent Scotti, one of the biggest suspected drug dealers in this county, he is fully capable of keeping this county safe during the period of growth and development that lies ahead."

Ya, ya, ya, and so on, Shea thought. He asked a few more questions, got the bullshit he needed to fill out the piece, and flipped his notebook closed.

"So is the D.A.'s office gonna fix Scotti up with a nice pre-election show trial?" he asked.

Purdy laughed. "Are we off the record?"

Shea laughed. "No."

"Well, then, I don't know the first thing about it. But hey, listen, don't let Sally Dawes and that trained Jewish terrier of hers go too hard on us, okay? Vince Scotti is a man who badly needs to be in prison for a long time—whether it gets me elected or not."

Shea tilted his head. "Hey. You know Sally, man. You're on your own. See you in the papers."

He started walking toward the stairs.

"Hey, wait. Wait."

Shea paused, looked back. Purdy stood in the hallway with his hands in his back pockets. He cut a rakish figure, smiling, disheveled, his red forelock on his brow.

"Really, Chris," he said. "Really. Listen."

Shea waited. "Yeah?" he said.

"Well, I mean, the opposition—I mean, our old friend Ralph Jones, lovable old Farmer Ralph—I mean, he's not perfect either, you know. Sally ought to have you fellas take a look at him sometime too, don't you think?"

Shea raised his hands. "I get em and write em, Whit. I don't make the assignments."

"Yeah, but I mean, if you had the story, I mean . . . I mean, you could go to Sally, if you had something on big fat Ralphie boy, couldn't you? If you had a story on fat Ralph?"

Shea stood there another second. Purdy didn't go on. Shea finally said, "Is there some particular story you have in mind?"

Purdy made a noise. "Hey. Don't look at me. Don't get me involved in that. No sir. Uh-uh. Ralph Jones and a certain pistol-packing and largely humorless county sheriff of our mutual acquaintance—I mean, those two go way back, they are old, old friends from, like, the dawn of time. I don't want to get involved in anything that might lose me my endorsement. I'm just saying . . . I mean, lookit, Chris, you're a good guy, an approachable kind of guy. I couldn't say this to just anybody. All I'm saying is: You gotta use your head a little on this story. You don't just go off where Sally sends you every time, right?"

Shea couldn't help smiling. He pulled his cigarette pack from his shirt pocket. Shot a fresh butt into his mouth. "Where should I just go off, Whit? You tell me."

"Well, I mean, think about it," Purdy insisted. "I mean, think about this whole county being rezoned and all, right? After January first, there's gonna be a whole brand-new commercial corridor, snaking right through every town in the whole county. Plenty of new places for development. Malls, car lots, restaurants, corporate offices. The new county executive, all his appointees—they're going to control a lot of development money. In every town, Chris. Hickory too—Jonesy's Hickory too. Hickory maybe more than anyplace because Jones has kept all the development out until now. Think about that, Chris. That's all I'm saying."

Shea let out a curt laugh as he lit his cigarette. "Yeah? Go on."

"Oh no." Purdy started to back away. "No, no. Really. That's all I'm saying," he repeated. "You know. Just think about it."

Shea let out a puff of smoke. He watched through narrowed eyes as Purdy turned and walked down the hall, back toward that office where Mrs. Schneider was waiting. Purdy was reaching to unzip his fly even before he was completely out of sight.

By the time Shea and Merriwether finished writing up their convention stories, it was nearly one in the morning. Merriwether's wife had gone shopping in White Plains that day and had taken his car, so Shea gave him a lift home in his old Chevy.

For a long time, the two reporters traveled in silence, Shea smoking at the wheel, Merriwether leaning wearily against the window. They wound over the rutted pavement of Hickory Kingdom Road while, outside, in a night hung with moonlit mist, Shea saw the dark, empty expanses of wildflower fields rolling away to an obscure horizon. They made him think of Purdy again, about what he had said about Ralph Jones.

Jones had been running the town of Hickory now for almost fifteen years. In Shea's opinion, these empty, useless fields were his doing. Preserving the county's rural tradition, Jones called it. Keeping out the speculators, controlling development. He'd called it a lot of things over the years. But the simple truth, as far as Shea was concerned, was that Jones had sold out to the rich. For all his country-bumpkin manners, Jones was just the front man for the summer tourists and the mansion owners, the people who did not want their rural views spoiled by development. Oh, of course, people needed places to live and work, they said, but not here, not in our town. So Jones had let Hickory's old farms die out and had replaced them with absolutely nothing. That's why the town was falling apart the way it was. That's why the kids had nothing to do but hang out at the train tracks and get into trouble. Old Jonesy was preserving their rural traditions.

But then why had he finally agreed to the rezoning? That was Purdy's point, and it was a good question when you thought about it. The sheriff had spent years coordinating a plan that featured a countywide commercial corridor, a snake of business and development running through every town in the county. Jones had held out against the plan for a long time, but he'd gone along with the other towns in the end. Why? At the time, Shea had assumed that it had to do with Jones's campaign for county executive. If he was going to beat Purdy, he would have to appeal to the whole county, including the people who wanted development, the locals who needed places to live and work.

But was that the only reason? Did Purdy have something else on our fat little friend? And if he did, why was he holding back? Not because Jones and Dolittle were friends. It couldn't be that. They had been friends once, good friends, but it was a long time ago. A real long time. Their friendship ended for good and all the day Jones started talking to Sally, the day he became her main source on her Hemlock Cathedral pieces. He was the one who'd given her all that bullshit about how it snowed on the night of the Carol Marsh murder. It snowed. Jesus. There was no way Dolittle would hold off using something against Jones because of friendship, not anymore. . . .

"Did you see her tonight?"

"What?" Merriwether had spoken so suddenly that Shea was startled from his thoughts.

"Sally, I mean. Back at the office. Did you see the way she was?"

"Sally?"

"Yes. She was so pale. Did you notice that?"

"Oh. Yeah. I guess. I don't know."

"And the way she kept calling the sheriff's house. Over and over.

She looked so . . . angry that we hadn't interviewed him. I mean, what could we have done? . . . He left. He wasn't there."

"Ah, that's not the point," said Shea. "She was just pissed off, that's all. She can't stand the fact that Dolittle took over his party tonight."

"It's that next turn up on your left."

"Oh, yeah? No kidding? You're renting Fred Denkinger's cottage?"

"That's right."

"My wife says she sees him sneaking out of the porno shop in Wannawan all the time. She thinks he's some kind of creep." The Chevy bounced hard as he turned onto the packed-dirt hill that led up to the cottage gate.

Merriwether lit a cigarette. He sat without speaking as the Chevy strained up the hill.

For a while, Shea didn't say anything either. He didn't know what to say. He felt sorry for Merriwether more than anything. He was, apparently, the last guy in the office to realize he had fallen in love.

It was not much of a surprise really. Everybody fell a little bit in love with Sally at first. She really was sweet-tempered, gentle, the maternal type. And that voice, that smile. You had to be dead not to go for her in some way, even if she was kind of ugly. But Sid seemed to have taken it all a little too seriously. He couldn't keep his eyes off her, couldn't stop gabbing with her in the back of the office. Personally, Shea hated that sort of thing. He hated it when personal bullshit intruded on the workday. It was the whole problem with newspaper people. They all needed to get themselves wives or husbands and kids, a family. It would straighten their heads out, the lot of them. A person didn't understand anything until he had a family. That's how Shea felt. Kids and a family. They were the only things that made a man see sense. And friend Merriwether, he thought, would sure benefit from some good old common sense just about now.

All the same, Shea kept his mouth shut. He had a bad habit of burying people under advice sometimes.

The Chevy rumbled through the stone gate. Up a smaller dirt

drive to the cottage. Merriwether's Rabbit was in the driveway, which meant Mrs. Sid was back from her trip to White Plains. But the lights were off inside the house, and that meant she was asleep.

Shea brought the Chevy to a stop. Popped it into park. Listened to the smooth idle of the old V-6. He waited to see if Merriwether would say anything.

"She takes it so personally," Merriwether murmured after a moment.

"Look." Shea pointed his cigarette at him. "Let me tell you something. Okay? The thing is, Sid: They have no lives. People like her, like Rumplemeyer. I mean, Rumplemeyer, look, I love the guy like a brother, but he has no life. He lives at the newspaper. And Sally, she just . . . she has no life, Sid. I'm telling you."

Merriwether regarded him gravely but did not say anything. Shea pressed on; he couldn't stop himself.

"I mean, no matter what happens, no matter who they like or who their friends are, it's all about this, about work. It's always about work. Even their personal lives are about work."

"I don't understand. You mean she uses us."

"No, I don't . . ."

"You mean she's kind and sweet just to win us over to her side? So we'll cover stories the way she thinks is right? So we'll do what she wants."

Shea shook his head. He should have kept his mouth shut. It was coming out all confused. "All I'm saying," he said, "is, like: You have a life. You know? You have a wife, you could have some kids, you could have a life, a future. You gotta . . . protect that. Protect yourself. You gotta . . . avoid the occasion of sin. That's what I'm saying. Avoid the occasion of sin a little bit."

Merriwether drew slowly on his cigarette. That pretty face of his was very still and solemn.

Christ, Sid, Shea thought, *she's forty and lives with her fucking mother. Wake up. She's an emotional basket case.*

"Look," he said aloud. "Sally has problems. Okay? I mean, you've read the Hemlock Cathedral piece, right?"

Merriwether shook his head. "Only the first part."

207

Shea was jabbing his cigarette out in the ashtray. He stopped. His eyes widened. "Are you kidding? Are you kidding me? You didn't read Part Two? The part about the snow?"

"No, I . . . I never got around to finishing it, I guess. I don't know why."

"Oh, but that's the thing, that's the whole thing. That's what all this bullshit is about. Ever since then, ever since Sally wrote that, she's been at war with the sheriff, trying to make it stick, trying to prove she didn't . . ."

But now, all of a sudden, the yellow light above the cottage front door snapped on. The door opened and out stepped Mrs. Merriwether.

She was clutching a blue bathrobe closed at her throat. Under the light from the door, the slim, soft shape of her body stood out in silhouette.

"Sidney?" she called.

Shea glanced at her—and then froze. He stared at her through the windshield. It was a moment before he could force himself to stop. Finally, he turned back to Merriwether. In the dark car, Sid's chiseled features looked shadowy, his cheeks seemed pale and drawn.

I'll be a son of a bitch, Shea thought. *I'll be a dyed-in-the-wool son of a bitch.*

"I better go," said Merriwether. He smiled—kind of sadly. "Thanks for everything, Chris. Really."

"Yeah," Shea managed to say. "Yeah. Sure."

As he drove away, he saw Merriwether in his rearview mirror. He saw him walk to his wife and put his arm around her.

Christ, he thought, *I wonder how long it's going to take Rumplemeyer to get this out of me.*

It took five minutes. Less than five, depending where you started the clock.

About ten fifteen the next morning, Shea went over to the Courthouse Restaurant for his hard roll and a cup of coffee. Someone down at the plant had fucking butchered the last two graphs of his Purdy story last night. Shea wanted to work off his disgust with a few games of Jungle Man pinball before he went back to the office, called down to the city desk, and exploded in a ball of furious flame.

The restaurant was bustling. The breakfast crowd was just begin-ning to thin out. Deputies in khaki and government types in their sleek city suits sat at the tables over their last sip of coffee.

Shea had just put his first ball in play—and had taken out the M in the top left chute—when in came Ernie and Sally both—both amazingly early after the late convention night. Sally sat at the end of the counter with a cup of coffee. Ernie popped his quarter on Jungle Man's glass top to reserve the next game and leaned there watching. Now it was maybe 10:20.

"See what they did to your Purdy piece?" Rumple said.

"Yeah." The ball plummeted. Clear from the high bumpers down between the flippers and out of sight. It had scored maybe six points. "Shit! I swear this machine hates me."

"I spoke to Bernstein about it," Sally whispered. "He got the message. I mean, it's not like I hadn't edited the piece already."

Shea fired off another ball. Rumplemeyer grinned his Cheshire-cat grin. "You drove Fourth home last night, didn't you?" he said. Now it was about 10:22.

The ball lit the A. There was some good bumper action this time. "Yeah," said Shea. "His wife had his car." *Here he goes*, he thought.

"So'd you ask him why his father disowned him?"

"Oh gee, Ernie, somehow it didn't come up, all right? Now shut up, wouldja, I'm trying to play."

"Come on. Tell me what you got."

"No."

"Then you did get something."

"Would you shut up? I'm playing."

"You didn't ask him, but you got something, right? Well, did he just open up to you?"

Shea heard Sally laugh as he flippered the ball back to the high ground. "Rumple!" she said—but she didn't sound very stern about it.

Shea said: "He didn't tell me anything, Ernie. Forget about it, wouldja."

"He didn't tell you *anything*?" Rumplemeyer was practically on tiptoe, that's how excited he was. "So you just, like, *saw* some-thing that explained why he's all, like, poor and estranged from his father and everything? What could you just *see* that would be, like, so important it could . . . ?" There was a pause. Then: *"Oooooooh."*

Shea just barely caught the ball on the flipper's edge—but it looped up, headed for the side dump. . . . How the hell was he supposed to concentrate with Rumplemeyer on him like this?

"You saw his wife," Rumplemeyer declared after a second. "That's the only thing that could've been important enough. You saw his wife, and there was something about her that explained why Sid would get disowned. But what could . . . ?"

Shea heard Sally gasp behind him. He heard her coffee cup clatter on the saucer as she set it down.

The ball went down the side dump. Jungle Man began ringing up the bonus points. Shea checked his watch. It was 10:25.

Rumplemeyer laughed triumphantly. "She's black," he said.

She's black.

The words made Sally shiver. She was in the office now. Sitting in the dark, at her desk, alone.

She's black, she thought. *Oh boy, oh boy, oh boy.*

The day had ended early. Everyone had worked late at the convention last night and come in early this morning to do reaction pieces. By six, Shea and Merriwether were both ready to call it quits. And even Rumplemeyer had headed down to the plant to write up his day's stories a little before his usual time.

No one was left but Sally. Sitting at her desk at the rear. The lights off. The air-conditioning off, the warmth of the night beginning to seep in. Her hands were clasped, lying on her skirt. Her eyes were trained half-seeing on the box of an office: the crumpled papers on the desks, the litter on the carpeting. The shadows moved and shifted a moment as the headlights of a car streaked past.

Then the car was gone, the darkness thickened.

She's black, Sally thought. She shivered. *Oh boy.*

The thing was, she thought: He must have given up everything for her. He must have stood up to his bigoted, imperious father with a lion's courage. *But nay, Father,* he must have said, *for in sooth I do love her and set my earthly weal at naught lest I am in her arms.* Or words to that effect. His mother must have wept. *Oh my boy, my beamish boy.*

Corruption

And yet he, with upraised chin, with clear and marble brow, with cerulean eyes upraised to heaven—he must have surrendered every natural claim to Fortune and Privilege and strode away with stately step and all for the sake of Love. . . .

Jesus Christ, but she had it bad for this guy.

She let her head sink back. She closed her eyes. She whispered, "Aagh."

It was perfect, wasn't it? A real Sally Dawes Special: She had fallen in love with a man for all the same reasons she couldn't have him. What more could she possibly ask from a relationship?

She lowered her head. She moved a hand to the corner of her eye and caught a tear there before it fell.

Yes, and what first attracted you to him, Miss Dawes?

Well, counselor, it was that sense of honor and sacrifice that caused him to give up everything for a woman other than myself.

She sighed aloud. Oh, McGoo, you have definitely done it again.

She took another long breath. Swiped at the other eye. She ought to be going down to the plant herself soon, she thought. Edit the day's stories. Go home early. Mom was probably warming up the old TV even now. "I have such a crush on that newsman," Mom always said. Good old Mom. Irritating, banal—you hadda love her.

She swiveled in the chair and stood. Brushed her limp hair back with her hand. She let her eyes travel over the darkened room. A last check. She wandered—aimlessly—down the aisle. Then she was standing at Merriwether's desk, her hand resting on the surface of it.

Behind her, the back door opened. She turned and saw Merriwether in the flesh.

He didn't seem to notice her, at first. She watched him, the shape of him, standing there in the open doorway with the night at his back. He scanned the room. Then he moved in, the door swinging shut behind him. She said nothing, watching him, watching his shadow. He moved to her desk quickly.

She saw him there, bending over, reaching down. She heard the rumble as he slid open her desk drawers. When he straightened, he

211

had something in his hand. He held it up: a folder. He slapped it down on the desktop.

"Did you have anything else?" he said suddenly.

Sally caught her breath. "What?"

"Did you have anything besides the snow?"

Even in the dark, she could sense his eyes, the steady blue gaze, the disapproval. "What are you doing?" she said. "What are you doing here?"

"I'm sorry." He moved away from her desk, came down the aisle a few steps toward her. Running his fingers up through his blond hair. Distraught—she could see it in the gesture, hear it in his voice. "I came back to read it, that's all. I've been thinking about it all day."

"The story . . ."

"The story about the Hemlock Cathedral. Shea reminded me of it last night."

Sally closed her eyes, lowered her head. Chris, she thought. He would.

"I started thinking about it," Merriwether went on. "And, of course, I realized what it was. I just wanted to know, I guess, if you had anything else. Besides the snow, I mean."

Nodding slowly, Sally raised her eyes to his. "No," she said. "Not much anyway."

He stopped. Nodded back. Sat against the nearest desk—Shea's. Rubbed his chin. Forced a smile at her. She shrugged, smiled back.

"Randall wanted it," she heard herself whisper.

"Shank?"

"He was bureau chief up here then. The bureau had only just opened, and Randall was their hotshot city editor, so they sent him up here to start it. Sort of the last outpost of the Sutcliffe newspaper empire." There was a sudden orange flare. She turned away, narrowed her eyes as Merriwether lit a cigarette. "I'd been . . . away. Away from the paper for a while, and when I came back . . . Well, Randall helped me get my job back. They assigned me up here with him. I was one of his reporters." Merriwether did not say anything, did not react. He just waited, smoked, watched her. Sally swallowed and went on: "Randall knew the editor-in-chief spot was going to open within a year and this was his audition pretty much. If he could run the Auburn bureau, get it started, get it off the ground, he was a shoo-in for promotion. Only the thing was, the bureau wasn't going well, you know, because . . . the sheriff . . . I mean, he wouldn't talk to us. He wouldn't tell us anything, the simplest things. He even tried to keep everyone else in the county from talking to us. It was worse in some ways even than it is now. And poor Randall, he was . . . I mean, he just was livid. He just started to hate the sheriff. With a passion, really. He was sure the sheriff was hiding something."

"So he assigned you to ruin him."

"He assigned me to find out what was going on. To get the story on what he was hiding. Why he would never talk to the press. I mean, we knew what he was."

"Did you?"

"Yes. I don't care what Chris says. I don't care what anyone says. The sheriff is dirty. He's an arrogant, macho, dirty . . ." She stopped. She let out a shaky breath. "But we couldn't prove it," she said. "Randall and I. We couldn't prove it, and Randall . . ." She made a small gesture with one hand. "He just jumped the gun, that's all. He started to promo the story right away, the minute he assigned it to me. He went big with it. He just assumed we'd get what we needed. I don't know, he was desperate to make the bureau work and, anyway . . . Before I even had a chance to get anything, before I'd even started doing interviews, he was running banners in the Sunday paper: *Next Week: A Startling Exposé of Sheriff Dolittle* . . ." She raised both hands. "And I didn't have a thing."

"Yes, but . . . still." Merriwether shook his head at her. "I mean: You accused him of murder. You accused him of murdering Hank McGee, the best friend he ever had in the world. All because of the *snow?*"

"You have to understand," she said, and she hated the sound of her voice, she hated to hear herself pleading with him like that. "You have to understand, I . . . felt like I understood him. Dolittle. I had . . . this *image* of him, this picture of him in my mind."

"You accused him of murder, Sally."

"Listen to me. I had this image of Dolittle standing in the Hemlock Cathedral with . . . with Carol Marsh, this little murdered seven-year-old girl he and Jones had found in the woods. He was, he was looking down at her and . . ." She reached her hand out toward him, but he watched her impassively. He shook his head at her. "What do you want me to say, Sidney?" she whispered. "I needed the job. I had nowhere else to go."

He nodded, lowered his eyes at last.

"And I did . . . connect with him, with Dolittle," she went on softly after a moment. "No matter what you think. I did see this image of him, in my mind. In the Cathedral. With the girl and . . . it just . . . came to me, that's all. You remember how he and Jones had come into the Cathedral? And they'd been hunting, and they saw her, the little girl, they saw her foot sticking out where she was buried in the snow."

"Yes, yes, yes, I remember," said Merriwether.

"Well, it just occurred to me . . . I had this image of him, and it occurred to me: that there was snow. See? There was snow on the ground. It had snowed, I mean, the night before, the night the little girl went off to see her grandmother, the night Hank McGee was supposed to have raped her and killed her." She raised her hand again but he didn't even look at her this time. "You see? Dolittle and Jones and McGee—these three friends—they had joined the Highway Department together. That's what they did then, the three of them. And it snowed the night of the girl's murder and the highway trucks were called out. There are records. I checked them. The highway trucks were out that night because of the snow. Sanding the roads, shoveling them. When I mentioned it to Ralph Jones, he said he thought he remembered it. He said it was the first time anyone had even asked him about it and he was almost sure Hank McGee was assigned to a truck with Dolittle that night. The night when the girl was supposed to have been killed."

"He was almost sure." Merriwether's voice was practically sepulchral. The tip of his cigarette moved slowly up and down. "Almost sure, Sally. After how many years? I mean, the time of death in these things—it's never that well established in the first place, is it? And there were ballistics tests too. Linking McGee's rifle to the bullet that killed the little girl."

Sally felt her face go hot. She turned away, turned her back on him, looked out the window at a blur of street lamps, the night.

"I had a theory."

There was a pause. A sheriff's cruiser drove by with a soft whoosh. Sally watched it pass. *They can see us, they can look right in,* she thought, *and see us together.*

Then Merriwether said, "You had a theory?"

"Yes." She cleared her throat. "I mean . . . this was a sex killing. Right? The little girl was killed by . . . by a deviant of some kind. A terrible, a sick person. And if it was Hank McGee who did it, well, then . . . I mean, he was this person, this sick man. And the thing is: What must he have meant to Dolittle? You see what I'm saying? They were so close, the two of them. Dolittle with his alcoholic father and his dead mother, and Hank McGee all romantic and fired up, inspiring him, you know. I mean, I think Dolittle just . . . worshiped McGee. I think Dolittle would've just done . . . anything for him. Anything McGee said." She turned back to face him, trying to keep her lips from trembling. "And what if McGee *was* sick? What if he was the sort of person who could do something as terrible as killing that poor little girl . . . And what if he wanted Dolittle to come along with him?"

"What? What are you talking about?"

"What if he talked Dolittle into doing something with the little girl, something terrible, and it showed Dolittle something . . . a part of himself that he just couldn't bear to see? . . . It's just a theory. I'm just saying there *could* have been a reason."

"Oh, Jesus, Sally." Merriwether stood off the desk.

"And then . . ." She swallowed hard. "And then what if Dolittle *led* Jones out to the Cathedral the next day. What if Dolittle made sure he and Jones discovered the girl together. What if he sent Jones off to get help so that he could stand there, alone in the Cathedral with the girls' body, so he could plant the rifle shell that was the only real proof against McGee. And then he could blame McGee for it, for everything. Not just in front of the county and the public, but in his own mind too. He could . . . *erase* . . . the thing that he and McGee had done together to the little girl."

"Jesus. You didn't print that. You couldn't have."

"No."

"But you *implied* it."

"Yes."

"Right in the newspaper?"

"Yes."

"Because it *snowed?*"

She brought her hand up to cover her eyes. "Yes," she said softly. "All right? Yes. Can we stop now?"

"Don't you know how . . . *true* something like that looks? When it's printed on the page?"

"Can we stop now?"

"I mean, no wonder he treats us the way he does . . ."

"He was always like this, Sidney. Always."

". . . especially if he's innocent. The man must practically be on fire for revenge half the time, and the other half he probably lives in sheer terror that you'll . . ." his voice faded. "That you'll do it to him again," he said faintly.

Sally let her hand fall, clasped it with her other before her skirt. "You know, don't you?" she said. "You know how I feel about you."

He ignored this. With slow, deliberate movements, he crushed out his cigarette in Shea's ashtray. He put his hands in his pockets. Ambled toward her casually. Smiled at her slightly through the shadows when they stood face-to-face. It was a terrible smile. She felt the terrible weight of it inside her.

"We already have done it, haven't we?" he said. "We've done it to him again already in a way."

"No."

"Yes. With the Wocek piece. We've accused him of gunning down Teddy Wocek with no proof at all."

"That's different, Sidney."

"Yes." He gave a sharp laugh. "It's different, all right. I'm involved in it now."

"What?"

"You *got* me involved in it. With all your *sweetness*. Step by step. That's what all this you-know-how-I-feel-about-you business is. Isn't it? That's all you're up to."

"Don't do that. Don't say it. It's mean."

"You're just trying to bring everybody in on it. Get everyone to agree that you were right, that you were perfectly right about what happened in the Hemlock Cathedral."

"Don't," she told him softly.

"It's not the sheriff trying to erase what he did with Hank McGee. It's you trying to erase what you did to the sheriff."

She shook her head.

"Christ, what if he wins, Sally? What if this Purdy of his actually wins the election?"

"Don't analyze me. I hate that."

"It'll be like having the whole county declare you were in the wrong, won't it? It'll be like everyone rising up with one voice to say you sold out for a job, you attacked Dolittle out of some weird obsession, that you use . . ."

"You're just doing this . . ."

". . . you use everyone. You draw them in. With your *sweetness*. You draw them in to confirm your version of things. . . ."

"You're just doing this to stop it from happening. To stop it from happening with us."

". . . this weird little world of yours of, of, of conspiracy and corruption that doesn't even exist." He stopped. "What? What did you say? What does that mean? I don't know what you're talking about."

"Yes, you do. You want to stop it from happening with us, don't you? You want . . . You want . . ." She saw him—saw his lips working, his eyes feverish. She lowered her voice. Whispered, "You're just trying to stop this from happening with us."

He shook his head, his mouth still moving, his eyes nearly glowing, wild. He reached out and put his hand on her cheek. "It's a bit late for that," he said. And he drew her to him and kissed her.

She tensed and caught her breath. *Oh shit*, she thought. And she kept meaning to pull away. All through it. His lips pressed against her lips and then her cheek and then her lips again and his tongue pressed into her mouth, his hands into her back, and she kept meaning to pull back from him, and she didn't. He touched his mouth to her ear. He whispered, "You're so beautiful."

"Don't say that. I'm not," she said. She was afraid she might start to cry.

Now his hands were inside her blouse, under her bra, on her breasts, and she was kissing him back, holding the back of his head with both hands, holding him to her, her eyes filling as she kissed him.

"What are we going to do?" She whispered it into his mouth. "We have to stop."

He took her by the shoulders, pressed down on her, kissing her, lowered her under him gently to the floor.

"What are we going to do?" she said again.

The carpet smelled of old cigarettes. It was dank and sour, dotted with lint and dirt and bits of paper. Breathless, the reporter, her reporter, was kissing her throat, opening her blouse, exposing her breasts, kissing them, Christ, she didn't even know if he'd locked the door. What if someone came back? What if the sheriff drove by outside? . . .

His hand was beneath her skirt now, inside her underwear, working it down over her thighs.

Uh—excuse me but—what the hell am I doing?

He climbed onto her, and she felt him come up inside her, easily—but with a shock that made her gasp.

"God, I love you, Sally," he said.

"Oh," she cried out softly. "Oh no."

She buried her face against him. She held on to him as hard as she could.

218

PART IV

THE HICKORY KINGDOM

TWELVE

The Scotti Trial
Part One:
Opening Statements

MONDAY, OCTOBER 22

THE TREES ACROSS the lake were changing now: the maples, oaks, and elms between the white houses. They leaned out over the water and their new colors, gold and scarlet, brown and orange, blended on the surface as the lake was riffled by the cool breeze. Merriwether watched them from a window in the court anteroom, leaning on the sill with one hand, holding a cigarette in the other. He could just make out—in the dense cluster of forest beyond the boating club—he could just make out the stand of paper birches, the white of their trunks, the yellow of their leaves, behind the red maples nearer the water's edge.

That was their place, his and Sally's among those birches, hidden from the road and the surrounding homes. Just watching it, he felt lonely for her, for the autumn smell of the leaves out there, and the two of them lying on the rough blanket with the trees all around them. The way her hair moved on her forehead when the wind rose, the way her eyes almost seemed to plead with him . . .

He drew a breath, looked away, lowered his gaze to the flag hanging from the courthouse wall just outside, just beneath the window. Emily often lay asleep when he got home, a book open on the floor beside the mattress. Often she curled against him as he slid into bed and rested her head on his chest. Her raven hair had a rich, secret smell that he loved especially and he liked to watch her brush it in the evening. Tomorrow, he often thought as he held her, I will get home in time to watch her brush her hair.

Then he would lull himself to sleep, daydreaming that she had died in a plane crash and he was free to be with Sally.

Just then, he heard a commotion in the stairwell: voices. He turned. There was a blast of light and they bubbled out of the well, erupted into the room: reporters with pads and pens, radio newsmen jutting microphones, photographers with their periscope strobes exploding, even a TV crew with a minicam and a small spotlight careening over the upturned faces. They moved to the courtroom's double doors like a single creature, throwing out pods, oozing across the little hall. Speaking as if in a single voice, "Would you look this way, do you feel you're a political victim, do you feel the upcoming election has anything to do with the scheduling of your trial? . . ." The double doors swung in, and Vince Scotti—his thin face moving above the others—pushed out of the center of the beast and entered the courtroom. The doors swung shut and the beast, its nucleus gone, dissolved into some ten or fifteen individuals, milling about the anteroom.

Merriwether dropped his cigarette on the floor, crushed it under his heel. He walked to the courtroom doors, where now a young woman stood before the TV minicam, talking into a microphone.

". . . a murder which shattered the quiet summer of this peaceful exurban community," she said.

"Pardon me," said Merriwether. He squeezed past her and entered the court.

He could not help but feel the drama of the thing around him. Not just his own stake in it—his chance to cover the county's big murder trial— but the rest of it too: the crowded courtroom pews, the reporters from as far away as New York and Stamford crammed into the first two rows, the cumulative intensity of all those staring eyes. There was the memory of Billy Thimble—which had brought out the press and the crowds in the first place—and the way his body had been found in the Hudson by the swimming boy. And then there was the shooting of Teddy Wocek at Scotti's arrest, and the idea, which the D.A.'s Office had been spreading around, that Scotti was some sort of exurban Mafia don. All of it gave the room an aura of breathlessness. Merriwether felt it in his chest as he held his thin pad open on his knee, his ballpoint poised over the page.

And of course, he thought, the court itself was like a theater, wasn't it? If you happened, that is, to go in for the ancient drama of sacrifice. There was Judge Posey—a portly, cherub-cheeked older man—lordly over all in his black robes on his high bench. The jury—a mechanic, a librarian, a retired supermarket manager, God knew what other peasants—welded into a formidable *deus ex machina* in the box under the towering, arched and mullioned windows. The protagonist—the sacrifice himself—Vince Scotti—wearing a spiffy three-piece pinstripe, slouching beside his lawyer at one of the two long counsel tables, his legs stretched out comfortably underneath it and, as far as Merriwether could tell from his profile, a sneer on his face for the entire proceeding.

And, pacing smoothly before the jury box—strophe, antistrophe—there was senior A.D.A. Michael Stern, a lean, stooped, shaggy-haired, hawk-faced Jew, maybe forty. Cheap black suit wrinkled on his bent back. Sharp eyes set deep beneath his high brow. Spinning out his opening statement in a dramatic rumble.

"Betrayal was the motive. Cocaine was the key," he said. "Billy Thimble—a good, a decent man, a good husband, a fine father—was seduced by the drug. He was enslaved by the drug cocaine until he was willing to do anything to pay for it—yes, he was even willing to sell drugs himself. But—" He raised a finger as he paced back and forth. "But when he came to his senses, when he realized what he was doing—not only to himself but to the wife and child who loved him—he resolved to go to the police. He resolved to risk his life to help end the reign of Vincent Scotti and the scourge of drugs he has spread throughout this county.

"However, ladies and gentlemen of the jury, Billy Thimble never got the chance to perform that heroic act. Because Vincent Scotti, and his two accomplices, murdered him. Brutally murdered him and tied his body to a cinder block and *sank* it into the depths of the Hudson River."

Merriwether, sitting in the second pew next to a woman from the *Daily News*, scribbled in his pad—*good husband father . . . seduced by drug . . . willing to do anything pay for it . . .* as fast as he possibly could.

When Stern was finished, when he had slouched back to his counsel table to the right of the judge's bench, Posey nodded to the left, to the defense. Merriwether flexed his writing hand as he watched Douglas O'Day rise and walk toward the jurors. It was clear right off that the defense was far ahead in the grooming department, at any rate. O'Day was a sleek, square-jawed fellow, his ash-blond hair short and elegantly coiffed. He was wearing a very appropriate double-breasted wool suit—a Versace, it looked like to Merriwether—just on the light side of gray, perhaps a touch too flashy in the lapel but very nice.

He stood at the center of the jury box, one hand in his pocket, the other raised.

"My client, Vincent Scotti," he began—and he spoke in a mild, instructive voice, "is not necessarily someone you're going to like or admire," he began.

. . . not necessary someone you like or admire. Merriwether's pen raced across the page.

"His father, as the prosecution was good enough to point out, is a convicted felon, an accused member of organized crime. And Vince, as a teenager, did work for his father's contracting firm as you were told. What you were not told, however, is that Vincent and his father had a falling-out more than ten years ago and have not spoken to each other since. Or that Vincent made numerous efforts at honest, gainful employment before turning to his present life."

O'Day paused here to press a finger thoughtfully to his pale lips.

. . . numerous efforts honest . . . employ before present life, Merriwether scribbled.

"But that present life does include selling drugs," said O'Day. "The defense acknowledges that. And Vince Scotti was involved in a drug deal with John Barnes and Teddy Wocek on the night of July nineteenth, when the police broke in and arrested him for Billy Thimble's murder."

. . . drug deal w/ JB and TW on night J 19 when police arrested him . . .

Now, O'Day raised his hand, raised his voice, and, without moving, eyed the jurors one by one. "But Vincent Scotti," he announced, "was not arrested because of a petty drug deal. He does not come before you charged with dealing drugs or even possessing drugs. He is charged with the murder of Billy Thimble, and the defense will show that that murder he did not commit." He turned his hand gracefully in the air. "Why would he, ladies and gentlemen? Vince Scotti had no motive for killing Billy Thimble. Why would he? They were friends. They did business together. Oh no." He shook his head. His eyes sorrowful now and mild. "Oh no," he said again. "The defense will show that it was John Barnes and Teddy Wocek who murdered Billy Thimble. They murdered him because he was beginning to cut in on their drug territories. They murdered him out of greed and envy and without a thought of remorse. And Vincent Scotti wasn't even there."

. . . drug territories, wrote Merriwether, *greed, envy . . . wasn't there . . .*

"So why is Vince Scotti in this courtroom today?" Douglas O'Day continued quietly. "Ladies and gentlemen, the defense is going to show that Vince Scotti has been dragged into this courtroom and charged with this crime not because he *committed* murder—but because he *witnessed* a murder. That's right. Vincent Scotti witnessed the murder of Teddy Wocek by the investigators of the Auburn County Sheriff's department."

. . . witnessed the murder of . . . What? Merriwether stopped writing. His lips parted. He looked up.

"On the evening of July nineteenth," O'Day said, "investigators of the Auburn County Sheriff's Department burst into a house on Sheep Pasture Road with their guns blazing. In that brutal, negligent, and incompetent action, they gunned down seventeen-year-old Teddy Wocek, who was unarmed and defenseless at the time." And once again, sadly, he cast his eye from one of them to the next. "Vincent Scotti witnessed that act, ladies and gentlemen. Vincent Scotti vowed to tell the truth about that killing. And so the Sheriff's Department framed him. They framed him for the murder of Billy Thimble. They convinced one of the real killers—John Barnes—to lie about Teddy

Wocek's killing, to cover up for the trigger-happy homicidal negligence of the sheriff's men, and to implicate Vincent Scotti in the murder of Billy Thimble. And because John Barnes agreed to tell those lies in his so-called confession, the charge of murder against *him* has been dropped." O'Day nodded, slowly, again and again, staring at the jurors. "But Vincent Scotti is still determined to tell the truth. He's going to tell it here in this courtroom, ladies and gentlemen. That's why he's on trial today."

Merriwether sat still, his pen hovering above the page. He let out a breath, a long sigh, long and forlorn. O'Day was claiming that John Barnes was allowed to cop a plea so he would cover up the sheriff's killing of Teddy Wocek. That Scotti was being hit with the murder rap only to keep the cover-up alive. Good heavens, Merriwether thought, Shea was right, we've given Scotti his defense. He's taken it right out of the newspaper, right out of the *Champion*. It was lifted wholesale from Rumplemeyer's story about Mrs. Wocek. It's the Wocek Piece Defense.

And won't it make the sheriff look bad if it works, he thought.

He turned his eyes from O'Day to the defendant.

And won't that make my pretty Sally happy.

Vince Scotti shifted slowly in his chair. He looked at Merriwether over his shoulder. He stared at him dully. He smiled.

THIRTEEN

"Where the Fuck Is She?"

TUESDAY, OCTOBER 23– THURSDAY, OCTOBER 25

1

ON LINCOLN GREEN, an oompah band was playing. It was sort of a funny thing, Dolittle thought.

They were up on the stage, on a wooden platform erected at one end of the narrow sward. Four fat guys in Tyrolean hats and peasant overalls playing tubas and trombones and accordions. There was a white banner hung above them, strung from a telephone pole to a lamppost. "Octoberfest," it said. It flapped in the breeze, glistened in the autumn sun. At the stage corners, two overweight high school girls—blondes with their hair in coils—kicked up chubby legs from under frothy dirndl skirts.

And all around, over the thin stretch of grass, the people were gathering in clusters: carrying paper plates and plastic forks to the folding tables; jostling around the makeshift stoves where bratwurst sizzled in cast-iron skillets; standing in line before the metal kegs, holding out their steins to the streams of gurgling beer. The quaint white train station house stood on one end of the green; the redbrick stores of Main Street ran along two sides; the high hills that gave the town of Lincoln its Alpine feel surrounded them. . . .

And it was just a funny thing, Dolittle thought, that it would all still be here; a year from now, say. He coughed slightly as he moved his eyes across the green again. His face looked gaunt; his eyes were sunken and deeply ringed. He coughed again. A funny thing.

On the left side of the grass, tied to a telephone pole with a piece of string, there was a small campaign sign. It fluttered and bounced against the wooden pole. It wasn't much, just a white sign with red letters. SELECT PURDY FOR COUNTY EXECUTIVE, it said. AUBURN'S FUTURE.

Standing in front of the sign, right at the edge of the green, was Purdy himself. Looking good. Jacket slung over his shoulder, sleeves rolled up on his muscular arms, red hair shining in the sun, smile gleaming. He was pressing the flesh, talking the talk whenever a crowd formed around him.

"Development doesn't have to mean destroying the county, that's the main thing. It doesn't have to mean drugs and all those city problems. The new town master plans have shown we can work together for cautious progress. And if you want to know how we handle those drug dealers who do come in—why, just take a look at the newspapers. . . ."

His teeth flashed. The sheriff watched him. The sheriff leaned against the Civil War memorial—a concrete stele, a brass plaque full of names. He leaned an elbow on the base and watched quietly, keeping his breathing as shallow as he could to keep from hitting the dark spot down in his lungs.

Purdy was doing all right, he thought. The election was so close now, and there hadn't been a major fuck-up yet. The polls—what few polls there were—showed the race was too close to call, but the Scotti trial ought to put them over the top. Purdy was dancing to the right music anyway, singing the right tune.

And he'd still be here, Dolittle thought. Like the stores and the train station and the high hills. Purdy would still be here a year down the line; still talking, smiling, breathing; maybe even running the county . . .

Dolittle saluted and grinned as Jerry Schmit from the hardware store (one DWI, one public urination) went by him. He grinned and tipped a wink at Virginia Horstman's daughter too. She was nearly thirty; Dolittle could remember the night she was born.

He watched her as she strode across the grass. He watched her until his eyes came to rest on Ralph Jones.

Jones had a sign too. Over on the other side of the grass. His was stapled to a thin wooden post; the post was driven into the ground. RALPH JONES FOR COUNTY EXECUTIVE, the sign said. THE MAN FOR THE COUNTY.

Jones stood in front of it, grinning, shaking hands, slapping backs, grinning some more.

He was obese, Jones was. Always had been, even when he and Dolittle were young. Now, Dolittle guessed, he must've weighted close to three hundred pounds. He wore a woolen shirt, a loud plaid that seemed to expand for yards from every side of him. He wore jeans so huge you could've clothed a Third World country with the waistband alone. He had a big, square head with lots of jowls melting off it, dewlaps wobbling and stretching every time he grinned. It was a simple, friendly face and he wore thick square glasses that made it look even friendlier. Dolittle could hear his country stutter drift to him where he stood.

"Now, now, now, now, now, now, Tom, now Tom," he said to the man just in front of him. "Don't you, don't you get me wrong here, y'unnerstand. Doncha go listening to every, every, everything you hear from a certain fella across the way now. It's not that I'm sayin no progress, nosir. Nosir. You know me fer twenty years, ya know I wouldn't say that. Nosir. Only I don't see why we gotta all go hog-wild with greed neither. Sell off everything we have, all the, all the good stuff we got in the county. Now we got new areas of commercial development. Let's take it slow, that's all I'm saying. Preserve some o' what we got for our kids and our grandkids. Don't go squanderin it all. Hey, Mrs. P.!" he shouted suddenly. "How about some more of that bratwurst? This campaigning makes a man mighty hungry."

Dolittle couldn't help it: He laughed once, shook his head. Coughed.

229

Jones would be here too. In a year. Jones. Christ. Ralph Jones would be here forever.

With one last tremendous *PAH*, the band stopped playing. The boys laughed and scattered, heading for the beer kegs with outstretched steins.

As the new quiet fell over the green, Dolittle let out a long, moaning breath. "Just keep yourself under control," he said. His voice rasped out of him. He sounded like a ninety-year-old man.

Undersheriff Benoit spat on the ground. Hands in his back pockets, he stood next to Dolittle, leaned one shoulder against the Civil War monument. He watched his own foot ground his phlegm into the grass.

"I'm under fucking control," he said. "It's the situation that's fucked-up, that's all. We gotta take care of the situation. I mean, you just remember, Mr. Control, that we are all in this together."

When he looked up, Dolittle could see the mean little glitter of Benoit's eyes.

A year from now he might be the sheriff, Dolittle thought.

He smiled easily. "I would never forget that, Henry," he said.

Benoit returned the smile, his face breaking into harsh jags. "Good. Then let's talk about Sally Dawes and her pet Jew. Let's talk about Ernie fucking Rumplemeyer."

The sheriff tried to draw a deeper breath, but he coughed as it came out; coughed again, more harshly. His chest felt raw.

"Hey there, Sheriff!" someone called from across the grass.

He looked up and grinned. There was George Gruber, stuffing some sort of wurst into his gristly face. A carpenter, George was. A nice guy. Bribed Ted Danning for that variance last year.

Dolittle looked at Benoit again. The grin faded. "There'll come a time to take care of Rumplemeyer. There'll come a time to take care of Dawes and Rumplemeyer both."

"Rumplemeyer is hanging out around the Hickory train tracks asking for Cindy by fucking name," Benoit said. "There's only one reason no one's talked so far and that's because they're afraid I'll kick their ass. The time has fucking come to take care of Rumplemeyer now. Sheriff sir," he added thickly.

230

The sheriff shook his head, made a sound in the corner of his mouth: Tsk, tsk. "What's the plan, drop him in a well?"

"I can take care of Rumplemeyer."

"Forget it. Jesus. What's he gonna find out, Henry? What're the kids down there gonna tell him?"

"What? You think they don't know where your daughter is? You think kids don't know everything that happens to other kids? They know, Sheriff."

"She tried to kill herself. She's in a hospital. If Dawes tries to use that, she'll probably win us sympathy votes. They can't get in to interview her, and even if they did, she's crazy, no one will believe her."

"I'm not talking about fuckin *votes.*" Benoit had to strangle his voice in his gullet in order to keep from screaming. "I'm talking about the fact that I have to testify next week in the Scotti trial. In a court of fucking law. Under a fucking oath. You know what their fucking defense is, Cy. You know what they're gonna do to me. They're gonna say I murdered poor, defenseless little Teddy Wocek."

The sheriff tried to clear his throat. He felt the mucus boiling in there. "Police conspiracy theories are about as old as lawyers, Henry. They may buy them in the Bronx, but not in Auburn. Anyway, O'Day's a has-been. He hasn't had a big case since the Norville killings in Poughkeepsie. He lives off his reputation and about a quart of Bushmills a day. He's cruising on style. You'll be fine."

Dolittle straightened off the monument. "You'll be fine," he said again. He slapped Benoit on the shoulder. "Now I gotta go put my arm around Purdy and grin like an idiot. Warm people's hearts with our closeness."

"I'm gonna take care of Rumplemeyer," Benoit said. "I'm gonna send that little fuckhead a message. You gonna stop me, Sheriff?"

Dolittle sighed, a hollow sound.

Fuck, fuck, fuck, he thought. But there was nothing he could do. Not now, with the election less than two weeks away. He just hoped he lived long enough to do this bastard in, that's all.

He lifted his shoulders in an amiable shrug. Smiled his country smile and tipped Benoit an easygoing wink.

"What you do off duty, out of uniform, and in the pitch-black dead of night, is none of my business," he said. "But if it gets back to me, if it damages my boy's chances in this election, well, son, I will personally turn your balls to powder."

He walked off across the grass.

2

Cindy woke up at seven-thirty the next morning. That's when they all woke up, so she did too. She lay in bed for a few moments and the room seeped into her mind like smoke. The windows, the grated windows, too high on the wall to show anything but the sky. The worn, torn, colorless carpet. The three other beds with the three other girls sitting up on them. The door, open, always propped open, onto the hall.

The other girls got up and began to make their beds. Even the girl who talked to herself all the time made her own bed. So Cindy got up and made her bed just like they did, the green blanket flat as a board, the little tucks tight at the corners. When the other three went to the bathroom, she did too. They shared the bathroom with another room, so there were eight girls in there all together.

After that, the girls went out into the hall, a long hall with pale green walls and other open doors. Cindy followed right behind.

She was pretending to be one of them.

They walked down the hall like zombies, like something out of the movies: *Night of the Living Dead.* Dragging their feet, dangling their arms. And Cindy did it too, letting her mouth hang open a little, making her eyes stare straight ahead. Oh, Teddy would've laughed, Teddy would really have just whooped it up if he'd seen her like this. But she couldn't think about that now, not during the day. Because when she did think about it, she suddenly pictured in her head the sky so blue above the tops of the big hemlock trees and the clouds going over like in a movie and Teddy kissing her—and it made the tears well up in her eyes as she dragged her feet down the hall, down the long hall. If they saw that, she thought—the nurses, even the orderlies—if they saw that, they would know she was not really like the others, that she was still herself inside, that she was hiding from them.

They shuffled into the dining hall, a dingy cafeteria really. No light came down to it through the grated windows high on the wall. The room felt cramped and small to Cindy, but the long tables there and the wooden chairs around seemed to go on in rows and rows forever. The girls filed in and sat down at their table.

They were still in their green gowns. Cindy hated that. She hated being in her stupid green gown in front of everybody. The nurses and orderlies laughed at them, she was sure of it. Hiding it behind those thin Miss Prissy smiles they wore. As if the girls were just little children to be taken care of. It was all crap, if you asked her. Those smiles especially. Those smiles disappeared in a big, big hurry if you started screaming. If you told them, Let me the fuck out of here, you asshole pieces of shit. They didn't smile then. Then they practically broke your arm while they held you down. The fat black one: Roberta? She would even sit on you while they stuck a needle into your arm to make you pass out. Sometimes they even strapped you to your bed, just left you there shrieking for your mommy to come and get you out, shrieking, Don't leave me here, oh God, oh God. They didn't smile then, no, not if you did that.

But Cindy didn't do that anymore. She was smarter now. Now she pretended to be just like the others.

The orderlies brought the food to the tables. Always the same fucking thing: cereal on Monday, pancakes on Tuesday, cereal with fruit on Wednesday, today. You were supposed to get all excited about the fruit. A special treat they called it. A big fucking deal.

Cindy ate without talking. Some of the other girls did talk as they ate, but if you asked Cindy, they talked in weird mutant voices. They giggled and made disgusting faces. Most of them ate without talking, so she did too. When they were done, they scraped their plates and bowls into the garbage can, then stacked them on the metal tray. Then they all went zombie-ing back down the hall to the all-purpose room. It was a big bright playroom with large windows—still grated, of course—and card tables and old furniture and even a TV.

She stayed there for an hour. You could play cards or games or do puzzles there or read or watch TV, though only old Popeye cartoons were on now. Cindy just sat in a chair by one of the big windows. She looked out through the wire mesh.

The hospital was on top of a steep hill. When she looked out the window, she could see other hills in the distance against the sky, and ranges of hills beyond those. The hills were covered with trees and they looked very pretty. With the leaves all different colors, they looked like a box of Trix cereal with its different fruit flavors (lemon yellow, raspberry red, orange orange . . .): The leaves had the same kind of soft colors the sugary cereal had.

Cindy looked out and wondered if the other kids had asked about her when she didn't come back to school this year. Not that she wanted to be in tenth grade anyway. You had to take stupid science with Mr. Becker, and everybody knew what an asshole he was. And she knew three separate people who had to take his class over again in the summer before he'd give them a passing grade, so fuck that shit too. . . .

But she had to stop thinking about that now. It was like Teddy. It made her eyes fill with tears. The nurses were bringing around the Dixie cups filled with medication now, and if they saw her crying, it would give everything away.

For the same reason, she didn't argue about the pills anymore either. That made them suspicious, so she just took them when they brought them to her. The pills didn't do anything to her anyway really. Made her head feel heavy, that was all. And anyway, after she took the pills, she was allowed to go back to her room and get dressed finally.

She went back down the long hall, dragging her feet, dangling her arms. She brushed her teeth and got into her jeans and T-shirt. Almost as soon as she was finished, the nurse came to take her to see Dr. Bloom.

She saw Dr. Bloom every other day. Mondays, Wednesdays, and Fridays. He was a bigwig, the head of the hospital or something, Cindy wasn't sure. None of the other girls got to see him, and Cindy figured she only did because her father was the sheriff. Not that it was a big privilege or anything. She thought the guy was basically a piece of shit.

Corruption

Dr. Bloom was long, skinny and bald and wore thick, stupid-looking glasses. He always sat slouched in his big black leather swivel chair behind his big I'm-an-important-doctor glass desk. He always had his hands together under his nose like he was praying. And he would swivel back and forth, back and forth, so that Cindy had to watch his shiny dome move from the framed degree on the paneled wall behind him to her left, to the one in the middle, to the one on the right, back to the middle, and so on for forty-five fucking minutes.

And he always started the same way: "So how are you feeling today, Cindy?"

And she always answered the same way: "I want to get out of here."

She could never keep from crying when she said that. It was the same today. She started crying then, and she would go on crying through the whole session. She would cry until she got back to her room.

"Why do you think you *are* here?" he said. That too was what he always said.

And she recited, "Because I cut my wrists."

"And do you remember *why* you cut your wrists?"

"Because . . . because of Teddy . . ." She could just get it out, she was sobbing so hard—it was so fucking humiliating. "Because he died."

"And do you remember *how* he died?"

"They shot him."

"*Who* shot him, Cindy?"

"You *know* this." But that didn't matter: He just looked at her. They had to go through the whole thing. As always. "My father's men shot him. . . ."

"And why did they shoot him?"

She didn't fight him anymore the way she used to. She knew there was no point to it. Weeping, she just gave him what he wanted: "Because Teddy shot at them when they tried to arrest him. All right?"

"And you can understand that now, can't you?" Back and forth, swiveling back and forth, the light flashing off his bald head.

She could hardly get the word out to answer. "Yes."

"And you understand why they had to arrest Teddy, don't you?"

"Because of . . . because of Billy Thimble . . ." She hated to take a Kleenex from the box on his desk, but she had to, to blow her nose, dry her cheeks. She was sobbing like a baby.

"Because Billy Thimble was murdered, isn't that right?"

"All right, all right: yes!"

"And it wasn't your father who murdered Billy Thimble, was it?"

"No."

"Who was it?"

"Stop it. Don't make me."

But he would make her, swiveling back and forth. He always did. "Who *was* it, Cindy?"

"Vince Scotti and John Barnes," she said sullenly.

He insisted: "Come on now. Who else, Cindy?"

"Teddy!" she cried out. She knew he would not stop until she said it. She covered her face with her hands. "It was Teddy. All right? Is that what you want? It was Teddy."

When she lay in her bed that night, her voice, her sobs, the words she shouted at the swiveling doctor, seemed to echo and bounce off the walls of her brain. She had to say them. She knew she had to say them. She had to fool the doctor just like she had to fool everyone else in here.

But she also knew something else. She knew a secret. She knew the Truth. And she was the only one who knew.

She clutched it to herself as she lay there. She crossed her arms over it and held it inside herself. She didn't know how long she could keep it in there, how long she could keep it from just rising up and bursting out of her lips. It was like a living thing in her, like some kind of demon, trying to break out. Nobody else knew. Nobody else had figured it out. And when the things she said to Dr. Bloom echoed in her head like this, she just wanted to scream it, to scream the Truth out at everyone. Shit, if she wasn't careful, she was going to become one of those girls who scream things all of a sudden. One of those girls who just starts screaming in the hall or in the all-purpose room, just screaming things at nobody, at the ceiling, at the wall.

I know the Truth! she would scream. *I know the secret! Me!*

Everyone would think she really *was* crazy then.

236

She clutched the sheets up under her chin. She clenched her jaw so the sobs only escaped as little squeaks. The tears rolled silently down the side of her face, into her ears, onto her pillow.

Mama, she thought.

If Mama would come, if Mama would only come, if she would just visit, just once, if anyone would just visit once so she wouldn't be so all alone by herself, all the fuck fucking alone, then she could tell them, her friends, her mother, she could tell them the secret, and then Dr. Bloom wouldn't matter, she could just go on lying to Dr. Bloom. If only . . .

Oh, Teddy.

If only *he* would come, if he could come right out of his grave, like someone in the horror movies, his shirt all torn, the bones showing through the muscle, his face half flesh, half skull, the teeth gritted: REVENGE! She could see the poster for it outside the theater . . . If Teddy would come.

But no one came. She cried harder, the sobs squeaking out more loudly, her nose running into the sheets. No one even visited. And soon the words would just bubble up out of her—*except, except*—and she would say it out loud, and Dr. Bloom would know, he would know what she knew, he would know that she had figured out the whole thing. And then—

And then they would never let her go. Her father would never let her go and no one would rescue her and no one would even remember her after a while.

She opened her mouth, gasped for air as quietly as she could. *Oh Mama, Oh Mama, Mama . . .*

They had all forgotten her probably already. Probably no one even wondered anymore where the fuck she was.

3

Where the fuck is she? wondered Ernie Rumplemeyer.

Normally, it was the sort of question an intrepid, hardworking reporter would ask his attentive, interested, and intelligent editor. But

was she in the office this windy Thursday afternoon? Noooooo. Rumplemeyer was here, rocking back and forth in his chair so fast he could
feel a breeze on his beard. And Shea was here, right at his desk,
cigarette in his teeth, diligently typing some piece of capitalist pro-
paganda about the proposed connector road or whatever. Doreen was
here, wonking into the phone as always. Alice was here, clipping
feature ideas.

But Sally—their editor, their fearless leader, the commander in
chief of the bureau—where, pray tell, was she? She was over at the
Courthouse Restaurant, that's where. She was just entering her second
hour of lunch with her star Courtroom Reporter. Sidney "Murder Is
My Beat" the Fourth. Sidney the Dilettante Merriwether. Who had
not only been assigned to the best fucking murder trial up here since
the glacier receded but was also monopolizing all the editorial guidance in the place.

Right, Rumplemeyer thought. *The only editorial guidance he's getting is: "Oh baby, now, now, now."*

And Sally could have spent her evenings caning the future ace of
the everloving *New York Times,* for Christ's sake.

The phone rang and Rumplemeyer, rocking forward, snatched it
up angrily. *"Champion."*

A woman's voice came back to him. Not a woman's, no. A girl's.
"Ernest Rumplemeyer please."

"Yeah. Hi. That's me. Who's this?"

"I can't . . . I can't tell you that."

"Uh . . . What? You can't tell me who you are?"

"No. No. But I have a story for you. Okay? I want you to meet
me in the Hickory Pine Forest tonight at ten o'clock."

Rumplemeyer stopped rocking. He grinned. *Wow,* he thought,
what a neat phone call!

"Yeah, okay," he said. "I can do that. Where do you want to
meet, where in the forest?"

There was a long pause, a low cough. Then the girl said, "Have
you ever heard of the Hemlock Cathedral?"

Rumplemeyer had never been there before, but when he walked into
the Hemlock Cathedral that night, it somehow felt familiar to him.

Like the Empire State Building or the Arc de Triomphe or Paul Newman's face, the shape of the place stood out from the mundane in relief; it had the reality of fame. Now, here, in person, he thought, were the actual towering conifers swaying against the cloud-blown night sky and the white stones squatting on the dark floor. Here was the spot near the rim of the circular clearing where Jones and Dolittle first saw the foot of the dead little girl protruding from the mound of snow. There was the place where Dolittle stood deciding—he remembered it all from Sally's story. And there was the forest—moonlit, shadowy, tortuous—all around him. And the cold October wind was blowing through the trees and the twigs were crunching and the brush quivering as bears probably lumbered toward the scent of him to tear his heart out and eat it while the last few drops of blood in his veins kept him alive long enough to hear his mother's voice. . . .

Oh, Ernie, get out of here before you're killed and leave me all alone just like your father did you're all alike it's giving me oh I feel a sudden, Ernest. I'm serious. I can't breathe. . . .

He shivered. He hugged his shoulders. The gathering wind blew his corduroy coat out around him. It was ten o'clock—three minutes past—and there was no sign of her—whoever she was—his mystery date. She was nowhere to be seen. He should have brought a flashlight, he thought. He'd probably never find his way back to the road. It was probably all some kind of Dolittle trick: The old lure-em-out-here-sneak-up-on-em-and-sacrifice-em-to-some-minor-forest-deity routine.

"Mr. Rumplemeyer?"

"Yaaa-aa-aha!" Rumplemeyer replied. He jumped half a foot off the ground, spun in midair, and saw her.

She was standing just within the circle of hemlocks. A small girl, a teenager. With a cap of black hair, a kiss-me-quick curl on her forehead. She looked pretty, but he couldn't make her out too well; her face was gray and unfocused in the dim light.

"I know you been asking around about Cindy," she said. She was wearing a long belted coat; she kept her hands clasped together in front of it; the hem of it fluttered in the wind. "I wanted to tell you because it was my fault what happened. It was all my fault."

Rumplemeyer blinked at the little figure framed against the

hunkered night woods. *Is this really happening?* he thought. She looked like a little phantom standing there.

"Tell me what?" he said. "Like what do you want to tell me?"

"I was the one who told originally, see," the girl said—almost proudly, Rumplemeyer thought. "I told my brother about the meeting—the one in the house with Teddy and Vince and John. I told my brother and he told the police, see. And Cindy got all upset because she thought her father killed Teddy because of her, because they were, like, together. You know? Anyway, that's what Cindy said. Oh shit. Shit, it was my fault. I shouldn't've said anything and now they . . ."

A strong wind surged across the open space, loud in the treetops. The girl took a half step forward, the skirt of her coat dancing around her bare calves.

Rumplemeyer held his hand up in front of him, narrowed his eyes. He had to raise his voice above the noise. "Now they what? Where is she?"

"Lookit," said the girl, "I could get in big trouble for telling you this, okay? So you have to, like, not say anything about where you heard it. I saw in a movie about that, that a reporter has to do that if someone tells him to."

"I won't tell," Rumple called to her as the wind blew up again.

And over the wash of the trees, she called back, "Well, I don't know this for sure, okay? But my friend's sister has a boyfriend who's a deputy? And she told me he says that Cindy had to be put in a hospital."

"In the hospital?"

"For killing herself, for trying to kill herself. They put her away."

Branches creaked and cracked around them as the wind moved on, as it fanned out through the forest.

"Which hospital did she . . . ?" Rumplemeyer began.

But then there was a loud skitter in the leaves behind him and he swiveled to look.

When he turned back, the girl was gone.

The wind dropped. The rattle of the leaves became a whisper. All alone in the clearing, Rumplemeyer looked beyond the place where she'd been, into the broad cavern of forest.

Corruption

And then there was her voice. A whisper in the whisper of the wind. It came from nowhere.

"Don't say it was me, okay? I'm not supposed to tell."

Oh, I mean, wow, was that dramatic, or what?

Chugging back to the office in his Volks, Rumple kept the radio blasting, felt the rhythm of it, the pure bassline, pounding in his chest.

Oh yes!

Steering the little bug over the twists and dips of Stillwater Lane, past the rows of Quiet Desperation Housing the sheriff was so proud of.

Listen to this, you clockpunchers! he thought.

And he sang—shrieked—along with the driving bass:

"Meet me in the forest at ten P.M.—uh!—I can't tell you my name. Yeah, meet me in the forest again and again. I'm so glad you ca-ame. . . ."

Tell us, Mr. Rumplemeyer, is it true you began the most glorious journalistic career in American history in a leaky box of a newspaper called the, heh, heh . . . Champion?

Yes, my son. I can still see it now . . .

And, by jingo, he could see it now, up ahead to the right, the storefront window dead and dark, staring out at the swaying elms. He turned the Bug down the alley beside it and putted into the back parking lot. Just wanted to go inside and get his bag, call down to Sally at the plant, let her know he was getting close to solving *The Mystery of Cindy Dolittle.*

I can't tell you my na-ame . . .

Braking with a screech, he stopped the car in the dead center of the lot—not even in a designated spot—just right in the center. He loved doing that late at night when no one was there.

"Bum bum bum bum bum," he sang with the music.

And then he killed the engine, shutting off the song on that last bum.

"Meet me in the forest at 10:00 P.M., I say meet me at the Hemlock Cathedral wo-wo."

He hopped out, slammed the door behind him. Started scuttling across the lot to the bureau, jutting his head to the beat, snapping his fingers. Casting a quick look around to see if anyone else was parked here. But it was too dark to see anything and . . .

Rumplemeyer pulled up short. Stopped. Stood for a second, trying to figure out what was bothering him, what was so strange.

Getting dark, too dark to see, I feel I'm knockin on heaven's . . .

The street lamp. The halogen lamp that was usually on back here. It was out tonight.

"Ooh, ooh, ooh," said Rumplemeyer aloud.

A long breath hissed out of him. He looked around again. Darkness. That's all there was. The wavering shapes of trees at the edge of the lot. The shapes of cars. There were two cars over there against the storm fence . . .

He cleared his throat. "Uh boy . . ."

He started heading for the office door again. Faster now, his bowed legs swinging around hard. He reached for the doorknob. He was still ten yards away but he reached for the doorknob anyway. The door was just becoming visible to him. He could just make out its rectangle of gray metal. It was getting closer to him, clearer to him. . . .

And then a figure—a huge figure—stepped in front of it.

Oh fuck.

Rumplemeyer halted on his heels. He was breathing hard. He peered through the gloom at the hulking creature, an enormous silhouette against the door's dimly glinting metal. For the beat of two breaths he stood motionless, and the Monster stood motionless, confronting him. Then Rumplemeyer spun around. He took three quick steps back to his car. . . .

But a figure was standing there now, too. A smaller figure, but lean and coiled. It stood waiting. It stood ready.

Oh no. Oh no. I'm fucked. Rumplemeyer thought. *I can't believe I'm so fucked, oh no.*

Slowly, the lean figure pushed away from the car. Slowly, he came toward Rumplemeyer, still crouched, still taut, his hands out from his sides. Rumplemeyer swung around in place, back to the door again.

The huge figure there was also on the move. Also coming toward him. Slowly.

Corruption

Rumplemeyer's throat was tight, so tight, he thought he would choke. His heart was beating so hard it felt as if it would explode. The small figure behind him prowled in closer like a leopard. The huge figure in front of him rocked forward heavily like a giant. Rumplemeyer wanted to burst into tears like a baby. He couldn't believe they were doing this, that they were actually going to do this to him. . . .

Again, he spun to the smaller one. He could see the creature's eyes in the night, he could see them burning, he could hear its breath. He spun to the large one. He was right there, right on top of him, looming over him, staring down. Rumplemeyer could see the gleam of his teeth.

"Just don't . . ." he cried out.

The big one hit him. A stinging clout on the ear.

"Ow!"

Rumplemeyer stumbled to the side, tumbled down into gravel. He felt his knees ripped open as he slid forward onto his hands. He felt the flesh scraped off his palms. He braced himself there, on all fours. He shook his head. His head rang; it was filled with ringing. Tears sprang into his eyes.

One of the men above him chuckled. They came toward him. Rumple heard their shoes go *chunk, chunk* on the gravel as they closed in.

He lay down flat. He lay on his side on the piercing pebbles and curled himself into a ball. He lay at the two men's feet. He put his hands up to cover his head. The tears spilled out of his eyes now. His nose started running.

"Go ahead, you shits," he said. His voice trembled. Snot ran into his mouth. "I hate you. I fucking hate you so fucking much, you shits. You shits."

"Act like a man, you mewling piece of garbage."

A big hand grabbed Rumplemeyer's shoulder. He cried out. The hand started to drag him to his feet.

Then, suddenly, there was a loud crack—a flash of light.

Oh God, they shot me, now I'll be dead, oh no. Rumplemeyer went on crying.

But the hand had let him go, had dropped him back to the ground. The light was still shining; it was shining down on him steadily. Rumplemeyer peeked through his fingers to see what it was. . . .

243

It was a radiant beam. A soft and radiant beam pouring down on him. And in the beam . . . In the beam, there was the image of an angel. No. Not the image. An angel, wafting toward him, floating toward him gently among motes and sparkles. So beautiful, Rumplemeyer thought. An angel with golden hair flowing to his shoulders, with the face of perfection lustrous with heavenly fire . . .

"Fourth!" Rumple screamed. "Help! Help!"

And the angel kept coming, kept floating forward, unafraid. Floating toward him in the light from the office door. And the men—Rumple peeked at them through his fingers too, and son of a bitch, they were falling back, falling away into the surrounding darkness step by step as Merriwether came on step by step. The thugs were falling, dimming, fading, as if they were being forced down into their natural habitat of blackness by the sheer candescent righteousness of this approaching being, this seraphim, yes, he was, he *was* an Angel, he'd been an Angel of the Lord all along, that was it, it all made sense to Rumplemeyer now, it explained everything, hooray, hooray. . . .

He reached his hand up, and Merriwether took hold of it.

"Why, Rumplemeyer," he said quietly. "How delightful to see you like this."

He pulled, and Rumplemeyer scrambled to his feet. Merriwether caught him, threw an arm around his waist to hold him upright, and started dragging him to the door.

Nauseous, weary, the inside of his head throbbing, Rumplemeyer lifted his eyes into the light as it flowed out brilliantly from the office into the lot. There she was. He saw her. Sally. Waiting for him at the heart of the beam. Reaching for him, the mother of them all. It was just like one of those near-death experiences you read about in the *Enquirer.* He was saved. He was saved. Hallelujah. Hallelu . . . Only . . . Wait a minute. . . . Wait a minute. . . .

"Hey, Fourth . . ." Rumple managed to raise his eyes to Merriwether. He managed a feeble grin. "How come you two had the lights out in here? Huh?"

"Oh, do be civilized, Rumplemeyer," Merriwether said—and dumped him into Sally's waiting arms.

FOURTEEN

The Scotti Trial
Part Two: Mrs. Thimble

FRIDAY, OCTOBER 26

HE THOUGHT OF her, lifted in his arms, pressed against the wall, her hands clasped behind his neck, her legs around him; her skirt bunched up (oh, his cock stiffened in his slacks at the thought of it), her skirt bunched up and her head flung back against the bulletin board, her hair spilling down, her mouth open. . . .

And then, when it was over, that voice of hers, that whisper. She had asked him again. He had sat beside her on the floor behind her desk. He had held her, and she had rested her head on his shoulder and whispered: "What are we going to do, Sidney? What are we going to do?"

"This is . . . an *evil* man."

"Objection!"

Merriwether looked up dully. The defense attorney, O'Day, was standing at his table, his finger raised. Stern, the prosecutor, was leaning on the rail of the jury box.

"Yes," said Judge Posey in his pinched, nasal twang. "The jury will disregard that. We're not interested in your opinions about the defendant, Mrs. Thimble."

245

The housewife in the witness chair hung her head. Wrung her handkerchief in her hands, twined it round her reddened knuckles. Dishpan hands, Merriwether thought vaguely. Kindly crow's-feet at the corners of sad, gentle eyes. Her white lips curved down, quivering as she nodded slowly. O'Day settled back into his chair beside Vincent Scotti.

Where are we? Merriwether thought. He looked down at his notebook. The top page bore the heading *Nancy Thimble.* The rest of the page was blank. *Uh-oh.* He seemed to have fallen behind.

"Let me rephrase the question, Mrs. Thimble." The jurors' eyes followed the assistant district attorney as he left their box and slouched across the floor to stand directly in front of the witness. He jutted his hawk face at her. "Before July of last year, when your husband met Vincent Scotti, did you consider William Thimble to be a good husband?"

"Yes." She was close to tears.

"Was he a good father?"

"Very good, yes."

"He was kind to you and your son?"

"Yes, he was very . . . " She looked up at the ceiling, her eyes glistening in the daylight. The slate-gray sky filled the mullioned windows. "He was silly," she said. "Funny, I mean. He made a lot of jokes. Very young-acting, just like he was in college. He made me laugh. . . . " She could not go on. She lowered her head again. Twisted the handkerchief in her hands.

Made her laugh, Merriwether wrote. Then, in the pause, he took a quick glance over at Scotti. The defendant was still slumped in the chair next to O'Day, his long legs stretched out under the counsel table. He was still sneering, regarding the victim's wife through half-lidded eyes as if she were an object of derision.

Merriwether fell to gazing at him dreamily. At his long, relaxed frame, his thick-lipped sneer. His mind drifted away again, back to last night, the time with Sally. Soon, he was barely aware of the courtroom anymore. He was thinking about Rumplemeyer, remembering how Rumplemeyer had stumbled in after those two thugs assaulted him in the parking lot. . . . The way he had pushed away from Sally, practically fallen into the office bathroom, too hurried to close the door; the way he had bent over the toilet, vomiting. The raw purple bruise had been damp and shiny beneath his beard. It had sent a chill into Merriwether's groin.

Sally had been on the phone by then, calling the state police. Wiping the last tears from her cheeks with the heel of her free hand. He, Merriwether, had leaned against a desk. He had watched her and smoked a cigarette glumly. He had thought: *Now it will be in the paper. That I was here. That I was here with her.* Earlier that night, he had told Emily he would be interviewing a lawyer for background on the trial. He had lied to her.

What *were* they going to do? It was a good question.

In front of him now, Scotti shrugged and glanced over at his lawyer. He laughed, Scotti, out of the corner of his mouth.

". . . after he met Vince Scotti, Billy started to change," Mrs. Thimble was saying on the witness stand. "He was the same outside. Still joking around and everything. But it was like there was another person inside him who was telling him to do that. The inside person made Billy act the same, joke around the same way he did before and be funny and everything. But it was just to fool me, so I wouldn't get suspicious. The person inside him—he was only thinking about the drugs."

O'Day began to object but apparently thought better of it and settled back into his chair.

Merriwether began taking notes again. . . . *thinking about drugs,* he scribbled vaguely.

Stern went on, his voice deep, his tone solemn. "Mrs. Thimble, did there come a time when you confronted your husband about this change in his behavior?"

She nodded. Gulped. "Yes. In June. Late June. About two weeks before Billy . . . died. I . . . I had just put little Will to bed. And I came downstairs, and I saw Billy sitting on the sofa. We have a sofa in our living room and he was . . . just sitting on it in the dark. And when he looked up, he saw me, standing at the bottom of the stairs, you know, looking at him. And he just . . . he just made this kind of noise. And he started to cry."

The courtroom was very quiet. The jurors, most with their hands folded in their laps, sat still, watching the woman respectfully. In the pews, there were only a few curious townies now, old men mostly; they were motionless and silent. The crowds and the out-of-town press had virtually vanished after the trial's opening day. Even Buzzy Farquharson was gone, and WAUB's Dog Saunders only dropped in occasionally to get some sound bytes from the lawyers. Merriwether sat alone in the second pew, his pen moving over the notepad. . . . *started to cry.*

"And what happened then?" said Stern softly.

"He told me . . . He said he'd had to start selling drugs for Vincent Scotti. He said he had to do it for the money. But he said he hated it. He said he couldn't bear it and . . ."

"Objection." O'Day was on his feet again, speaking quietly. "Hearsay, Your Honor."

"Uh, no," said Posey. "No, I'll allow that."

"Go on, Mrs. Thimble," the prosecutor said.

Mrs. Thimble nodded. "He said he couldn't bear it. He said it was tearing at him inside, killing him. I remember I sat next to him on the couch and he . . . he just put his head in my lap and cried."

"And did you advise your husband at that time, Mrs. Thimble?" Stern asked.

"Yes," she said—her voice broke—the tears began. She shook her head and lowered her face. "I told him he had to go to the police. I told him he had to do the right thing so little Will would know he . . . did what was right, the right thing." She sobbed and Merriwether—writing *Will know did that*—looked up. And she, Mrs. Thimble, looked up at him—at everyone—at the whole courtroom. "And he was going to do it too . . ." she said.

"Oh, objection!"

The woman turned to O'Day. "Well, he was!"

"Mrs. Thimble," said Judge Posey quietly. "You can only testify to what you know . . ."

She lowered her head again, holding her handkerchief to her eyes. "I'm sorry," she said softly. "But I *do* know. He was going to go to the police."

"Mrs. Thimble," said the judge. "You just can't know that."

Merriwether watched her, his lips parted, his pen against the notepad, unmoving.

"I'm his wife," she whispered. "I do know. I'm his wife."

Christ. Oh, Christ, Christ, Christ, thought Merriwether. He buried his face in his hands.

I do know. I'm his wife. I know.

Christ, Christ, Christ, Christ, Christ.

He was in the court men's room now, alone. The trial had let out for lunch. When he raised his face again, looked up into the mirror over the sink, he saw the two toilet stalls behind him. The one urinal next to them. And his own miserable face.

I'm his wife. I know.

He groaned and turned away from the reflection. He leaned against the sink. Lit a cigarette. Pulled the smoke in hungrily and let it out again in a thin stream, shaking his head.

At least the newspaper story about Rumplemeyer hadn't said much. Rumple couldn't identify his attackers, and Randall Shank—who was phoned at home by the city editor—refused to print Sally's angry insinuations that the sheriff was somehow involved. In the end, there were only three paragraphs on the local page under the headline REPORTER ASSAULTED. Not much at all really. Still, he had thought it best to tell Emily before she saw it for herself.

I'm his wife. I'm his wife. I know.

Emily had listened to his tale without remark. She had made all the appropriate noises of shock and sympathy for the profligate Rumplemeyer. But then, later, as he was leaving for work, she had said, all innocence, "So Sally was there too?" Standing in the doorway, her voice small, her body tense, diamonds of coffee skin showing through the lacework of her nightgown . . .

Merriwether drew in another breath of smoke now and shuddered. Still leaning there against the sink, he thought of the first time he had ever kissed Emily. They had been standing on the porch of her house on Cambridge Street. He had held her by the shoulders with great solemnity, and the snow had floated down over the lawn, going golden in the light from the porch lantern. And she had looked up at him. She had looked up at him with such . . . such adoring joy that he had had to have her. Even before he loved her, he had known she was the woman he had to have. Not just because of the way she looked, but the way she talked, the way she read, the way she worked her thoughts out for him, hesitant, faltering, until he nodded his encouragement to her, gave her his approval. And then when *he* talked: all that idiocy he came out with then. The philosophy and the literary claptrap and the grand plans for his grand magazine. He envied his children—the children he and Emily wanted to have; he envied them that they would see those encouraging eyes of hers, that patient smile, when they talked *their* claptrap and made *their* plans. . . .

"Ah, God," said Sidney Merriwether the Fourth. He lowered his chin to his chest. He did not think he would be able to stand it if she ever found out about Sally.

There was a thump and a whisper outside the door. The door swung in, and Vincent Scotti limped in after it.

The dark man snorted when he saw Merriwether. Long and slim in his charcoal suit, he limped past to the urinal and stood before it with his back to the reporter. Merriwether dropped his cigarette to the floor, crushing it underfoot. Eyed the door, but didn't move. He took a breath. Surely this was one of those opportunities at which the perceptive journalist leapt. . . .

Scotti flushed the urinal and turned around, zipping his fly. Thumped slowly back to the sink. One corner of his mouth twisted in something like a smile as Merriwether stepped out of his way. Looping his cane over the sink's edge, Scotti bent down to wash his hands. Merriwether, his own hands in his pockets, stood behind him. Watching. Like the veriest idiot—watching a man wash his hands in the bathroom.

Scotti straightened, saw Merriwether in the mirror, and gave a thick laugh.

" 'I Pissed with a Murderer,' by Face," he said.

Merriwether offered his most wintry smile. "Any waste you excrete around me, Vince, is strictly off-the-record."

With another dull laugh, Scotti tore a towel from the wall dispenser, and dried his hands, still sneering at Merriwether's reflection. "Pretty funny testimony today, huh."

"Was it? I must've missed that part."

"Oh, Face. Don't tell me. Don't tell me you're a sucker for, like, the Crying Wife routine. I mean, don't tell me you're one of these guys, you see some cunt, she puts one ring on her finger and another ring through a guy's dick and calls herself a wife, so you get all choked up? Is that it? 'I'm his wife. I know.' That gives you goose bumps. Jesus!" He dashed his crumpled towel into the garbage can. Turned. "Let me show you something."

He reached into his jacket and Merriwether fought to keep his eyes from widening in terror. But instead of a gat, a heater, a roscoe, the man brought out his wallet, flipped it open, held it up. Merriwether found himself looking at a snapshot of a woman. She was a sweet-faced woman of around thirty. She had a lush spill of auburn hair, a soft swell of breasts against her I'M THE MOMMY sweatshirt. And she had a child in her arms, a blond, pink-cheeked little girl, shyly smiling.

"I got a wife too," Scotti said. "She's got a cunt too, and a ring too. She cries too." He glanced at the photo himself. "Had to send her to New York, get the kid away from this shit. They both cry every day." He slipped the wallet back inside his jacket. "So write about that. Write about that for a change."

Scotti took up his cane. Limped a step toward Merriwether. "Because the rest of it is bullshit, Face. Billy Thimble was a lying coked-up piece of human shit." He laughed again: heh. "He was going straight, all right. He was going to the police, for sure. Oh yeah. He told me all about it."

"He told you he was going to the police?"

"Yeah. Big man. He had a big bill with me; he owes me a lot of money. And he tells me, he's bragging, he says Sheriff Fuckhead owes him. He tells me, he says he's gonna make Sheriff Fuckhead pay him some big money. Big money. So what do I do like a jackass, right? I waited. I liked the idea of getting paid with Sheriff Fuckhead's money. So I waited for him to collect."

Scotti smiled, to himself it seemed. Then, without another word, he limped toward the door.

Merriwether watched him, wondering what to say. Surely, he should say something. Ask a question or something. "What . . ."

Scotti stopped, his hand on the door. "What could Sheriff Fuck . . . uh, Dolittle possibly owe Billy Thimble?"

Scotti cast a long sneer back over his shoulder. "Why don't you find out? You're a reporter, right?" He laughed. "Face." And he pushed through the door.

FIFTEEN

In the Birch Trees

MONDAY, OCTOBER 29–
WEDNESDAY, OCTOBER 31

"VI-SISSY-TUDES! Vi-sissy-tudes?" Shank threw the printout sheet
down on his desk. "Just 'cause he knows Greek, Sally, doesn't mean
he can put it in my goddamned newspaper!"

She huddled in the chair before the editor in chief, huddled
inside herself, thinking, *I don't care.* "I caught it, Randall, it never
ran," she whispered.

The egg-shaped little tyrant strode to the window, posed there,
legs akimbo, hands on hips. "I can't have you rewriting all his stuff
every day."

"I'm not rewriting . . ."

"And what was that bullshit graph about Scotti's wife and daughter? How he had to get them out of town and whatnot. I mean, shit.
The victim had a family too, you know. Billy What's-his-name had a
family too, and he's dead."

I don't care, she thought. "Sidney's just trying to stay in Scotti's
good graces, Randall. He's walking a fine line."

"Yeah, between incompetence and unemployment. I want him
off the trial. I want Rumplemeyer on it."

253

Sally looked down at the hands clasped on her skirt. She whispered: "You'll have to fire me."

"What did you say?"

"You'll have to fire me, Randall."

"You're fired."

"Fine."

"Oh come on, Sally, you're not fired. Sit down."

She had hardly risen; she sank back down. Shank sighed. Rubbed his eyes with his hand. Sally braced herself, thinking, *I don't care. Whatever you say to me, even if you say all the things you always say. I don't care . . .*

But Shank merely sagged before his parking-lot backdrop. "I got some big-time shit this morning, Sally. *Big-*time shit."

"Well, I'm sorry, Randall." *But I don't actually care.*

"The suits upstairs, they called me up there. I had to stand in front of a big desk, all these executives staring at me. Talking to me about the Sutcliffe newspaper organization expects this and requires that. I mean, I hate shit like that. Man!" He gave a high-pitched whine and leaned back against the wall.

"Because Sidney used the word vicissitudes in a story?" Sally said. "I can't believe that." *And do I care? Uh, no.*

"It's not just that," said Shank. "Not just that. It's this Rumplemeyer thing too. Getting beat up in a parking lot? I mean, shit, *I* know he deserves it, but it's just the kind of thing makes these executive types sit up and take notice. You know what I'm saying? They're actually reading the goddamned paper now and I'm telling you, Sally, that means trouble." Throwing his hand up suddenly, he stalked back to his desk. "They want Merriwether off the trial, you hear? They want Rumplemeyer in the courtroom, not off wasting his time on some bullshit story about this Teddy Wocek punk." He dropped into his chair, swung around to her. "I mean, they're not asking me politely, Sal. You understand?"

After a moment's thought, Sally shook her head. "Not exactly, no. But Sidney's doing a good job on the trial and I made the assignment and he's going to stay."

Shank closed his eyes, laid his head against the rest, putting the chair into the short arc of a comfort-swivel, back, forth, back. "All right. All right," he said. He opened his eyes. "Look. Forget about Merriwether. Okay? Forget him. Just reassign Scoop Hairball for me. How's that? Just keep the fuzzy little turd out of trouble for a few days, just until the election's over."

A laugh escaped her. "Are you telling me you want me to take Rumplemeyer off a story because of police intimidation?"

"What am I, talking Swahili? Of course that's what I'm telling you, how much clearer can I say it?"

"No, Randall. He's on a story. I don't understand this. What is going on?"

Shank lengthened the arc of the swivel. "Shit, shit, shit." He sighed. He pointed a stubby finger at her. It swiveled with him. "You gotta see the light here, Sally. It's over."

"What's ov . . . ?"

"The election," said Shank. "The election is over. The election is Tuesday, one week from tomorrow, and Purdy's gonna win. Purdy and every other piece of shit who'll give Sheriff Dolittle a political blow job are gonna be running that county from top to bottom. After Tuesday, Auburn is Dolittle Land, and you better just get used to it. With power like that, jobs to give away and zoning rights and building permits and tax breaks, even the state boys are gonna fall in line with him. Even the governor."

Sally stared at him. "You mean someone reached them," she said slowly. "Your friends upstairs, the Sutcliffe gang: Some power boy called them up and leaned on them and told them to get rid of Rumple, get him off the Wocek story. It's not about Sidney at all, is it?"

"Damn it, Sally," Shank squeaked. "No one had to call them. No one has to pressure the executives here. They *are* the power boys. This is what they're thinking about all the time."

"Well, forget it, Randall, I'm . . ."

"Sally . . ."

"Forget it," she said.

He sighed again and his swiveling chair slowly settled to a halt. He regarded her steadily. She felt the full force of his piggy little stare. "Well, then, let me tell you something, old friend," he said after an eternity. "Whatever it is you and Rumplemeyer are up to up there,

255

whatever you eventually dig up on our revered and respected Auburn County sheriff, it had better be awfully good. It better be good, and it better be solid. None of this *it snowed* bullshit."

"Oh, Randall!"

"And one more thing," Shank told her. "You better get it before Tuesday. It better be right there on the front page for all to see before the votes are cast. 'Cause if it's not, girl, he will win, you hear me. And if he wins, you are shit on his heel, I guarantee it."

She did not answer him. She stood up angrily.

"And as for Merriwether . . ." Shank said.

She faced him with fierce eyes. "What about him?"

Shank still studied her, but his voice was softer now, almost gentle. "He's a married man, you know."

Sally lowered her eyes as her cheeks grew hot. "I do know, Randall," she whispered.

But I don't care.

That night, she met him by the lake again. Waited in the birch wood, leaning against the white trunk of a tree. The bright yellow leaves, silver in the moonlight, rattled above her in the chill wind, fluttered down around her, skittered over the forest floor—and to hell with Randall Shank because it was fabulous, she couldn't even have dreamed it. And when she saw the headlights of his Rabbit up by the road, her throat felt thick with fear and excitement. And then came his footsteps under the sound of the wind, and her hands clenched at her sides. There was his slim figure moving down the slope, hurrying to get to her, and then he was there, his breath on her, his hands on her shoulders. He kissed her. "Sally." Reared back to look at her, his blue eyes all melodrama and deep soul: He was so young, it made her ache.

There wasn't much art to him—he had her down on their blanket in another minute, her blouse opened, her bra askew, her skirt at her waist, her underwear stripped away—and he got so hard for her so fast, pistoned into her with such abandon—Christ, out here in the woods and all, the whole thing was like adolescence—although not, in fact, like her adolescence—but like those other girls', prettier girls', like their adolescence—and where, by the by, was her disdain for them now—where, come to think of it, was her dignity now, her middle-aged composure while she squealed and thrashed to keep from screaming outright, trying to hold back from this boy just a little of herself, just a token, trying . . . until she bid ta-ta to such considerations, a fond toodle-oo to the whole cramped, miserable nonorgasmic world, and excused herself from it to go rocketing off the ceiling of the universe where, just as she had always imagined, one didn't give much of a good goddamn.

When it was over, he lay with his head on her breast, and she stoked his blond hair and kissed it, breathing in the scent of him, not wondering—for a minute, maybe for ten—what on earth they were going to do, because basically, just then, she was ready to do whatever it took.

Basically, just then, she was ready to do anything.

But when she spoke to him after a while, the first thing she said was about Emily.

"Did she see the story? Your wife? About Ernie getting beaten up? Did she see it?"

"I told her about it," he murmured. "It was all right. I don't think she knows."

"Oh, she knows," said Sally. She bit her lip. "I'll bet anything she knows."

Merriwether withdrew from her; softly kissed her breast good-bye. He rolled away to lie on his back, his arm slung across his forehead. She followed his somber gaze up into the swaying latticework of branches; saw the stars appearing through it, washed out by the gibbous moon.

He said it first tonight: "What *are* we going to do, Sally?"

She sat up on the blanket. Straightened her clothes a little. Reached for the sweater that lay on the ground nearby. It was getting chilly. "We won't be able to come here anymore soon, that's for sure." She laughed. "There won't be any leaves, for one thing."

"I hadn't thought of that. How embarrassing. *Love Nest Bared by Autumn Wind.*"

"Please turn to page three." She wrapped the sweater over her shoulders, held it closed in front of her. In a minute, he was behind her, touching her hair, kissing the back of her neck.

"I can't stop thinking about Emily," she said. "I keep thinking about how you went through so much, you and her, the two of you."

Merriwether sighed. Left off kissing her. "How do you mean?" he said wearily.

"I just mean, you gave up . . . everything for each other . . . breaking with your mother and father. . . . Isn't that what happened? Didn't you break with them over her, over Emily?"

"Oh, I don't know. Sort of." She heard him shifting on the blanket. "My mother is no longer living, first of all. And my father . . . Well . . . My father and I have a long-standing philosophical disagreement: He wants me to be a eunuch and I want him dead."

She smiled. "Still. You must have really loved her to . . . go on with it. When he disowned you. You must really have loved her. Didn't you?"

There was a long silence. Off through the dark trees, she saw the faint glimmer of the lake, the moon on the water.

"I do," said Merriwether then. "I do love her, my love."

She pressed her lips together. She started these things on purpose—she was sure of it. She did it just to make herself suffer.

"I loved a man named Jerry once," she said. "It was awful."

She heard the pop and sizzle of his match, smelled the cigarette smoke drift to her, mingle with the smell of the autumn leaves. "Was it?"

"Oh was it. Oh boy. He was a jazz musician, a saxophone player. All thin and starved with these big deep . . . kind of hot eyes, and this red beard . . . I don't know what it was about him. I was working out of White Plains then, with Randall. Randall was the city editor. He was really pissed when I quit." She laughed. "Jerry said he had to go to New Orleans to get work, and I had some money . . . some money my father had left me. . . ."

"You don't have to tell me this, you know."

"Don't you want me to?" He didn't answer. She closed her eyes, shook her head, reveled in the pain, the old pain still warm in her after all this time. "I'd never really *been* in love with anyone before, you know. And I convinced myself, like: Hallelujah, this is it. Practically went out and hired a string quartet to follow me around playing the theme to *Love Story*. And Randall, meanwhile, he was livid, he was stomping around, screaming at me—'He's the lowest of the low, Sally, the scum of the earth. A monster, a demon . . .' And I thought, typical Randall hyperbole. You know?"

When she opened her eyes, the gleam of the lakewater glistened, unfocused. "Unfortunately, in this case, he was taking an ill-timed stab at understatement. Jerry was worse than he said. Just awful. A heroin addict, for one thing. Which it seems to me I must've known before we went South, but it somehow . . . slipped my mind. Or something." She felt Merriwether's hand on her shoulder, reached up to touch it, take it. "And when my money ran out, there were all kinds of . . . other women and . . . everything. I came home—I was stringing for AP to bring in some money—and I came home one day and found this woman in bed with him . . . right there in bed with him. We had a hellacious fight. He yelled; I cried."

"And that was when you came back to the paper."

She didn't answer—couldn't. She had punished herself past the limit and had to fight off tears.

Merriwether went on: "And they sent you up to the new Auburn bureau to work with Shank. And that was when you worked on the Hemlock Cathedral piece. I see now."

"Randall really went to the wall to get me my job back. They were pretty pissed at me for quitting in the first place."

"And that was when you came up with your . . . theory about the sheriff. Was it?"

"Uh-huh." She swiped at the edge of her eyes. The lake, the forest, they were just a blur now. "Except . . ." she said. "Except all of that happened a year later."

There was a beat. Then: "A year? I don't . . . What do you mean, a year?"

"I mean I stayed with him," Sally whispered. "With Jerry. I stayed with him for almost a year."

"After he cheated on you like that?"

"Yes." Merriwether was silent—frowning, she imagined; sitting behind her and frowning with disapproval, silently asking himself why

. . . "After he cheated on me a lot. After a lot of things. I stayed. I stayed with him." And still he just sat behind her like a log, probably staring at her, probably speechless with horror. Thank heavens the wind rose and the trees started racketing again so she didn't have to listen to his steady breathing anymore or feel his judgment on her or wait for him to . . .

"He hit me, Sidney," she said softly. Her voice broke: She had never told anyone. "He used to hit me."

Merriwether took her by the shoulders. He drew her back. She saw his smooth and marble face above her.

"Don't," she said. "Don't look at me. I'm so ugly when I cry. I hate it, stop. . . ."

He did stop. For a second. He paused in the act of laying her down, his eyes uncertain. But then, finally, he came through. Laying her back on the blanket despite her protests, murmuring to her so gently she thought it would break her heart; kissing her cheek though she turned her face away; drinking her tears—and getting hard again too; Jesus, he was so young.

She looked up at him, nose to his nose. She snuffled.

"Well, to hell with the saxophone player," he whispered. "I'm taking all his records back first thing tomorrow." Sally laughed. "Except that really good one with 'My Blue Heaven' on it . . . All right, all right, that one too." He kissed her lips softly. "Just one question? Can I ask one question?"

"You sound like Rumplemeyer."

"Just one question."

"All right. What is it then?"

"Did you come with him the way you come with me?"

"Sidney!"

"It's all right, it's not personal. I'm taking a survey."

She looked up, studied his face, each part of it. "What if I say yes?"

"Then you don't go on to the lightning round."

She kissed him. "No. I didn't."

He began pushing up her skirt again, and she watched his face as he did it. Trailed her fingers over his cheek, felt the soft stubble of his beard. She tugged him down until her lips were pressed against his ear. "I thought he was the only chance I'd ever have," she said.

He was inside her again, covering her, kissing her, brushing back her hair and basically basically, yeah—she would do anything she had to do.

2

At three the next afternoon, Dolittle stood alone in the Tahitian Lounge at the top of Dutchman's Mountain. He leaned against the end of the long bar. He lifted a brandy snifter to his lips and sipped the sting off the rim of it. With a small breath, he lowered the glass again and swirled the brandy impatiently.

The place was dead empty except for him and the bartender at the bar's other end. The Dutchman was the county's only ski resort and there was never much business here before the winter. The emptiness made the place look cheap. Imitation thatch sticking out from under the eaves, phony torches flickering on the wall, wooden island gods in every nook and cranny and, in honor of Halloween, a cardboard jack-o'-lantern taped to one of the windows and a couple of cardboard black cats as well. The whole place just felt cheap and wrong.

Dolittle glanced at his watch. It was 3:03. He glanced back along the bar toward the front of the room and the front door. He didn't have time for this. Standing here. Drinking in the middle of the day. With Halloween tomorrow, the kids would be out in full force starting trouble. He had to get back to the department in time to go over the duty rosters and the patrol maps, and make sure all the investigators were on call and oversee statements to the press and so on. It was one of the busiest nights of the year . . . And it fell just one week before the election too.

He raised his glass, tipped back a whole half of the snifter, felt it burning in him, coughed thickly. It made his lungs feel a little better at least. Cleared the congestion out of them. He set the glass on the bar.

Tapping his fingers against the wood, he looked out through the wall of windows. Past the Dutchman's curling peak, he could see his own mountain, Wapataugh, and its whole rolling range. He could look straight down over the tops of the trees in the Hickory Pine Forest. He could see the brown tonsure of open ground that marked the Hemlock Cathedral.

One week, he thought. *Just one more week.*

He heard the door open behind him. He turned and saw Ralph Jones come in.

The fat man trundled casually down the length of the bar. His jeans were blown up like a balloon and his plain woolen farmer's shirt was stretched tight over his belly. He waved to the barkeep as he went past.

"A Bud would be great there, friend. Yup, yup, yup," he said.

He stood in front of Dolittle, blinking behind those big glasses. For a moment, Dolittle thought Jones would offer him his pudgy hand.

But the big flaccid face just screwed itself up into a wink and Jones said simply, "Cy." And then turned to face the bar.

His great belly pressed against the wood, his elbows rested on it, his foot rested on the rail. The bartender slapped a foaming glass of beer down in front of him. Jones nodded.

"Thanks, thanks, thanks," he said with a sigh. He lifted the glass and slurped in the foam.

"Ahhh," he said. Shook his head. "That's good beer. That's good beer."

Dolittle very nearly laughed. "Come on, Ralph, cut the shit," he said. "You wanted to talk to me."

"Yeah. Yeah. Yeah, yeah, yeah." He took another sip and then turned away from the bar. One hand in his jeans pocket, one wrapped around his glass, he moseyed over to the window. "Wanted to talk to you," he muttered with a sigh. And he stood there, staring out at the view. At the forest. At the dark brown circle of open ground.

"How far you planning to take this thing, Cy?" he said finally. The hand in his pocket began to shake the keys in there: jingle, jingle, jingle. One corner of Dolittle's mouth lifted. That sound, those keys:

262

That was always a sure sign that Jones was thinking politics, plotting strategy. Dolittle just watched his back. The fat man would get around to the point sooner or later.

Step by step, Jones waddled around until he was facing him again. "Thing is, thing is, Cy," he said. "I got this call, this call from Chris Shea over there at the *Champion.* Yup. Yup. Right over there at the *Champion* he was. Got a call from him. Asked me—you know what he asked me?"

Dolittle sipped his brandy. "No."

"He asked me why I'd gone and approved your rezoning plan after I said it was bad for the county. He said Purdy was making some kind of a fuss about it."

"What?"

"Yup. That's what he said. That's what he said, Cy. He said Purdy's been after him for weeks about it."

It was a moment before Dolittle could answer. The surprise and the rage hit him that hard. Purdy had gone off on his own, gone off to the press on his own. *I'll kill him,* Dolittle thought, stone-faced. *I'll squeeze his balls till his eyes fucking explode.*

"Ach," he said finally out loud. "You know the press. It's bullshit."

"Well. Well. I'll tellya. I'll tellya. There's a lotta bullshit over there, no doubt, nosir. Lotta bullshit with Sally and whatnot. But that Chris, that Shea, he's a good guy, a straight guy. He wouldn't tell me Purdy'd said it, he wouldn't just make that up out of his head." Jones shook his big square face solemnly, shivering his dewlaps.

Dolittle had to fight down his anger. He felt his chest tightening. He tried to breathe and coughed a little. All the same, he tilted his head to one side and smiled, crinkling his eyes. "Well," he drawled softly. "Purdy is Purdy."

And Jones said, "Nope. Nope-nope-nope-nope." He tipped his beer glass at him. "Purdy's not Purdy. Purdy's you, Cy. That's who Purdy is." The hand worked the keys in his pocket: jingle, jingle, jingle. "You came to me, came to me, you said, Ralphie, you said, Ralphie, I want to coordinate the town master plans so the county can develop as a whole. Don't gotta say nothing, don't gotta give up your rural-county stance. Just gotta let the planning board do their thing, stay out of the way. Isn't that right? Showed me the map you wanted. Isn't that right?"

The sheriff lifted his snifter and took a breath of it, trying to clear the cloud from his lungs, trying to stay cool. He could feel the sweat gathering on his forehead.

"You must've liked that map pretty good, Ralphie-boy," he said. "A little too much, it turned out."

At that, Jones came thumping back to the bar, good and steamed. Set the beer glass down hard. Blinked furiously behind those glasses.

"You think I don't know what Purdy's up to here, Cy? Heck, Billy Thimble was already hitting me up for—for hush money or whatever you wanna call it."

Dolittle snorted, trying to look as if he'd known that all along.

"Sure, he was always weaseling around me, Thimble was, trying to get more, trying to get extra. For his drugs, I guess. Shoot, I wouldna paid him either if I'd figured he'd go to you anyway."

"Well, don't be too hard on him," Dolittle said. "He didn't exactly come to me. He was busted for possession with intent to sell. He struck a bargain with me to keep out of jail."

"Yeah. Yeah, I figured it was some setup like that."

A long breath rippled through Jones's jowls. The jingle of his keys stopped. He took his hand out of his pocket and laid it on the enormous expanse of his belly. "Well. I guess I just wanted to ask you to your face," he said. "I wanted to ask you: You gonna push this to the limit? You gonna put this in the paper? We got seven days to the election, just exactly seven days. You gonna scandal me, Cy? I wanted to ask you."

Dolittle didn't answer him. Go ask fucking Purdy, he wanted to say; he seems to be running his own fucking campaign. But he didn't say it. He didn't say anything.

"Okay," said Jones after another moment. He wrestled a money clip out of his tight pants. Slapped a bill down on the bar. He walked past Dolittle, stumping toward the door.

Then he stopped, though. He stopped and turned around. The slack flesh of his face furrowed as he narrowed his eyes behind the thick lenses.

"Thing is," he said. "Thing is, I wantcha to know: If I do read about this in the papers, I may just go over there myself, over to the *Champion*. I may just go on over and talk to Sally Dawes myself. Ask her: How convenient is it that Billy Thimble turned up dead when he did? Who's the one to benefit from that? Who benefits most? I might just ask her that, Cyrus. It might just get her thinking."

Dolittle's soft rasp became a growl in his throat. He felt the hot pulse of his anger in him, like his heartbeat, uncontrollable. "You were always good at talking to Dawes, Ralph. That seems to be something you do real well."

"I'm just telling you, Cy. We're not kids anymore. You can't just take me."

"I can take you," Dolittle said. He was trembling now. "I could always take you."

Jones pointed a fat finger at him. "Just shut your boy up, Cy. Shut Purdy up but good."

He turned and waddled out of the bar.

Oh, I'll shut him up, all right, Dolittle thought. He pulled his Caddy into the courthouse parking lot with a screech of tires. *That stupid son of a whore. I'll nail him shut.*

What the fuck had Purdy been thinking about? Opening his mouth like that. Going to Shea behind his back. One week before the fucking election. One last, stupid week. Did he think Dolittle was losing his grip? Or that he wasn't tough enough to use the information he had? Or did he think the sheriff was breathing so bad, he'd better plan for his own future, a future without the sheriff's protection? Was that it? What the fuck was he thinking of? Putting Dolittle in this position. Making it so Ralph Jones could come right up to him, tell him off like that, threaten him like that:

I may just go and talk to Sally Dawes myself. It may just get her thinking.

Dolittle stepped out of the car. Slammed the door behind him. Strode across the parking lot quickly, coughing lightly with every step.

You try to do a thing, he thought. Just a thing that you believe in. Not a clean thing maybe, not a pure thing, nothing's pure. But you take on a decent business, if you can, a job for the good of your territory, your

265

little piece of the world, whatever it is. And you do your job day by day, every day you do it, making your choices. And they just sit there. They just sit there, waiting for you. People in rooms. People in closed rooms whispering one to the other. They sit there, waiting for you to make your move. Your big move, your last move to finish the job. They sit and sit there, holding your work up to their desk lamps. Turning it this way and that until the light catches the dirt on it, until they can show the dirt to everyone. Look there. This is a dirty man. Telling everyone. People in rooms who never did anything. Day after day. Saying those things about you, until sometimes you looked back at your life, your own life, and you didn't know whether it was what it was or what they said it was. You didn't know anymore whether to be proud or to be ashamed. And that ruined it, ruined everything.

Dolittle reached the front of the courthouse. He marched up the stairs between the columns. He went in through the doors.

The deputies and secretaries scattered in front of him as he steam-rolled down the hall, his long legs taking long strides. They ran into offices. They bowed their heads over their desks.

Purdy, he thought. Purdy and Benoit too. My life's work threatened by those two. Bozo and Godzilla. One of them playing footsie with the press behind my back, the other trying to beat up a reporter in his own goddamned parking lot. . . .

He pushed into his office and slammed the door behind him. He stepped to his desk. Snatched up the phone.

"Sheriff."

Dolittle paused only a second when he saw Undersheriff Benoit leaning against the wall there. The arrogant, ambitious, marked-for-vengeance son of a bitch. The sheriff practically snarled, putting the phone to his ear.

Benoit leaned against the wall like one of the goddamn juveniles at the train track. Leg bent back, foot braced against the wall. Same arrogant smile as a punk kid.

Dolittle started punching the buttons with his finger. He was calling Purdy's office. "What the fuck are you doing in here?" he said.

Benoit smiled even a little more. "Well, I thought I'd tell you something. There's something I thought you might want to know."

"Shouldn't you be overseeing Halloween, Undersheriff?"

Benoit ignored the question and went on. "You know that thing that happened out in the *Champion* parking lot? With Dawes and the other guy coming out of the office?"

"Yeah, I know." The sheriff punched the last number hard. "Another brilliant Benoit operation. I know all about it."

"Yeah, well the reason we didn't figure they were in there, see, was cause the lights were out. Right?"

Benoit kept smiling. Dolittle wanted to knock his head against the wall. He didn't even answer. He stood listening as Purdy's phone began to ring.

"So I started thinking," Benoit said.

"Real bad idea, Henry."

"I had O'Hara follow up on it. It's just what I figured it was."

The phone rang again. The sheriff rapped the desk impatiently.

"Dawes and that guy, that Merriwether guy, the one with the colored wife? Him and Dawes are out in the woods practically every night. They're banging each other's brains out out in the woods every night. See? That's why the lights were out in there. They're banging each other."

The ringing stopped. Purdy's secretary came on the line: "Supervisor's Office."

But Dolittle had lowered the phone from his ear. He was holding it down by his neck. He was just holding it and staring at Benoit.

"What?" he said.

"I'm telling you," Benoit answered in a stage whisper. "They're fucking each other's brains out, the two of them. I mean, maybe we could use that."

"Hello?" said the secretary.

"Maybe we could use that somehow," Benoit said.

Dolittle laid the phone down softly in its cradle.

3

The sunlight was turning orange when Emily Merriwether ran out of words. It came in from the window behind her as she sat at her desk, her fingers rattling over the computer keyboard.

She typed, and the words blinked on in amber in the fathomless gray monitor:

"If author-ity itself becomes suspect, if its illusion, that is, can't be preserved in the face of understanding that it *is* an illusion, if, in effect, the impulse toward scandal, the urge to unearth the human center, so topples the icon of utterance that utterance becomes impossible, then . . . yyyyyyyyyyyyyy," she typed suddenly. "Why do we have to know? Everything. All the time. Do we have to? Some things can be secret, there can be secret things and if not, then . . ."

That was as far as she got. Her racing hands just froze suddenly. The amber cursor pulsed at her from the screen—pulsed, pulsed—but would not move again. And as she gazed at it, that "then . . ." that uncompleted—uncompletable—resolution of the condition seemed to sit atop her thoughts like an anvil. Not only could she not come up with the next word, but she knew—with a terrible, hollow panic— knew that she *would* not come up with the next word. That the passion to do it had failed her. That she did not even care.

So complete, in fact, was her indifference, that it thoroughly surprised her when, bowing her head and throwing her hands up over her face, she burst into a fit of uncontrollable weeping.

Later, she went out into the yard. It was early evening now. The sun just down behind the western hills. The sky still blue. The air cool and brittle. She had to hug her sweater closed around her as she stood in the cold grass, scanning the scene. It was very quiet. Barely a bird singing in the hickories. Barely a cricket in the wide field, which was violet with asters now. Off in the far hills, the pastels had developed great brown gaps where the leaves were falling. It was Halloween, Emily realized.

She looked down the dirt path to the gate. She wished some kids would come in their costumes—she had bought some chocolate bars for them when she did the shopping Monday. But there was no one; the cottage was too far from the road.

Her eyes moved on. At the rim of the big yard, she saw her garden: pale green, colorless really; weeds growing, spiraling out of a carpet of brown leaves. Emily looked at it a long time, sadly. Inside the house, she could hear the phone ringing. After a while, the sound made her grimace and close her eyes. He was calling to say he would be late again. She knew it. She wouldn't answer.

She went to bed at nine. She did that a lot these days. She didn't like to, but she couldn't seem to help it. She just got so tired so early—and frequently slept until her husband got up at eight the next morning. Just lonely, that's all. Depressed. She had to get out, make some friends, not depend on Sidney so much. Probably why her thesis dried up like that, working on it all the time, too much. And with Sidney working so hard on this trial now, staying so late night after night . . .

She opened her eyes, and he was there. The familiar hiss of the shower behind the bathroom door. She must have dozed. What time was it? Only eleven by the bedside clock. The hiss stopped. The bathroom door snapped open. He stepped out and she could see him, through the bedroom doorway, in the light of the living room. Naked, slim, white as snow. Still drying himself, wringing out his long hair. He turned the light off and padded toward her in the dark. She could make out his figure, a shadow, standing above her bed.

"Are you having an affair?" she asked him.

He laughed. "What are you doing awake?"

"Worrying that you're having an affair."

"Oh."

"Are you?"

"Several. I'm working my way through the female members of the jury."

She smiled up at him in the dark. "Sid-ney."

"Sweet-heart. I'm covering a murder trial. When exactly do I have time to have an affair?"

She felt the mattress sag under his weight as he sat down beside her. He laid his hand on her hair. She reached up and took hold of it, brought it to her lips, kissed it. It smelled of soap and water. "I don't know. You come home so late."

"Right." With a weary sigh, he lay down next to her. "I'm turning eight hours of testimony into a thin column of type every day. And doing it as slowly as only I can."

She put her head on his chest. Nestled against him. Closed her eyes and breathed in the scent of him as he stroked her hair. "Your heart is beating so hard."

"Is it?"

She lay and listened; the pounding slowed. "I can't write at all anymore," she said.

"What do you mean? Why not?"

"I don't know. I was doing the chapter about Blake today, all that stuff about Milton being afraid to declare his true poet's allegiance to hell. . . ."

"That Blake. What a kidder."

She rapped him on the chest. "It's not funny."

"Ow."

"It just got—I don't know—so complicated and I . . . I just didn't care anymore."

He held her closely, hand on her shoulder, and she bit her lip, hiding away in his body heat. She felt that she was lying to him, not telling him about how she had cried. . . .

"It'll pass," he said. "Look at Milton himself—he was blind, and he never let that stop him. Jolly old Milton, they used to call him. Blind as a bat, happy as a fool."

She laughed. "Sidney."

"Jaunty as a june bug, crazy as a loon."

"Stop. It's serious."

"It's not. How can you say you don't care about your doctorate?"

"Why should I care about it? You don't." It came out of her that quickly—she could hardly believe she had said it. Immediately, she played cute—toyed with his chest, pouted. "All you care about is that dumb trial."

He cleared his throat. "Ahem." Rolled over so that she was under him. Pressed close, his breath flowing down over her. "Is that right?" he said.

She kept toying with his chest. "That's all you talk about. Your dumb murderer friend. I don't see what's so interesting about a dumb murderer."

"Mm." He kissed her. "What's that got to do with your doctorate?"

Emily tilted her chin up at him defiantly. "Because I only care about what you care about."

"Ah. Of course. How silly of me." He kissed her throat. She stretched beneath him.

"And that's why you can't have an affair," she said.

"Oh really?" He kissed her lips hard. He was hard against her. "Why's that?"

She held the kiss as long as she could. Glad for the dark, glad he couldn't see her eyes. "Because if you stop caring about me," she said hoarsely, "then I'll die."

SIXTEEN

The Scotti Trial
Part Three:
Undersheriff Benoit

THURSDAY, NOVEMBER 1

WELL! THOUGHT SIDNEY Merriwether, *I am a miserable piece of human horseshit.*

He sat in the second pew. His pen worked across the page. He wrote without thinking. Undersheriff Benoit was on the stand.

The undersheriff, husky, round-headed, granite-cheeked, moved his sharp black eyes over the room. Hands folded in his lap. Big shoulders hunched forward. Absolutely horrible jacket—some sort of gayly elaborate plaid. All county officialdom needed a new tailor, as far as Merriwether was concerned.

"Uh, after we entered the house on Sheep Pasture Road," Benoit said, "we proceeded to the room upstairs. We knocked on the door."

"And what, if anything, happened then?" asked Stern.

Benoit shifted his shoulders under the plaid. "At the first knocking on the door, I announced that we were police officers and requested that they, the people inside, open up."

"And what, if anything, happened then?"

"Um, then, there was a gunshot. A bullet came through the door narrowly missing myself and the other officers. We, uh, hid, you

272

know, behind the wall. And we could hear, like, movements inside the room that I took to be people scrambling around. That's when I determined that we should enter."

"And did you enter at that time with the other officers?"

"Yes, I did."

"And what did you see?"

"Well, it was all confusion. There was a lot of confusion. Everybody was running around every which way. At the time, my attention was occupied by one man because he in particular was firing a gun at me."

"And did you at some point come to identify this individual?"

"Yes, we came to identify this individual as Theodore Wocek."

Stern moved to the evidence table in front of the judge's bench. "Do you recognize this gun?" He held up a small, blocky, silver-handled pistol. An identification tag dangled from the trigger guard.

"Yes, sir," said Benoit. "That's Mr. Wocek's gun."

"And he fired this gun at you?"

"Yes, sir."

"And what happened then?"

"Well, then, as I say, there was a lot of confusion. One of the suspects, Vincent Scotti, was trying to escape through a window. And another one, Mr. John Barnes, had put his hands up to surrender. But at that particular moment, like I said, Mr. Wocek was firing in my direction. So at that time I opened return fire upon him, uh, resulting in his death."

his death . . . wrote Merriwether blandly in his notebook.

He thought, *I am a husband from hell.*

He wished he were more like Vince Scotti, actually.

He strode angrily along the sidewalk by the lake. He kicked through the fallen leaves lying on the concrete. They swirled up into the cool air. Tumbled down again on either side of him. He strode on.

It was lunch hour now but he hadn't eaten. The thought of going to the Courthouse Restaurant was almost intolerable. The lawyers would be there. The cops. Even Scotti himself. All eating their hamburgers and french fries. Sitting a table away from each other. Even

Sally might be there. She came by sometimes looking to have lunch with him. . . . The thought of it. The thought of her . . .

I thought I'd never have another chance at love, Sidney.

Jesus. He preferred to go hungry.

He laughed bitterly as he kicked along. He passed half-aware under the flaming orange of a maple tree. A sign was strung around the waist of the tree, tied there like an apron: VOTE FOR PURDY, TUESDAY, NOVEMBER 6. The water to his right glittered gunmetal blue in the noon sun. He wished he was more like Vince Scotti. That's all there was to it.

Just *look* at Scotti, he thought. Just *look* at him. The way he just *sits* there. Sleepy-eyed—*sneering*, for God's sake. Like the black hat in a silent movie. And why not? If you're going to play the villain, you might as well put some spirit into it, right? Throw it back in the faces of the police. The witnesses. The jury. Christ, especially the jury. Frowning down at him. Judging him. Lowering over him with their . . . plebeian morality.

And what was a jury, after all, but one Joe Doakes after another? A mechanic after a librarian after a retired supermarket manager? The sort of people one *tipped* on a particularly friendly day. And there they were: *judging* him with their dull stares, their slurry flews, their thick hands settled in their laps like cement, spinster squints bugging out at the dirty thrill of him like lobstery peduncles, mean, stupid, scandalized faces scrunched like crumpled thumbprints in the intensity of their disapproval, the Twelve Crumpled Thumbprints of the Bourgeoisie, that's what they were, suckers for cops and confessions and crying wives. . . .

Merriwether stopped, out of breath. Moved to the edge of the sidewalk and gazed blindly out at the shivering water. Shoved his hands in his pockets. Shook his head.

And just look at Scotti, he thought. How he just *slouched* there. How he just *sneered*. Pulling off his villainy with more élan than any of them had ever brought to their so-called decency. And he was accused of *murder*, for Christ's sake? Murder!

And what was he—what was Merriwether—accused of? A little adultery? A little dabbling in the woods? Why should he squirm in torment? Why should he play the flagellant? Why should he take it out on himself? He should be more like Scotti. That's all. That's all there was to it.

He snorted. Pulled out his cigarettes. Shot one into his mouth and fired it up. Blew smoke out at the lake, at the far shore, the small pines there showing beryl now through the naked branches of the other trees . . .

He cocked his eyebrow at them. He sneered boldly. He thought of Emily. . . .

If you stop caring about me, I'll just die.

"Shit!" he said. He tossed his cigarette into the grass.

The Husband from Hell.

He returned to the courtroom early. Strolled sullenly across the empty anteroom, an unlit cigarette dangling between his lips. He pushed into the bathroom, stood at the urinal, pissed. When he was done, he went to the sink and washed his hands. He brushed a lock of golden hair out of his eyes with his fingers. He reached into his shirt pocket for a match. . . .

Whereupon there came from the stall behind him an absolute explosion of flatulence—a thunderous fart—followed by the pitter-patter of little pieces of shit hitting toilet water. On the instant, the room was filled with a stench of human waste so powerful that Merriwether reeled.

"Hey, Face," came the dull voice from behind the stall door. "That's what I think of today's testimony."

Merriwether burst out laughing. "Ah, Vince, always the *mot juste.*" He lit the cigarette and spread the smoke around him: Scotti was letting off a series of smaller reports, and the smell was appalling.

"Just remember . . . uh . . . this," Scotti grunted. "Benoit and Barnes, Stern, Dolittle—" His voice was strained on the last word. "They're all the same guy, they're all, like, just the same, full of . . ." There was another small splash. "Shit," he concluded with a heavy sigh.

"You mean the part about Wocek firing on them." Merriwether shook his head, trying to clear the fumes out of it.

"Hell, yes," Scotti said from behind the stall. "I mean, what? Three fucking cops come in there like a fucking locomotive, you think

anyone's gonna fucking shoot at them? Wocek and Barnes were piss-
ing their pants, they were so fucking scared. Had their hands in the
air. Benoit just fucking blew that boy away."

Merriwether tried to draw on his cigarette—and nearly gagged on
the room's smell. "You saw all this while you were going out the
window, I take it."

There was shifting within the stall. The tearing of paper. "Fuck,
yes. Read your own newspaper, Face. The only person who fired on
anybody is the cops. And the other . . . " The rest of the sentence was
washed away by the sudden blast of rushing water. When it subsided,
Merriwether heard Scotti buckling his belt. "And Johnny Barnes is
just the same," he was saying. "Wait'll you hear his so-called confession. Every word is garbage, Face. He's covering for the cops. He's
gonna try to make it look like Wocek was this big-time gangster. So
Barnes gets off for murder, and the sheriff gets off for shooting Wocek.
Everybody's happy. The only thing is: Teddy wasn't even there when
Billy Thimble got done. See? He wasn't even there in the first place."

The bolt of the stall door shot back. The door swung in. The
stench wafted out, and Scotti stepped out with it, his cane clomping
on the tiles. He stopped in the doorway, regarded Merriwether through
eyes almost cataracted with disdain.

"What?" he said. "What're you looking at?"

"How do you know, Vince?" Merriwether asked him. "How do
you know whether Wocek was there or not?"

Scotti smiled. "Hey, can I tell you something? Off the record this
time?"

Merriwether nodded.

"No, I'm serious," said Scotti. "Off the record. Because this is
something very personal to me, and I don't want it in the paper like
that stuff you wrote about my wife and kid and everything."

"All right," said Merriwether.

"Word of honor."

"Yes, yes, of course."

"I'm guilty," Scotti said. He came forward, chasing Merriwether
from before the sink, bending to it to wash his hands. "Now fuck you,"
he said.

SEVENTEEN

Christopher Shea Discovers the Hickory Kingdom

MONDAY, NOVEMBER 5

ON THE DAY before the election, Christopher Shea was at the county office building by 9:00 A.M. It was a small concrete block of a place, a few pilasters carved into the face of it so it wouldn't look blank and odd beside the old courthouse. Shea was on the front steps when the county clerk, Margaret Mulligan, unlocked the glass door.

She pushed it out and held it open for him.

"Hey, Chris," she said. "How you doin?"

"Fine, Margaret," Shea said. He slipped inside.

"How's your mom?"

"She's fine. How's everything at your house?"

"Oh good. Fine."

She let the door whisper shut. Shea felt a pang of regret for the clear, sweet, cool blue autumn sky he was leaving behind him. For the softly colored trees around Lake Tyler. For the reflection of the leaves painted on the lakewater. It was going to be hours before he saw them again. He sighed and lumbered down the hall wearily.

This, he thought, *is going to take fucking forever.*

*   *   *

He'd been up all night. Just lying on his side in the dark. Or rolling over to lie on his other side sometimes. Sometimes he'd snuggle up against his wife, Rosie, but he had to stop that because her nightgown had ridden up on her hip, and the touch of her bare backside just got him going. It was a bad time of month for that, even if he'd been willing to wake her up. Another kid right now and he'd have to go into his father's contracting business.

So he lay on his back some more and thought about baseball. Wondering who the Mets would trade over the winter. Trying to name the team's entire roster. Then, soon, he was not thinking about baseball anymore, but about the sheriff again and Purdy and Jones and the election on Tuesday, just one day away.

When the baby emitted a soft little syllable of complaint from the next room, Shea was up like a shot.

"I'll get it."

His wife had not even stirred.

Gratefully, Shea took the kid out of her crib and began to carry her back and forth across the dark nursery. It made him feel better. To have the little thing cradled in his great arms, to pace the floor with her, to sing to her in his toneless murmur. The only creature on earth that would ever listen to him sing with that kind of rapture. Or any kind of rapture, or any kind of pleasure. He was glad for the company and for something to do.

Finally, Rosie spoiled the party. She came to the doorway, clutching her nightgown shut and squinting at him. "Is she all right?"

Shea had to admit that the baby was fine, that it was the baby, in fact, who was rocking the father. Rosie came to him and dug the child out of his arms. The hulking red-haired man stood on the braid rug under the Mickey Mouse mobile, tugging at his nose, bereft, as she set the kid back in her crib.

"Why are you still awake?" Rosie asked him when they were in bed again.

"I've been thinking. I've been thinking about quitting my job."

"Again?"

"I can't work with these people, Rosie. It's, like, all a game to them. They don't live here, they don't care what happens. It's not a community to them, it's just . . . some kind of staging ground for their goddamned sophisticated lives."

"Oh, Chris," said Rosie sleepily. She had closed her eyes.

"It is. It is," Shea whispered. "I mean, Rumplemeyer wants to start trouble so he can get good clips to show *The New York Times*. Merriwether wants to start trouble so Sally'll put out for him. And Sally wants to start trouble because . . . she's got nothing better to think about, she needs a goddamned husband, that's why."

"Well . . ." Rosie's voice had dropped to a distant murmur. "Why can't you just ignore them? Why can't you just do your job?"

"How can I do my job? How can I do my job? Whatever I do, they're gonna use it. They're gonna make it part of their grand scheme."

Rosie's head tilted to one side. She shook it, opening her eyes for a second. "You mean, you're afraid to do your job because you might find something that helps them?"

"No. No, that's not it," Shea said, annoyed. Then he fell silent. He stared through the darkness, to the place where his daughter's night light gleamed. "Yes," he said softly. "Yeah. That is right."

Rosie snored beside him.

So here he was, first thing in the morning. In the County Office Building. In the records room on the ground floor. With one day left before the voting started. There were no windows here. The place—a small room just off the clerk's office—was a dark maze of short corridors formed by the tall shelves and the broad reading tables. The shelves were filled with huge record books lying on rollers, lying on their side so that the gray-white bindings showed. Shea went to the shelves with the bindings marked "Deeds."

He had brought the new master plan for the town of Hickory with him, though he knew it pretty well by heart. He knew, for instance, that the new commercial corridor would be almost entirely adjacent to Highway 17. County Highway 17: Hickory Kingdom Road. That meant, Shea realized, that almost all the development in that area would be subject to the approval of the county planning director, an appointee of the county executive. That Jones, in other words, who already controlled the town planning board, which also had a heavy say, would, if he beat Purdy to the executive post, have almost absolute control over the development of the town.

This, as Shea knew, was no small thing. The pol who controls development can tip his friends off to which land to buy. The land can be bought cheap and then instantly resold for many times the price when the development plans become public. As an advanced form of patronage it provided plenty of money for loyal friends and plenty of power for the guy in charge. Especially in a town like Hickory, with so much land still lying untouched.

What Shea wanted to know, then, was who'd been buying up the rezoned land.

The deed books were in chronological order, so Shea had to guess at a year. He guessed two years before the master plan was approved. Rolled the first book off the shelf and dragged it—it weighed a ton—to the table. He sat on a stool, wishing for a cigarette. He drew the huge cover back, fanning the big pages over one by one. Photocopied deeds. He leaned down to study them. The way they were written made it practically impossible to figure out what land they referred to: "Ten acres two steps east of Earl's potato patch running to the border of Aunt May's old refrigerator has now become the property . . ."

"Cripes," he whispered, turning page after page.

It took him forty-five minutes—three books—to find the first parcel. Ten acres of wildflower fields right up by Merriwether's cottage. A concern called Country Acres had bought it three years ago.

"Country Acres," said Shea.

Hoisting himself down off the stool, he went back to the shelves. To the smaller books this time, the ones marked "Names." These were incorporation papers, listing the names of local companies when they were newly created or when their names were changed. They also told the names of the companies' principal owners. The books were listed alphabetically here, which made it easy to find Country Acres. Easy to find the names of its owners. There was John Feller, an acquaintance of Shea's father who owned the miniature golf course up on Route 20. Richard Avery, the landlord to most of the stores by the Hickory train tracks.

And—you guessed it, folks—there was the Great One himself—Ralphie "I Am a Greedy Guy" Jones.

At the sight of the name, Shea smirked and shook his head. He'd been expecting as much, but all the same his heart was beating pretty hard as he got up again and returned to the books of deeds.

Another thirty minutes, and he had found another parcel. Six acres near the train tracks. Who owned it? Country Acres. Ten minutes more and he found another: five Country Acres at the curve at the base of Merriwether's hill. All of them were bought before the master plan was announced to the public—but obviously after the sheriff had shown it to Jones.

Talk about a Hickory Kingdom, thought Shea. Ralph Jones didn't want to be elected: He wanted to be crowned.

There were other people around him in the room now. Two or three guys from the law offices wandering past the shelves, sliding out the books. All the same, Shea chuckled out loud when he thought of the look on Rumplemeyer's face when he brought him this little tidbit. Here election day was tomorrow, and Rumple the Mad was practically frantic to find Cindy Dolittle and prove that the sheriff was running some kind of Evil Empire over there at the courthouse. And now, Shea had a little piece of *proven* information—ready to run today—that could easily cost Jones the election even if it only made the paper tomorrow morning.

Shea went into the clerk's office and pleaded with Margaret Mulligan to give him some change—which she did, for his mother's sake. He then dragged his deed books to the ancient Xerox machine in the corner. He started the old thing sliding back and forth—*ka-chunk, ka-chunk*—running off one copy of each deed.

But what about the sheriff? he thought as he watched the machine work. Why hadn't he wanted Purdy to let this stuff get out? Obviously, either he'd given Jones the go-ahead to buy up the land in order to get his approval for the rezoning. Or else he was just afraid it would look that way if it got into the newspaper. Still, all in all, the information was far more likely to hurt Jones than Purdy. Shea thought the sheriff was likely to come up a winner when the truth got out.

The machine was done. Shea gathered his copies together. He

patted them into a pile. He ran his eyes quickly over the top sheet one more time.

And that's when he noticed it. The name signed at the bottom of the deed. The lawyer who'd worked out the deal, worked up the deed, signed it as the representative of Country Acres.

Shea's face went pale as he laid the sheets down on the table and began going through them one by one.

There it was. There it was. The same name was on every deed. The same guy had handled all of Country Acres' land dealings.

"What the hell does that mean?" Shea whispered.

The name was William Thimble.

EIGHTEEN

The Scotti Trial
Part Four: John Barnes

MONDAY, NOVEMBER 5

"William Thimble," said John Barnes. "Yeah, I knew him pretty good. I met him, like, several times before we, you know, actually killed him."

The courtroom was full again. Reporters, lawyers, courthouse workers, old men and women with time on their hands—everyone who had vanished after the first day was back now, crowding the pews. Merriwether, in his usual seat in the second row, was practically crushed between Dog Saunders and a TV newswoman up from the city. They, like everyone, were watching Barnes.

The afternoon sun spilled through the tall, arching windows. The entire front of the court—the jury box, the counsel tables, the witness stand, the judge's bench—was spotlit by the hazy shafts of light. Barnes sat in his chair, watching the prosecutor with an attentive, childlike tilt of his head. A teenager, looking uncomfortable in a clean white shirt, a dark jacket, a dark tie. He rubbed his hands together nervously.

Stern, holding the center of the floor, boomed out his questions with great round tones—Merriwether thought he would start to roll his *R*'s in a minute. This was his star witness, after all. Neatly timed for the day before the election.

"And did you know Teddy Wocek?"

"Uh. Yeah. Yes. Yeah." Barnes's voice was flat, thick, dull. He whipped his head back to clear the shock of black hair from his forehead.

"Did you know Vincent Scotti?"

"Yeah, I knew him too."

"Can you identify Mr. Scotti in this courtroom today?"

"Uh, yes, I can identify him in this courtroom today sitting right over there behind that table next to that man."

Scotti slouched, watched sleepily; sneered.

"All right, then, Mr. Barnes," Stern went on briskly. "Could you tell us how you came to be involved with Mr. Scotti?"

"I, uh, came to be involved with Mr. Scotti," Barnes said, "because, uh, at the time, this was two years ago, I was in mechanic school, and I had been, at that time, purchasing marijuana from an acquaintance of mine when he, this acquaintance, said, you know, uh, 'Hey,' you know, 'Vince says you're a good customer. . . .' "

"Objection," O'Day murmured softly. He didn't bother to stand.

"Yes, sustained," Judge Posey said. He pinched the bridge of his nose wearily. "Uh, Mr. Barnes, don't say what people said, just what you did. Unless, uh, Mr. Scotti was actually present at the time."

Barnes looked at the judge, then back at the prosecutor. His expression never changed.

"What happened as a result of this conversation with your acquaintance?" Stern said.

"As a result of this conversation with my acquaintance, I went to Vince's, Mr. Scotti's, house," said Barnes. "And we sat around. And it was in October, I remember, because we had the series on TV. And Vince had, he had this big TV. And Vince said, you know, 'This is a fifty-inch screen I have.' And I said, 'Oh,' you know, 'that's really good, Vince.' Because it was, you know, like, really good. So we watched the game, you know, and smoked a couple joints, had a couple of beers. And then, you know, Vince said, 'This stuff,' meaning these drugs that we were smoking, he said, 'This stuff is very good.' And I said, 'Yeah, you know, it is,' because, uh, you know it was very good stuff. And Vince said, you know, 'You could make a lot of money selling this stuff to people at your mechanic school and, uh, other places.' And I said, 'Vince, what do you mean?' cause, like, I didn't know, you know, what he meant, okay? And then, Vince, he got up and went into another room, and he came back with a small suitcase he had. And he opened it and showed me it was filled with bags of marijuana."

"Objection," said O'Day, half rising this time.

"Uh . . ." Judge Posey wagged his head. "Mr. Barnes, how do you know it was marijuana?"

"Because we smoked some of it, and I sold, uh, the rest of it and, uh, no one ever complained."

A wave of laughter crested quickly in the pews, then fell away. The teenager smirked at the audience a little.

"Overruled," the judge said. "Go ahead."

"So you began selling marijuana for Mr. Scotti," Stern said. "Anything else?"

Barnes rubbed his nose. "Uh, pills, you know, cocaine sometimes. Whatever. Just to sell to my friends, you know."

"And was one of these friends Theodore Wocek?"

"Uh, yes, he was. Theodore, uh, Mr. . . . Teddy—he went to the mechanic school with me, but only sometimes, part time, like. Because he had to work."

"And did he ever sell drugs, in your experience?"

"Yes, in my experience, he did."

"And in your experience did he ever go to Mr. Scotti's house to get these drugs?"

"Yes, he, uh, he did that. In my experience."

Stern nodded once, turned aside and strolled away, turned back, strolled back. "Now you testified," he said, with a roll of his hand, "that there came a time when you became acquainted with William Thimble."

"Yeah," Barnes said. "There came a time when I became acquainted with Billy, William Thimble, when Teddy and I were at Vince's house, getting our, you know, whatever, our supplies."

"Your supplies of drugs."

"Yeah."

285

"Do you remember when this was?"

"This was, uh, I think in January because I remember we had the Super Bowl on TV. And, you know, the doorbell rang and the next thing I know Vince has got this kind of skinny, nervous guy there. Um, and Vince, uh, has, like, his arm around him and he says, Vince says, you know, like, 'This is the big real estate man Billy Thimble. He's a client of mine.' And Teddy and I said, 'Oh,' you know, 'that's really good, Vince,' or something 'cause, you know . . . And then, you know, we all sat around together and watched the game, you know, and smoked a couple of joints, had a couple of beers. And Vince said, you know, 'Billy is going to be working for me too, now.' And I said, 'Oh,' you know. And then, you know, we did some, uh, Vince brought out some cocaine to sort of, you know, celebrate. And, you know, Billy was very smiling, and sort of making jokes a lot. Vince said he was the Court Jester."

Hands clasped behind his back, the A.D.A. took another pace about, staring grimly at his shoes. "So then how would you characterize your relationship with Mr. Thimble?"

"I would characterize it as, you know, very smiling. You know. Good."

"You weren't angry at him? You weren't angry he'd cut into your business?"

"No, because, you know, I had my places to sell to and he was at other places. You know."

Nodding, the prosecutor paced. Barnes watched him. The judge on his bench leaned his round head on his palm. O'Day took notes. Scotti smiled. The jurors, hands in their laps, looked on. The audience shifted through the long silence.

"Tell us," said Stern, "what happened on the evening of July the tenth."

Barnes nodded. "Okay, you know," he said. "On that evening, I had to go and see Vince at his house. Because I had to purchase, you know, whatever. Some pills and stuff. And Vince was there with Teddy Wocek and they had the baseball game on the big TV, you know? "The Mets and the Cubs. So we all sat together a while and watched it. And so, you know, we smoked a couple of joints, had a couple of beers and, uh, pretty soon, I hear the doorbell, you know, and I think, uh, 'What's this?' And, you know, it's Billy. Billy Thimble. And Vince goes to let him in. And he comes in. And he watches the game with us for a while and, uh, he was all laughing and making jokes. So, uh, okay, you know?"

He shifted uncomfortably in his collar. Someone coughed in the back of the room. The traffic whispered at the courtroom windows. Motes floated in the rays of the sun.

"And we all sat around for a while," said John Barnes. "And, you know, we smoked a couple of joints, had a couple of beers, and pretty soon I have to get up and, uh, you know, go to the bathroom. So I do that. And I'm not thinking anything, and I come out of the uh, bathroom, and there's Vince standing right there in the door. In the hall, you know, looking at me. So, uh, okay, you know. I say, 'Vince,' you know, 'what is this?' And Vince, he says, all of a sudden, 'Go get something to use, you know, because we're going to take Billy down to the river and do him.' So I said, like 'Vince,' you know, 'what do you mean?' Because, like, I didn't know what he meant, okay? And he said, 'Get a tire iron or a baseball bat or something because, uh . . . to hit Billy with,' you know. 'We're going to take Billy down to the river and when I stop the car, you hit him, and we're going to do him.' So, uh, okay, you know. I went out into the garage, you know, and I found a tire iron that was there. And I put it in back of Vince's car."

The A.D.A. handed him a snapshot from the evidence table. "Can you identify this photograph, Mr. Barnes?" he asked.

"Uh, yes," said Barnes. "I can identify this photograph as Vince's car."

"Let the record show the witness identified exhibit J, a photograph of a navy-blue Cadillac. Go on, Mr. Barnes."

Again, the witness snapped his head to clear his hair away. Watching him from the pews, Merriwether caught himself brushing absently at his own hair.

"So, uh, okay," Barnes said again. "I went back, uh, into the living room, you know. And I sat down and watched the game some more cause I think, uh, the Mets were losing at this point. And we all sat around, you know, drinking beers and smoking joints and like that, you know. And after a while, I think it was, like, the seventh inning, Vince says, 'Hey, Billy.' And Billy says, like, 'What?' you know. And

Vince says, 'Let's go down to the river, you know, and do some of this cocaine that I've got.' And, you know, Billy, uh, you can see he wants cocaine, but he says, like, 'Why can't we do it here, Vince, and watch the game?' you know. And Vince says, you know, 'Because it'll be better at the river' or something. So Billy says, 'Okay,' you know.

"So, okay. So we go out into the car, you know. And Vince and Billy get in front and Teddy and I get in the backseat. And that's where the tire iron is on the floor, okay? And there's also a bag there, like, what you call a duffelbag, on the floor where Teddy is, you know. So it's there too. And we start to drive around, listening to the game on the radio, you know. So after a while, you know, Billy starts saying, like 'Vince, when are we going to do this cocaine?' you know. And Vince says, like, 'I want to wait until it's a little darker.' Because it's, like, already the postgame show, you know, but it isn't dark yet it's just, like, what you might call evening or something like that, you know. So, okay, so, you know, so we drive down into these, like, winding roads, you know, that go down to, like, a back way to the river, okay? And, like, Billy is being really laughing, you know, and making a lot of jokes about the baseball game. And we're all, like, laughing a lot at Billy's jokes, you know. And it's very, like, happy, everybody, in the car. So, okay. So, then, we get to this road, Shoreview Lane, you know. Which is, like, just a small road near the highway down at the river, you know. And we come to a stop sign and Vince, he, like, stops the car, okay. And he sort of, like, turns in his seat and, you know, like, looks at me. So, okay, you know, so Billy's saying, like, 'What is it, Vince? Why are we stopping the car?' 'Cause he's wondering, you know. And Vince, you know, gets all excited, and he says to me, you know, like, 'Do it now.' So okay. So, okay, so I pick up the tire iron and I hit Billy over the head with it. Only I don't do it so good because I guess, like, I'm nervous or something. So I try to hit him again only now Billy's got his hands up, you know, and he's saying, like, 'Ow, ow,' and like that, you know? And trying to get out of the car. Only Vince is, like, trying to hold him, you know, only he can't because he can't get across the, like, the seat with his bad leg, you know? And Teddy is kind of, like, bending over at this point unzipping his bag.

"So, like, Billy says, like, 'Vince, Vince, what is this?' you know?

Corruption

And he opens the door and kind of falls out. So, like, I open the door and I get out. And so does Vince and Teddy. And now I see for the first time, you know, that Teddy has a shotgun which, like, he must have taken out of his bag, you know. And he is holding it in his hands and pointing it at Billy. And Billy is like kind of out of it, you know. Just kind of walking around in the road in front of the headlights, you know, like he doesn't know where he is. Okay? And there is all blood on his head and on the side of his, like, face. And, you know, he is saying, 'Vince, Vince, what is this?' you know and, you know, like, 'Why are you doing this thing to me, Vince?' Like that, because he doesn't know, right? So, okay, you know—now Vince has gotten out of the car too, which has took him a long time because of his leg, you know. And he says to Teddy, he says, like, 'Shoot him,' you know. 'Shoot the motherfucker.' And Billy is kind of wandering around with his hands out, you know, looking, like, I don't know. And he turns to Teddy, and Teddy shoots him with the shotgun."

Barnes rubbed his nose. "So, like, okay, you know," he said. "Then, like, I saw this kind of, like, this kind of, like, wind in front of Billy's shirt, you know. And I thought, So, okay, you know. Because you could see like all of Billy's front, like, his stomach, was all opened up, you know. Like this black hole there, only with all blood all over. But Billy, like, he just kept walking around, you know? Like he's waving his hands around at us, you know, and sort of, like, reaching out for us and reaching out for Vince and saying, like, 'Vince, Vince, like, please,' you know. Like: 'Don't do this,' you know. So, like, Vince, he was, like, getting, like, you know, angry, you know, 'cause like Billy is still doing this. So I mean, like, okay, you know? So Vince went back into the car, you know, and he got out his pistol, this pistol he had from the glove compartment. Only, like, while he was in the car, you know, um, uh . . . whatsis . . . uh, Billy—Billy, he, like, finally falls down, okay? And he's, uh, like, crawling on the ground, on the street and, uh . . . Like, we can see him because he's in the headlights, all right. And now Vince has to go after him, you know, like, limping with his cane, you know, and his pistol in his other hand, you know, and Billy is trying to crawl away."

A truck's steam horn sounded on the street outside. Merri-wether—many in the audience; the jurors too—glanced up at the

289

windows a moment, then back at Barnes. The boy took a glass of water from the rail before him, sipped it, set it down with a satisfied gasp. He went on.

"Okay. So now, like, Billy can't, like, crawl so fast anymore. So Vince gets to be standing over him and pointing the pistol down at him, at his head. And Billy just, like, looks up at him, you know. From crawling. And he says, like, he just says, like, 'Vince, Vince,' you know? Like that. So Vince, like, shoots him in the head, you know. And Billy just sort of—he sort of, like, jumps with his body and then, like, falls down flat on the ground, you know, and just, like, lies there. His whole front, the whole front of his face, has sort of, like, just blown up, you . . . sort of, like, you know, a firecracker, you know, except with blood all over." Barnes spread his hands a moment to demonstrate.

"So, okay, you know. So we looked at him for a little while, and you know, Vince says to us, like, 'Okay, you know, so that's it. So let's put him in the car.' You know? So Teddy and I go over to Billy, you know. And we, like . . . Teddy takes his arms and I take his feet, and, you know, we pick him up. Only then Billy kind of, like moans, okay? So, you know, like, I say, 'Vince.' I say, 'He's still breathing.' Because, I mean, as you would think, I don't like this very much, okay? But Vince says, like, 'No. No, he's dead. Put him in the car.' Like that. So Teddy and I, we put Billy in the car, you know. Which is not an easy thing because of the many things, you know, of pushing him and pulling him from the other side. But finally we get him in there. And then Vince tells us for Teddy to get in the front seat and for I to sit in the back with Billy. And I say, you know, I say, 'Vince, why do I have to do that?' because, like, I mean, this is . . . already, I'm upset about this and this is something extra. You know? So, okay, so I get in the backseat with Billy. And he is lying across the backseat and I can see close up that he has no, like, face or anything on that part of him, his face part. And, like, his insides or what you would call his stomach is all open and there is all blood. But the only thing is, because I am sitting there, I can hear he is still making these little, like, small noises like he is breathing. Which I say to Vince, I say, you know, like, 'Vince. Billy is still alive.' Okay? And so I have to, according to

Vince, you know, sit on Billy while we're driving to the river. You know, in case Billy should still have some things he can do.

"So, okay, you know. So that's how we drive to the, uh, river. And Vince, you know, he drives the car over, like . . . there are train tracks there on top of, like, this hill, you know. And he drives the car over them, these tracks, so we are on top of the hill, you know. And we can look down at the river. So at this time, you know, it would almost be, like, night but still not all dark because we can see, like, all the river and, like, some of up in the sky, you know. So we leave Billy in the car, you know, and get out. And Vince has some, uh, beers and stuff, you know, in the trunk which he brought with also a rope and a cinder block. So he says, like, 'We have to rest,' you know, 'and wait until it is more, like darkness.' So we do this. And we sat around, you know, kind of watching the river, and we smoked a couple of joints, drank a couple of beers, and I very much enjoyed this part, you know, because we had been working so hard.

"So by then, it has gotten to be darkness and Vince says, 'So, okay, you know.' And Teddy says, like, 'Vince, what are we going to do?' you know, because, like, we don't know what is going to happen next with this. And Vince says, like, 'We are going to tie Billy up, you know, and sink him in the river. With, like, the cinder block, okay?' So, okay, you know, so that's what we do. Teddy and me, we get Billy out of the car and lie him down on, like, the grass that is on the hill, you know. And by this time, Billy is not making the breathing noises but only lying there in the grass, you know. So, okay, so Vince brings us the rope, you know, and I wrap it around Billy a few times and tie it to the cinder block, okay? Which I'm the one who's the expert in this because of I was in the Boy Scouts at an earlier time. So then Teddy and me . . . because Vince, you know, he can't come down the hill on account of his bad leg. So Vince, you know, he stands at the top of the hill, helping us with a flashlight, holding a flashlight, you know. And Teddy and me, we put the cinder block on Billy's chest, you know. Kind of balanced. And we pick him up—Teddy takes, like, his feet, and I, like, take his shoulders, you know. And we pick him up and carry him down the hill to the side of the river, okay. So, okay, so, you know, like, Vince is up on the hill holding the flashlight. And we hear him say down to us, like, you know. 'Heave him in.' Like, meaning Billy, throw Billy in the river, you know. Only this is very heavy, you know, Billy, because he has the cinder block on his chest, too. And it was very hot and I was very sweating at this time, all right? So Teddy and me, we heaved Billy into the river, only he doesn't go very far, you know. Only out a few feet from the shore so he can't sink, you know. Or, like, he sinks, but not very far, you know, because it's so shallow and you can still see him, like, just under the water, kind of, like shivery down there. So I look up the hill, you know, and I see Vince's flashlight. And I hear him say, like, 'Drag him in, drag him in,' you know. Like that, very excited because, uh, I guess he doesn't want anyone to see us doing this, you know. So I climb down into the water, you know. And I take Billy's rope and I start to drag it out, you know, further into the water, okay? And so I'm like maybe about, I don't know, up to like my legs, my thighs, in the river, okay, dragging Billy. And this is when Billy's hand takes hold of my arm, all right? I mean, like, I see him, I see his fingers kind of grab hold of my arm, like, my wrist, you know. And this is, like, the scariest thing that has ever happened in my life up to that point, okay. I mean, this is, like . . . I was so scared, I scream. And I fell down in the water. And, like, I let go of Billy, you know, and I pulled my arm away from him because he was, like, holding on to me, I thought, although Vince said this was just, like scientific, you know, because of his muscles being tight or something, you know. But I don't know this then, okay? So then, like, I could only give Billy one more shove, you know, because I was so, like, upset. And this sent him out into the water where there was a drop, you know, and he sank down finally. So I, like, at this point, just went back to the ground, like, as fast as I could. And I say to Teddy, you know, I say, 'Let's go,' you know, because I want to get out of there as fast as I can, you know, because this is, like, very upsetting to me. Only now, you know, like, Vince, up on the hill, you know, he shines his flashlight out into the river, and he says, like, 'Billy is not deep enough.' And when I look, okay? I can see, like, this sort of, like, a white thing of Billy, like what you could call his reflection, sort of, sort of floating, like, right just under the water. And I just, like, stood there, you know, and I looked up at the flashlight, you know, 'cause, like, no way am I going, like, back in the water with Billy, you know. And I say, like, 'Vince, what do we do?' you know. And Vince says, like, 'Throw rocks at him and see if he goes down,' you know. And so, okay, you know, me and Teddy start finding the biggest rocks we can find, you know. Like boulders almost, and we start throwing them at Billy until, finally, you know, he sinks down so we can't see him.

"So, okay, you know. So we climb back up the hill to where Vince is, okay. And we have to sit down from so much work, you know, because now, when I look at Vince's watch, you know, I see it is almost eleven and we have been doing this for, like, three hours already, you know. So we sit down, you know, on the hill and we sort of watch the river, you know, waiting to see if Billy is going to come back up or anything. And we smoke a couple of joints and have some beers, you know. And I remember I say to Vince, I say, 'Vince. Vince, why did we do this thing?' you know. Because I, like, don't know, okay. And Vince says, like, 'This is something we had to do. We had to do this thing,' okay? So . . ." Barnes gave a small shrug. "So okay," he said. "So, okay. You know?"

The boy's voice ceased and he stared blankly at the prosecutor. For a moment, the courtroom was quiet, and the audience and the jury stared back at him. The judge rested his head on his hand. O'Day wrote thoughtfully on his yellow pad. Vincent Scotti looked down at the counsel table, smiled wryly, shook his head. The traffic noises went on, and a few birds whistled underneath the building's eaves.

And then the judge said softly, "I think this might be a good time to break for the day."

There was one breath from everyone, and everyone rose. The jurors were led from the box by the bailiff. Barnes was led out a side door by a deputy. Merriwether stood in the crowded pew as those to his left filed out into the aisle. For a moment after the path was clear, he still stood there, holding up the progress of the people to the right of him. He stood there, watching Scotti. The dark man's shoulders shook with silent laughter.

"Come on, Fourth, move it out, it's dinnertime," Dog Saunders said.

"What?" said Merriwether. "Oh. Sorry." He moved out of the pew, into the aisle. Filed up toward the doors with the crowd.

He wanted a cigarette badly and stopped by the window to light one up. He leaned on the sill with one hand, holding his cigarette at his waist with the other, looking out over the flagpole, out over the lake, out at the trees on the far sides, the shower of their leaves in the wind.

The crowd moved to the stairwell behind him. And out of the subdued murmur of their voices came a voice at his shoulder. A soft drawl—hoarse, strained.

"Mr. Merriwether."

He turned from the window and found himself confronting a tall man with a pleasant face. A crinkled, easygoing face, with thinning hair brushed straight back and friendly crow's-feet at the corners of the eyes. The man wore sharply creased black slacks and a black vest over a white shirt.

"Sheriff Dolittle," Merriwether said.

The man nodded, smiled; even winked slightly. "I want you to do me a favor, son," he said. He sounded congested, as if he had a cold.

"Yes?" said Merriwether.

"I want you to tell your editor—Miss Dawes—that I would like to meet with her tonight at ten o'clock. All right?"

"Yes, of course," said Merriwether. "I'll be happy to."

Dolittle tipped him another wink. "Good." he said. "Tell her to meet me in the woods on the northwest side of Lake Tyler." He smiled again. "In the stand of birches there."

It was a second before Merriwether understood, and when he did, he couldn't speak to answer.

In the silence, the sheriff added, "Your place, that is." He started moving away.

Merriwether stood at the window and watched him. The sheriff threaded through the thinning crowd, pushed into the courtroom. The doors swung shut behind him.

Merriwether closed his eyes.

PART V

WAITING FOR RUMPLEMEYER

MONDAY, NOVEMBER 5

9:17 P.M.

So THEN IT was the eve of the election.

Alone, Merriwether sat in the *Champion* office writing the story of Barnes's confession. A cigarette burned in the ashtray on his desk, sending up a wavering line of smoke to the ceiling. The Selectric clattered loudly.

According to Barnes, he and Wocek then carried Thimble's body down the slope to the river side. Merriwether wrote. *Scotti called orders from the top of the ledge and shone a flashlight down on them, Barnes said, while the two prepared to throw the body in the river.*

Under the pounding of the machine, Merriwether heard the back door crack open. He kept typing, kept watching the black lines of words roll up out of the machine.

It took three hours to sink the body, Barnes said.

Now he heard the footsteps coming toward him down the aisle. The thump of a cane, the dragging whisper of a bum foot. He backspaced, crossed out the last sentence, began again.

Three hours . . . He crossed that out. *It took three hours . . .*

Closer and closer the footsteps came as he typed faster and faster.

297

. . . to sink the body . . . He crossed that out. *The body . . .* He crossed that out. *The body . . .*

With a sharp breath, Merriwether stopped typing. Spun in his chair to face the aisle.

No one was there. He was alone in the office. His shoulders sagged. He wiped the sweat from around his lips.

9:24

Half an hour more, and they would start to get ready for bed. In bed, that was the best time. Then she could think again.

Cindy knelt in the big chair by the window of the hospital's all-purpose room. She stared through the grate, out the window. There was nothing to see in the dark out there but her own reflection on the glass, staring back in through the wires. Poor fucking person, she thought—the sad way she looked, her sweatshirt all baggy, her short hair all scraggly, her mouth hanging open . . .

Poor fucking person, Teddy, what they fucking did to her. Not fair, man. It isn't fair.

She shook her head, her lips getting puffy, her eyes damp. It *wasn't* fair. It really wasn't . . . but she couldn't think about that now, or she would cry, and they would know. They would know she was just pretending to be crazy.

From across the room, the sound of the television set came to her. A comedy was on; she could tell from the shrill voices and the canned laughter. The other girls were all gathered around the TV, some crowded together on the sofa, some sitting on the various plastic chairs, some sitting cross-legged on the floor. All of them stared at the set. Some of them made noises. One laughed loudly at all the wrong times; another shouted now and then. One girl on the floor kept talking to herself in a low undertone.

Half an hour, Cindy thought. Just half an hour more.

She'd made it through the day so far. She'd been just like the rest of them: No one could tell the difference. She'd made it through her session with Dr. Bloom even.

Who shot him, Cindy? That's right. And why did they shoot him? . . .

She'd answered all his questions right. She hadn't even started crying until they got to the Teddy-getting-killed part.

And it wasn't your father who murdered Billy Thimble, was it?

She'd answered dutifully: No. And she hadn't told her secret. She'd kept it down for another day. Kept it to herself for another day.

And now, in just half an hour, she could get ready for bed. Go to bed and think about being Out There again. Close her eyes and think about being Out There in the trees. Lying on the damp pine needles. Lying on her back, out of breath, in the open circle of tall hemlocks. Waiting—breathing—waiting—for the shape moving toward her through the fog. The Thing Like a Man moving toward her through the forest fog, breaking out of the fog so she could see that it was . . .

She gasped aloud, her eyes wide. A face was hanging outside the window. It was just hanging out there in the open air above the mountainside. Just staring in at her. Just floating above nothing like a . . .

No. No, she saw now: It was a reflection, a reflection on the pane like her own reflection there.

She turned quickly and faced the little man who had snuck up beside her. It was a doctor. A new doctor . . . But strange, Cindy thought. A strange-looking doctor. He didn't look doctorlike somehow. She could tell he *was* a doctor because he was in one of those pale blue coats they wore, all those pens in his pocket, but . . . he had this huge bush of a beard, and shaggy hair, stooped shoulders . . . And that big, weird grin on his face. He didn't look like a doctor at all, in fact. In fact, he looked . . . familiar somehow. Yes, she'd seen him before. Out There . . . somewhere . . .

Cindy's heart beat hard. The doctor looked down at his own hand. He was holding a photograph, a photograph of her. She recognized it from her old middle-school yearbook. He looked at it, then back up at her face.

"Cindy?" He whispered her name—as if it was a secret, as if he was here on some secret mission to her. "Are you Cindy Dolittle?"

Slowly, Cindy's mouth opened wide. "I know who . . . "

"Ssh! Ssh!" He held up his hand frantically.

Cindy looked around. The girls were still watching the television. No one had turned to look at them. The nurse—the huge black nurse—Roberta; "the Tank," they called her—was busy too. She was at the nurses' station in the far corner. The nurses' station was a small room next door with a counter looking out on the all-purpose room. There was another nurse—the little one named Janet—behind the counter, and she was handing paper cups filled with medication to Roberta. Roberta was setting the cups out carefully on a long folding table.

Cindy looked at the little man again. Now she started whispering too.

"You were at Teddy's funeral," she said. "Weren't you? I saw you talking to Mrs. Wocek."

The man nodded. "Yeah, that's right, that's right."

Cindy just kept gaping at him—she could feel her own mouth hanging open like a fish's mouth.

"Are you, like, a Real Person? From Out There?" she hissed.

"No, no," the man said. "I'm a reporter. From a newspaper."

"But . . ." Cindy's voice was very small. It squeaked. "But can you help me? Can you help me?"

The funny little man came forward another step. He lowered himself to one knee in front of her. He put his own hand over hers.

"Yes," he whispered. "I can help you. Yes."

9:26

Christ, look at her, she's fucking crazy, Rumplemeyer thought.

He knelt before Cindy, holding her hand in his. He could see the scar on her wrist, the dark red line fading back into the skin. And when he looked up, he saw the teenager's wild, darting eyes. Jesus. He had maybe two minutes before that nurse in the corner—the one who looked like a cross between a black sumo wrestler and an atom bomb disguised as a black sumo wrestler—came over here, picked him up,

Corruption

placed him in the crack of her ass and squeezed until the top of his head blew off. Two minutes at most—and here he was stuck with a nutcase, a dull-faced, square-faced little teen with dishwater hair falling all over her face, and her mouth hanging open, and eyes like pinballs, shooting off in all directions. . . .

"Listen," he whispered desperately. "You've got to, like, listen, okay? And answer my questions really, really fast, okay?"

She nodded, openmouthed. "Yeah. Okay."

Yeah, right, thought Rumplemeyer, *right after she does her impersonation of a drooling eggplant.* "Why did they put you in here, Cindy?"

She blinked. Her lips came together, opened again. *Come on, come on,* Rumplemeyer thought. He glanced back over his shoulder to see Nurse Kaboom. She was taking pills from another nurse behind a counter, dropping the pills into Dixie cups, setting the cups in rows on the table beside her. The wooden double doors that led out into the hall were right in back of Rumple so his exit was clear. He still had time.

"Because I cut my wrists," Cindy whispered to him.

"Right." Rumplemeyer faced her, nodded. "Right, right. Like, why . . . why'd you do that?"

"Because of Teddy. Because he died."

And then Cindy started to cry.

I'm a dead guy, thought Rumplemeyer. *It's, like, not funny how dead I am.*

She put her hands over her face and her whole body shook. She was trying to keep it quiet, but a steady, rhythmic squeaking leaked out through her fingers.

"Ssh," Rumplemeyer said. "Ssh, ssh."

Cindy hiccuped loudly. Rumplemeyer looked over and saw Nurse Killyou pause in her work. The humongous woman glanced up—

I am so totally dead.

—then turned back to her Dixie cups, plopping in another pair of pills.

Rumplemeyer swung back to Cindy, clutched the girl's hand harder. Tears ran down her cheeks. Yellow snot ran over her upper lip.

"Who killed him, Cindy? Do you know who killed Teddy? Can you tell me? Can you tell me?"

301

She yanked her hand away from him and stretched back against the seat of the cushioned chair, taut, as if electricity were running through her.

"I told you already," she said—her whisper strained, almost breaking into full voice. "I already told Dr. Bloom today. I'm not supposed to have to do it again. It's not fair."

"What?"

"My father's men killed Teddy because he shot at them when they tried to arrest him. All right? Is that what you want me to say? All right?"

"What? Wait. Is that true?" said Rumplemeyer.

"What? What?"

"What you just said—that Wocek shot at the police. That the police killed him in self-defense. Is that true? Are you sure of that?"

She looked at him, baffled, snot-stained, waving her hands all around: an utter fruitcake. She started making those squeaky crying noises again: *eek, eek, eek* . . . She lowered her chin to her chest.

"What do you want me to say? I don't know the right answer anymore. Please . . . I just want to go to bed . . . Okay? I just want to go to bed."

Shit, thought Rumplemeyer.

"It's okay," he whispered. He took her hand back. He patted it gently. "Ssh. Ssh. It's okay. Really. I just wanted to know, like . . . why you were here, okay? I thought maybe, like, they put you here because . . . " He shook his head sadly. "But now I know. It's okay." He smiled, his own eyes growing damp. "Now I know."

The girl frowned at him angrily. Defiantly, she dragged her sweatshirt sleeve across her nose, smearing the snot all over her face. For Rumplemeyer, it was a truly disgusting moment. He swallowed hard and patted her hand some more.

"They put me in here because I know who killed Billy Thimble," Cindy said aloud.

"Ssh . . . ssh . . . It's okay. It's . . ." Rumplemeyer stopped. He stared at her. "What?"

"I know who killed Billy Thimble."

"Billy Thimble? I thought Vince Scotti killed Billy Thimble."

She pulled her back straight and, still crying, glared down her nose at him almost haughtily. "He did."

"He did. Right."

"Except . . ." said Cindy.

"Except?" said Rumplemeyer, his heart hammering.

"Uh . . . Doctor?"

Oh no. It was . . . the Fluty Trill of Nurse Death. Rumplemeyer turned toward her, hiding his face in his sleeve as best he could. She was still standing by the medication table, but she had paused in her work and was looking directly at him. Her eyes were narrowed, her lips tight: She did not like what she was seeing.

"Just a minute, Nurse, I'll be, like, right with you, okay?"

The nurse didn't answer—and Rumplemeyer didn't dare glance around to see if she was still watching him. Maybe she was steamrolling across the room toward him right this minute. Already baring her ass in preparation . . .

Frantically, he raised his eyes to Cindy. "Except what?"

Cindy shook her head once, and the words rushed out of her. "Except Daddy told me . . . He's the one who told me that Billy was going to turn Scotti in." She snuffled, trying to control her voice, keep it down. "Just 'cause he caught me and Teddy together. That's why. We weren't doing anything. We were just in my room together. Shit. We could've gone in the woods." She wiped her face with her baggy sleeve again. "And he threw Teddy out and then he told me."

"He told you," said Rumplemeyer.

"He said, like, you know: 'That Teddy and all his fucking friends, you know, they're going to get fucking arrested soon because Billy Thimble is going to turn Scotti over to me.' " She gave a deep grimace. "Big man," she said.

"Doctor, could I speak to you for a moment please?" He glanced back and saw Nurse Castastrophe—still in her corner, but turned full around now. Hands on her massive hips, massive head tilted to one side. Eyes glowering like an eagle's. Definitely an I'm-gonna-squeeze-that-man-between-my-ass-halves look.

"Just a moment please, nurse," said Rumplemeyer. As long as she stayed there, he had time to make a dash for the doors. He looked up at Cindy. "And you told Teddy, right? And Teddy told Vince."

Cindy was crying too hard now to speak softly. But she nodded. "Daddy never told me anything else. He never told me *anything* before. Ever. He *wanted* this to happen. You see? That's why he told. He wanted Billy to get killed just so he could kill Teddy. That's why. Because he saw me and Teddy on the bed. And we weren't even *doing* anything, we were just . . ."

"Excuse me, Doctor," said Nurse Buttocks. "Do I *know* you? . . ."

Rumplemeyer knelt there—he couldn't move, could only stare at Cindy, shaking his head. The girl had collapsed completely. Sitting in the chair, speechless, shaking up and down with the force of her crying.

"I said, *excuse* me, Doctor!"

"Are you . . . ?" Cindy gasped for air. "Are you going to make me stay here now? Are you going to make me stay here forever?"

Rumplemeyer patted her hand. "I'm gonna get you out of here if I have to, like, tear this fucking place apart. Okay?"

She nodded uncertainly.

"Okay?" said Rumplemeyer.

"Okay," Cindy said.

"Doctor!"

And with that, the nurse charged at him across the room.

"But not right now," Rumplemeyer said. "Bye." And jumping to his feet, he humped it hard for the doors.

"Hey, you!" screamed the onrushing nurse. Rumplemeyer felt the floor tremble under him.

Wo, he thought.

And he made like a nose—and ran.

9:38

A high wind rose, and a shower of leaves fell on the dirt path. The trees lining the path dipped and swayed as Merriwether drove by them. His deadline was midnight and the Barnes story wasn't done yet, but he had left the office. He had come home to see Emily.

The Rabbit pulled through the stone gate. Merriwether saw the cottage and cursed miserably. The lights were out in there. Emily must be asleep already. It seemed she went to bed earlier every day, he thought. He pulled the Rabbit to the end of the drive and shut it down. Stepped out.

The wind was strong and steady. It blew his hair back off his brow. The hickories at the edge of the yard cracked and groaned as they bent and straightened; they rattled the last of their leaves. White clouds went black and silver as they sailed swiftly over the moon. Merriwether walked slowly to the cottage door.

He let himself in. Closed the door softly behind him. Listened a moment before coming forward—then moved into the room on the balls of his feet. Threading through the furniture—past the shapes of the table, the sofa, the chairs—he came into the bedroom. He stood in the dark until his eyes adjusted, until he saw her, lying under the covers on the mattress.

He pulled a canvas chair up beside her. Got an ashtray from the bookshelf. Sat down and held the ashtray on his lap. He put a cigarette between his lips, lit a match, and looked at his wife on the bed beneath him.

The flame light wavered yellow on her coffee skin. Her black hair curled on her cheek. Her lips were parted slightly. She lay on her side, the covers pushed down around her waist. He could see the curve of her breast rise and fall steadily under her white nightgown.

He lit the cigarette, waved out the match. The dark narrowed down around the cigarette's glow. He thought of how her eyes would look if he had to tell her. He thought of the sound of her voice. And he would have to tell her. Now that the sheriff knew. Now that it was sure to come out. His heart felt like a stone.

He glanced at his watch. It was ten o'clock. Sally would be meeting with the sheriff any minute.

10:00

She saw him down there, down among the gray shadows of the birches. Saw his silhouetted figure standing still, leaning back on his hips, hands in his pockets. Waiting for her, looking right up at her. She had to pause a minute before she could do it, before she could go down the hill to meet him, because she had run down the same hill just four nights before, like a girl in a story, a young girl, kicking up the leaves.

The wind moved through with the snap and clatter of branches. She put her hands in the pockets of her skirt and walked down, braking her progress with the sides of her feet.

Dolittle stood just that way—leaning back on his hips, hands in his pockets—until she reached him. She stopped while there was still maybe ten feet between them. All the same, she felt the familiar birches surround them both, saw the same lakewater through the branches, silver with the moon, saw the old moon, going in and out of the clouds, through the high branches. There was enough light to make the sheriff's craggy, friendly face dimly visible, to make his eyes glitter in the dark.

"It sure is a nice spot, Sally," he said softly. "I'll give that to you. I got there a little early, and it's a nice old spot, it is." She saw him lift his shoulders. "Cold, though. Don't you guys get all cold?"

"This was cruel, Sheriff." It came out in that same schoolgirl whisper but it was steady enough. "It was just plain mean—even for you."

"Even for me, huh?" He coughed—hard. She heard him fight to heave in his breath and she thought, *Good.* She hoped he was sick. She hoped he was dying.

"Yeah," he said. He spit into the leaves. Ambled away from her to lean against a birch. Gazed up toward the road. He chuckled. "Yeah, I guess it was sort of nasty, at that. I mean, there you are: You wait for something all this time, your whole life really. Then it finally comes along and what happens? Someone puts their hands all over it. Makes it seem dirty and low-down where it seemed good before. That's what it's like, isn't it?"

Sally didn't answer him.

"Yeah," the sheriff drawled again. "Yeah, I know how that feels, Sally. I know *exactly* how that feels." He coughed some more—and made an old man's grating sound as he pulled his breath in. Sally still didn't say anything. Just watched him, afraid only that she might cry—her throat was thick with it—but strangely calm aside from that.

306

With another cough, Dolittle straightened against the tree. "It's that element of doubt that does it," he said. "You know? I mean, as long as you got no one to bother you, it all just seems right somehow, doesn't it? I mean, you might know it's wrong in the usual sense, by the usual rules, you know. But, man, it sure seems right in a . . . a kind of bigger way. Doesn't it? Like it's 'meant to be.' That sort of thing."

"Yes." Sally started to murmur the word but bit it back.

The sheriff shook his head. "Hell, then someone comes along, starts asking questions. Starts saying how maybe it's all a mistake. Maybe the usual rules apply to you too. And that just does it—that puts the doubt in there. Makes it seem all . . . dirty. And low-down." She heard him make a soft, hoarse noise. She thought he was laughing at her. "And I hate to be the one to break this to you, darling. But once you got that doubt thing in there, it *never* goes away. Never."

He had hardly finished the last word before another fit of coughing hit him. He had to bend over, holding on to the tree with one hand. Sally stood watching, coldly at first. But after a minute or so, she started to think maybe he really *was* sick. Goddamn it, maybe she should go to him, try to help. . . .

Finally, though, the fit eased, passed. Dolittle straightened with a low, guttural curse.

She had to say something. "Are you all right?"

"Yeah," he said.

"You sound sick."

"Yeah, hell. I guess I am, a little."

The wind swirled down to them and Sally hugged her shoulders. The tall man still braced himself against the tree, breathing hard. Why couldn't he just skip it, she thought, why couldn't he just skip it and get right to the blackmail? She pressed her lips together tightly, watching him, waiting.

"It makes everything seem a little more important," he told her. "Being sick."

"Does it?" she said coolly.

"Yeah. Yeah, it does." With a grunt, he pushed off the tree and came toward her. Crossing the distance with that slow, arrogant cowboy stride. He stood over her, and she could see, looking up at him,

307

how tired he seemed, his eyes sunken, his cheeks drawn. She looked away from him, down at her shoes.

"Well," he said. "How about it, Sally?" He snorted. "Come on. I got you fair and square. A woman your age. Cavorting out in the woods with a boy like that. A married boy. Well, I'm not saying you'll be run out of town on a rail or anything. Not anymore, not even in Auburn." He rubbed the side of his head with an open hand. "Still in all, if I make it public, it'll get awful dirty for you. You know it will. The wife'll get involved. There'll be charges. Recriminations. Lies and then apologies and some more lies. And the whole story will come out. All public. Every minute of it. Every word, I'll see to it. It'll be awful hard for you to function as a journalist with people looking down at you, laughing at you." He gave her a soft, sympathetic *tsk-tsk.* "Not to mention your bosses down in White Plains. I don't think they'll take too kindly to the whole idea. It could get you fired, Sally. And then, the most important thing . . . "

"All right!" She raised her eyes to his and his glittered down at her. She wanted to punch him. "I get the picture."

"The most important thing," he went on quietly, "is that you will lose him. You've got to know that. Maybe you hope it'll force the issue. He'll leave his wife for you, or she'll leave him and he'll come to you. But no, you're a smart girl, Sally. You've got to know, down in your heart . . ."

"What do you want, Sheriff? Just get to it, all right?"

He paused. Smiled with one corner of his mouth, his eyes crinkling. "I want you to lay off, Sally. That's all. Lay off Wocek and tell Rumplemeyer to lay off my daughter. One year. Hell, one more year and I'll be gone, almost for certain. Then it won't matter what you do."

"You know I can't . . ." She had the speech all planned, her noble journalist speech, but she barely got that much out. Her throat felt like it had shut completely.

The sheriff reached for her—she didn't have time to pull away. He put his hand on her arm: a big warm hand that held her firmly. "Down in your heart, you've got to know you'll lose him," he said gently. "If it comes to a crisis, I mean. You've got to know it's true."

Sally felt the blood rush to her cheeks, the tears to her eyes.

"He's just passing through this county," the sheriff told her quietly. "You and me, Sally, we're here for the duration."

Sally cried out angrily and wrenched herself free.

10:11

Dolittle felt sorry for her. Small, hunched, ugly woman. Uglier now with her cheeks mottled, her lips puffy, her eyes ringed with mascara. Middle-aged, lonely. Probably let herself believe she was going to get away with it. Run off to some little house with a garden. Little white picket fence. The cock stands up, and the brain shuts down: probably the same way for women too; the same principle applies.

He shook his head, looked at her. She had turned her back on him now and she stood before him trembling. Like a little animal caught in a trap, he thought, just waiting for the coup de grâce.

"Christ, Sally. A year," he said. He was hoarse—his chest was beginning to hurt with all this talking. "What the hell is so goddamned important that it can't wait a year?"

She wouldn't answer him, just stood there, 120 pounds of ticked-off female, showing him her back.

"You're gonna lose your job. You're gonna lose your boyfriend, you know you are." He threw his hand up. "And I'm gonna win the goddamned election anyway." Still—the silent treatment. "Christ!" he said. "A year from now I'm gonna be goddamned dead and you know what? You're gonna wonder what all the fuss was about."

"No," she said softly. He could just hear her under the rising wind. "No, I won't."

"Ah!" He walked away from her, deeper into the birch wood. Stood there with his hands on his hips, looking out toward the dark water, the reflection of the moon. It was loud out here tonight, loud with the wind in the branches. Cold, too. These little lovebirds must've really gone at each other, humping away just to stay warm half the time. The sheriff let out a thin breath. Must've been kind of fun, too. He was almost jealous of them. . . .

He cursed, swung around on her. "What is it?" he called to her.

"What the hell is it about me anyway that gets under your bonnet so damned much? Would you explain that to me, Sally? My smile, my hairstyle, what the hell is it?"

Finally, she showed him her face again. All set and grim, little chin jutting out at him. She was one riled lady, all right. "It's not you personally," she said, prissy as you please. "I'm a newspaperwoman, Sheriff. It's the things you do with your office that . . . get under my bonnet."

Exasperated, Dolittle jammed his hands in his back pockets now. Raised his head and sighed up at the moon. "Well, that is very high-minded of you, Sally. It truly is. Utter bullshit, of course, but high-minded bullshit, there's no denying. It's not me personally, it's my office," he repeated. "And just what is it about the way I run my office that you don't like? If I may ask."

That at least got a small smile out of her. "Well, for one thing, I find the idea of a law officer committing blackmail like this a little disturbing."

"Oh, goodness, do you? You find that a little disturbing." And now, he started coughing again, and he could tell it wouldn't be long before it really got going on him. Still, he fought to breathe, to go on. He said, "You didn't find it so disturbing when the feds gave us those whatchamacallem—those housing funds two years ago. And we built the whole community up in the southeast corner? Low-income families and all that shit. I seem to recall a glowing editorial by you, Sally, about the board of supervisors and how they'd finally seen the light. Hallelujah and whatnot." She didn't say anything, just stood there sulking on him. "You think those houses wouldn't have gone to Al Schneider's mother-in-law? Huh? You think he didn't have thirty-five deeply personal friends and close relations in mind to give those houses to? Not to mention the contracts to build them. Hell, if I didn't just happen to know about how Al likes to waggle his pud in front of Boy Scouts every now and again. . . ."

She reared back and gave him her that's-disgusting pout.

"Well, it's the ugly truth, Sally."

"I know it's true," she said. "But it's not right."

"Sally . . ." He tried to shout it at her, but it came out as a rasp.

He moved toward her, one hand out, rasping on. "I don't give a diddly *shit* about what's right. Or fair. Or any of that newspaper Crusader Rabbit crap. I'm trying to do *good* here, Sally. For this *county*. So it doesn't get *eaten* by the goddamned developers and peddled off by the goddamned politicians and . . ."

But the phlegm boiled up painfully into his throat and he reached out until his hand hit a tree. He caught hold of it and leaned there. Coughed with thick, rumbling noises. Coughed and coughed. Coughed until there was no breath left in him, until the dead leaves under his shoes seemed to wheel around and around and he thought he would suffocate, right then, just standing there.

Then she was standing beside him. Her small, thin hand was on the crook of his arm. He caught his breath and dragged in the cool night air gratefully.

"Do you want me to call a doctor?" she asked him—her voice had softened too.

He shook his head at her, but it was nearly a minute before he could speak. "Sally," he whispered. "Sally . . ."

She cocked her head at him, waited.

"This is the last chance," he said. "For you and me both. Come on, Sally. One year. One last year."

Her lips started trembling again, and her eyes filled up with tears. But her hand stayed on his arm a moment longer, and he began to think maybe . . .

And then she was running away from him, kicking through the leaves, the leaves blowing down around her as she faded from him among the trees, faded until a cloud blew across the moon and the woods grew dark—and she was gone.

The sheriff pushed off the tree stiffly. Cleared his throat. Spat on the ground.

10:20

For a long time, Merriwether didn't move. He was on his third cigarette now, but he just held it between his fingers, letting it burn. On the mattress beneath him, Emily slept without stirring. He watched her breathing evenly, gently; her still face peaceful, unaware.

You don't really love her, he thought.

That's what his father had told him. The Dragon King. Upright in his studded-leather throne, behind his outsized oak desk. His bald head, fringed with silver, had tilted back so that his chin jutted haughtily: It was his Don't-mess-with-me-you-spineless-mother's-boy pose. *You can't love her,* he'd said. *Your cultures are too different. You're just doing this to get at me. That's all. Some kind of . . . misguided rebellion. To get at me. Well, you got me, boy. All right? Are you satisfied? Are you satisfied now?*

It was funny really; it was really pretty funny. Just before the old man had spoken, Merriwether had been thinking almost the same thing about *him.* He'd been thinking that the Dragon King didn't really care what color his wife was, that he'd just jumped on an excuse to wield power in the affair, to have his say, to have control.

Still, long after Merriwether had marched out of the third-floor study, long after he'd trotted down the sweeping stairway to the front hall, he had continued to argue with the bastard in his mind:

Different cultures? Yes, of course, she's an English major, I'm in Classics—it can never be. Then there's the fact that she's brilliant and beautiful—a sound mind in an incredible body. She believes in me, she's sweet-tempered, witty, good with children . . . She can even cook a little. How could I have imagined that I wanted anything from her that didn't have to do with you? You unbearable fuck!

But, of course, his father's Pronouncements: They had their existence in some privileged celestial terrain, above argument, beyond insult, immune even to reality.

You don't really love her. You're just doing this to get at me.

Merriwether sat with the cigarette held by his brow, his elbow propped on the wooden arm of the director's chair. He looked down at his sleeping wife and he wondered if it was true.

He thought about being rid of her all the time now, didn't he? He daydreamed that she had died. In a plane crash or a fire. That would make it easy anyway. He wouldn't have to tell her; he wouldn't have to lose her. He wouldn't have to see that look of hurt and betrayal in her eyes.

Maybe he *didn't* really love her then; if he could imagine her dead like that. Maybe the passion for defiance, the bitter goodness of being *right*, had just convinced him that he had to stand up to his father, had to marry her, *had* to love her. Maybe the romantic poverty of the house on Mass. Ave, the office of *Helios* in the cellar, the floor carpeted with papers, the books scattered everywhere, and he in his chair at the corner table beneath the window, curled before the computer like a question mark, his hands dancing over the keyboard, the ideas seeming to crystallize in the very air, looking up to find her watching him, Emily, watching him with her head tilted to one side, smiling that wistful, faithful smile as if she treasured this moment of his idealism but trusted he would surmount its inevitable collapse so that . . .

Christ, what the hell was he thinking about? Of course he loved her, she was his life, he had always loved her, she was the life he had always wanted, she was . . .

The phone rang in the other room.

"God damn it," Merriwether whispered. He placed his cigarette in the ashtray, set the ashtray on the floor. Got up quickly. Couldn't even have a goddamned epiphany without the goddamned phone ringing every second. He hurried into the living room as it rang again. It was probably Sally or someone from the plant: Sorry to break into your moment of crisis, chum, but we do need the Barnes piece by midnight. . . . He had to get the phone before it woke up Emily.

It began to ring a third time just as he reached it. He took it up.

"Hello," he said sharply.

"Fourth! Thank God!"

"Rumplemeyer?"

10:21

"Where the hell is everyone?" Rumplemeyer loosened his grip on his own hair, falling back against the glass wall of the phone booth. "I called, like, the office. I called the plant. I called, like, Sally's house. Shea's. I even called the Courthouse Restaurant."

"And yet you phoned me before trying Mel's Park N' Shop. I'm flattered, Rumplemeyer, truly."

Rumplemeyer grinned wickedly into the receiver. "Yeah, well, it's not like I don't trust you to get a story right, Fourth. I mean, you're almost as good as a real reporter."

"Wonderful. Remember those two men who beat you up? You don't happen to have their number, do you?"

Merriwether's dry, familiar voice came to him over the line and it was a nice sound to hear out here. Out here, by the side of a dark mountain road with the wind moaning in the trees and the moon dancing eerily behind the clouds the way it often does just before a chain-saw-wielding psychopath steps out of the bushes and slices someone really decent to pieces. And with the booth he was in sitting at the edge of a lot, a weed-grown, shattered-to-gravel lot with a dilapidated old service station on it, a ruin of stucco next to a sagging garage of rotten wood, a perfect place for the dead to walk, especially if they happened to be dead mechanics.

"Listen," he said, bouncing rapidly on his toes. "I've been hiding in a hospital broom closet for the last twenty minutes, and I'm pretty sure the police are looking for me, okay?"

"Perfectly fine, yes. Good of you to call. Bye now."

"The thing is if I, like, get arrested, I may not make it back in time for deadline. And the other thing is: I just got an interview with Cindy Dolittle."

Even Fourth shut up at that. Rumplemeyer looked up and down the road. Empty: a twisting two-lane with hills of fingery trees on one side and a sharp drop into more of these same fingery trees on the other. The only comfort in sight was his Bug, squatting faithfully beside the booth, motor running, lights off, ready to get him the fuck out of there.

"Fourth? Are you there?"

"Yes, yes. I was just getting a pen. Go on."

Attaway. Fourth. Come through, you shallow WASP, you.

"Okay," Rumplemeyer said. "Cindy says Dolittle, like, set Thimble up. Okay? Dolittle told her that Thimble was going to rat on Scotti, knowing she would tell her boyfriend, Wocek, and that he would tell Scotti and Scotti would kill him. Okay? The point is, like: Dolittle put the word out through his daughter that Thimble was gonna turn over. It's an old cop trick. He set Thimble up to be murdered."

"But why?"

"Well, Cindy says the sheriff wanted to get Thimble killed so he could kill Wocek for fucking his daughter."

"Oh, come on, Rumplemeyer, that's insane."

"Well, she's in an asylum, Fourth, what do you want?"

"But maybe it *was* because Thimble was planning to blackmail the sheriff," Merriwether said.

"What?"

"That's what Brer Scotti says."

"Scotti said that? He said Billy Thimble was trying to blackmail the sheriff?"

"Well, he implied it, at least. He said Thimble was expecting the sheriff to give him money."

"But for what? What could Billy Thimble blackmail Dolittle for?"

"Ah, Scotti neglected to mention that. Still, it could explain why the sheriff might want to put out the word on Billy T."

"Sure. Sure. And then . . . then Dolittle had Wocek shot down in the raid so that Wocek wouldn't tell that he'd gotten the information from Cindy."

"Don't get carried away, Rumplemeyer."

"No, no, really, I mean even tonight, even with the vote tomorrow: if the voters found out the sheriff had actually *caused* the murder . . ."

"I don't know if we could . . ."

"Listen," Rumplemeyer said. "I'm coming back right now, okay? Just find Sally, okay? Just tell her, okay?"

"Right-ho."

"Thanks."

Rumplemeyer hung up.

Right-ho, he thought. *Fuck me blind.*

He folded open the door of the booth and stepped out into the night. It was not, he had noticed, a good night to step out into. Howling wind. Thin branches bowing this way and that like the arms of dancers in some cultic ritual. Shadows creeping over the ground like snakes, rising against the trees like demons . . .

315

Rumplemeyer yanked open his car door and practically leapt inside, slamming the door shut, hammering the lock into place with his fist.

"Car, do your stuff," he said. He knocked the gearshift into first with the heel of his palm. Shot onto the road before he even had his lights on.

And off he putted—lights shining now—bounding down the mountain, chugging around the bend.

"Ooh baby, baby, baby," he sang in a high-pitched shriek. "I have nailed yooooou, you fascist fuck. Ooh, baby, baby, baby. You are a sheriff who is shit out of luck. You put your daughter in a hole, and now the story can be tole; and when I've written 'bout your crimes . . . I'm goin to da *New York Ti-yi-yimes* . . ."

Suddenly, his rear window flared white. White lights—headlights—were sweeping down the mountain at him.

Rumplemeyer held his breath, squinted into his rearview. "Ooh, baby, baby," he murmured, "don't let the cops arrest me, pleeeese . . ."

The lights came on—they came on fast—got brighter, broader, obliterating the glass. . . . Rumplemeyer pressed down harder on the gas pedal. The Volkswagen jerked, farted, and continued down the hill at exactly the same speed.

"Ooh, baby . . ."

Maybe it's just a truck, Rumplemeyer thought as the lights got bigger, drew closer. It had to be a truck. *It must be a truck bearing down too fast to brake. It must be about to crash into me and . . .*

There was nothing behind him now but the onrushing light.

"Oooh . . . shit . . ."

Rumplemeyer swung the wheel over, nudged the Volks into the left lane, the oncoming lane. The car sailed blind around a curve, flirting with the steep shoulder into the woods. . . .

Come on, he thought. *Pass me, you asshole. Come on, come on, come on.*

There was the sound of a gunned engine. The headlights pressed closer and then pulled up next to him.

It was a car. Not a truck. A long boat of a thing, racing alongside him. Holding there, alongside him. Just holding there. It wouldn't pass. . . .

"Come on!" Rumplemeyer screamed.

Another blind curve lay up ahead. The Volks hurtled toward it and Rumplemeyer was sure a tractor-trailer would come careening around it any second.

"Come on!"

With a quick, decisive motion, the other car veered toward him. It slapped hard into the Volks's side. Rumplemeyer squealed. He fought the wheel. The Volks skidded across the lane. He felt its tires slip over the edge of the pavement; he felt them dig into the soft earth.

The steering wheel wrestled itself out of his hands. The Volks lifted up onto two tires. Rumplemeyer screamed.

The Volks pitched over the side of the hill.

It plunged into the woods. He saw the bony branches grip at his windshield. Saw his lights skew wildly over the trunks of trees. The car bounced hard beneath him.

Rumplemeyer shrieked . . .

And there was a jolt. There was the sound of glass shattering; metal crumpling in. The car stopped short and Rumplemeyer was thrown forward, his brow punching into the hard wheel. "Oof!"

And that was it. Everything was suddenly quiet. Just like that. Rumplemeyer lay still, leaning to one side, his hair splayed against the window. He was dazed. He wasn't sure what was happening. He saw light; he saw light and branches waving. Odd angles of trees; the whole world at odd angles. He felt a thick trickle on his forehead. Reached up and touched it gingerly with his fingertips. Looked at the fingers. It was blood, all right.

"Shit," he said. "Those motherfuckers."

One day, when he *was* on the *Times*, he was going to write a goddamned *book* about them so everyone would know.

With a groan, he pulled the door handle back, shouldered out the door. It resisted a second, then gave with a hollow pop. Rumplemeyer rolled stiffly out into the forest, gripping the door's edge, standing and staggering on wobbly legs. He was definitely going to miss deadline now. It was all going to be up to Fourth. Which meant it was all going to be fucked up. And he'd have to share a byline too—the thought made him groan again as he stepped slowly out in front of the Volks, holding on to the hood, bent over in pain.

A twig snapped. He looked up. Undersheriff Henry Benoit was standing before him.

Benoit wore a light blue polo shirt and an open windbreaker. He looked as if he'd been called from home in a hurry. He stood with his legs akimbo, framed against the trees as they swayed in the stark shadows thrown by the Bug's headlights. He was carrying a tire iron in his right hand. As Rumplemeyer looked up at him, the undersheriff raised the tire iron across his chest, back over his shoulder like a whip. He smiled.

Uh-oh, Rumplemeyer thought. He put his hands up. "Okay, like, wait, okay?" he said. "Just listen, okay?"

But Benoit brought the tire iron around full force. Rumplemeyer saw it—it was weird the way time seemed to slow down—and he saw the fury twisting Benoit's face, and the singing, black blur of the iron as it came at him. It seemed he had all the time in the world to think and react—to dive to the side, hunch his shoulders, duck his head down. . . .

But the thing hit him anyway. He felt the painless jar of it denting his temple. Then he was dead.

10:23

After Merriwether hung up on Rumplemeyer, he stood by the table a moment, his hand still on the phone. He half expected Emily's voice to sound behind him. He half expected to turn and find her there. But when he looked around, he could see her through the bedroom door-way—he could see her still sleeping—and he felt a sort of sick relief. As long as she slept, the time had not yet come. The moment of reckoning was not yet upon him.

He folded up his notes and put them in his pocket. Walked heavily to the cottage door. He paused there a second, looking down. There was something he was forgetting. . . .

But it didn't matter; he couldn't bear to stay anymore. He couldn't bear to go back in there and see her again. It was awful enough—the innocence of her sleep. And, God, if she opened her eyes, if she looked at him—if he finally had to tell her. . . . He did not know how he was going to live with the sight of her pain. He pushed outside.

The moon was high overhead—free of the clouds—and the fields were bright. The wind had grown stronger and the hickories bent hard to one side on a long loud breath of it. All around him, Merriwether saw the silver fields moving with the wind and heard the sough of the wind in the distant hills. He walked to his car with his jacket blowing open, his hair blowing back. When he slid into the Rabbit and shut the door, muting the roar of the night, he still felt the wind on every side of the car, buffeting, swirling.

He drove to the stone gate. He paused there again, his foot easing down on the brake. He saw the dead leaves on the dirt path tumbling by, racing before the wind. He saw them whip up into the air and tumble in circles before his eyes. He shivered at the wheel. Wild night. It was a wild, nervy night.

He pushed the gas down and drove out through the gate.

10:27

He had forgotten his cigarette. He had left it burning in the ashtray by Emily's bed. The smoke rose from it into the darkness. The ash lengthened, the paper grayed, curling down toward the filter. Soon, the weight of the filter counterbalanced the remaining tobacco. The cigarette dropped from the ashtray's edge and rolled over the wooden floor. It rolled toward the bed until it touched the edge of Emily's sheet. The cigarette kept burning, smoking. In another moment, the edge of the sheet began to smolder too. Emily lay sleeping. A brown dime of char appeared in the fabric of the sheet. A wisp of smoke rose from it. The char began to glow red. The sheet seemed as if it would burst into flame.

But the tobacco in the cigarette was all consumed now. The filter burned for another second or so, then went out. Without the cigarette to fuel it, the sheet soon stopped smoldering. The wisp of smoke rising from it dissipated, faded away. There was no fire.

Emily slept.

10:33

Shea was at one with his car tonight. The old Chevy, shooting around Lakeshore Road, speeding back to the bureau. His eyes and his headlights were glued to the double yellow lines on the highway. Everything else—the house lamps glittering red and white on the black water to his right, the forest depths alive with wind on the slope of ground to his left—had sunk into the vast semidarkness of his peripheries.

Shea and his car were racing to the office against the midnight deadline. He had a story. A hell of a story. And it had to be told tonight. Before election day.

There was a small, tight smile on his pale face as he drove. He was pretty pleased with himself. It had taken some smarts to nail this one down. Sure, Rumplemeyer might have his dramatic meetings in the forest in the dead of night, but Shea was no slouch himself when it came to a bit of reportorial flair. He had just pulled off the age-old political technique called "the whipsaw"—and he had pulled it off on the age-old politicians themselves.

First, he had gone to Jones with the copies of the deeds. Ralph, he had said, Purdy is saying you bought up the town of Hickory on the basis of prior knowledge of the new master plan.

And Jones had replied: Chris (or actually: wuh, wuh, wuh, wuh, well, uh, Chris. The fat man was sweating like a pig too). Anyway: Chris, he'd said, Billy Thimble made most of those deals without this poor country boy really understanding what he was doin, yup, yup, yup. Then he tried to blackmail me about it, sayin he'd tell everybody. Well, I didn't mind givin the poor fella a little money. But then the sheriff busted him for selling cocaine and the little weasel used the deeds to buy his way out of it.

So Shea had gone to Purdy.

Whitman, he had said, Jones is saying the sheriff got the goods in this scandal by letting a cocaine dealer go free.

Well, now, Chris, Purdy had replied, brushing his hair back out of his eyes and smiling his gleaming white smile. Now, Chris, Billy Thimble gave us that information to clear his guilty conscience, and for absolutely no other reason, doncha know. It was only afterward, when that ol' devil cocaine took control of his soul that he stooped to blackmailing us. He claimed he would go to the press and announce—of all things!—something no one in his right mind could ever believe, mind you, announce that the honest and upright Sheriff Cyrus Dolittle had arrested him on drug charges, and that he was allowed to buy his release with the scandalous information on Jones. And that's the truth right there, Chris, that's all I'm trying to say. . . .

Shea's Chevy came up out of the woods and bumped onto Main Street. Shea relaxed behind the wheel as he drove the last short stretch to Stillwater Lane.

The only thing that still puzzled Shea was, why didn't Dolittle want to use the information? Sure, when Thimble was still alive, he couldn't use it because he'd have to pay off Thimble to keep him quiet. But once Thimble was dead, why didn't he let Purdy just scream it from the rooftops?

Well, it didn't matter. It was a good story. A hell of a story to break on election day: JONES BOUGHT UP COMMERCIAL CORRIDOR WITH HELP OF MURDER VICTIM. CHARGES SHERIFF TRADED DEALER FOR HIS FREEDOM.

It wouldn't say much for Dolittle's campaign techniques, but it was sure to ruin Jones. And Sally would be forced to lead with it too. It was just too big to bury.

He was on Stillwater now. He pulled up under the elms across the street from the bureau. The lights were still on in the office and he could see Sally sitting alone in the back.

She was sitting at her desk and staring into the empty air.

10:33

In his home on Wapataugh Mountain, Sheriff Dolittle stood at the picture window, gazing through his own reflection at the night. His wife was upstairs in bed. He could hear her breathing, breathing hard, hoarsely. Whatever that bastard Steinbach was giving her, it sure as hell knocked her out cold. He hardly ever saw her these days; by the time he came home, she was fast asleep.

He shook his head. That sound she made though, that breathing, it was beginning to irk him. That raw sound. It was worse than his own breathing, almost. It was almost the way his mother sounded, upstairs in her bed, at the end.

Well, she'd be better soon, he thought. All this hysteria would be over after tomorrow. After the election—say, a week or two after—things would be sure to settle down. He could go get his own lungs checked on without it becoming a campaign issue. He could bring Cindy home and she and her mother could have a good cry on each other's shoulders. After tomorrow, it would all be over.

Somehow, he thought—and he smiled a little to himself as he stood there—somehow, he had managed to get through it. He'd kept the pieces in place, the strings clenched tightly in his fist; he'd stopped it all from unraveling. Looking through the image of his own gaunt face, looking through the shadows of it out at the dark, he could almost feel the texture of his achievement, it was almost palpable: a warm, luxurious blanket of silence lying like peace over the night county; the certain knowledge in his heart that he was going to prevail. There might not be much time left to him, but there would be time enough, anyway, to make a start.

The bare tips of the maple branches tap-danced on the pane. There was a wind from the west out there, growing stronger, it sounded like. He heard the dead leaves rattling along the grass, and he thought of Sally, running through the forest with the leaves falling all around her. He thought of her fading away from him, fading into the night as she ran, and he saw the forest fading as the moon went dim behind a cloud. And when the forest had faded in his mind completely, when it had become so dark that it was hard to call the image forth, then he saw the other forest as he stood there in his house, the old forest with its circle of snow-covered earth, its white boulders, capped with the snow, rising out of it. White sleeves of snow hung on the sagging boughs, and lanes of snow weaved between the trees. The pines and hemlocks soared toward the sky all around him. And in the shabby mound of snow and leaves just before his feet, Dolittle saw the girl again, the little girl, her sweet face peaceful as if she were sleeping unaware; her clothes in shreds; her white legs splayed . . . and the blood there, between her legs, the brown clot of blood which seemed darker amid the brilliance of the surrounding snow. It held his eyes, the blood. It funneled his vision down to the fine point of itself until all the forest, all the world, seemed to have been reduced to that stain, that blot, and there was such clarity to it, such simplicity, that he knew—knew with a welling, almost spiritual, precision—the course he had to take, the thing he had to do. . . .

The phone rang in the other room. The sheriff blinked and straightened.

Well, whatever—it's over now, he thought.

The phone rang again.

He thought, *It's over.*

10:35

Merriwether parked the Rabbit in back of the bureau and walked across the lot to the office door. Leaves skipped and chittered along the asphalt all around him. The wind was growing stronger. It made his eyes tear. He hunched his shoulders against the cold, stuffed his hands deep in the pockets of his overcoat. He took long strides to reach the door quickly.

When he stepped inside, he saw Sally sitting there. Alone at her desk among the empty desks. The empty desks looked abandoned, with old papers and folders lying stacked and bunched and crumpled on top of them. The typewriters sat silent on their adjoining tables.

Sally swung around in her chair and faced him. He came toward her, his face taut and creased with tension and with pain. She stood up, looking at him through tears, shaking her head, trying to speak. The door swung closed behind him.

"He'll tell," she managed to whisper.

"Yes," he said. "Of course."

"I'm never going to stop loving you. I'll never stop loving you."

"Sally . . ."

He reached for her.

But then Shea pushed in through the front door, and Merriwether's hand dropped to his side. There was no time for the lovers to say anything else.

10:45

"You can't run it, Sally," Shea said. "We've got to wait for Rumplemeyer."

Sally had just told him what she was planning to do, and Shea stood in the aisle, jabbing his cigarette in her direction. She was sitting at her desk again. She just seemed to be staring at the old carpet. Her mouth was turned down, her brow deeply furrowed, but Shea could not tell if she was listening to him or not. Merriwether wasn't much help either. He was sitting in his own chair now, still wearing his overcoat. He was hunched forward, his hands clasped on his lap. He was staring at his typewriter, at his unfinished story on the Scotti trial. He looked like his mind was a thousand miles away.

Christ, thought Shea. He didn't know what the hell he had blundered into, but it was sure something. Talk about a bull in a china shop. Here were these two poor lovesick souls trying to mingle their hearts' desire or whatever it was they were trying to do, and here was he—big, bad Christopher Shea—brutally interrupting them with such crude, minor issues as, oh, politics and truth, and the fact that it was one hour and fifteen minutes before deadline on the eve of the most important fucking election in the county's history. . . .

"Sally," he said.

She shifted a little. Raised her eyes to him briefly, wearily, as if he were a jackhammer and she had a headache. "I'm sorry, Chris. What did you say?"

"We have to wait. . . ."

"For Rumplemeyer? We don't even know where Rumplemeyer is."

"Well, we called the cops—he hasn't been arrested. Where else can he be? He's got to be here soon."

Sally massaged her temples with one hand.

"You ever know Rumplemeyer to miss a deadline?" Shea insisted. But she only sighed, she didn't answer him. He turned away.

He jabbed his cigarette out in the ashtray on his desk. He ran his fingers up through his hair. He wanted to pull his hair out in handfuls. She was driving him crazy. She was going to do it again: hammer the sheriff again, go after him one last time. Shea couldn't stand it.

He glanced up at her where she sat in her chair. He thought, Look at her. Depressed, defeated. She's finished, and she knows it. After tomorrow, the old man's hold on the county's politics will be so vast, so tight, she might never get anyone to speak out against him again. And that's what it's all about to her. Tonight, this last time, while there's still a faint hope of tripping Dolittle up, of spiking the election, Sally wants to give it to him but good.

Shea simply could not believe what she was planning to do. The lengths she'd go to, the depth of her obsession. She was going to run his land-grab story—but she wanted to run it under one heading in conjunction with Merriwether's trial piece and with information that Rumplemeyer had called in from some phone booth out in the middle of nowhere. And these three stories, the way Sally was going to put them together, would combine into a single tale of murder and conspiracy that would hit the stands just as voters went to the polls.

And it was nuts. This story of hers. It was just nuts, thought Shea. The gist of the three stories, as Sally saw them, was this: Billy Thimble, a real estate lawyer and a drug addict, had been arrested last spring by Sheriff Dolittle. To get off the hook, he'd given the sheriff information on Ralph Jones's land dealings in Hickory. Then, desperate to support his drug habit, Thimble had turned around and blackmailed the sheriff. He threatened to reveal that Dolittle was letting criminals like himself go if they offered to help him gain his political goals. So, according to Sally, the sheriff set Billy Thimble up by telling his daughter, Cindy, that Thimble was going to turn in Vincent Scotti. The sheriff knew the information would go through Cindy to Teddy Wocek and then to Scotti and that Thimble would then have to run for it—he'd be in no position, anyway, to blackmail anybody. As it turned out, Mr. Scotti took the direct route and blew Thimble's head off. So now the sheriff's only problem was that Cindy and Wocek were left as witnesses to his role in the killing. So, when Dolittle had Scotti arrested for the crime, he also conveniently had Wocek blown away. And then he had his own daughter committed to a mental institution to keep her silent too.

It was, as far as Shea was concerned, the stupidist theory ever constructed that didn't involve John F. Kennedy.

"Sally," he said, he begged her. "Just listen to me, all right? Just listen." He stood over her at her desk. He held his hands out to her. "Even if you accept for a minute that Cindy Dolittle is not completely buggy . . . Okay? I mean, it's a big if, but if you accept it . . . Maybe you're still coming to the wrong conclusions. Maybe Billy Thimble *was* the sheriff's informant. Maybe Dolittle blabbed about it to his daughter by mistake, okay? That could have happened. And I mean, that's just *assuming* Cindy is telling the truth." He spread his hands. Sally just sat there morosely. "But to say that Dolittle purposely had Billy Thimble whacked by a mobster; to say he had his daughter's boyfriend murdered, his own daughter put in the loony bin . . . Sally . . . I mean . . ." His hands fell, slapped to his sides. "I'm sorry, Sally, but it's nuts. I don't know how else to put it. It's just nuts." He pulled another cigarette out of the pack in his pocket. He waggled it at her. "We've gotta wait for Rumplemeyer. We have to ask him . . ."

Suddenly, it seemed, Sally could take no more. She threw her hands up before her face, waved them around as if to chase away mosquitoes. "Enough, Chris, enough, all right?" she said—harshly for her. She stood up. They confronted each other in the aisle, the big hulking man and the slight woman, her eyes only half raised to him. "You just don't know what's at stake," she whispered. "You don't know how much is at stake."

"At stake?" Shea took a step toward her. "At stake?" he said. "Sally . . . Sally—if we run this—if we run this and the sheriff's people win tomorrow—it's going to be war. You understand? That's what's at stake. It's gonna be worse than war. Dolittle will close this bureau down. He'll squeeze us out. The news, our distributors—he'll hit us everywhere. He'll go right through White Plains if he has to. And you, you personally . . ." Shea felt his heart begin to beat more rapidly. He knew he was running off at the mouth again. He knew he was going too far. But he couldn't stop himself. "Whatever you want to hide about your life, whatever you want to protect, that's where he'll come for you." Sally looked up at him fully now. He thought he saw a flash of hatred in her eyes, and her mouth was a thin gray line. "Well, he will, Sally. If you go at him with this—this theory—this unsubstantiated stuff—you'll leave yourself wide open, and he will come after you with everything he's got. Everything. You understand? You can't win, you can't . . ."

"Chris." Her hand rose to him. A small, thin hand, wrinkled and frail. To Shea's amazement, she still managed one of her sweet, motherly little smiles. She still managed to speak in that gentle girlish voice of hers. "You've made your point. Okay? You've made your point. I have to think about it."

Shea stood aside as she moved past him. She went down the aisle toward the storefront window, its wide expanse of glass dark with the night. Merriwether, Shea could see now, had raised his face from the story in his typewriter. He was watching Sally move down the aisle. As Sally came toward him, their eyes met, locked. Sally was turned away from him, but Shea could see the expression on Merriwether's face, and for a moment he felt sorry for both of them. *The poor bastards,* he thought.

Slowly, as Sally came near him, Merriwether rose to his feet. He kept his eyes on her face, and Shea saw her profile now. The plain, sorry, old maid's face, gazing at him desperately.

Merriwether's voice was hoarse. "You *could* hold on to it, Sally, you know. Shea's right. We don't really have it solid yet. We could hold on to it for a while. We could wait for Rumplemeyer to come back and clear up a few points, at least. Maybe if we held off a little, just held off until . . ."

"After the election." Her whisper was barely audible.

Merriwether looked away from her for a second, as if he were ashamed. But he looked back again quickly. "Maybe then the sheriff wouldn't be so vindictive," he said. "Maybe he wouldn't be so quick to . . . to try to ruin you. Ruin all of us."

Shea straightened, surprised: Even with him standing right there, even with him watching, Sally reached out her hand to Merriwether. Merriwether snapped it up in both his own, held it tightly for a moment. They didn't say anything, but the way their gazes were going at each other, *straining* at each other, it almost seemed . . . Well, Shea became embarrassed by the intimacy of it finally and turned his head away, lit his cigarette.

When he looked back, Sally slowly pulled her hand free. She looked into Merriwether's eyes another moment. Merriwether sank back into his chair.

"I have to think about it," Sally said.

And she moved away from him, to the storefront window.

11:00

Sally stood at the window, looking through her own reflection at the dark of night. She could hear the steady shush and crackle of the police scanner on the file cabinet at the back of the room. The voices that broke from it sometimes sounded like voices shouting through a rising wind. There was a power line down in Wannawan, one voice called. A car had driven off the road in Hickory, called another, and the driver was apparently dead. A burglary had been reported on Bullet Hole Road. . . .

Sally was also aware of the two men behind her, the pressure of their thoughts and feelings for her. The pressure of their stares at her back.

She slipped her hands into her pockets of her skirt. *I'm going to have to stop at the Lincoln Pharmacy on the way home*, she thought. That was the only drugstore that would be open at this time of night, and her mother had to have her medicine by tomorrow. If her mother woke up in the morning and did not find her arthritis pills on the bedside table, Sally would never hear the end of it.

She glanced automatically down at her watch. It was 11:01. She ought to ask Sidney to phone the power company to check on how many people in Wannawan had lost their lights. Shea could check with the cops on the traffic fatality in Hickory. She raised her eyes back to the window. She peered into her reflection. She saw the street lamp outside on Stillwater Lane. Her thoughts drifted back to her mother.

Corruption

Mom had been kind of cranky lately, she thought. Moaning and complaining; symptoms and infirmities. Making little remarks about Sally's late hours. She must have begun to suspect that there was a man in the picture: That always did make her nervous, Sally thought. She was afraid of being left behind in her old age or something.

Maybe this weekend, they could drive to Kent together, just the two of them. Mother would like that; she liked to see the falls. They could bring the folding chairs and have a picnic on the lawn. Gaze up at the tumble of bright water over the high rocks and down into the stream below. They could chatter between themselves in fits and starts about Mrs. Donovan next door and her nasty dog, or the rising price of groceries, or the weather and whatnot. It would calm Mother down a little. In fact, Sally always found these outings kind of peaceful herself.

And it's over anyway, she thought suddenly. *That's the point, isn't it? It's all over, everything.*

She took her hands from her pockets and held her shoulders, hugged herself and shivered as if she were cold. If you just could know, she thought. If you could know just for a minute. What was true, what was going to happen. If you could know anything at all to guide yourself by. It would be so much easier to know what to do.

She shivered again, hugged herself more tightly. She wished they would stop watching her. Chris and Sidney. She wished they would stop standing there behind her, waiting for her to figure it out, to decide what to do. She didn't *know* what to do. She didn't even know how she was supposed to approach it, what she was supposed to be thinking about, how she was supposed to distinguish between what she did think and what she only felt. If she killed the story, was it because she wanted to hold on to Merriwether? If she ran the story, was it because she was so obsessed with destroying Dolittle that she was willing to unleash this scandal, this suffering, on the man she loved? And what if the story just wasn't true? And how was she supposed to know what was true and what wasn't? How did you *ever* know really?

Sally closed her eyes. She felt dizzy for a moment. She had the sensation of rushing forward, falling forward, out of control. It was a strange, unmoored, and dreamy feeling, as if everything that supported her had dropped away, as if nothing else existed, nothing

329

besides herself. Maybe it was true, then. Maybe she had made it all up, the whole world, and now it was gone, and she was falling through nothingness. . . .

She began to feel queasy and opened her eyes. She saw her own face, her own plain face, reflected on the pane. She saw the street lamps beyond it and the night filling in the spaces in the reflection. It was all steady enough, all real enough, all standing still. *It's over,* she thought again. And she felt that too as a heavy, solid thing inside her: the knowledge that he would leave her, that whichever way it went, the sheriff was right, Merriwether would leave her. If she ran the story and the sheriff struck back and made a scandal of them, Merriwether would leave to try to save his marriage. In his heart, he would never forgive her for it, and he would certainly never come back. If she killed the story, he would stay a while longer, a few weeks maybe, a month, no more than that. Then the threat of discovery would rise up in his mind again, and he would start to be afraid, and he would leave her. And he would go back to his wife, because she was right for him and he loved her. Maybe he loved Sally too, but Emily was right for him, so he'd go back to her. One way or the other, he was going to leave.

Sally let out a bitter, nasty little puff of laughter. These journalistic decisions are murder, she thought. She shook her head, lowering her chin to hide her twisted smile from the two men behind her.

Oh, what are we going to do? she wondered wearily. *Whatever are we going to do?*

And weary she really was. Weary almost past caring, it felt like. It was not as if, after all, she could change anything. The sun was going to rise tomorrow, and the people would go to the polls and Purdy or Jones would become the county's first executive, one or the other as the voters decided. Probably it would be Purdy. And probably all the sheriff's men would be his legislature. And nothing she ran in the newspaper was going to change that, not this late in the day. She'd lost that battle. If there had been a battle. If it hadn't just been in her imagination. If she and Dolittle all these years had been locked in some sort of dire struggle for the heart and soul of this stupid meaningless little county, well, the struggle was over now, and Sally had lost. Oh, maybe if she hammered at the sheriff long enough, she could slow him down a little. Expose a few of his backroom deals, force people to recognize how much power he had, how much had gone on without their knowing. Maybe if she got something really good, really solid, she could weaken the sheriff enough so he would have to compromise and Jones could get a toehold again.

Or maybe not. Either way, Shea was right, the price was going to be terrible, it was going to be like war. And was it worth that? Had it ever been worth that? She just didn't know anymore. Strangely enough, she just could not remember anymore why it had ever seemed so very important to her. A year from now, or two years or five or sometime, the sheriff would be dead. The Dolittle empire would crumble and the county would fall into the hands of the Purdys and the Henry Benoits and the other scum Dolittle had raised up to obey him. Because that was what happened to empires, that was what always happened, and nothing she or anyone else did would make it much better or worse in the end.

And a year from now, or two years or five or possibly tomorrow, Sally would be sitting at the park in Kent, sitting on the folding chair next to her mother, talking about grocery prices and the neighbor's dog. And she would sit there and stare at the bright water tumbling over the falls into the stream below, and she would realize that this was her life. From now on. From now on until forever this was going to be her life, and so what the hell difference did it make really who controlled the planning boards and the real estate and the people of this little backwoods nowhere?

Sally was taken off guard by her emotion and almost started to cry. She fought the tears down but even so, even in the dark window, she could see her own eyes, the panic, even the terror in her own eyes. *Oh boy, oh boy, oh boy,* she thought—and she was not smiling at all now. *What have I been thinking of? All these years. What have I done?*

When Sally finally turned back from the window, she had not really decided anything. She did not even have a very clear idea of what she had just been thinking about. She had no idea at all how much or how little she really knew. It was just that she felt the pressure of Shea and Merriwether behind her, so she finally turned around.

Shea was still standing in the aisle, smoking tensely, watching her, waiting for her to speak. And Merriwether—poor Sidney—still sat slumped at his desk, gazing at his unfinished story. He lifted his eyes to her when she turned and she looked into them and she felt it like a physical pang. He was in over his head in this thing, she thought, where he simply did not belong. She loved him so much, and she was so sorry. She wished she knew better: what would happen, what was true.

She turned away. She glanced up at the clock. She would have to make the scanner calls herself now. About the power line down in Wannawan. And the death in Hickory, the driver of the car.

She looked at the men again.

"It's getting late," she whispered to them. "We can't wait for Rumplemeyer."

Shea made a gesture of protest but cut it short. Letting out a harsh, angry burst of smoke, he plugged his cigarette into his mouth and left it here. He moved around the edge of his desk to his chair.

Merriwether only nodded once. He lowered his gaze. He stared at the half-written page in front of him, but Sally didn't think he was looking at it; she thought he was gazing right through it, gazing far away. He bit his lip. He lifted his fingers to the typewriter keys.

Shea, with another angry breath, yanked his chair away from his typing table and dropped into it. He shook his head as he rolled a page into the machine.

Sally smiled at them both gently. "We have to tell the story," she whispered.

There was silence for a long moment. And then they both began typing.